THE GHOST
OF A MODEL T

THE GHOST

OF A MODEL T

AND OTHER STORIES

The Complete Short Fiction
of Clifford D. Simak,
Volume Three

Introduction by David W. Wixon

OPEN **①** ROAD

INTEGRATED MEDIA
NEW YORK

All works reprinted with permission of the Estate of Clifford D. Simak.

"Leg. Forst." © 1958 by Royal Publications, Inc. © 1986 by Clifford D. Simak. Originally published in *Infinity Science Fiction*, v. 3, no. 4, April, 1958.

"Physician to the Universe" © 1963 by Ziff-Davis Publishing Company. © 1991 by the Estate of Clifford D. Simak. Originally published in *Fantastic Stories*, v. 12, no. 3, March, 1963.

"No More Hides and Tallow" © 1945 by Real Adventures Publishing Co., Inc. © 1973 by Clifford D. Simak. Originally published in *Lariat Story Magazine*, v. 14, no. 12, March, 1946.

"Condition of Employment" © 1960 by Galaxy Publishing Corporation. © 1988 by the Estate of Clifford D. Simak. Originally published in *Galaxy Magazine*, v. 18, no. 4, April, 1960.

"City" © 1944 by Street & Smith Publications, Inc. © 1972 by Clifford D. Simak. Originally published in *Astounding Science Fiction*, v. 33, no. 3, May, 1944.

"Mirage" © 1950 by Ziff-Davis Publishing Co. © 1978 by Clifford D. Simak. Originally published in *Amazing Stories*, v. 24, no. 10, October, 1950, under title "Seven Came Back."

"The Autumn Land" © 1971 by Mercury Press, Inc. © 1999 by the Estate of Clifford D. Simak. Originally published in *The Magazine of Fantasy & Science Fiction*, v. 41, no. 4, October, 1971.

"Founding Father" © 1957 by Galaxy Publishing Corp. © 1985 by Clifford D. Simak. Originally published in *Galaxy Science Fiction*, v. 14, no. 1, May, 1957.

"Byte Your Tongue!" © 1980 by Random House, Inc. Originally published in STELLAR SCIENCE FICTION STORIES #6, ed. by Judy-Lynn del Rey, Ballantine Books.

"The Street That Wasn't There" © 1941 by H-K Publications, Inc. Originally published in *Comet*, v. 1, no. 5, July, 1941.

"The Ghost of a Model T" © by 1975 by Robert Silverberg and Roger Elwood. Originally published in EPOCH, edited by Robert Silverberg and Roger Elwood, Berkley Publishing Corp., 1975.

Copyright © 2016 by the Estate of Clifford D. Simak

Cover design by Jason Gabbert

978-1-5040-3946-8

Published in 2016 by Open Road Integrated Media, Inc.
180 Maiden Lane
New York, NY 10038
www.openroadmedia.com

CONTENTS

CLIFFORD D. SIMAK AND "CITY": THE SEAL OF GREATNESS

_____

"It would have been different, he thought, if we could have stayed on Earth, for there we would have had normal human contacts. We would not have thought so much, or brooded; we could have rubbed away the guilt on the hides of other people."

—Clifford D. Simak in "Shadow Show"

In this, the third volume of Clifford D. Simak's collected short fiction, you find the story "City," reprinted in its original magazine version.

If there is a single work for which Clifford D. Simak is most known, it is the book City. Most people call City a novel, but it is actually a compilation of eight short stories laced together by interstitial materials to form a work that functions as a novel. And since those eight stories were all once published individually, they are included as such in this volume.

Simak fans of a purist disposition may be pleased to know, however, that this collection features the original magazine versions of the stories from City. Most of them were altered, to various extents, for the book, which was put together some years later. But this volume preserves the original versions, heretofore unavailable.

As it happens, the earlier stories were not projected to be part of any series. "Desertion," which appears as the fourth episode in

City, was actually written before any of the others: Cliff's journals show that it had been sold to John W. Campbell Jr. (who would publish the story in Astounding), before "City" itself was sent to him. This lends credence to the theory that "Desertion" was inserted into the series after the fact to provide a basis for the following story, Paradise.

The City stories, in their compiled form, demonstrate Clifford D. Simak's passage from apprenticeship to craftsman as a writer. His own words confirm that transition: "From that time on, for the most part, I was in control of my writing efforts rather than floundering around, trying to find myself as a writer."

Yet, he added, "there was still much that I had to learn." And later, speaking of a time when he reread the City volume in its entirety, he said: "I ached to rewrite the tales." But that, he continued, was unrealistic: "The ache to rewrite was a gut reaction— a sadness that in the '40s I had not done as good a writing job as I could have done in the '70s. I realized, however, that those stories could only have been written in the '40s, that in the '70s I would have been incapable of writing them. In the intervening years I undoubtedly had become a better writer, but I had lost something in the process."

Thus, the author who wrote the version of "City" in this volume might be described as a different man, and a different writer, than the author who would pen his later works. But I sincerely hope that he is still someone you would like to know.

—David W. Wixon

LEG. FORST.

This story was originally published in the April 1958 issue of Infinity Science Fiction; *and Cliff's fragmented journals give a slightly better view of how the story developed than is usually the case: only four days passed between the time (in May 1957) he first mentioned that he was working on the "Stamp story," to his referring to it as "Spore," then finally to his use of the name "Leg.Forst." The story went quickly for him, which I suspect came about at least in part because of its subject matter. Cliff actually commented, within days of having begun to write it, that it was a "Better story than I thought it was."*

And it is a charming little story. But you, average reader, might not fully understand that—not unless you (like Cliff and like myself) are a stamp collector, too.

The term "Leg.Forst." represents a clever counterfeit of the sort of term familiar to collectors serious enough to have spent time perusing the various stamp-collecting catalogs and journals. And Clyde Packer's views about the avocation, which so puzzled those who came into contact with him, were clearly written by someone all too familiar with both the way collectors were viewed by others (with opinions starting at gentle amusement and quickly deteriorating), and the way collectors refuse to be affected by such opinions. (In Cliff's defense, let me hastily add that he was not the same sort of deep-down, driven stamp collector as Clyde Packer: Cliff, aware of the difference, called himself a "stamp accumulator," not a "stamp collector.")

—*dww*

CHAPTER I

When it was time for the postman to have come and gone, old Clyde Packer quit working on his stamps and went into the bathroom to comb his snow-white hair and beard. It was an everlasting bother, but there was no way out of it. He'd be sure to meet some of his neighbors going down and coming back and they were a snoopy lot. He felt sure that they talked about him; not that he cared, of course. And the Widow Foshay, just across the hall, was the worst one of them all.

Before going out, he opened a drawer in the big desk in the middle of the cluttered living room, upon the top of which was piled an indescribable array of litter, and found the tiny box from Unuk al Hay. From the box he took a pinch of leaf and tucked it in his cheek.

He stood for a moment, with the drawer still open, and savored the fullsome satisfaction of the taste within his mouth—not quite like peppermint, nor like whiskey, either, but with some taste akin to both and with some other tang that belonged entirely to itself. It was nothing like another man had ever tasted and he suspected that it might be habit-forming, although PugAlNash had never informed him that it was.

Perhaps, he told himself, even if Pug should so try to inform him, he could not make it out, for the Unukian's idea of how Earth's language should be written, and the grammar thereof, was a wonder to behold and could only be believed by someone who had tried to decipher one of his flowery little notes.

The box, he saw, was nearly empty, and he hoped that the queer, faithful, almost wistful little correspondent would not fail him now. But there was, he told himself, no reason to believe he would; PugAlNash, in a dozen years, had not failed him yet. Regularly another tiny box of leaf arrived when the last one was quite finished, accompanied by a friendly note—and all franked with the newest stamps from Unuk.

Never a day too soon, nor a day too late, but exactly on the dot when the last of the leaf was finished. As if PugAlNash might know, by some form of intelligence quite unknown to Earth, when his friend on Earth ran out of the leaf.

A solid sort, Clyde Packer told himself. Not humanoid, naturally, but a very solid sort.

And he wondered once again what Pug might actually be like. He always had thought of him as little, but he had no idea, of course, whether he was small or large or what form his body took. Unuk was one of those planets where it was impossible for an Earthman to go, and contact and commerce with the planet had been accomplished, as was the case on so many other worlds, by an intermediary people.

And he wondered, too, what Pug did with the cigars that he sent him in exchange for the little boxes of leaf—eat them, smoke them, smell them, roll in them or rub them in his hair? If he had hair, of course.

He shook his head and closed the door and went out into the hall, being doubly sure that his door was locked behind him. He would not put it past his neighbors, especially the Widow Foshay, to sneak in behind his back.

The hall was empty and he was glad of that. He rang almost stealthily for the lift, hoping that his luck would hold.

It didn't.

Down the hall came the neighbor from next door. He was the loud and flashy kind, and without any encouragement at all, he'd slap one on the back.

"Good morning, Clyde!" he bellowed happily from afar.

"Good morning, Mr. Morton," Packer replied, somewhat icily. Morton had no right to call him Clyde. No one ever called him Clyde, except sometimes his nephew, Anton Camper, called him Uncle Clyde, although he mostly called him Unk. And Tony, Packer reminded himself, was a worthless piece—always involved in some fancy scheme, always talking big, but without much to show for it. And besides, Tony was crooked—as crooked as a cat.

Like myself, Packer thought, exactly like myself. Not like the most of the rest of them these days, who measured to no more than just loud-talking boobies.

In my day, he told himself with fond remembrance, I could have skinned them all and they'd never know it until I twitched their hides slick off.

"How is the stamp business this morning?" yelled Morton, coming up and clapping Packer soundly on the back.

"I must remind you, Mr. Morton, that I am not in the stamp business," Packer told him sharply. "I am interested in stamps and I find it most absorbing and I could highly recommend it—"

"But that is not just what I meant," explained Morton, rather taken aback. "I didn't mean you dealt in stamps . . ."

"As a matter of fact, I do," said Packer, "to a limited extent. But not as a regular thing and certainly not as a regular business. There are certain other collectors who are aware of my connections and sometimes seek me out—"

"That's the stuff!" boomed Morton, walloping him on the back again in sheer good fellowship. "If you have the right connections, you get along O.K. That works in any line. Now, take mine, for instance . . ."

The elevator arrived and rescued Packer.

In the lobby, he headed for the desk.

"Good morning, Mr. Packer," said the clerk, handing him some letters. "There is a bag for you and it runs slightly heavy. Do you want me to get someone to help you up with it?"

"No, thank you," Packer said. "I am sure that I can manage."

The clerk hoisted the bag atop the counter and Packer seized it and let it to the floor. It was fairly large—it weighed, he judged, thirty pounds or so—and the shipping tag, he saw with a thrill of anticipation, was almost covered with stamps of such high denominations they quite took his breath away.

He looked at the tag and saw that his name and address were printed with painful precision, as if the Earthian alphabet was something entirely incomprehensible to the sender. The return address was a mere jumble of dots and hooks and dashes that made no sense, but seemed somewhat familiar, although Packer at the moment was unable to tell exactly what they were. The stamps, he saw, were Iota Cancri, and he had seen stamps such as them only once before in his entire life. He stood there, mentally calculating what their worth might be.

He tucked the letters under his arm and picked up the bag. It was heavier than he had expected and he wished momentarily that he had allowed the clerk to find someone to carry it for him. But he had said that he would carry it and he couldn't very well go back and say he'd rather not. After all, he assured himself, he wasn't quite that old and feeble yet.

He reached the elevator and let the bag down and stood facing the grillwork, waiting for the cage.

A birdlike voice sounded from behind him and he shivered at it, for he recognized the voice—it was the Widow Foshay.

"Why, Mr. Packer," said the Widow, gushingly, "how pleasant to find you waiting here."

He turned around. There was nothing else for it; he couldn't just stand there, with his back to her.

"And so loaded down!" the Widow sympathized. "Here, do let me help you."

She snatched the letters from him.

"There," she said triumphantly, "poor man; I can carry these."

He could willingly have choked her, but he smiled instead. It was a somewhat strained and rather ghastly smile, but he did the best he could.

"How lucky for me," he told her, "that you came along. I'd have never made it."

The veiled rebuke was lost on her. She kept on bubbling at him.

"I'm going to make beef broth for lunch," she said, "and I always make too much. Could I ask you in to share it?"

"Impossible," he told her in alarm. "I am very sorry, but this is my busy day. I have all these, you see." And he motioned at the mail she held and the bag he clutched. He whuffled through his whiskers at her like an irate walrus, but she took no notice.

"How exciting and romantic it must be," she gushed, "getting all these letters and bags and packages from all over the galaxy. From such strange places and from so far away. Someday you must explain to me about stamp collecting."

"Madam," he said a bit stiffly, "I've worked with stamps for more than twenty years and I'm just barely beginning to gain an understanding of what it is all about. I would not presume to explain to someone else."

She kept on bubbling.

Damn it all, he thought, is there no way to quiet the blasted woman?

Prying old biddy, he told himself, once again whuffling his whiskers at her. She'd spend the next three days running all about and telling everyone in the entire building about her strange encounter with him and what a strange old coot he was. "Getting all those letters from all those alien places," she would say, "and bags and packages as well. You can't tell me that stamps are the only things in which he's interested. There is more to it than that; you can bet your bottom dollar on it."

At his door she reluctantly gave him back his letters.

"You won't reconsider on that broth?" she asked him, "It's more than just ordinary broth. I pride myself on it. A special recipe."

"I'm sorry," he said.

He unlocked his door and started to open it. She remained standing there.

"I'd like to invite you in," he told her, lying like a gentleman, "but I simply can't. The place is a bit upset."

Upset was somewhat of an understatement.

Safely inside, he threaded his way among piles of albums, boxes, bags and storage cases, scattered everywhere.

He finally reached the desk and dropped the bag beside it. He leafed through the letters and one was from Dahib and another was from the Lyraen system and the third from Muphrid, while the remaining one was an advertisement from a concern out on Mars.

He sat down in the massive, upholstered chair behind his desk and surveyed the room.

Someday he'd have to get it straightened out, he told himself. Undoubtedly there was a lot of junk he could simply throw away and the rest of it should be boxed and labeled so that he could lay his hands upon it. It might be, as well, a good idea to make out a general inventory sheet so that he'd have some idea what he had and what it might be worth.

Although, he thought, the value of it was not of so great a moment.

He probably should specialize, he thought. That was what most collectors did. The galaxy was much too big to try to collect it all. Even back a couple of thousand years ago, when all the collectors had to worry about were the stamps of Earth, the field even then had become so large and so unwieldy and so scattered that specialization had become the thing.

But what would a man specialize in if he should decide to restrict his interest? Perhaps just the stamps from one particular planet or one specific system? Perhaps only stamps from beyond a certain distance—say, five hundred light-years? Or covers, perhaps? A collection of covers with postmarks and cancellations showing the varying intricacies of letter communication throughout the depths of space, from star to star, could be quite interesting.

And that was the trouble with it—it all was so interesting. A man could spend three full lifetimes at it and still not reach the end of it.

In twenty years, he told himself, a man could amass a lot of material if he applied himself. And he had applied himself; he had worked hard at it and enjoyed every minute of it, and had become in certain areas, he thought with pride, somewhat of an expert. On occasion he had written articles for the philatelic press, and scarcely a week went by that some man well-known in the field did not drop by for a chat or to seek his aid in a knotty problem.

There was a lot of satisfaction to be found in stamps, he told himself with apologetic smugness. Yes, sir, a great deal of satisfaction.

But the mere collection of material was only one small part of it—a sort of starting point. Greater than all the other facets of it were the contacts that one made. For one had to make contacts—especially out in the farther reaches of the galaxy. Unless one wanted to rely upon the sorry performance of the rascally dealers, who offered only what was easy to obtain, one must establish contacts. Contacts with other collectors who might be willing to trade stamps with one. Contacts with lonely men in lonely outposts far out on the rim, where the really exotic material was most likely to turn up, and who would be willing to watch for it and save it and send it on to one at a realistic price. With far-out institutions that made up mixtures and job lots in an attempt to eke out a miserly budget voted by the home communities.

There was a man by the name of Marsh out in the Coonskin system who wanted no more than the latest music tapes from Earth for the material that he sent along. And the valiant priest at the missionary station on barren Agustron who wanted old tobacco tins and empty bottles which, for a most peculiar reason, had high value on that topsy-turvy world. And among the many others, Earthmen and aliens alike, there was always PugAlNash.

Packer rolled the wad of leaf across his tongue, sucking out the last faded dregs of its tantalizing flavor.

If a man could make a deal for a good-sized shipment of the leaf, he thought, he could make a fortune on it. Packaged in small units, like packs of gum, it would go like hot cakes here on Earth. He had tried to bring up the subject with Pug, but had done no more than confuse and perplex the good Unukian who, for some unfathomable reason, could not conceive of any commerce that went beyond the confines of simple barter to meet the personal needs of the bargaining individuals.

The doorbell chimed and Packer went to answer it.

It was Tony Camper.

"Hi, Uncle Clyde," said Tony breezily.

Packer held the door open grudgingly.

"Since you are here," he said, "you might as well come in."

Tony stepped in and tilted his hat back on his head. He looked the apartment over with an appraising eye.

"Some day, Unk," he said, "you should get this place shoveled out. I don't see how you stand it."

"I manage it quite well," Packer informed him tartly. "Some day I'll get around to straightening up a bit."

"I should hope you do," said Tony.

"My boy," said Packer, with a trace of pride, "I think that I can say, without fear of contradiction, that I have one of the finest collections of out-star stamps that anyone can boast. Some day, when I get them all in albums—"

"You'll never make it, Unk. It'll just keep piling up. It comes in faster than you can sort it out."

He reached out a foot and nudged the bag beside the desk.

"Like this," he said. "This is a new one, isn't it?"

"It just came in," admitted Packer. "Haven't gotten around as yet to figuring out exactly where it's from."

"Well, that is fine," said Tony. "Keep on having fun. You'll outlive us all."

"Sure, I will," said Packer testily. "What is it that you want?"

"Not a thing, Unk. Just dropped in to say hello and to remind you you're coming up to Hudson's to spend the week-end with us. Ann insisted that I drop around and nudge you. The kids have been counting the days—"

"I would have remembered it," lied Packer, who had quite forgotten it.

"I could drop around and pick you up. Three this afternoon?"

"No, Tony, don't bother. I'll catch a stratocab. I couldn't leave that early. I have things to do."

"I bet you have," said Tony.

He moved toward the door.

"You won't forget," he cautioned.

"No, of course I won't," snapped Packer.

"Ann would be plenty sore if you did. She's fixing everything you like."

Packer grunted at him.

"Dinner at seven," said Tony cheerfully.

"Sure, Tony. I'll be there."

"See you, Unk," said Tony, and was gone.

Young whippersnapper, Packer told himself. Wonder what he's up to now. Always got a new deal cooking, never quite making out on it. Just keeps scraping along.

He stumped back to the desk.

Figures he'll be getting my money when I die, he thought. The little that I have. Well, I'll fool him. I'll spend every cent of it. I'll manage to live long enough for that.

He sat down and picked up one of the letters, slit it open with his pocketknife and dumped out its contents on the one small bare spot on the desk in front of him.

He snapped on the desk lamp and pulled it close. He bent above the stamps.

Pretty fair lot, he thought. That one there from Rho Geminorum XII, or was it XVI, was a fine example of the modern classic—designed with delicacy and imagination, engraved with loving care and exactitude, laid on paper of the highest quality, printed with the highest technical precision.

He hunted for his stamp tongs and failed to find them. He opened the desk drawer and rummaged through the tangled rat's-nest he found inside it. He got down on his hands and knees and searched beneath the desk.

He didn't find the tongs.

He got back, puffing, into his chair, and sat there angrily.

Always losing tongs, he thought. I bet this is the twentieth pair I've lost. Just can't keep track of them, damn 'em!

The door chimed.

"Well, come on in!" Packer yelled in wrath.

A mouselike little man came in and closed the door gently behind him. He stood timidly just inside, twirling his hat between his hands.

"You Mr. Packer, sir?"

"Yes, sure I am," yelled Packer. "Who did you expect to find here?"

"Well, sir," said the man, advancing a few careful steps into the room, "I am Jason Pickering. You may have heard of me."

"Pickering?" said Packer. "Pickering? Oh, sure, I've heard of you. You're the one who specializes in Polaris."

"That is right," admitted Pickering, mincing just a little. "I am gratified that you—"

"Not at all," said Packer, getting up to shake his hand. "I'm the one who's honored."

He bent and swept two albums and three shoe boxes off a chair. One of the shoe boxes tipped over and a mound of stamps poured out.

"Please have a chair, Mr. Pickering," Packer said majestically.

Pickering, his eyes popping slightly, sat down gingerly on the edge of the swept-clean chair.

"My, my," he said, his eyes taking in the litter that filled the apartment, "you seem to have a lot of stuff here. Undoubtedly, however, you can lay your hands on anything you want."

"Not a chance," said Packer, sitting down again. "I have no idea whatsoever what I have."

Pickering tittered. "Then, sir, you may well be in for some wonderful surprises."

"I'm never surprised at anything," said Packer loftily.

"Well, on to business," said Pickering. "I do not mean to waste your time. I was wondering if it were possible you might have Polaris 17b on cover. It's quite an elusive number, even off cover, and I know of not a single instance of one that's tied to cover. But someone was telling me that perhaps you might have one tucked away."

"Let me see, now," said Packer. He leaned back in his chair and leafed catalogue pages rapidly through his mind. And suddenly he had it—Polaris 17b—a tiny stamp, almost a midget stamp, bright blue with a tiny crimson dot in the lower left-hand corner and its design a mass of lacy scrollwork.

"Yes," he said, opening his eyes, "I believe I may have one. I seem to remember, years ago . . ."

Pickering leaned forward, hardly breathing.

"You mean you actually . . ."

"I'm sure it's here somewhere," said Packer, waving his hand vaguely at the room.

"If you find it," offered Pickering, "I'll pay ten thousand for it."

"A strip of five," said Packer, "as I remember it. Out of Polaris VII to Betelgeuse XIII by way of—I don't seem to remember by way of where."

"A strip of five!"

"As I remember it. I might be mistaken."

"Fifty thousand," said Pickering, practically frothing at the mouth. "Fifty thousand, if you find it."

Packer yawned. "For only fifty thousand, Mr. Pickering, I wouldn't even look."

"A hundred, then."

"I might think about it."

"You'll start looking right away? You must have some idea."

"Mr. Pickering, it has taken me all of twenty years to pile up all the litter that you see and my memory's not too good. I'd have not the slightest notion where to start."

"Set your price," urged Pickering. "What do you want for it?"

"If I find it," said Packer, "I might consider a quarter million. That is, if I find it . . ."

"You'll look?"

"I'm not sure. Some day I might stumble on it. Some day I'll have to clean up the place. I'll keep an eye out for it."

Pickering stood up stiffly.

"You jest with me," he said.

Packer waved a feeble hand, "I never jest," he said.

Pickering moved toward the door.

Packer heaved himself from the chair.

"I'll let you out," he said.

"Never mind. And thank you very much."

Packer eased himself back into the chair and watched the man go out.

He sat there, trying to remember where the Polaris cover might be buried. And finally gave up. It had been so long ago.

He hunted some more for the tongs, but be didn't find them.

He'd have to go out first thing in the morning and buy another pair. Then he remembered that he wouldn't be here in the morning. He'd be up on Hudson's Bay, at Tony's summer place.

It did beat hell, he thought, how he could manage to lose so many tongs.

He sat for a long time, letting himself sink into a sort of suspended state, not quite asleep, nor yet entirely awake, and he thought, quite vaguely and disjointedly, of many curious things.

But mostly about adhesive postage stamps and how, of all the ideas exported by the Earth, the idea of the use of stamps had caught on most quickly and, in the last two thousand years, had spread to the far corners of the galaxy.

It was getting hard, he told himself, to keep track of all the stamps, even of the planets that were issuing stamps. There were new ones popping up all the blessed time. A man must keep everlastingly on his toes to keep tab on all of them.

There were some funny stamps, he thought. Like the ones from Menkalinen that used smells to spell out their values. Not five-cent stamps or five-dollar stamps or hundred-dollar stamps, but one stamp that smelled something like a pasture rose for the local mail and another stamp that had the odor of ripe old cheese for the system mail and yet another with a stink that could knock out a human at forty paces distance for the interstellar service.

And the Algeiban issues that shifted into colors beyond the range of human vision—and worst of all, with the values based on that very shift of color. And that famous classic issue put out, quite illegally, of course, by the Leonidian pirates who had used, instead of paper, the well-tanned, thin-scraped hides of human victims who had fallen into their clutches.

He sat nodding in the chair, listening to a clock hidden somewhere behind the litter of the room, ticking loudly in the silence.

It made a good life, he told himself, a very satisfactory life. Twenty years ago when Myra had died and he had sold his interest in the export company, he'd been ready to curl up and end it all, ready to write off his life as one already lived. But today, he thought, he was more absorbed in stamps than he'd ever been in the export business and it was a blessing—that was what it was, a blessing.

He sat there and thought kindly of his stamps, which had rescued him from the deep wells of loneliness, which had given back his life and almost made him young again.

And then he fell asleep.

The door chimes wakened him and he stumbled to the door, rubbing sleep out of his eyes.

The Widow Foshay stood in the hall, with a small kettle in her hands. She held it out to him.

"I thought, poor man, he will enjoy this," she said. "It's some of the beef broth that I made. And I always make so much. It's so hard to cook for one."

Packer took the kettle.

"It was kind of you," he mumbled.

She looked at him sharply.

"You are sick," she said.

She stepped through the door, forcing him to step back, forcing her way in.

"Not sick," he protested limply. "I fell asleep, that's all. There's nothing wrong with me."

She reached out a pudgy hand and held it on his forehead.

"You have a fever," she declared. "You are burning up."

"There's nothing wrong with me," he bellowed. "I tell you, I just fell asleep, is all."

She turned and bustled out into the room, threading her way among the piled-up litter. Watching her, he thought: My God, she finally got into the place! How can I throw her out?

"You come over here and sit right down," she ordered him. "I don't suppose you have a thermometer."

He shook his head, defeated.

"Never had any need of one," he said. "Been healthy all my life."

She screamed and jumped and whirled around and headed for the door at an awkward gallop. She stumbled across a pile of boxes and fell flat upon her face, then scrambled, screeching, to her feet and shot out of the door.

Packer slammed the door behind her and stood looking, with some fascination, at the kettle in his hand. Despite all the ruckus, he'd spilled not a single drop.

But what had caused the Widow . . .

Then he saw it—a tiny mouse running on the floor.

He hoisted the kettle in a grave salute.

"Thanks, my friend," he said.

He made his way to the table in the dining room and found a place where he could put down the kettle.

Mice, he thought. There had been times when he had suspected that he had them—nibbled cheese on the kitchen shelf, scurryings in the night—and he had worried some about them making nests in the material he had stacked all about the place.

But mice had a good side to them, too, he thought.

He looked at his watch and it was almost five o'clock and he had an hour or so before he had to catch a cab and he realized now that somehow he had managed to miss lunch. So he'd have some of the broth and while he was doing that he'd look over the material that was in the bag.

He lifted some of the piled-up boxes off the table and set them on the floor so he had some room to empty the contents of the bag.

He went to the kitchen and got a spoon and sampled the broth. It was more than passing good. It was still warm and he had no doubt that the kettle might do the finish of the table top no good, but that was something one need not worry over.

He hauled the bag over to the table and puzzled out the strangeness of the return address. It was the new script they'd started using a few years back out in the Bootis system and it was from a rather shady gentle-being from one of the Cygnian stars who appreciated, every now and then, a case of the finest Scotch.

Packer, hefting the bag, made a mental note to ship him two, at least.

He opened up the bag and upended it and a mound of covers flowed out on the table.

Packer tossed the bag into a corner and sat down contentedly. He sipped at the broth and began going slowly through the pile of covers. They were, by and large, magnificent. Someone had taken the trouble to try to segregate them according to systems of their origin and had arranged them in little packets, held in place by rubber bands.

There was a packet from Rasalhague and another from Cheleb and from Nunki and Kaus Borealis and from many other places.

And there was a packet of others he did not recognize at all. It was a fairly good-sized packet with twenty-five or thirty covers in it and all the envelopes, he saw, were franked with the same stamps—little yellow fellows that had no discernible markings on them—just squares of yellow paper, rather thick and rough. He ran his thumb across one and he got the sense of crumbling, as if the paper were soft and chalky and were abrading beneath the pressure of his thumb.

Fascinated, he pulled one envelope from beneath the rubber band and tossed the rest of the packet to one side.

He shambled to his desk and dug frantically in the drawer and came back with a glass. He held it above the stamp and peered through it and he had been right—there were no markings on the stamp. It was a mere yellow square of paper that was rather thick and pebbly, as if it were made up of tiny grains of sand.

He straightened up and spooned broth into his mouth and frantically flipped the pages of his mental catalogue, but he got no clue. So far as he could recall, he'd never seen or heard of that particular stamp before.

He examined the postmarks with the glass and some of them he could recognize and there were others that he couldn't, but that made no difference, for he could look them up, at a later time, in one of the postmark and cancellation handbooks. He got the distinct impression, however, that the planet, or planets, of origin must lie Libra-wards, for all the postmarks he could recognize trended in that direction.

He laid the glass away and turned his full attention to the broth, being careful of his whiskers. Whiskers, he reminded himself, were no excuse for one to be a sloppy eater.

The spoon turned in his hand at that very moment and some of the broth spilled down his beard and some spattered on the table, but the most of it landed on the cover with the yellow stamp.

He pulled a handkerchief from his pocket and tried to wipe the cover clean, but it wouldn't wipe. The envelope was soggy and the stamp was ruined with the grease and he said a few choice cusswords, directed at his clumsiness.

Then he took the dripping cover by one corner and hunted until he found the wastebasket and dropped the cover in it.

CHAPTER II

He was glad to get back from the weekend at Hudson's Bay.

Tony was a fool, he thought, to sink so much money in such a fancy place. He had no more prospects than a rabbit and his high-pressure deals always seemed to peter out, but he still went on talking big and hung onto that expensive summer place. Maybe, Packer thought, that was the way to do it these days; maybe if you could fool someone into thinking you were big, you might have a better chance of getting into something big. Maybe that was the way it worked, but he didn't know.

He stopped in the lobby to pick up his mail, hoping there might be a package from PugAlNash. In the excitement of leaving for the weekend, he'd forgotten to take along the box of leaf and three days without it had impressed upon him how much he had come to rely upon it. Remembering how low his supply was getting he became a little jittery to think that more might not be forthcoming.

There was a batch of letters, but no box from Pug.

And he might have known, he told himself, that there wouldn't be, for the box never came until he was entirely out. At first, he recalled, he wondered by what prophetic insight Pug might have known when the leaf was gone, how he could have gauged the shipping time to have it arrive exactly when there was need of it. By now he no longer thought about it, for it was one of those unbelievable things it does no good to think about.

"Glad to have you back," the clerk told him cheerfully. "You had a good weekend, Mr. Packer?"

"Tolerable," growled Packer, grumpily, heading for the lift.

Before he reached it, he was apprehended by Elmer Lang, the manager of the building.

"Mr. Packer," he whinnied, "I'd like to talk to you."

"Well, go ahead and talk."

"It's about the mice, Mr. Packer."

"What mice?"

"Mrs. Foshay tells me there are mice in your apartment."

Packer drew himself up to the fullness of his rather dumpy height.

"They are your mice, Lang," he said. "You get rid of them."

Lang wrung his hands. "But how can I, Mr. Packer? It's the way you keep your place. All that litter in there. You've got to clean it up."

"That litter, I'll have you know, sir, is probably one of the most unique stamp collections in the entire galaxy. I've gotten behind a little in keeping it together, true, but I will not have you call it litter."

"I could have Miles, the caretaker, help you get it straightened out."

"I tell you, sir," said Packer, "the only one who could help me is one trained in philately. Does your caretaker happen to be—"

"But, Mr. Packer," Lang pleaded, "all that paper and all those boxes are nesting places for them. I can do nothing about the mice unless I can get in there and get some of it cleared away."

"Cleared away!" exploded Packer. "Do you realize, sir, what you are talking of? Somewhere hidden in that vast stock of material, is a certain cover—to you, sir, an envelope with stamps and postmarks on it—for which I have been offered a quarter million dollars if I ever turn it up. And that is one small piece of all the material I have there. I ask you, Lang, is that the sort of stuff that you clear away?"

"But, Mr. Packer, I cannot allow it to go on. I must insist—"

The lift arrived and Packer stalked into it haughtily, leaving the manager standing in the lobby, twisting at his hands.

Packer whuffled his mustache at the operator.

"Busybody," he said.

"What was that, sir?"

"Mrs. Foshay, my man. She's a busybody."

"I do believe," said the operator judiciously, "that you may be entirely right."

Packer hoped the corridor would be empty and it was. He unlocked his door and stepped inside.

A bubbling noise stopped him in his tracks.

He stood listening, unbelieving, just a little frightened.

The bubbling noise went on and on.

He stepped cautiously out into the room and as he did he saw it.

The wastebasket beside the desk was full of a bubbling yellow stuff that in several places had run down the sides and formed puddles on the floor.

Packer stalked the basket, half prepared to turn and run.

But nothing happened. The yellowness in the basket simply kept on bubbling.

It was a rather thick and gooey mess, not frothy, and the bubbling was no more than a noise that it was making, for in the strict sense of the word, he saw, it was not bubbling.

Packer sidled closer and thrust out a hand toward the basket. It did not snap at him. It paid no attention to him.

He poked a finger at it and the stuff was fairly solid and slightly warm and he got the distinct impression that it was alive.

And immediately he thought of the broth-soaked cover he had thrown in the basket. It was not so unusual that he should think of it, for the yellow of the brew within the basket was the exact color of the stamp upon the cover,

He walked around the desk and dropped the mail he'd picked up in the lobby. He sat down ponderously in the massive office chair.

So a stamp had come to life, he thought, and that certainly was a queer one. But no more queer, perhaps, than the properties of many other stamps, for while Earth had exported the idea of their use, a number of peculiar adaptations of the idea had evolved.

And now, he thought a little limply, I'll have to get this mess in the basket out of here before Lang comes busting in.

He worried a bit about what Lang had said about cleaning up the place and he got slightly sore about it, for he paid good money for these diggings and he paid promptly in advance and he was never any bother. And besides, he'd been here for twenty years, and Lang should consider that.

He finally got up from the chair and lumbered around the desk. He bent and grasped the wastebasket, being careful to miss the places where the yellow goo had run down the sides, He tried to lift it and the basket did not move. He tugged as hard as he could pull and the basket stayed exactly where it was. He squared off and aimed a kick at it and the basket didn't budge.

He stood off a ways and glared at it, with his whiskers bristling. As if he didn't have all the trouble that he needed, without this basket deal! Somehow or other, he was going to have to get the apartment straightened out and get rid of the mice, He should be looking for the Polaris cover. And he'd lost or mislaid his tongs and would have to waste his time going out to get another pair.

But first of all, he'd have to get this basket out of here. Somehow it had become stuck to the floor—maybe some of the yellow goo had run underneath the edge of it and dried. Maybe if he had a pinch bar or some sort of lever that he could jab beneath it, he could pry it loose.

From the basket the yellow stuff made merry bubbling noises at him.

He clapped his hat back on his head and went out and slammed and locked the door behind him.

It was a fine summer day and he walked around a little, trying to run his many problems through his mind, but no matter what he thought of, he always came back to the basket brimming with the yellow mess and he knew he'd never be able to get started on any of the other tasks until he got rid of it.

So he hunted up a hardware store and bought a good-sized pinch bar and headed back for the apartment house. The bar, he knew, might mark up the floor somewhat, but if he could get under the edge of the basket with a bar that size he was sure that he could pry it loose.

In the lobby, Lang descended on him.

"Mr. Packer," he said sternly, "where are you going with that bar?"

"I went out and bought it to exterminate the mice."

"But, Mr. Packer—"

"You want to get rid of those mice, don't you?"

"Why, certainly I do."

"It's a desperate situation," Packer told him gravely, "and one that may require very desperate measures."

"But that bar!"

"I'll exercise my best discretion," Packer promised him. "I shall hit them easy."

He went up the lift with the bar. The sight of Lang's discomfiture made him feel a little better and he managed to whistle a snatch of tune as he went down the hall.

As he fumbled with the key, he heard the sound of rustling coming from beyond the door and he felt a chill go through him, for the rustlings were of a furtive sort and they sounded ominous.

Good Lord, he thought, there can't be that many mice in there!

He grasped the bar more firmly and unlocked the door and pushed it open.

The inside of the place was a storm of paper.

He stepped in quickly and slammed the door behind him to keep the blowing paper from swooping out into the hall.

Must have left a window open, he thought. But he knew he had not, and even if he had, it was quiet outside. There was not a breath of breeze.

And what was happening inside the apartment was more than just a breeze.

He stood with his back against the door and watched what was going on and shifted his grip on the bar so that it made a better club.

The apartment was filled with a sleet of flying paper and a barrage of packets and a snowstorm of dancing stamps. There were open boxes standing on the floor and the paper and the stamps and packets were drifting down and chunking into these, and along the wall were other boxes, very neatly piled—and that was entirely wrong, for there had been nothing neat about the place when he had left it less than two hours before.

But even as he watched, the activity slacked off. There was less stuff flying through the air and some of the boxes were closed by unseen hands and then flew off, all by themselves, to stack themselves with the other boxes.

Poltergeists! he thought in terror, his mind scrambling back frantically over all that he had ever thought or read or heard to grasp some explanation.

Then it was done and over.

There was nothing flying through the air. All the boxes had been stacked. Everything was still.

Packer stepped out into the room and stared in slack-jawed amazement.

The desk and the tables shone. The drapes hung straight and clean. The carpeting looked as if it might be new. Chairs and small tables and lamps and other things, long forgotten, buried all these years beneath the accumulation of his collection, stood revealed and shining—dusted, cleaned and polished.

And in the middle of all this righteous order stood the waste-basket, bubbling happily.

Packer dropped the bar and headed for the desk.

In front of him a window flapped open and he heard a swish and the bar went past him, flying for the window. It went out the window and slashed through the foliage of a tree, then the window closed and he lost sight of it.

Packer took off his hat and tossed it on the desk.

Immediately his hat lifted from the desk and sailed for a closet door. The closet door swung open and the hat ducked in. The door closed gently on it.

Packer whuffled through his whiskers, He got out his hand-kerchief and mopped a glistening brow.

"Funny goings-on," he said to himself.

Slowly, cautiously, he checked the place. All the boxes were stacked along one wall, three deep and piled from floor to ceiling. Three filing cabinets stood along another wall and he rubbed his eyes at that, for he had forgotten that there were three of them—for years he'd thought that he had only two. And all the rest of the place was neat and clean and it fairly gleamed.

He walked from room to room and everywhere it was the same.

In the kitchen the pots and pans were all in place and the dishes stacked primly in the cupboard. The stove and refrigerator had been wiped clean and there were no dirty dishes and that was a bit surprising, for he was sure there had been. Mrs. Foshay's kettle, with the broth emptied out of it and scrubbed until it shone, stood on the kitchen table.

He went back to the desk and the top of it was clear except for several items laid out, as if for his attention:

Ten dead mice.

Eight pairs of stamp tongs.

The packet of covers with the strange yellow stamps.

Two—not one—but two covers, one bearing a strip of four and the other a strip of five Polaris 17b.

Packer sat down heavily in his chair and stared at the items on the desk.

How in the world, he wondered—how had it come about? What was going on?

He peeked around the desk edge at the bubbling basket and it seemed to chortle at him.

It was, he told himself, it *must* be the basket—or, rather, the stuff within the basket. Nothing else had been changed, no other factor had been added. The only thing new and different in the apartment was the basket of yellow gook.

He picked up the packet of covers with the yellow stamps affixed and opened the drawer to find a glass. The drawer was arranged with startling neatness and there were five glasses lying in a row. He chose the strongest one.

Beneath the glass the surface of the stamps became a field made up of tiny ball-like particles, unlike the grains of sand which the weaker glass he had used before had shown.

He bent above the desk, with his eye glued to the glass, and he knew that what he was looking at were spores.

Encysted, lifeless, they still would carry life within them, and that had been what had happened here. He'd spilled the broth upon the stamp and the spores had come to life—a strange alien community of life that settled within the basket.

He put the glass back in the drawer and rose. He gathered up the dead mice carefully by their tails. He carried them to the incinerator shaft and let them drop.

He crossed the room to the bookcases and the books were arranged in order and in sequence and there, finally, were books that he'd lost years ago and hunted ever since. There were long rows of stamp catalogues, the set of handbooks on galactic cancellations, the massive list of postmarks, the galactic travel guides, the long row of weird language dictionaries, indispensable in alien stamp identification, and a number of technical works on philatelic subjects.

From the bookcase he moved to the piled-up boxes. One of them he lifted down. It was filled with covers, with glassine envelopes of loose stamps, with sheets, with blocks and strips. He dug through the contents avidly, with wonder mounting in him.

All the stamps, all the covers, were from the Thuban system.

He closed the box and bent to lift it back. It didn't wait for him. It lifted by itself and fitted itself in place.

He looked at three more boxes. One contained, exclusively, material from Korephoros, and another material from Antares and the third from Dschubba. Not only had the litter been picked up and boxed and piled into some order, but the material itself had been roughly classified!

He went back to the chair and sat down a little weakly. It was too much, he thought, for a man to take.

The spores had fed upon the broth and had come to life, and within the basket was an alien life form or a community of life forms. And they possessed a passion for orderliness and a zest for work and an ability to channel that zest into useful channels.

And what was more, the things within the basket did what a man wanted done.

It had straightened up the apartment, it had classified the stamps and covers, it had killed the mice, it had located the Polaris covers and had found the missing tongs.

And how had it known that he wanted these things done? Read his mind, perhaps?

He shivered at the thought, but the fact remained that it had done absolutely nothing except bubble merrily away until he had returned. It had done nothing, perhaps, because it did not know what to do—until he had somehow told it what to do. For as soon as he had returned, it had found out what to do and did it.

The door chimed and he got up to answer.

It was Tony.

"Hi, Unk," he said. "You forgot your pajamas and I brought them back. You left them on the bed and forgot to pack them."

He held out a package and it wasn't until then that he saw the room.

"Unk!" he yelled. "What happened? You got the place cleaned up!"

Packer shook his head in bewilderment. "Something funny, Tony."

Tony walked in and stared around in admiration and astonishment.

"You sure did a job," he said.

"I didn't do it, Tony."

"Oh, I see. You hired someone to do it while you were up at our place."

"No, not that. It was done this morning. It was done by that!"

He pointed at the basket.

"You're crazy, Unk," said Tony, firmly. "You have flipped your thatch."

"Maybe so," said Packer. "But the basket did the work."

Tony walked around the basket warily. He reached down and punched the yellow stuff with a stuck-out finger.

"It feels like dough," he announced.

He straightened up and looked at Packer.

"You aren't kidding me?" he asked.

"I don't know what it is," said Packer. "I don't know why or how it did it, but I'm telling you the truth."

"Unk," said Tony, "we may have something here!"

"There is no doubt of that."

"No, that's not what I mean. This may be the biggest thing that ever happened. This junk, you say, will really work for you?"

"Somehow or other," said Packer. "I don't know how it does it. It has a sense of order and it does the work you want. It seems to understand you—it anticipates whatever you want done. Maybe it's a brain with enormous psi powers. I was looking at a cover the other night and I saw this yellow stamp . . ."

Packer told him swiftly what had happened.

Tony listened thoughtfully, pulling at his chin.

"Well, all right, Unk," he said, "we've got it. We don't know what it is or how it works, but let's put our thinking into gear. Just imagine a bucket of this stuff standing in an office—a great big, busy office. It would make for efficiency such as you never saw before. It would file all the papers and keep the records straight and keep the entire business strictly up to date. There'd never be anything ever lost again. Everything would be right where it was supposed to be and could be located in a second. When the boss or someone else should want a certain file—bingo! It would be upon his desk. Why, an office with one of these little buckets could get rid of all its file clerks. A public library could be run efficiently without any personnel at all. But it would be in big business offices—in insurance firms and industrial concerns and transportation companies—where it would be worth the most."

Packer shook his head, a bit confused. "It might be all right, Tony. It might work the way you say. But who would believe you? Who would pay attention? It's just too fantastic. They would laugh at you."

"You leave all that to me," said Tony. "That's my end of the business. That's where I come in."

"Oh," said Packer, "so we're in business now."

"I have a friend," said Tony, who always had a friend, "who'd let me try it out. We could put a bucket of this stuff in his office and see how it works out."

He looked around, suddenly all business.

"You got a bucket, Unk?"

"Out in the kitchen. You'd find something there."

"And beef broth. It was beef broth, wasn't it?"

Packer nodded. "I think I have a can of it."

Tony stood and scratched his head. "Now let's get this figured out, Unk. What we want is a sure source of supply."

"I have those other covers. They all have stamps on them. We could start a new batch with one of them."

Tony gestured impatiently. "No, that wouldn't do. They are our reserves. We lock them tight away against emergency. I have a hunch that we can grow bucket after bucket of the stuff from what we have right here. Pull off a handful of it and feed it a shot of broth—"

"But how do you know—"

"Unk," said Tony, "doesn't it strike you a little funny that you had the exact number of spores in that one stamp, the correct amount of broth, to grow just one basket full?"

"Well, sure, but . . ."

"Look, this stuff is intelligent. It knows what it is doing. It lays down rules for itself to live by. It's got a sense of order and it lives by order. So you give it a wastebasket to live in and it lives within the limits of that basket. It gets just level with the top; it lets a little run down the sides to cement the basket tight to the floor. And that is all. It doesn't run over. It doesn't fill the room. It has some discipline."

"Well, maybe you are right, but that still doesn't answer the question—"

"Just a second, Unk. Watch here."

Tony plunged his hand into the basket and came out with a chunk of the spore-growth ripped loose from the parent body.

"Now, watch the basket, Unk," he said.

They watched. Swiftly, the spores surged and heaved to fill the space where the ripped-out chunk had been. Once again the basket was very neatly filled.

"You see what I mean?" said Tony. "Given more living room, it will grow. All we have to do is feed it so it can. And we'll give it living room. We'll give it a lot of buckets, so it can grow to its heart's content and—"

"Damn it, Tony, will you listen to me? I been trying to ask you what we're going to do to keep it from cementing itself to the floor. If we start another batch of it, it will cement its bucket or its basket or whatever it is in to the floor just like this first one did."

"I'm glad you brought that up," said Tony. "I know just what to do. We will hang it up. We'll hang up the bucket and there won't be any floor."

"Well," said Packer, "I guess that covers it. I'll go heat up that broth."

They heated the broth and found a bucket and hung it on a broomstick suspended between two chairs.

They dropped the chunk of spore-growth in and watched it and it stayed just as it was.

"My hunch was right," said Tony. "It needs some of that broth to get it started."

He poured in some broth and the spores melted before their very eyes into a black and ropy scum.

"There's something wrong," said Tony, worriedly.

"I guess there is," said Packer.

"I got an idea, Unk. You might have used a different brand of broth. There might be some difference in the ingredients. It may not be the broth itself, but some ingredient in it that gives this stuff the shot in the arm it needs. We might be using the wrong broth."

Packer shuffled uncomfortably.

"I don't remember, Tony."

"You have to!" Tony yelled at him. "Think, Unk! You got to—you have to remember what brand it was you used."

Packer whuffled out his whiskers unhappily.

"Well, to tell you the truth, Tony, it wasn't boughten broth. Mrs. Foshay made it."

"Now, we're getting somewhere! Who is Mrs. Foshay?"

"She's a nosy old dame who lives across the hall."

"Well, that's just fine. All you have to do is ask her to make some more for you."

"I can't do it, Tony."

"All we'd need is one batch, Unk. We could have it analyzed and find out what is in it. Then we'd be all set."

"She'd want to know why I wanted it. And she'd tell all over how I asked for it. She might even figure out there was something funny going on."

"We can't have that," exclaimed Tony in alarm. "This is our secret, Unk. We can't cut in anyone."

He sat and thought.

"Anyhow, she's probably sore at me," said Packer. "She sneaked in the other day and got the hell scared out of her when a mouse ran across the floor. She tore down to the management about it and tried to make me trouble."

Tony snapped his fingers.

"I got it!" he cried. "I know just how we'll work it. You go on and get in bed—"

"I will not!" snarled Packer.

"Now listen, Unk, you have to play along. You have to do your part."

"I don't like it," protested Packer. "I don't like any part of it."

"You get in bed," insisted Tony, "and look the worst you can. Pretend you're suffering. I'll go over to this Mrs. Foshay and I'll tell her how upset you were over that mouse scaring her. I'll say you worked all day to get the place cleaned up just because of that. I'll say you worked so—"

"You'll do no such thing," yelped Packer. "She'll come tearing in here. I won't have that woman—"

"You want to make a couple billion, don't you?" asked Tony angrily.

"I don't care particularly," Packer told him. "I can't somehow get my heart in it."

"I'll tell this woman that you are all tuckered out and that your heart is not so good and the only thing you want is another bowl of broth."

"You'll tell her no such thing," raved Packer. "You'll leave her out of this."

"Now, Unk," Tony reasoned with him, "if you won't do it for yourself, do it for me—me, the only kin you have in the entire world. It's the first big thing I've ever had a chance at. I may talk a lot and try to look prosperous and successful, but I tell you, Unk . . ."

He saw he was getting nowhere.

"Well, if you won't do it for me, do it for Ann, do it for the kids. You wouldn't want to see those poor little kids—"

"Oh, shut up," said Packer. "First thing you know, you'll be blubbering. All right, then, I'll do it."

It was worse than he had thought it would be. If he had known it was to be so bad, he'd never have consented to go through with it.

The Widow Foshay brought the bowl of broth herself. She sat on the bed and held his head up and cooed and crooned at him as she fed him broth.

It was most embarrassing.

But they got what they were after.

When she had finished feeding him, there was still half a bowl of broth and she left that with them because, she said, poor man, he might be needing it.

CHAPTER III

It was three o'clock in the afternoon and almost time for the Widow Foshay to come in with the broth.

Thinking of it, Packer gagged a little.

Someday, he promised himself, he'd beat Tony's brains out. If it hadn't been for him, this never would have started.

Almost six months now and every blessed day she had brought the broth and sat and talked with him while he forced down a bowl of it. And the worst of it, Packer told himself, was that he had to pretend that he thought that it was good.

And she was so gay! Why did she have to be so gay? Toujours gai, he thought. Just like the crazy alley cat that ancient writer had penned the silly lines about.

Garlic in the broth, he thought—my God, who'd ever heard of garlic in beef broth! It was uncivilized. A special recipe, she'd said, and it was all of that. And yet it had been the garlic that had done the job with the yellow spore-life—it was the food needed by the spores to kick them into life and to start them growing.

The garlic in the broth might have been good for him as well, he admitted to himself, for in many years, it seemed, he had not felt so fine. There was a spring in his step, he'd noticed, and he didn't get so tired; he used to take a nap in the afternoon and now he never did. He worked as much as ever, actually more than ever, and he was, except for the widow and the broth, a very happy man. Yes, a very happy man.

He would continue to be happy, he told himself, as long as Tony left him to his stamps. Let the little whippersnapper carry the load of Efficiency, Inc.; he was, after all, the one who had insisted on it. Although, to give him credit, he had done well with it. A lot of industries had signed up and a whole raft of insurance companies and a bunch of bond houses and a good scattering of other lines of business. Before long, Tony said, there wouldn't be a business anywhere that would dare to try to get along without the services of Efficiency, Inc.

The doorbell chimed and he went to answer it. It would be the Widow Foshay, and she would have her hands full with the broth.

But it was not the widow.

"Are you Mr. Clyde Packer?" asked the man who stood in the hall.

"Yes, sir," Packer said. "Will you please step in?"

"My name is John Griffin," said the man, after he was seated. "I represent Geneva."

"Geneva? You mean the Government?"

The man showed him credentials.

"Okay," said Packer a bit frostily, being no great admirer of the government. "What can I do for you?"

"You are senior partner in Efficiency, Inc., I believe."

"I guess that's what I am."

"Mr. Packer, don't you know?"

"Well, I'm not positive. I'm a partner, but I don't know about this senior business. Tony runs the show and I let him have his head."

"You and your nephew are sole owners of the firm?"

"You bet your boots we are. We kept it for ourselves. We took no one in with us."

"Mr. Packer, for some time the Government has been attempting to negotiate with Mr. Camper. He's told you nothing of it?"

"Not a thing," said Packer. "I'm busy with my stamps. He doesn't bother me."

"We have been interested in your service," Griffin said. "We have tried to buy it."

"It's for sale," said Packer. "You just pay the price and—"

"But you don't understand. Mr. Camper insists on a separate contract for every single office that we operate. That would run to a terrific figure—"

"Worth it," Packer assured him. "Every cent of it."

"It's unfair," said Griffin firmly. "We are willing to buy it on a departmental basis and we feel that even in that case we would be making some concession. By rights the government should be allowed to come in under a single covering arrangement."

"Look," protested Packer, "what are you talking to me for? I don't run the business; Tony does. You'll have to deal with him. I have faith in the boy. He has a good hard business head. I'm not even interested in Efficiency. All I'm interested in is stamps."

"That's just the point," said Griffin heartily. "You've hit the situation exactly on the head."

"Come again?" asked Packer.

"Well, it's like this," Griffin told him in confidential tones. "The government gets a lot of stamps in its daily correspondence. I forget the figure, but it runs to several tons of philatelic material every day. And from every planet in the galaxy. We have in the past been disposing of it to several stamp concerns, but there's a disposition in certain quarters to offer the whole lot as a package deal at a most attractive price."

"That is fine," said Packer, "but what would I do with several tons a day?"

"I wouldn't know," declared Griffin, "but since you are so interested in stamps, it would give you a splendid opportunity to have first crack at a batch of top-notch material. It is, I dare say, one of the best sources you could find."

"And you'd sell all this stuff to me if I put in a word for you with Tony?"

Griffin grinned happily. "You follow me exactly, Mr. Packer."

Packer snorted. "Follow you! I'm way ahead of you."

"Now, now," cautioned Griffin, "you must not get the wrong impression. This is a business offer—a purely business offer."

"I suppose you'd expect no more than nominal payment for all this waste paper I would be taking off your hands."

"Very nominal," said Griffin.

"All right, I'll think about it and I'll let you know. I can't promise you a thing, of course."

"I understand, Mr. Packer. I do not mean to rush you."

After Griffin left, Packer sat and thought about it and the more he thought about it, the more attractive it became.

He could rent a warehouse and install an Efficiency Basket in it and all he'd have to do would be dump all that junk in there and the basket would sort it out for him.

He wasn't exactly sure if one basket would have the time to break the selection down to more than just planetary groupings, but if one basket couldn't do it, he could install a second one and between the two of them, he could run the classification down to any point he wished. And then, after the baskets had sorted out the more select items for his personal inspection, he could set up an organization to sell the rest of it in job lots and he could afford to sell it at a figure that would run all the rest of those crummy dealers clear out on the limb.

He rubbed his hands together in a gesture of considerable satisfaction, thinking how he could make it rough for all those skinflint dealers. It was murder, he reminded himself, what they got away with; anything that happened to them, they had coming to them.

But there was one thing he gagged on slightly. What Griffin had offered him was little better than a bribe, although it was, he supposed, no more than one could expect of the government. The entire governmental structure was loaded with grafters and ten percenters and lobbyists and special interest boys and others of their ilk. Probably no one would think a thing of it if he made the stamp deal—except the dealers, of course, and there was absolutely nothing they could do about it except to sit and howl.

But aside from that, he wondered, did he have the right to interfere with Tony? He could mention it to him, of course, and Tony would say yes. But did he have the right?

He sat and worried at the question, without reaching a conclusion, without getting any nearer to the answer until the door chimes sounded.

It was the Widow Foshay and she was empty-handed. She had no broth today.

"Good afternoon," he said. "You are a little late."

"I was just opening my door to come over when I saw you had a caller. He's gone now, isn't he?"

"For some time," said Packer.

She stepped inside and he closed the door. They walked across the room.

"Mr. Packer," said the Widow, "I must apologize. I brought no broth today. The truth of the matter is, I'm tired of making it all the time."

"In such a case," he said, very gallantly, "the treats will be on me."

He opened the desk drawer and lifted out the brand new box of PugAlNash's leaf, which had arrived only the day before.

Almost reverently, he lifted the cover and held the box out to her. She recoiled from it a little.

"Go ahead," he urged. "Take a pinch of it. Don't swallow it. Just chew it."

Cautiously, she dipped her fingers in the box.

"That's too much," he warned her. "Just a little pinch. You don't need a lot. And it's rather hard to come by."

She took a pinch and put it in her mouth.

He watched her closely, smiling. She looked for all the world as if she had taken poison. But soon she settled back in her chair, apparently convinced it was not some lethal trick.

"I don't believe," she said, "I've ever tasted anything quite like it."

"You never have. Other than myself, you may well be the only human that has ever tasted it. I get it from a friend of mine who lives on one of the far-out stars. His name is PugAlNash and he sends it regularly. And he always includes a note."

He looked in the drawer and found the latest note.

"Listen to this," he said.

He read it:

Der Fiend: Grately injoid latter smoke you cent me. Ples mor of sam agin. You du knot no that I profetick and wach ahed for you. Butt it be so and I grately hapy to perform this taske for fiend. I assur you it be onely four the beste. You prophet grately, maybee.
Your luving fiend,
PugAlNash

He finished reading it and tossed it on the desk.

"What do you make of it?" he asked. "Especially that crack about his being a prophet and watching ahead for me?"

"It must be all right," the widow said. "He claims you will profit greatly."

"He sounds like a gypsy fortune-teller. He had me worried for a while."

"But why should you worry over that?"

"Because I don't want to know what's going to happen to me. And sometime he might tell me. If a man could look ahead, for example, he'd know just when he was going to die and how and all the—"

"Mr. Packer," she told him, "I don't think you're meant to die. I swear you are getting to look younger every day."

"As a matter of fact," said Packer, vastly pleased, "I'm feeling the best I have in years."

"It may be that leaf he sends you."

"No, I think most likely it is that broth of yours."

They spent a pleasant afternoon—more pleasant, Packer admitted, than he would have thought was possible.

And after she had left, he asked himself another question that had him somewhat frightened.

Why in the world, of all people in the world, had he shared the leaf with her?

He put the box back in the drawer and picked up the note. He smoothed it out and read it once again.

The spelling brought a slight smile to his lips, but he quickly turned it off, for despite the atrociousness of it, PugAlNash nevertheless was one score up on him. For Pug had been able, after a fashion, to master the language of Earth, while he had bogged down completely when confronted with Pug's language.

I profetick and wach ahed for you.

It was crazy, he told himself. It was, perhaps, some sort of joke, the kind of thing that passed for a joke with Pug.

He put the note away and prowled the apartment restlessly, vaguely upset by the whole pile-up of worries.

What should he do about the Griffin offer?

Why had he shared the leaf with the Widow Foshay?

What about that crack of Pug's?

He went to the bookshelves and put out a finger and ran it along the massive set of *Galactic Abstracts.* He found the right volume and took it back to the desk with him.

He leafed through it until he found *Unuk al Hay.* Pug, he remembered, lived on Planet X of the system.

He wrinkled up his forehead as he puzzled out the meaning of the compact, condensed, sometimes cryptic wording, bristling with fantastic abbreviations. It was a bloated nuisance, but it made sense, of course. There was just too much information to cover in the galaxy—the set of books, unwieldy as it might be, would simply become unmanageable if anything like complete-ness of expression and description were attempted.

X-lt.kn., int., uninh. hu., (T-67), tr. intrm. (T-102) med. hbs., leg. forst., diff. lang . . .

Wait a second, there!

Leg. forst.

Could that be legend of foresight?

He read it again, translating as he went:

X-little known, intelligence, uninhabitable for humans (see table 67), trade by intermediaries (see table 102), medical herbs, legend (or legacy?) of foresight, difficult language . . .

And that last one certainly was right. He'd gained a working knowledge of a lot of alien tongues, but with Pug's he could not even get an inkling.

Leg. forst.?

One couldn't be sure, but it could be—it could be!

He slapped the book shut and took it back to the shelf.

So you watch ahead for me, he said.

And why? To what purpose?

PugAlNash, he said, a little pleased, someday I'll wring your scrawny, meddling neck.

But, of course, he wouldn't. PugAlNash was too far away and he might not be scrawny and there was no reason to believe he even had a neck.

CHAPTER IV

When bedtime came around, he got into his flame-red pajamas with the yellow parrots on them and sat on the edge of the bed, wiggling his toes.

It had been quite a day, he thought.

He'd have to talk with Tony about this government offer to sell him the stamp material. Perhaps, he thought, he should insist upon it even if it meant a loss of possible revenue to Efficiency, Inc. He might as well get what he could and what he wanted when it was for the taking. For Tony, before they were through with it, probably would beat him out of what he had coming to him. He had expected it by now—but more than likely Tony had been too busy to indulge in any crookedness. Although it was a wonder, for Tony enjoyed a dishonest dollar twice as much as he did an honest one.

He remembered that he had told Griffin that he had faith in Tony and he guessed that he'd been right—he had faith in him and a little pride as well. Tony was an unprincipled rascal and there was no denying it. Thinking about it, Packer chuckled fondly. Just like me, he told himself, when I was young as Tony and was still in business.

There had been that triple deal with the bogus Chippendale and the Antarian paintings and the local version of moonshine from out in the Packrat system. By God, he told himself, I skinned all three of them on that one.

The phone rang and he padded out of the bedroom, his bare feet slapping on the floor.

The phone kept on insisting.

"All right!" yelled Packer angrily. "I'm coming!"

He reached the desk and picked up the phone.

"This is Pickering," said the voice.

"Pickering. Oh, sure. Glad to hear from you."

And had not the least idea who Pickering might be.

"The man you talked with about the Polaris cover."

"Yes, Pickering. I remember you."

"I wonder, did you ever find that cover?"

"Yes, I found it. Sorry, but the strip had only four. I told you five, I fear. An awful memory, but you know how it goes. A man gets old and—"

"Mr. Packer, will you sell that cover?"

"Sell it? Yes, I guess I told you that I would. Man of my word, you realize, although I regret it now."

"It's a fine one, then?"

"Mr. Pickering," said Packer, "considering that it's the only one in existence—"

"Could I come over to see it sometime soon?"

"Any time you wish. Any time at all."

"You will hold it for me?"

"Certainly," consented Packer. "After all, no one knows as yet that I have the thing."

"And the price?"

"Well, now, I told you a quarter million, but I was talking then about a strip of five. Since it's only four, I'd be willing to shave it some. I'm a reasonable man, Mr. Pickering. Not difficult to deal with."

"I can see you aren't," said Pickering with a trace of bitterness.

They said good night and Packer sat in the chair and put his bare feet up on the desk and wiggled his toes, watching them with a certain fascination, as if he had never seen them before.

He'd sell Pickering the four-strip cover for two hundred thousand. Then he'd let it get noised about that there was a five-strip cover, and once he heard that Pickering would be beside himself and frothing at the mouth. He'd be afraid that someone might get ahead of him and buy the five-stamp strip while he had only four. And that would be a public humiliation that a collector of Pickering's stripe simply couldn't stand.

Packer chortled softly to himself.

"Bait," he said aloud.

He probably could get half a million out of that five-strip piece. He'd make Pickering pay for it. He'd have to start it high, of course, and let Pickering beat him down.

He looked at the clock upon the desk and it was ten o'clock— a good hour past his usual bedtime.

He wiggled his toes some more and watched them. Funny thing about it, he wasn't even sleepy. He didn't want to go to bed; he'd got undressed from simple force of habit.

Nine o'clock, he thought, is a hell of a time for a man to go to bed. He could remember a time when he had never turned in until well after midnight and there had been many certain memorable occasions, he chucklingly recalled, when he'd not gone to bed at all.

But there had been something to do in those days. There had been places to go and people to meet and food had tasted proper and the liquor had been something a man looked forward to. They didn't make decent liquor these days, he told himself. And there were no great cooks any more. And no entertainment, none worthy of the name. All his friends had either died or scattered; none of them had lasted.

Nothing lasts, he thought.

He sat wiggling his toes and looking at the clock and somehow he was beginning to feel just a bit excited, although he could not imagine why.

In the silence of the room there were two sounds only—the soft ticking of the clock and the syrupy gurgling of the basket full of spores.

He leaned around the corner of the desk and looked at the basket and it was there, foursquare and solid—a basketful of fantasy come to sudden and enduring life.

Someday, he thought, someone would find where the spores came from—what distant planet in what misty reaches out toward the rim of the thinning galaxy. Perhaps even now the origin of the stamps could be determined if he'd only release the data that he had, if he would show the covers with the yellow stamps to some authority. But the covers and the data were a trade secret and had become too valuable to be shown to any one and they were tucked away deep inside a bank vault.

Intelligent spores, he mused—what a perfect medium for the carrying of the mail. You put a dab of them on a letter or a package and you told them, somehow or other, where the letter or the package was to go and they would take it there. And once the job was done, then the spores encysted until the day that someone else, or something else, should recall them to their labors.

And today they were laboring for the Earth and the day would come, perhaps, when they'd be housekeepers to the entire Earth. They'd run all businesses efficiently and keep all homes picked up and neat; they would clean the streets and keep them free of litter and introduce everywhere an era of such order and such cleanliness as no race had ever known.

He wiggled his toes and looked at the clock again. It was not ten-thirty yet and it was really early. Perhaps he should change his mind—perhaps he should dress again and go for a moonlight stroll. For there was a moon; he could see it through the window.

Damn old fool, he told himself, whuffling out his whiskers.

But he took his feet down off the desk and padded toward the bedroom.

He chuckled as he went, planning exactly how he was going to skin Pickering to within an inch of that collector's parsimonious life.

He was bending at the mirror, trying to make his tie track, when the doorbell set up a clamor.

If it was Pickering, he thought, he'd throw the damn fool out. Imagine turning up at this time of night to do a piece of business that could better wait till morning.

It wasn't Pickering.

The man's card said he was W. Frederick Hazlitt and that he was president of the Hazlitt Suppliers Corporation.

"Well, Mr. Hazlitt?"

"I'd like to talk to you a minute," Hazlitt said, peering furtively around. "You're sure that we're alone here?"

"Quite alone," said Packer.

"This is a matter of some delicacy," Hazlitt told him, "and of some alarm as well. I came to you rather than Mr. Anton Camper because I know of you by reputation as a man of proven business sagacity. I feel you could understand the problem where Mr. Camper—"

"Fire away," invited Packer cordially.

He had a feeling that he was going to enjoy this. The man was obviously upset and scared to death as well.

Hazlitt hunched forward in his chair and his voice dropped almost to a whisper.

"Mr. Packer," he confided in stricken horror, "I am becoming honest!"

"That's too bad," said Packer sympathetically.

"Yes, it is," said Hazlitt soberly. "A man in my position—in any business connection—simply can't be honest. Mr. Packer, I'll tell you confidentially that I lost out on one of the biggest deals in all my business life just last week because I had grown honest."

"Maybe," Packer suggested, "if you persevered, if you set your heart on it, you could remain at least partially dishonest."

Hazlitt shook his head dolefully. "I tell you, sir, I can't. I've tried. You don't know how hard I've tried. And no matter how I try, I find myself telling the truth about everything. I find that I cannot take unfair advantage of anyone, not even of a customer. I even found myself the other day engaged in cutting my profit margins down to a more realistic figure—"

"Why, that's horrible!" cried Packer.

"And it's all your fault," yelled Hazlitt.

"My fault," protested Packer, whuffling out his whiskers.

"Upon my word, Mr. Hazlitt, I can't see how you can say a thing like that. I haven't had a thing to do with it."

"It's your Efficiency units," howled Hazlitt. "They're the cause of it."

"The Efficiency units have nothing to do with you," declared Packer angrily. "All they do . . ."

He stopped.

Good Lord, he thought, they could!

He'd been feeling better than he'd felt for years and he didn't need his nap of an afternoon and here he was, dressing to go out in the middle of the night!

"How long has this been going on?" he asked in growing horror.

"For a month at least," said Hazlitt. "I think I first noticed it a month or six weeks ago."

"Why didn't you simply heave the unit out?"

"I did," yelled Hazlitt, "but it did no good."

"I don't understand. If you threw it out that should be the end of it."

"That's what I thought at the time, myself. But I was wrong. That yellow stuff's still there. It's growing in the cracks and floating in the air and you can't get rid of it. Once you have it, you are stuck with it."

Packer clucked in sympathy.

"You could move, perhaps."

"Do you realize what that would cost me, Packer? And besides, as far as I'm concerned, it simply is no good. The stuff's inside of me!"

He pounded at his chest. "I can feel it here, inside of me—turning me honest, making a good man out of me, making me orderly and efficient, just like it made our files. And I don't want to be a good man, Packer—I want to make a lot of money!"

"There's one consolation," Packer told him. "Whatever is happening to you undoubtedly also is happening to your competitors."

"But even if that were the case," protested Hazlitt, "it would be no fun. What do you think a man goes into business for? To render service, to become identified with the commercial community, to make money only? No, sir, I tell you—it's the thrill of skinning a competitor, of running the risk of losing your own shirt, of—"

"Amen," Packer said loudly.

Hazlitt stared at him. "You, too . . ."

"Not a chance," said Packer proudly. "I'm every bit as big a rascal as I ever was."

Hazlitt settled back into his chair. His voice took on an edge, grew a trifle cold.

"I had considered exposing you, warning the world, and then I saw I couldn't . . ."

"Of course you can't," said Packer gruffly. "You don't enjoy being laughed at. You are the kind of man who can't stand the thought of being laughed at."

"What's your game, Packer?"

"My game?"

"You introduced the stuff. You must have known what it would do. And yet you say you are unaffected by it. What are you shooting at—gobbling up the entire planet?"

Packer whuffled. "I hadn't thought of it," he said. "But it's a capital idea."

He rose stiffly to his feet. "Little old for it," he said. "But I have a few years yet. And I'm in the best of fettle. Haven't felt—"

"You were going out," said Hazlitt, rising. "I'll not detain you."

"I thank you, sir," said Packer. "I noticed that there was a moon and I was going for a stroll. You wouldn't join me, would you?"

"I have more important things to do, Packer, than strolling in the moonlight."

"I have no doubt of that," said Packer, bowing slightly. "You would, of course, an upright, honest business man like you."

Hazlitt slammed the door as he went out.

Packer padded back to the bedroom, took up the tie again.

Hazlitt an honest man, he thought. And how many other honest men this night? And a year from now—how many honest men in the whole wide world just one year from now? How long before the entire Earth would be an honest Earth? With spores lurking in the cracks and floating in the air and running with the rivers, it might not take so long.

Maybe that was the reason Tony hadn't skinned him yet. Maybe Tony was getting honest, too. Too bad, thought Packer, gravely. Tony wouldn't be half as interesting if he should happen to turn honest.

And the government? A government that had come begging for the spores—begging to be honest, although to be completely fair one must admit the government as yet did not know about the honesty.

That was a hot one, Packer told himself. An honest government! And it would serve those stinkers right! He could see the looks upon their faces.

He gave up the business of the tie and sat down on the bed and shook for minutes with rumbling belly laughter.

At last he wiped the tears out of his eyes and finished with the tie.

Tomorrow morning, bright and early, he'd get in touch with Griffin and arrange the package deal for the stamp material. He'd act greedy and drive a hard bargain and then, in the end, pay a bit more than the price agreed upon for a long-term arrangement. An honest government, he told himself, would be too honest to rescind such an agreement even if, in the light of its new honesty, it should realize the wrongness of it. For, happily, one of the tenets of honesty was to stay stuck with a bad bargain, no matter how arrived at.

He shucked into his jacket and went into the living room. He stopped at the desk and opened the drawer. Reaching in, he lifted the lid of the box of leaf. He took a pinch and had it halfway to his mouth when the thought struck him suddenly and he stood for a moment frozen while all the gears came together, meshing, and the pieces fell into a pattern and he knew, without even asking, why he was the only genuine dishonest man left on the entire Earth.

I profetick and wach ahed for you!

He put the leaf into his mouth and felt the comfort of it.

Antidote, he thought, and knew that he was right.

But how could Pug have known—how could he have foreseen the long, twisting tangle of many circumstances which must inevitably crystallize into this very moment?

Leg. forst.?

He closed the lid of the box and shut the drawer and turned toward the door.

The only dishonest man in the world, he thought. Immune to the honesty factor in the yellow spores because of the resistance built up within him by his long use of the leaf.

He had set a trap tonight to victimize Pickering and tomorrow he'd go out and fox the government and there was no telling where he'd go from there. Hazlitt had said something about taking over the entire planet and the idea was not a bad one if he could only squeeze out the necessary time.

He chuckled at the thought of how all the honest suckers would stand innocently in line, unable to do a thing about it—all fair prey to the one dishonest man in the entire world. A wolf among the sheep!

He drew himself erect and pulled the white gloves on carefully. He flicked his walking stick. Then he thumped himself on the chest—just once—and let himself out into the hall. He did not bother to lock the door behind him.

In the lobby, as he stepped out of the lift, he saw the Widow Foshay coming in the door. She turned and called back cheerfully to friends who had brought her home.

He lifted his hat to her with an olden courtesy that he thought he had forgotten.

She threw up her hands in mock surprise. "Mr. Packer," she cried, "what has come over you? Where do you think you're going at this time of night, when all honest people are abed?"

"Minerva," he told her gravely, "I was about to take a stroll. I wonder if you might come along with me?"

She hesitated for an instant, just long enough to give the desired small show of reluctance and indecision.

He whuffled out his mustache at her. "Besides," he said, "I am not an honest person."

He offered her his arm with distinguished gallantry.

PHYSICIAN TO THE UNIVERSE

Originally published in the March 1963 issue of Fantastic Stories, *"Physician to the Universe" displays a level of obsession and anger seldom seem in stories by Cliff Simak. In his other works, Cliff has described outer space as "the great uncaring," but when he uses those words here, he's talking about a swamp. The swamp, however, is not the enemy here; rather, the enemy is the human fear that leads to tyranny.*

—dww

He awoke and was in a place he had never seen before. It was an unsubstantial place that flickered on and off and it was a place of dusk in which darker figures stood out faintly. There were two white faces that flickered with the place and there was a smell he had never known before—a dank, dark smell, like the smell of black, deep water that had stood too long without a current to stir it.

And then the place was gone and he was back again in that other place that was filled with brilliant light, with the marble eminence looming up before him and the head of the man who sat atop this eminence and behind it, so that one must look up, it seemed, from very far below to see him. As if the man were very high and one were very low, as if the man were great and one, himself, were humble.

The mouth in the middle of face of the man who was high and great was moving and one strained to catch the sound of words, but there was only silence, a terrible, humming silence that shut one out from this brilliant place, that made one all alone and small and very unimportant—too poor and unimportant to hear the words that the great man might be saying. Although it seemed as if one knew the words, knowing there were no other words the great man might be allowed to say, that he had to say them because, despite his highness and his greatness, he was caught in the self-same trap as the little, humble being who stood staring up at him. The words were there, just beyond some sort of barrier one could not comprehend, and if one could pierce that barrier he'd know the words without having heard them said. And it was important that he know them, for they were of great concern to him—they were, in fact, about him and they would affect his life.

His mind went pawing out to find the barrier and to strip it from the words and even as he did, the place of brilliance tilted and he was back again in the dusk that flickered.

The white faces still were bent above him and one of the faces now came closer, as if it were floating down upon him—all alone, all by itself, a small white-faced balloon. For in the dark one could not see the body. If there were a body.

"You'll be all right," the white face said. "You are coming round."

"Of course I'll be all right," said Alden Street, rather testily.

For he was angry at the words, angry that here he could hear the words, but back in that place of brilliance he could hear no words at all—words that were important, while these words he had heard were no more than drivel.

"Who said I wouldn't be all right?" asked Alden Street.

And that was who he was, but not entirely who he was, for he was more than just a name. Every man, he thought, was more than just a name. He was many things.

He was Alden Street and he was a strange and lonely man who lived in a great, high, lonely house that stood above the village and looked out across a wilderness of swampland that stretched toward the south until it went out of sight—farther, much farther than the human eye could see, a swamp whose true proportions could be drawn only on a map.

The house was surrounded by a great front yard and a garden at the rear and at the garden's edge grew a mighty tree that flamed golden in the autumn for a few brief hours, and the tree held something of magnificent importance and he, Alden Street, was tied in with that great importance.

He sought wildly for this great importance and in the dusk he could not find it. It had somehow slipped his grasp. He had had it, he had known it, he'd lived with it all his life, from the time of childhood, but he did not have it. It had left him somehow.

He went scrabbling after it, frantically, for it was something that he could not lose, plunging after it into the darkness of his brain. And as he scrambled after it, he knew the taste again, the bitter taste when he had drained the vial and dropped it to the floor.

He scrabbled in the darkness of his mind, searching for the thing he'd lost, not remembering what it was, with no inkling of what it might have been, but knowing he would recognize it once he came across it.

He scrabbled and he did not find it. For suddenly he was not in the darkness of his brain, but back once more in the place of brilliance. And angry at how he'd been thwarted in his search.

The high and mighty man had not started speaking, although Alden could see that he was about to speak, that at any moment now he would start to speak. And the strange thing of it was that he was certain he had seen this all before and had heard before what the high, great man was about to say. Although he could not, for the life of him, recall a word of it. He had been here before, he knew, not once, but twice before. This was a reel re-run, this was past happening.

"Alden Street," said the man so high above him, "you will stand and face me."

And that was silly, Alden thought, for he was already standing and already facing him.

"You have heard the evidence," said the man, "that has been given here."

"I heard it," Alden said.

"What have you, then, to say in your self-defense?"

"Not a thing," said Alden.

"You mean you don't deny it?"

"I can't deny it's true. But there were extenuating circumstances."

"I am sure there were, but they're not admissible."

"You mean that I can't tell you . . ."

"Of course you can. But it will make no difference. The law admits no more than the commission of the crime. There can be no excuses."

"I would suppose, then," said Alden Street, "there is nothing I can say. Your Honor, I would not waste your time."

"I am glad," said the judge, "that you are so realistic. It makes the whole thing simpler and easier. And it expedites the business of this court."

"But you must understand," said Alden Street, "that I can't be sent away. I have some most important work and I should be getting back to it."

"You admit," said the high, great man, "that you were ill for twenty-four full hours and failed most lamentably to report your illness."

"Yes," said Alden Street.

"You admit that even then you did not report for treatment, but rather that you were apprehended by a monitor."

Alden did not answer. It was piling up and there was no use to answer. He could see, quite plainly, that it would do no good.

"And, further, you admit that it has been some eighteen months since you have reported for your physical."

"I was far too busy."

"Too busy when the law is most explicit that you must have a physical at six month intervals?"

"You don't understand, Your Honor."

His Honor shook his head. "I am afraid I do. You have placed yourself above the law. You have chosen deliberately to flout the law and you must answer for it. Too much has been gained by our medical statutes to endanger their observance. No citizen can be allowed to set a precedent against them. The struggle to gain a sound and healthy people must be accorded the support of each and every one of us and I cannot countenance . . ."

The place of brilliance tilted and he was back in the dusk again.

He lay upon his back and stared up into the darkness, and although he could feel the pressure of the bed on which he lay, it was as if he were suspended in some sort of dusky limbo that had no beginning and no end, that was nowhere and led nowhere, and was, in itself, the terminal point of all and each existence.

From somewhere deep inside himself he heard the questioning once again—the flat, hard voice that had, somehow, the sound of metal in it:

Have you ever taken part in any body-building program?

When was the last time that you brushed your teeth?

Have you ever contributed either time or money to the little leagues?

How often would you say that you took a bath?

Did you at any time ever express a doubt that sports developed character?

One of the white faces floated out of the darkness to hang above him once again. It was, he saw, an old face—a woman's face and kind.

A hand slid beneath his head and lifted it.

"Here," the white face said, "drink this."

He felt the spoon against his lips.

"It's soup," she said. "It's hot. It will give you strength."

He opened his mouth and the spoon slid in. The soup was hot and comforting.

The spoon retreated.

"Where . . ." he said.

"Where are you?"

"Yes," he whispered, "where am I? I want to know."

"This is Limbo," the white face said.

Now the word had meaning.

Now he could recall what Limbo was.

And he could not stay in Limbo.

It was inconceivable that anyone should expect that he should stay in Limbo.

He rolled his head back and forth on the thin, hard pillow in a gesture of despair.

If he only had more strength. Just a little while ago he had had a lot of strength. Old and wiry and with a lot of strength left in him. Strong enough for almost anything at all.

But shiftless, they had said back in Willow Bend.

And there he had the name. He was glad to have it back. He hugged it close against him.

"Willow Bend," he said, speaking to the darkness.

"You all right, old timer?"

He could not see the speaker, but he was not frightened. There was nothing to be frightened of. He had his name and he had Willow Bend and he had Limbo and in just a little while he'd have all the rest of it and then he'd be whole again and strong.

"I'm all right," he said.

"Kitty gave you soup. You want some more of it?"

"No. All I want is to get out of here."

"You been pretty sick. Temperature a hundred and one point seven."

"Not now. I have no fever now."

"No. But when you got here."

"How come you know about my temperature? You aren't any

medic. I can tell by the voice of you that you aren't any medic. In Limbo, there would be no medic."

"No medic," said the unseen speaker. "But I am a doctor."

"You're lying," Alden told him. "There are no human doctors. There isn't any such a thing as doctors any more. All we have is medics."

"There are some of us in research."

"But Limbo isn't research."

"At times," the voice said, "you get rather tired of research. It's too impersonal and sterile."

Alden did not reply. He ran his hand, in a cautious rubbing movement, up and down the blanket that had been used to cover him. It was stiff and hard to the touch, but seemed fairly heavy.

He tried to sort out in his mind what the man had told him.

"There is no one here," he said, "but violators. What did you violate? Forget to trim your toe-nails? Short yourself on sleep?"

"I'm not a violator."

"A volunteer, perhaps."

"Nor a volunteer. It would do no good to volunteer. They would not let you in. That's the point to Limbo—that's the dirty rotten joke. You ignore the medics, so now the medics ignore you. You go to a place where there aren't any medics and see how well you like it."

"You mean that you broke in?"

"You might call it that."

"You're crazy," Alden Street declared.

For you didn't break into Limbo. If you were smart at all, you did your level best to stay away from it. you brushed your teeth and bathed and used one of the several kinds of approved mouth washes and you took care that you had your regular check-ups and you saw to it that you had some sort of daily exercise and you watched your diet and you ran as fast as you could leg it to the nearest clinic the first moment you felt ill. Not that you were often ill. The way they kept you checked, the way they made you live, you were very seldom ill.

He heard that flat, metallic voice clanging in his brain again, the disgusted, shocked, accusatory voice of the medic disciplinary corps.

Alden Street, it said, *you're nothing but a dirty slob.*

And that, of course, was the worst thing that he could be called. There was no other label that could possibly be worse. It was synonymous with traitor to the cause of the body beautiful and healthy.

"This place?" he asked. "It's a hospital?"

"No," the doctor said. "There's no hospital here. There is nothing here. Just me and the little that I know and the herbs and other woods specifics that I'm able to command."

"And this Limbo. What kind of Limbo is it?"

"A swamp," the doctor said. "An ungodly place, believe me."

"Death sentence?"

"That's what it amounts to."

"I can't die," said Alden.

"Some day," the calm voice said. "All men must."

"Not yet."

"No, not yet. You'll be all right in a few more hours."

"What was the matter with me?"

"You had some sort of fever."

"But no name for it."

"Look, how would I know? I am not . . ."

"I know you're not a medic. Humans can't be medics—not practicing physicians, not surgeons, not anything at all that has to do with the human body. But a human can be a medical research man because that takes insight and imagination."

"You've thought about this a lot," the doctor said.

"Some," Alden said. "Who has not?"

"Perhaps not as many as you think. But you are angry. You are bitter."

"Who wouldn't be? When you think about it."

"I'm not," the doctor said.

"But you . . ."

"Yes, I of all of us, should be the bitter one. But I'm not. Because we did it to ourselves. The robots didn't ask for it. We handed it to them."

And that was right, of course, thought Alden. It had started long ago when computers had been used for diagnosis and for drug dosage computation. And it had gone on from there. It had been fostered in the name of progress. And who was there to stand in the way of progress?

"Your name," he said. "I'd like to know your name."

"My name is Donald Parker."

"An honest name," said Alden Street. "A good, clean, honest name."

"Now go to sleep," said Parker. "You have talked too long."

"What time is it?"

"It will soon be morning."

The place was dark as ever. There was no light at all. There was no seeing and there was no sound and there was the smell of evil dankness. It was a pit, thought Alden—a pit for that small portion of humanity which rebelled against or ignored or didn't, for one reason or another, go along with the evangelistic fervor of universal health. You were born into it and educated in it and you grew up and continued with it until the day you died. And it was wonderful, of course, but, God, how tired you got of it, how sick you got of it. Not of the program or the law, but of the unceasing vigilance, of the spirit of crusading against the tiny germ, of the everlasting tilting against the virus and the filth, of the almost religious ardor with which the medic corps kept its constant watch.

Until in pure resentment you longed to wallow in some filth; until it became a mark of bravado not to wash your hands.

For the statutes were quite clear—illness was a criminal offense and it was a misdemeanor to fail to carry out even the most minor precaution aimed at keeping healthy.

It started with the cradle and it extended to the grave and there was a joke, never spoken loudly (a most pathetic joke), that the only thing now left to kill a person was a compelling sense of boredom. In school the children had stars put against their names for the brushing of the teeth, for the washing of the hands, for regular toilet habits, for many other tasks. On the playground there was no longer anything so purposeless and foolish (and even criminal) as haphazard play, but instead meticulously worked out programs of calisthenics aimed at the building of the body. There were sports programs on every level, on the elementary and secondary school levels, on the college level, neighborhood and community levels, young folks, young marrieds, middle-aged and old folks levels—every kind of sports, for every taste and season. They were not spectator sports. If one knew what was good for him, he would not for a moment become anything so useless and so suspect as a sports spectator.

Tobacco was forbidden, as were all intoxicants (tobacco and intoxicants now being little more than names enacted in the laws), and only wholesome foods were allowed upon the market. There were no such things now as candy or soda pop or chewing gum. These, along with liquor and tobacco, finally were no more than words out of a distant past, something told about in bated breath by a garrulous oldster who had heard about them when he was very young, who might have experienced or heard about the last feeble struggle of defiance by the small fry mobs which had marked their final stamping out.

No longer were there candy-runners or pop bootleggers or the furtive sale in some dark alley of a pack of chewing gum.

Today the people were healthy and there was no disease—or almost no disease. Today a man at seventy was entering middle age and could look forward with some confidence to another forty years of full activity in his business or profession. Today you did not die at eighty, but barring accident, could expect to reach a century and a half.

And this was all to the good, of course, but the price you paid was high.

"Donald Parker," said Alden.

"Yes," said the voice from the darkness.

"I was wondering if you were still here."

"I was about to leave. I thought you were asleep."

"You got in," said Alden. "All by yourself, I mean. The medics didn't bring you."

"All by myself," said Parker.

"Then you know the way. Another man could follow."

"You mean someone else could come in."

"No. I mean someone could get out. They could backtrack you."

"No one here," said Parker. "I was in the peak of physical condition and I made it only by the smallest margin. Another five miles to go and I'd never made it."

"But if one man . . ."

"One man in good health. There is no one here could make it. Not even myself."

"If you could tell me the way."

"It would be insane," said Parker. "Shut up and go to sleep."

Alden listened to the other moving, heading for the unseen door.

"I'll make it," Alden said, not talking to Parker, nor even to himself, but talking to the dark and the world the dark enveloped.

For he had to make it. He must get back to Willow Bend. There was something waiting for him there and he must get back.

Parker was gone and there was no one else.

The world was quiet and dark and dank. The quietness was so deep that the silence sang inside one's head.

Alden pulled his arms up along his sides and raised himself slowly on his elbows. The blanket fell off his chest and he sat there on the bed and felt the chill that went with the darkness and the dankness reach out and take hold of him.

He shivered, sitting there.

He lifted one hand, cautiously, and reached for the blanket, intending to pull it up around himself. But with his fingers clutching its harsh fabric, he did not pull it up. For this, he told himself, was not the way to do it. He could not cower in bed, hiding underneath a blanket.

Instead of pulling it up, he thrust the blanket from him and his hand went down to feel his legs. They were encased in cloth—his trousers still were on him, and his shirt as well, but his feet were bare. Maybe his shoes were beside the bed, with the socks tucked inside of them. He reached out a hand and felt, groping in the dark—and he was not in bed. He was on a pallet of some sort, laid upon the floor, and the floor was earth. He could feel the coldness and the dampness of its packed surface as he brushed it with his palm.

There were no shoes. He groped for them in a wide semicircle, leaning far out to reach and sweep the ground.

Someone had put them someplace else, he thought. Or, perhaps, someone had stolen them. In Limbo, more than likely, a pair of shoes would be quite a treasure. Or perhaps he'd never had them. You might not be allowed to take your shoes with you into Limbo—that might be part of Limbo.

No shoes, no toothbrushes, no mouth washes, no proper food, no medicines or medics. But there was a doctor here—a human doctor who had broken in, a man who had committed himself to Limbo of his own free will.

What kind of man would you have to be, he wondered, to do a thing like that? What motive would you have to have to drive you? What kind of idealism, or what sort of bitterness, to sustain you along the way? What sort of love or hate, to stay?

He sat back on the pallet, giving up his hunt for shoes, shaking his head in silent wonderment at the things a man could do. The human race, he thought, was a funny thing. It paid lip service to reason and to logic, and yet more often it was emotion and illogic that served to shape its ends.

And that, he thought, might be the reason that all the medics now were robots. For medicine was a science that only could be served by reason and by logic and there was in the robots nothing that could correspond to the human weakness of emotion.

Carefully he swung his feet off the pallet and put them on the floor, then slowly stood erect. He stood in dark loneliness and the dampness of the floor soaked into his soles.

Symbolic, he thought—unintentional, perhaps, but a perfect symbolic introduction to the emptiness of this place called Limbo.

He reached out his hands, groping for some point of reference as he slowly shuffled forward.

He found a wall, made of upright boards, rough sawn with the tough texture of the saw blade unremoved by any planing, and with uneven cracks where they had been joined together.

Slowly he felt his way along them and came at last to the place they ended. Groping, he made out that he had found a doorway, but there was no door.

He thrust a foot over the sill, seeking for the ground outside, and found it, almost even with the sill.

Quickly, as if he might be escaping, he swung his body through the door and now, for the first time, there was a break in darkness. The lighter sky etched the outline of mighty trees and at some level which stood below the point he occupied he could make out a ghostly whiteness that he guessed was ground fog, more than likely hanging low above a lake or stream.

He stood stiff and straight and took stock of himself. A little weak and giddy, and a coldness in his belly and a shiver in his bones, but otherwise all right.

He put up a hand and rubbed it along his jaw and the whiskers grated. A week or more, he thought, since he had shaved—it must have been that long, at least. He tried to drive his mind back to find when he'd last shaved, but time ran together like an oily fluid and he could make nothing of it.

He had run out of food and had gone downtown, the first time in many days—not wanting to go even then, but driven by his hunger. There wasn't time to go, there was time for nothing, but there came a time when a man must eat. How long had it really been, he wondered, that he'd gone without a bite to eat, glued to the task that he was doing, that important task which he'd now forgotten, only knowing that he had been doing it and that it was unfinished and that he must get back to it.

Why had he forgotten? Because he had been ill? Was it possible that an illness would make a man forget?

Let's start, he thought, at the first beginning. Let's take it slow and simple. One step at a time, carefully and easily; not all in a rush.

His name was Alden Street and he lived in a great, high, lonely house that his parents had built almost eighty years ago, in all its pride and arrogance, on the mound above the village. And for this building on the mound above the village, for the pride and arrogance, his parents had been hated, but for all the hate had been accepted since his father was a man of learning and of great business acumen and in his years amassed a small-sized fortune dealing in farm mortgages and other properties in Mataloosa county.

With his parents dead, the hate transferred to him, but not the acceptance that had gone hand-in-hand with hate, for although he had a learning gathered from several colleges, he put it to no use—at least to no use which had made it visible to the village. He did not deal in mortgages nor in properties. He lived alone in the great, high house that now had gone to ruin, using up, bit by bit, the money his father had laid by and left him. He had no friends and he sought no friends. There were times when he did not appear on the village streets for weeks on end, although it was known that he was at home. For watching villagers could see the lights burning in the high and lonesome house, come nights.

At one time the house had been a fine place, but now neglect and years had begun to take their toll. There were shutters that hung crooked and a great wind years before had blown loosened bricks from the chimney top and some of the fallen bricks still lay upon the roof. The paint had peeled and powdered off and the front stoop had sunk, its foundation undermined by a busily burrowing gopher and the rains that followed. Once the lawn had been neatly kept, but now the grass grew rank and the shrubs no longer knew the shears and the trees were monstrous growths that almost screened the house from view. The flower beds, cherished by his mother, now were gone, long since choked out by weeds and creeping grass.

It was a shame, he thought, standing in the night. I should have kept the place the way my mother and my father kept it, but there were so many other things.

The people in the village despised him for his shiftlessness and his thoughtlessness which allowed the pride and arrogance to fall into ruin and decay. For hate as they might the arrogance, they still were proud of it. They said he was no good. They said that he was lazy and that he didn't care.

But I did care, he thought. I cared so very deeply, not for the house, not for the village, not even for myself. But for the job— the job that he had not selected, but rather that had been thrust upon him.

Or was it a job, he wondered, so much as a dream?

Let's start at the first beginning, he had told himself, and that was what he had meant to do, but he had not started at the first beginning; he had started near the end. He had started a long way from the first beginning.

He stood in the darkness, with the treetops outlined by the lighter sky and the white ghost fog that lay close above the water, and tried to swim against the tide of time back to that first beginning, back to where it all had started. It was far away, he knew, much farther than he'd thought, and it had to do, it seemed, with a late September butterfly and the shining gold of falling walnut leaves.

He had been sitting in a garden and he had been a child. It

was a blue and wine-like autumn day and the air was fresh and the sun was warm, as anything only can be fresh and warm when one is very young.

The leaves were falling from the tree above in a golden rain and he put out his hands to catch one of the falling leaves, not trying to catch any single one of them, but holding out his hands and knowing that one of them would drift into a palm—holding out his hands with an utter childish faith, using up in that single instant the only bit of unquestioning faith that any man can know.

He closed his eyes and tried to capture it again, tried to become in this place of distant time the little boy he had been on that day the gold had rained down.

He was there, but it was hazy and it was not bright and the clearness would not come—for there was something happening, there was a half-sensed shadow out there in the dark and the squish of wet shoes walking on the earth.

His eyes snapped open and the autumn day was gone and someone was moving toward him through the night, as if a piece of the darkness had detached itself and had assumed a form and was moving forward.

He heard the gasp of breath and the squish of shoes and then the movement stopped.

"You there," said a sudden, husky voice. "You standing there, who are you?"

"I am new here. My name is Alden Street."

"Oh, yes," the voice said. "The new one. I was coming up to see you."

"That was good of you," said Alden.

"We take care of one another here," the voice said. "We care for one another. We are the only ones there are. We really have to care."

"But you . . ."

"I am Kitty," said the voice. "I'm the one who fed you soup.

She struck the match and held it cupped within her hands as if she sought to protect the tiny flame against the darkness.

Just the three of us, thought Alden—the three of us arraigned against the dark. For the blaze was one of them, it had become one with them, holding life and movement, and it strove against the dark.

He saw that her fingers were thin and sensitive, delicate as some old vase fashioned out of porcelain.

She bent with the flame still cupped within her hand and touched it to a candle stub thrust into a bottle that, from the height of it, stood upon a table, although one could not see the table.

"We don't often have a light," said Kitty. "It is a luxury we seldom can afford. Our matches are so few and the candles are so short. We have so little here."

"There is no need," said Alden.

"But there is," said Kitty. "You are a new one here. We cannot let you go stumbling in the dark. For the first little while we make a light for you."

The candle caught and guttered, sending flickering shadows fleeing wildly. Then it steadied and its feeble glow cut a circle in the dark.

"It will soon be morning," Kitty told him, "and then the day will come and the light of day is worse than the darkness of the night. For in the day you see and know. In the dark, at least, you can think that it is not too bad. But this is best of all—a little pool of light to make a house inside the darkness."

She was not young, he saw. Her hair hung in dank strings about her face and her face was pinched and thin and there were lines upon it. But there was, he thought, back of the stringiness and the thinness and the lines, a sense of some sort of eternal youthfulness and vitality that nothing yet had conquered.

The pool of light had spread a little as the flame had settled down and now he could see the place in which they stood.

It was small, no more than a hut. There was the pallet on the floor and the blanket where he'd tossed it from him. There was a crazy-legged table upon which the candle stood and two sawed blocks of wood to serve as chairs. There were two plates and two white cups standing on the table.

Cracks gaped between the upright boards that formed the walls of the hut and in other places knots had dried and fallen out, leaving peepholes to the world outside.

"This was your place," he said. "I would not have inconvenienced you."

"Not my place," she said. "Harry's place, but it's all right with Harry."

"I'll have to thank him."

"You can't," she said. "He's dead. It is your place now."

"I won't need a place for long," said Alden. "I won't be staying here. I'll be going back."

She shook her head.

"Is there anyone who's tried?"

"Yes. They've all come back. You can't beat the swamp."

"Doc got in."

"Doc was big and strong and well. And there was something driving him."

"There's something driving me as well."

She put up a hand and brushed the hair out of her eyes. "No one can talk you out of this? You mean what you are saying?"

"I can't stay," he said.

"In the morning," she told him, "I'll take you to see Eric."

The candle flame was yellow as it flickered in the room and again the golden leaves were raining down. The garden had been quiet and he'd held out his hands, palms upward, so the leaves would fall in them. Just one leaf, he thought—one leaf is all I want, one leaf out of all the millions that are falling.

He watched intently and the leaves went past, falling all about him, but never a one to fall into his hands. Then, suddenly, there

was something that was not a leaf—a butterfly that came fluttering like a leaf from nowhere, blue as the haze upon the distant
hills, blue as the smoky air of autumn.

For an instant the butterfly poised above his outstretched palms
and then mounted swiftly upward, flying strongly against the
downward rain of leaves, a mote of blue winging in the goldenness.

He watched it as it flew, until it was lost in the branches of the
tree, and then glanced back at his hands and there was something
lying in his palm, but it was not a leaf.

It was a little card, two inches by three or such a matter, and it
was the color of the leaves, but its color came from what seemed
to be an inner light, so that the card shone of itself rather than
shining by reflected light, which was the way one saw the color
of the leaves.

He sat there looking at it, wondering how he could catch a
card when no cards were falling, but only leaves dropping from
the tree. But he had taken it and looked at it and it was not made
of paper and it had upon its face a picture that he could not
understand.

As he stared at it his mother's voice called him in to supper
and he went. He put the card into his pocket and he went into
the house.

And under ordinary circumstances the magic would have vanished and he never would have known such an autumn day again.

There is only one such day, thought Alden Street, for any man
alive. For any man alive, with the exception of himself.

He had put the card into his pocket and had gone into the
house for supper and later on that evening he must have put it
in the drawer of the dresser in his room, for that was where he'd
found it in that later autumn.

He had picked it up from its forgotten resting place and as he
held it in his hand, that day of thirty years before came back to
him so clearly that he could almost smell the freshness of the air
as it had been that other afternoon. The butterfly was there and

its blueness was so precise and faithful that he knew it had been imprinted on his brain so forcefully that he held it now forever.

He had put the card back carefully and had walked down to the village to seek out the realtor he'd seen the day before.

"But, Alden," said the realtor, "with your mother gone and all, there is no reason for your staying. There is that job waiting in New York. You told me yesterday."

"I've been here too long," said Alden. "I am tied too close. I guess I'll have to stay. The house is not for sale."

"You'll live there all alone? In that big house all alone?"

"There's nothing else to do," said Alden.

He had turned and walked away and gone back to the house to get the card out of the dresser drawer again.

He sat and studied the drawing that was on the face of it, a funny sort of drawing, no kind of drawing he had ever seen before, not done with ink or pencil nor with brush. What, in the name of God, he thought, had been used to draw it?

And the drawing itself? A many-pointed star? A rolled-up porcupine? Or a gooseberry, one of the prickly kind, many times enlarged?

It did not matter, he knew, neither how the drawing had been made, or the strange kind of stiff, silken fabric that made the card itself, or what might be represented in the drawing. The important thing was that, many years before, when he had been a child, he had sat beneath the tree and held out his hand to catch a falling leaf and had caught the card instead.

He carried the card over to a window and stared out at the garden. The great walnut tree still stood as it had stood that day, but it was not golden yet. The gold must wait for the coming of first frost and that might be any day.

He stood at the window, wondering if there'd be a butterfly this time, or if the butterfly were only part of childhood.

"It will be morning soon," said Kitty. "I heard a bird. The birds are astir just before first light."

"Tell me about this place," said Alden.

"It is a sort of island," Kitty told him. "Not much of an island. Just a foot or two above the water level. It is surrounded by water and by muck. They bring us in by heliocoptor and they let us down. They bring in food the same way. Not enough to feed us. Not enough of anything. There is no contact with them."

"Men or robots? In the ship, I mean."

"I don't know. No one ever sees them. Robots, I'd suspect."

"Not enough food, you say."

She shook her head. "There is not supposed to be. That's a part of Limbo. We're not supposed to live. We fish, we gather roots and other things. We get along somehow."

"And we die, of course."

"Death comes to everyone," she said. "To us just a little sooner."

She sat crouched upon one of the lengths of wood that served as a chair and as the candle guttered, shadows chased across her face so that it seemed the very flesh of it was alive and crawling.

"You missed sleep on account of me," he said.

"I can sleep any time. I don't need much sleep. And, besides, when a new one comes . . ."

"There aren't many new ones?"

"Not as many as there were. And there always is a chance. With each new one there's a chance."

"A chance of what?"

"A chance he may have an answer for us."

"We can always run away."

"To be caught and brought back? To die out in the swamp? That, Alden, is no answer."

She rocked her body back and forth. "I suppose there is no answer."

But she still held hope, he knew. In the face of all of it, she had kept a hope alive.

Eric once had been a huge man, but now he had shrunken in upon himself. The strength of him was there as it had always been, but the stamina was gone. You could see that, Alden told himself, just by looking at him.

Eric sat with his back against a tree. One hand lay in his lap and the other grubbed idly, with blunt and dirty fingers, at the short ground.

"So you're bent on getting out?" he asked.

"He talked of nothing else," said Kitty.

"You been here how long?"

"They brought me here last night. I was out on my feet. I don't remember it."

"You don't know what it's like."

Alden shook his head. "I don't intend to find out, either. I figure if I'm going, I'd best be going now before this place wears me down."

"Let me tell you," Eric said. "Let me tell you how it is. The swamp is big and we're in the center of it. Doc came in from the north. He found out, some way, the location of this place, and he got hold of some old maps. Geologic survey maps that had been made years ago. He studied them and figured out the best way for getting in. He made it, partly because he was strong and healthy . . . but mostly it was luck. A dozen other men could try it, just as strong as he was, and all of them might be lost because they weren't lucky. There are quicksand and alligators. There are moccasins and rattlesnakes. There is the killing heat. There are the insects and no water fit to drink.

"Maybe if you knew exactly the way to go you might manage it, but you'd have to hunt for the way to go. You'd have to work your way through the swamp and time after time you'd run into something that you couldn't get through or over and have to turn back and hunt another way. You'd lose a lot of time and time would work against you."

"How about food?"

"If you weren't fussy, food would be no trouble. You could find food along the way. Not the right kind. Your belly might not like it. You'd probably have dysentery. But you wouldn't starve."

"This swamp," asked Alden, "where is it?"

"Part in Mataloosa county. Part in Fairview. It's a local Limbo. They all are local Limbos. There aren't any big ones. Just a lot of little ones."

Alden shook his head. "I can see this swamp from the windows of my house. I never heard of a Limbo being in it."

"It's not advertised," said Eric. "It's not put on maps. It's not something you'd hear of."

"How many miles? How far to the edge of it?"

"Straight line, maybe thirty, maybe forty. You'd not be traveling a straight line."

"And the perimeter is guarded."

"Patrols flying overhead. Watching for people in the swamp. They might not spot you. You'd do your best to stay under cover. But chances are they would. And they'd be waiting for you when you reached the edge."

"And even if they weren't," Kitty said, "where would you go? A monitor would catch you. Or someone would spot you and report. No one would dare to help a refugee from Limbo."

The tree beneath which Eric sat was a short distance from the collection of huddled huts that served as shelter for the inhabitants of Limbo.

Someone, Alden saw, had built up the community cooking fire and a bent and ragged man was coming up from the water's edge, carrying a morning's catch of fish. A man was lying in the shade of one of the huts, stretched out on a pallet. Others, both men and women, sat in listless groups.

The sun had climbed only part way up the eastern sky, but the heat was stifling. Insects buzzed shrilly in the air and high in the light blue sky birds were swinging in great and lazy circles.

"Doc would let us see his maps?"

"Maybe," Eric said. "You could ask him."

"I spoke to him last night," said Alden. "He said it was insane."

"He is right," said Eric.

"Doc has funny notions," Kitty said. "He doesn't blame the robots. He says they're just doing a job that men have set for them. It was men who made the laws. The robots do no more than carry out the laws."

And Doc, thought Alden, once again was right.

Although it was hard to puzzle out the road by which man had finally come to his present situation. It was overemphasis again, perhaps, and that peculiar social blindness which came as the result of overemphasis.

Certainly, when one thought of it, it made no particular sense. A man had a right to be ill. It was his own hard luck if he happened to be ill. It was no one's business but his own. And yet it had been twisted into an action that was on a par with murder. As a result of a well-intentioned health crusade which had gotten out of hand, what at one time had been misfortune had now become a crime.

Eric glanced at Alden. "Why are you so anxious to get out? It'll do no good. Someone will find you, someone will turn you in. You'll be brought back again."

"Maybe a gesture of defiance," Kitty said. "Sometimes a man will do a lot to prove he isn't licked. To show he can't be licked."

"How old are you?" asked Eric.

"Fifty four," said Alden.

"Too old," said Eric. "I am only forty and I wouldn't want to try it."

"Is it defiance?" Kitty asked.

"No," Alden told her, "not that. I wish it was. But it's not as brave as that. There is something that's unfinished."

"All of us," said Eric, "left some unfinished things behind us."

The water was black as ink and seemed more like oil than water. It was lifeless; there was no sparkle in it and no glint; it soaked up the sunlight rather than reflecting it. And yet one felt that life must lurk beneath it, that it was no more than a mask to hide the life beneath it.

It was no solid sheet of water, but an infiltrating water that snaked its way around the hummocks and the little grassy islands and the water-defying trees that stood knee-deep in it. And when one glanced into the swamp, seeking to find some pattern to it, trying to determine what kind of beast it was, the distance turned to a cruel and ugly greenness and the water, too, took on that tint of fatal green.

Alden crouched at the water's edge and stared into the swamp, fascinated by the rawness of the green.

Forty miles of it, he thought. How could a man face forty miles of it? But it would be more than forty miles. For, as Eric had said, a man would run into dead-ends and would be forced to retrace his steps to find another way.

Twenty-four hours ago, he thought, he had not been here. Twenty four hours ago or a little more he had left the house and gone down into the village to buy some groceries. And when he neared the bank corner he had remembered that he had not brushed his teeth—for how long had it been?—and that he had not bathed for days. He should have taken a bath and brushed his teeth and done all the other things that were needful before he had come downtown, as he always had before—or almost every time before, for there had been a time or two as he passed the bank that the hidden monitor had come to sudden life and bawled in metallic tones that echoed up and down the street: "Alden Street did not brush his teeth today! Shame on Alden Street, he did not brush his teeth (or take a bath, or clean his fingernails, or wash his hands and face, or whatever it might be.)" Keeping up the clatter and the clamor, with the ringing of alarm bells and the sound of booming rockets interspersed between each shaming accusation, until one ran off home in shame to do the things he'd failed.

In a small village, he thought, you could get along all right. At least you could until the medics got around to installing home monitors as they had in some of the larger cities. And that might take them years.

But in Willow Bend it was not so hard to get along. If you just remembered to comply with all the regulations you would be all right. And even if you didn't, you knew the locations of the monitors, one at the bank and the other at the drugstore corner, and you could keep out of their way. They couldn't spot your shortcomings more than a block away.

Although generally it was safer to comply with the regulations before you went downtown. And this, as a rule, he'd done, although there had been a time or two when he had forgotten and had been forced to go running home with people standing in the street and snickering and small boys catcalling after him while the monitor kept up its unholy din. And later on that day, or maybe in the evening, the local committee would come calling and would collect the fine that was set out in the book for minor misdemeanors.

But on this morning he had not thought to take a bath, to brush his teeth, to clean his fingernails, to make certain that his toenails were trimmed properly and neat. He had worked too hard and for too long a time and had missed a lot of sleep (which, also, was a thing over which the monitor could work itself into a lather) and, remembering back, he could recall that he seemed to move in a hot, dense fog and that he was weak from hunger and there was a busy, perhaps angry fly buzzing in his head.

But he did remember the monitor at the bank in time and detoured a block out of his way to miss it. But as he came up to the grocery store (a safe distance from the bank and the drugstore monitors), he had heard that hateful metallic voice break out in a scream of fright and indignation.

"Alden Street is ill!" it screamed. "Everybody stay away from Alden Street. He is ill—don't anyone go near him!"

The bells had rung and the siren blown and the rockets been shot off, and from atop the grocery store a great red light was flashing.

He had turned to run, knowing the dirty trick that had been

played upon him. They had switched one of the monitors to the grocery, or they had installed a third.

"Stay where you are!" the monitor had shouted after him. "Go out into the middle of the street away from everyone."

And he had gone. He had quit his running and had gone out into the middle of the street and stayed there, while from the windows of the business houses white and frightened faces had stared out at him. Had stared out at him—a sick man and a criminal.

The monitor had kept on with its awful crying and he had cringed out there while the white and frightened faces watched and in time (perhaps a very short time, although it had seemed long), the disciplinary robots on the medic corps had arrived from the county seat.

Things had moved swiftly then. The whole story had come out. Of how he had neglected to have his physicals. Of how he had been fined for several misdemeanors. Of how he had not contributed to the little league programs. Of how he had not taken part in any of the various community health and sports programs.

They had told him then, in wrath, that he was nothing but a dirty slob, and the wheels of justice had moved with sure and swift precision. And finally he had stood and stared up at the high and mighty man who had pronounced his doom. Although he could not recall that he had heard the doom. There had been a blackness and that was all that he could remember until he had awakened into a continuation of the blackness and had seen two balloon-like faces leaning over him.

He had been apprehended and judged and sentenced within a few short hours. And it was all for the good of men—to prove to other men that they could not get away with the flouting of the law which said that one must maintain his fitness and his health. For one's health, said the law, was the most precious thing one had and it was criminal to endanger it or waste it. The national health must be viewed as a vital natural resource and, once again, it was criminal to endanger it or waste it.

So he had been made into a horrible example and the story of what had happened to him would have appeared on the front pages of every paper that was published and the populace thus would be admonished that they must obey, that the health laws were not namby-pamby laws.

He squatted by the water's edge and stared off across the swamp and behind him he heard the muted sounds which came from that huddled camp just a short ways down the island—the clang of the skillet or the pot, the thudding of an axe as someone chopped up firewood, the rustle of the breeze that flapped a piece of canvas stretched as a door across a hut, the quiet murmur of voices in low and resigned talks.

The swamp had a deadly look about it—and it waited. Confident and assured, certain that no one could cross it. All its traps were set and all its nets were spread and it had a patience that no man could match.

Perhaps, he thought, it did not really wait. Maybe it was just a little silly to imagine that it waited. Rather, perhaps, it was simply an entity that did not care. A human life to it was nothing. To it a human life was no more precious than a snake's life, or the life of a dragonfly, or of a tiny fish. It would not help and it would not warn and it had no kindness.

He shivered, thinking of this great uncaring. An uncaring that was even worse than if it waited with malignant forethought. For if it waited, at least it was aware of you. At least it paid you the compliment of some slight importance.

Even in the heat of the day, he felt the slimy coldness of the swamp reaching out for him and he shrank back from it, knowing as he did that he could not face it. Despite all the brave words he had mouthed, all his resolution, he would not dare to face it. It was too big for a man to fight—it was too green and greedy.

He hunkered in upon himself, trying to compress himself into a ball of comfort, although he was aware that there was no comfort. There never would be comfort, for now he'd failed himself.

In a little while, he thought, he'd have to get up from where he crouched and go down to the huts. And once he went down there, he knew he would be lost, that he would become one with those others who likewise could not face the swamp. He would live out his life there, fishing for some food, chopping a little wood, caring for the sick, and sitting listless in the sun.

He felt a flare of anger at the system which would sentence a man to such a life as that and he cursed the robots, knowing as he cursed that they were not the ones who were responsible. The robots were a symbol only of the health law situation.

They had been made the physicians and the surgeons to the human race because they were quick as well as steady, because their judgment was unfrayed by any flicker of emotion, because they were as dedicated as the best of human doctors ever had been, because they were tireless and unthinking of themselves.

And that was well and good. But the human race, as it always did, had gone overboard. It had made the robot not only the good and faithful doctor, but it had made him guardian and czar of human health, and in doing this had concocted a metallic ogre.

Would there ever be a day, he wondered, when humans would be done for good and all with its goblins and its ogres?

The anger faded out and he crouched dispirited and afraid and all alone beside the black waters of the swamp.

A coward, he told himself. And there was a bitter taste inside his brain and a weakness in his belly.

Get up, he told himself. Get up and go down to the huts.

But he didn't. He stayed, as if there might be some sort of reprieve, as if he might be hoping that from some unknown and unprobed source he might dredge up the necessary courage to walk into the swamp.

But the hope, he knew, was a hollow hope.

He had come to the end of hope. Ten years ago he could have done it. But not now. He'd lost too much along the way.

He heard the footsteps behind him and threw a look across his shoulders.

It was Kitty.

She squatted down beside him.

"Eric is getting the stuff together," she told him. "He'll be along in a little while."

"The stuff?"

"Food. A couple of machetes. Some rope."

"But I don't understand."

"He was just waiting for someone who had the guts to tackle it. He figures that you have. He always said one man didn't have a chance, but maybe two men had. Two men, helping one another, just might have a chance."

"But he told me . . ."

"Sure. I know what he told you. What I told you, too. And even in the face of that, you never wavered. That is how we knew."

"We?"

"Of course," said Kitty. "The three of us. I am going, too."

It took the swamp four days to beat the first of them.

Curiously, it was Eric, the youngest and the strongest.

He stumbled as they walked along a narrow ridge of land, flanked by tangled brush on one hand, by a morass on the other.

Alden, who was following, helped him to his feet, but he could not stand. He staggered for a step or two, then collapsed again.

"Just a little rest," Eric panted. "Just a little rest and then I'll be able to go on."

He crawled, with Alden helping, to a patch of shade, lay flat upon his back, a limp figure of a man.

Kitty sat beside him and stroked his hair back from his forehead.

"Maybe you should build a fire," she said to Alden. "Something hot may help him. All of us could use a bit of something."

Alden turned off the ridge and plunged into the brush. The

footing was soft and soggy and in places he sank in muck half way to his knees.

He found a small dead tree and pulled branches off it. The fire, he knew, must be small, and of wood that was entirely dry, for any sign of smoke might alert the patrol that flew above the swamp.

Back on the ridge again, he used a machete to slice some shavings off a piece of wood and stacked it all with care. It must start on one match, for they had few matches.

Kitty came and knelt beside him, watching.

"Eric is asleep," she said. "And it's not just tuckered out. I think he has a fever."

"It's the middle of the afternoon," said Alden. "We'll stay here until morning. He may feel better, then. Some extra rest may put him on his feet."

"And if it doesn't?"

"We'll stay another day," he said. "The three of us together. That's what we said back there. We would stick together."

She put out a hand and laid it on his arm.

"I was sure you'd say that," she said. "Eric was so sure and he was so right. He said you were the man he had been waiting for."

Alden shook his head. "It's not only Eric," he declared. "It's not only us. It's those others back there. Remember how they helped us? They gave us food, even when it meant they might go a bit more hungry. They gave us two fishhooks out of the six they had. One of them copied the map that Doc had carried. They fixed up a pair of shoes for me because they said I wasn't used to going without shoes. And they all came to see us off and watched until we were out of sight."

He paused and looked at her.

"It's not just us," he said. "It's all of us . . . all of us in Limbo."

She put up a hand and brushed the hair out of her eyes.

"Did anyone," he asked her, "ever tell you that you are beautiful?"

She made a grimace. "Long ago," she said. "But not for years.

Life had been too hard. But once, I guess, you could have said that I was beautiful."

She made a fluttery motion with her hands. "Light the fire," she told him. "Then go and catch some fish. Laying over this way, we'll need the food."

Alden woke at the first faint edge of dawn and lay staring out across the inky water that looked, in the first flush of day, like a floor of black enamel that had just been painted and had not dried as yet, with the shine of wetness showing here and there. A great awkward bird launched itself off a dead tree stub and flapped ungracefully down to skim above the water so that little ripples ran in the black enamel.

Stiffly, Alden sat up. His bones ached from the dampness and he was stiff with the chill of night.

A short distance away, Kitty lay curled into a ball, still sleeping. He glanced toward the spot where Eric had been sleeping when he himself had gone to bed, and there was no one there.

Startled, he leaped to his feet.

"Eric!" he called.

There was no answer.

"Eric!" he shouted again.

Kitty uncoiled and sat up.

"He's gone," said Alden. "I just woke up and he wasn't there."

He walked over to where the man had been lying and the imprint of his body still was in the grass.

He bent to examine the ground and brushed his hand across it. Some of the blades of grass yielded to his touch; they were beginning to spring back, to stand erect again. Eric, he knew, had not left just a little while ago. He had been gone—for how long, for an hour, for two hours or more?

Kitty rose and came to stand beside him.

Alden got to his feet and faced her.

"He was sleeping when I looked at him before I went to sleep," he said. "Muttering in his sleep, but sleeping. He still had a fever."

"Maybe," she said, "one of us should have sat up to watch him. But he seemed to be all right. And we were all tired."

Alden looked up and down the ridge. There was nothing to be seen, no sign of the missing man.

"He might have wandered off," he said. "Woke up, delirious. He might just have taken off."

And if that were the situation, they might never find him. He might have fallen into a pool of water, or become trapped in muck or quicksand. He might be lying somewhere, exhausted with his effort, very quietly dying.

Alden walked off the ridge into the heavy brush that grew out of the muck. Carefully, he scouted up and down the ridge and there was no sign that anyone, except himself the afternoon before, had come off the ridge. And there would have been some sign, for when one stepped into the muck, he went in to his ankles, in places halfway to his knees.

Mosquitoes and other insects buzzed about him maddeningly as he floundered through the brush and somewhere far off a bird was making chunking sounds.

He stopped to rest and regain his breath, waving his hands about his face to clear the air of insects.

The chunking still kept on and now there was another sound. He listened for the second sound to be repeated.

"Alden," came the cry again, so faint he barely heard it.

He plunged out of the brush back onto the ridge. The cry had come from the way that they had traveled on the day before.

"Alden!" And now he knew that it was Kitty, and not Eric, calling.

Awkwardly, he galloped down the ridge toward the sound.

Kitty was crouched at the edge of a thirty-foot stretch of open water, where the ridge had broken and let the water in.

He stopped beside her and looked down. She was pointing at a footprint—a footprint heading the wrong way. It lay beside other footprints heading in the opposite direction, the footprints that they had made in the mud as they came along the ridge the day before.

"We didn't stop," said Kitty. "We kept right on. That can't be one of ours. You weren't down here, were you?"

He shook his head.

"Then it must be Eric."

"You stay here," he said.

He plunged into the water and waded across and on the other edge the tracks were going out—tracks heading back the way that they had come.

He stopped and shouted.

"Eric! Eric! Eric!"

He waited for an answer. There was nothing.

A mile farther on, he came to the great morass they had crossed the day before—the mile or more of muck and water that had eaten at their strength. And here, on the muddy edge, the tracks went into the sea of sucking mud and water and disappeared from sight.

He crouched on the shore and peered across the water, interspersed by hummocks that were poison green in the early light. There was no sign of life or movement. Once a fish (perhaps not a fish, perhaps only something) broke the water for an instant, sending out a circle of ripples. But that was all there was.

Heavily, he turned back.

Kitty still crouched beside the water's edge.

He shook his head at her.

"He went back," he said. "I don't see how he could have. He was weak and . . ."

"Determination," Kitty said. "And, perhaps, devotion, too."

"Devotion?"

"Don't you see," she said. "He knew that he was sick. He knew he couldn't make it. And he knew that we'd stay with him."

"But that's what we all agreed," said Alden.

Kitty shook her head. "He wouldn't have it that way. He is giving us a chance."

"No!" yelled Alden. "I won't let him do it. I'm going back and find him."

"Across that last stretch of swamp?" asked Kitty.

Alden nodded. "Probably he was just able to make it. He more than likely is holed up on the other side somewhere."

"And what if he didn't make it? What if he never got across?"

"Then I won't find him, of course. But I have to try."

"What I'm worried about," said Kitty, "is what you'd do if you did find him. What would you do about him? What would you say to him?"

"I'd bring him back," said Alden, "or I'd stay with him."

She lifted her face and tears were standing in her eyes. "You'd give him back his gift," she said. "You'd throw it in his face. You'd make this last great gesture of his mean absolutely nothing."

She looked at Alden. "You could do that?" she asked. "He has done a fine and decent thing. Thinking, perhaps, that it's the last chance he'll have for decency. And you wouldn't let him keep it?"

Alden shook his head.

"He'd do as much for you," she said. "He'd let you keep that final decency."

On the morning of the eighth day, Kitty moaned and tossed with fever. The day before had been a sunlit nightmare of mud and saw grass, of terrible heat, of snakes and mosquitoes, of waning hope and a mounting fear that stirred sluggishly in the middle of one's gut.

It had been crazy for them to try it, Alden thought, crazy from the very start—three people who had no right to try it, too out of condition, too ill-equipped, and in his case, at least, too old to try a thing like this. To cross forty miles of swamp took youth and strength, and all that any of the three of them had to qualify had been determination. Perhaps, he thought, a misplaced determination, each of them driven by something which, more than likely, they did not understand.

Why, he wondered, had Kitty and Eric wished to escape from Limbo?

It was something they had never talked about. Although perhaps they would have if there had been a lot of talk. But there had never been. There had been no time or breath for talk.

For, he realized now, there was no real escape. You could escape the swamp, but you could not flee from Limbo. For you became a part of Limbo. Once in Limbo and there was no place left for you in the outside world.

Had it been a gesture only, he wondered—a gesture of defiance. Like that foolish, noble gesture of Eric's in leaving them when he had fallen ill.

And the question of their decision back there came to haunt him once again.

All he had to do, even in the glare of noonday sun, was to shut his eyes and see it all again—a starving, helpless, dying man who had crawled off the path and hidden in a clump of tangled underbrush so he could not be found even if one, or both, of his companions should come seeking him. There were flies crawling on his face and he dare not (or could not?) raise a hand to brush them off. There was a gaunt, black bird sitting on a dead tree stump, waiting patiently, and there was an alligator that lay in the water watching and there were many crawling, creeping, hopping creatures swarming in the grass and in the stunted brush.

The vision never changed; it was a fixed and terrible vision painted in a single stroke by imagination, which then had walked away and let it stand in all its garish detail.

Now it was Kitty, lying there and moaning through clenched teeth—an old and useless woman as he was an old and useless man. Kitty, with her lined face and her straggly hair and the terrible gauntness of her, but still possessed of that haunting sense of eternal youth somehow trapped tight inside her body.

He should go, he thought, and get some water. Bathe her face and arms with it, force some down her throat. But the water was scarcely fit to drink. It was old and stagnant and it stank of rotted vegetation and it had the taste of ancient dead things one tried hard not to visualize.

He went over to the small pack that belonged to Kitty and from it he took the battered and fire-blackened sauce pan that was the one utensil they had brought along.

Picking his way carefully down the tiny island on which they'd spent the night, he approached the water's edge and scouted watchfully along it, seeking for a place where the water might appear a bit less poisonous. Although that, he knew, was foolishness; the water was the same no matter where one looked.

It was bitter water in a bitter swamp that had fought them for seven days, that had sought to trap them and had tried to hold them back, that had bit and stung them and tried to drive them crazy, that had waited, knowing there would come a slip or some misstep or fall that would put them at its mercy.

He shivered, thinking of it. This was the first time, he realized, that he had thought of it. He had never thought of it before; he had merely fought it. All his energy had been directed toward getting over that yard of ground ahead, and after that, another yard of ground.

Time had lost its meaning, measured only in a man's endurance. Distance had come to have no significance, for it stretched on every side. There would always be that distance; there would be no end to it.

It had been a murderous seven days and the first two of them he had known he could not make it, that there was not another day left in him. But each day there had been another day left in him and he'd made each day to its bitter end.

Of the three of them, he thought, he was the only one who still was on his feet. And another funny thing: He knew now that he had another day left in him, that he had many other days left in him. He could keep on forever, if it took forever. Now the swamp could never stop him. Somewhere in that terrible, tangled greenness he had found a hidden strength and had gotten second wind.

Why should this be, he wondered. What was that inner strength? From what source had it come?

Was it, perhaps, because his purpose had been strong?

And once again he stood at the window, wondering if there'd be a butterfly this time or if the butterfly were only a certain part of childhood. But never questioning for a moment that the magic still was there, that it had been so strong and shining that thirty years could not have tarnished it.

So he had gone outside and had sat beneath the tree as he had sat that day when he was a child, with his hands held out, palms up, and the strange card laid across one palm. He could feel the edge of magic and could smell the new freshness of the air, but it was not right, for there were no yellow leaves falling down the sky.

He had waited for the frost and when it came had gone out again and sat beneath the tree with the leaves falling through the air like slow-paced drops of rain. He had closed his eyes and had smelled the autumn air tainted with the faintest touch of smoke, and had felt the sunlight falling warm about him and it was exactly as it had been that day so long ago. The autumn day of boyhood had not been lost; it was with him still.

He had sat there with his hands held out and with the card across one palm and nothing happened. Then, as it had failed to do that day of long ago, a leaf came fluttering down and fell atop the card. It lay there for an instant, a perfect goldenness.

Then suddenly it was gone and in its place atop the card was the object that had been printed on the card—a ball of some sort, three inches in diameter, and with prickly spikes sticking out over it, like an outsize gooseberry. Then it buzzed at him and he could feel the buzzing spreading through his body.

It seemed in that instant that there was something with him, or that he was part of something—some thinking, living, (perhaps even loving) thing that quivered somewhere very close to him and yet very far away. As if this thing, whatever it might be, had reached out a finger and had touched him, for no other purpose than to let him know that it was there.

He crouched down to dip the water with the battered, blackened pan from a pool that appeared to be just a little cleaner and a little clearer than it had seemed elsewhere.

And there had been something there, he thought. Something that through the years he had become acquainted with, but never truly known. A gentle thing, for it had dealt with him gently. And a thing that had a purpose and had driven him toward that purpose, but kindly, as a kindly teacher drives a student toward a purpose that in the end turns out to be the student's own.

The little buzzing gooseberry was the gateway to it, so long as the gooseberry had been needed. Although, he thought, such a word as gateway was entirely wrong, for there had been no gateway in the sense that he had ever seen this thing, or come close to it or had a chance to find out what it was. Only that it was, that it lived and that it had a mind and could communicate.

Not talk—communicate. And toward the end, he recalled, the communication had been excellent, although the understanding that should have gone with communication had never quite come clear.

Given time, he thought. But there had been an interruption and that was why he must get back, as quickly as he could. For it would not know why he had left it. It would not understand. It might think that he had died, if it had a concept that would encompass a condition such as death. Or that he had deserted it. Or that somehow it had failed.

He dipped the sauce pan full of water and straightened, standing in the great hush of the morning.

He remembered now. But why had he not remembered sooner? Why had it escaped him? How had he forgotten?

From far away he heard it and, hearing it, felt the hope leap in him. He waited tensely to hear it once again, needing to hear it that second time to know that it was true.

It came again, faint, but carrying unmistakably in the morning air—the crowing of a rooster.

He swung around and ran back to the camping site.

Running, he stumbled, and the pan flew from his hand. He scrabbled to his feet and left the pan where it had fallen.

He rushed to Kitty and fell on his knees beside her.

"Just a few more miles!" he shouted. "I heard a rooster crowing. The edge of the swamp can't be far away."

He reached down and slid his hands beneath her, lifted her, cradling her, holding her tightly against him.

She moaned and tossed.

"Easy, girl," he said. "We're almost out of it."

He struggled from his knees and stood erect. He shifted her body so that it rode the easier in his arms.

"I'll carry you," he said. "I can carry you all the way."

It was farther than he'd thought. And the swamp was worse than it had ever been—as if, sensing that this stumbling, stubborn creature might slip out of its grasp, it had redoubled its trickery and its viciousness in a last attempt to seize and swallow him.

He had left the little food they'd had behind. He'd left everything behind. He had taken only Kitty.

When she achieved a sort of half consciousness and cried for water, he stopped beside a pool, carried water to her in his cupped hands, bathed her face and helped her drink, then went on again.

Late in the afternoon the fever broke and she regained full consciousness.

"Where am I?" she asked, staring at the green-blackness of the swamp.

"Who are you?" she asked, and he tried to tell her. She did not remember him, or the swamp, or Limbo. He spoke to her of Eric and she did not remember Eric.

And that, he recalled, had been the way it had been with him. He had not remembered. Only over hours and days had it come back to him in snatches.

Was that the way it would be with her? Had that been the way it had been with Eric? Had there been no self-sacrifice, no hero-ism in what Eric did? Had it been a mere, blind running from the pit of horror in which he awoke to find himself?

And if all of this were true, whatever had been wrong with him, whatever caused the fever and forgetfulness, was then the same as had happened to Kitty and to Eric.

Was it, he wondered, some infection that he carried?

For if that were true, then it was possible he had infected everyone in Limbo.

He went on into the afternoon and his strength amazed him, for he should not be this strong.

It was nerve, he knew, that kept him going, the sheer excite-ment of being almost free of this vindictive swamp.

But the nerve would break, he knew. He could not keep it up. The nerve would break and the excitement would grow dull and dim and the strength would drain from him. He'd then be an aged man carrying an aged woman through a swamp he had no right to think he could face alone, let alone assume the burden of another human.

But the strength held out. He could feel it flowing in him. Dusk fell and the first faint stars came out, but the going now was easier. It had been easier, he realized, for the last hour or so.

"Put me down," said Kitty. "I can walk. There's no need to carry me."

"Just a little while," said Alden. "We are almost there."

Now the ground was firmer and he could tell by the rasp of it against his trouser legs that he was walking in a different kind of grass—no longer the harsh, coarse, knife-like grass that few in the swamp, but a softer, gentle grass.

A hill loomed in the darkness and he climbed it and now the ground was solid.

He reached the top of the hill and stopped. He let Kitty down and stood her on her feet.

The air was clean and sharp and pure. The leaves of a nearby tree rustled in a breeze and in the east the sky was tinged with the pearly light of a moon.

Back of them the swamp, which they had beaten, and in front of them the clean, solid countryside that eventually would defeat them. Although eventually, Alden told himself, sounded much too long. In a few days, perhaps in a few hours, they would be detected and run down.

With an arm around Kitty's waist to hold her steady as she walked, he went down the hill to eventual defeat.

The rattletrap pickup truck stood in the moonlit farmyard. There were no lights in the house that stood gaunt upon the hilltop. The road from the farmyard ran down a long, steep hill to join the main road a half mile or so away.

There would be no ignition key, of course, but one could cross the wires, then shove the truck until it started coasting down the hill. Once it was going, throw it into gear and the motor would crank over and start up.

"Someone will catch us, Alden," Kitty told him. "There is no more certain way for someone to find out about us. Stealing a truck . . ."

"It's only twenty miles," said Alden. "That's what the signpost said. And we can be there before there is too much fuss."

"But it would be safer walking and hiding."

"There is no time," he said.

For he remembered now. It had all come back to him—the machine that he had built in the dining room. A machine that was like a second body, that was like a suit to wear. It was a two-way schoolhouse, or maybe a two-way laboratory, for when he was inside of it he learned of that other life and it learned of him.

It had taken years to build it, years to understand how to assemble the components that those others, or that other, had provided. All the components had been small and there had been thousands of them. He had held out his hand and thought hard of yellow leaves falling in the blue haze of autumn air and there had been another piece of that strange machine put into his hand.

And now it stood, untenanted, in that faded, dusky room and they would be wondering what had happened to him.

"Come on," he said to Kitty, sharply. "There is no use in waiting."

"There might be a dog. There might be a . . ."

"We will have to chance it."

He ducked out of the clump of trees and ran swiftly across the moonlit barnyard to the truck. He reached it and wrenched at the hood and the hood would not come up.

Kitty screamed, just once, more a warning scream than fright, and he spun around. The shape stood not more than a dozen feet away, with the moonlight glinting off its metal and the Medic Disciplinary symbol engraved upon its chest.

Alden backed against the truck and stood there, staring at the robot, knowing that the truck had been no more than bait. And thinking how well the medics must know the human race to set that sort of trap—knowing not only the working of the human body but the human mind as well

Kitty said: "If you'd not been slowed up. If you'd not carried me . . ."

"It would have made no difference," Alden told her. "They probably had us spotted almost from the first and were tracking us."

"Young man," the robot said, "you are entirely right. I have been waiting for you. I must admit," the robot said, "that I have some admiration for you. You are the only ones who ever crossed the swamp. There were some who tried, but they never made it."

So this was how it ended, Alden told himself, with some bitterness, but not as much, perhaps, as he should have felt. For there had been, he thought, nothing but a feeble hope from the first beginning. He had been walking toward defeat, he knew, with every step he'd taken—and into a hopelessness that even he admitted.

If only he had been able to reach the house in Willow Bend,

that much he had hoped for, that much would have satisfied him. To reach it and let those others know he had not deserted.

"So what happens now?" he asked the robot. "Is it back to Limbo?"

The robot never had a chance to answer. There was a sudden rush of running feet, pounding across the farmyard.

The robot swung around and there was something streaking in the moonlight that the robot tried to duck, but couldn't.

Alden sprang in a low and powerful dive, aiming for the robot's knees. His shoulder struck on metal and the flying rock clanged against the breastplate of the metal man. Alden felt the robot, already thrown off balance by the rock, topple at the impact of his shoulder.

The robot crashed heavily to the earth and Alden, sprawling on the ground, fought upright to his feet.

"Kitty!" he shouted.

But Kitty, he saw, was busy.

She was kneeling beside the fallen robot, who was struggling to get up and in her hand she held the thrown rock, with her hand raised above the robot's skull. The rock came down and the skull rang like a bell—and rang again and yet again.

The robot ceased its struggling and lay still, but Kitty kept on pounding at the skull.

"Kitty, that's enough," said another voice.

Alden turned to face the voice.

"Eric!" he cried. "But we left you back there."

"I know," said Eric. "You thought I had run back to Limbo. I found where you had tracked me."

"But you are here. You threw the rock."

Eric shrugged. "I got to be myself again. At first I didn't know where I was or who I was or anything at all. And then I remembered all of it. I had to make a choice then. There really wasn't any choice. There was nothing back in Limbo. I tried to catch up with you, but you moved too fast."

"I killed him," Kitty announced, defiantly. "I don't care. I meant to kill him."

"Not killed," said Eric. "There'll be others coming soon. He can be repaired."

"Give me a hand with the hood on this truck," said Alden. "We have to get out of here."

Eric parked the rattletrap back of the house and Alden got out.

"Come along now," he said.

The back door was unlocked, just as he had left it. He went into the kitchen and switched on the ceiling light.

Through the door that opened into the dining room, he could see the shadowy framework of the structure he had built.

"We can't stay here too long," said Eric. "They know we have the truck. More than likely they'll guess where we were headed."

Alden did not answer. For there was no answer. There was no place they could go.

Wherever they might go, they would be hunted down, for no one could be allowed to flaunt the medic statutes and defy the medic justice. There was no one in the world who would dare to help them.

He had run from Limbo to reach this place—although he had not known at the time what he was running to. It was not Limbo he had run from; rather, he had run to reach the machine that stood in the dining room just beyond this kitchen.

He went into the room and snapped on the light and the strange mechanism stood glittering in the center of the room.

It was a man-size cage and there was just room for him to stand inside of it. And he must let them know that he was back again.

He stepped into the space that had been meant to hold him and the outer framework and its mysterious attachments seemed to fold themselves about him.

He stood in the proper place and shut his eyes and thought of falling yellow leaves. He made himself into the boy again who had sat beneath the tree and it was not his mind, but the little boy mind that sensed the goldenness and blue, that smelled the wine of autumn air and the warmth of autumn sun.

He wrapped himself in autumn and the long ago and he waited for the answer, but there was no answer.

He waited and the goldenness slid from him and the air was no longer wine-like and there was no warm sunlight, but a biting wind that blew off some black sea of utter nothingness.

He knew—he knew and yet he'd not admit it. He stood stubbornly and wan, with his feet still in the proper place, and waited.

But even stubbornness wore thin and he knew that they were gone and that there was no use of waiting, for they would not be back. Slowly he turned and walked out of the cage.

He had been away too long.

As he stepped out of the cage, he saw the vial upon the floor and stooped to pick it up. He had sipped from it, he remembered, that day (how long ago?) when he had stepped back into the room after long hours in the cage.

They had materialized it for him and they'd told him he should drink it and he could remember the bitter taste it had left upon his tongue.

Kitty and Eric were standing in the doorway, staring at him, and he looked up from the vial and stared in their direction.

"Alden," Kitty asked, "what has happened to you?"

He shook his head at her. "It's all right," he told her. "Nothing's happened. They just aren't there, is all."

"Something happened," she said. "You look younger by twenty years or more."

He let the vial fall from his hand. He lifted his hands in front of him and in the light from overhead he saw that the wrinkles in the skin had disappeared. They were stronger, firmer hands. They were younger hands.

"It's your face," Kitty said. "It's all filled out. The crow's feet all are gone."

He rubbed his palm along his jaw and it seemed to him that the bone was less pronounced, that the flesh had grown out to pad it.

"The fever," he said. "That was it—the fever."

For he remembered dimly. Not remembered, maybe, for perhaps he had never known. But he was knowing now. That was the way it had always worked. Not as if he'd learned a thing, but as if he'd remembered it. They put a thing into his mind and left it planted there and it unfolded then and crept upon him slowly.

And now he knew.

The cage was not a teacher. It was a device they had used to study man, to learn about his body and his metabolism and all the rest of it.

And then when they had known all that need be known, they had written the prescription and given it to him.

Young man, the robot in the barnyard had said to him. But he had not noticed. Young man, but he had too many other things to think about to notice those two words.

But the robot had been wrong.

For it was not only young.

Not young alone—not young for the sake of being young, but young because there was coursing in his body a strange alien virus, or whatever it might be, that had set his body right, that had tuned it up again, that had given it the power to replace old and aging tissue with new.

Doctors to the universe, he thought, that is what they were. Mechanics sent out to tinker up and renovate and put in shape the protoplasmic machinery that was running old and rusty.

"The fever?" Eric asked him.

"Yes," said Alden. "And thank God, it's contagious. You both caught it from me."

He looked closely at them and there was no sign of it as yet, although Eric, it seemed, had begun to change. And Kitty, he thought, when it starts to work on her, how beautiful she'll be!

Beautiful because she had never lost a certain part of beauty that still showed through the age.

And all the people here in Willow Bend—they, too, had been exposed, as had the people who were condemned to Limbo. And perhaps the judge as well, the high and mighty face that had loomed so high above him. In a little while the fever and the healthy youthfulness would seep across the world.

"We can't stay here," said Eric. "The medics will be coming."

Alden shook his head. "We don't need to run," he said. "They can't hurt us now."

For the medic rule was ended. There was now no need of medics, no need of little leagues, no need of health programs.

It would take a while, of course, for the people to realize what had happened to them, but the day would come when they would know for sure and then the medics could be broken down for scrap or used for other work.

He felt stronger than he'd ever felt. Strong enough, if need be, to walk back across the swamp to Limbo.

"We'd not got out of Limbo," Kitty told him, "if it hadn't been for you. You were just crazy enough to supply the guts we needed."

"Please remember that," said Alden, "in a few more days, when you are young again."

NO MORE HIDES AND TALLOW

This story, which was published in the March 1946 issue of Lariat
Story Magazine, *features as a minor character the only Native
American to appear in Cliff's westerns— and it should be noted
that this particular "Indian Joe" seems to have more in common
with his namesake in "Huckleberry Finn"—a renegade who spent
his time hanging out with white criminals—than with most of the
stereotypical Indians in some westerns.*

*More importantly, though, this story reflects Cliff Simak's con-
stant efforts to push the envelopes of the genres he worked in. In
this case, he used the western genre to demonstrate the effect of the
American Civil War on the frontier economy. For some time after
the war, there was virtually no market for the cattle that had run
wild on the range while many of the men were away fighting. And
the people struggling to make a living from cattle, who had no way
to bring them to the northern and eastern markets, just killed the
animals in order to ship the hides and tallow from Texas seaports—
leaving the rest of the carcasses to rot. It was the idea of driving
cattle north to meet up with a railroad that would begin to pump
money back into the frontier economy.*

—dww

I

Lieutenant Ned Benton pulled the buckskin to a halt, sat a little straighter in the saddle, as if by sitting thus he might push the horizon back, see a little farther.

For here was a thing that he had hungered for, a thing that he had dreamed about through four years of blood and sweat, fears and hunger, cold and heat. Dreamed it in the dust of Gettysburg and the early morning mists of Mississippi camps, through the eternity of march and counter-march, of seeming victory and defeat that at last was deadly certain. A thing that had been with him always through the years of misery and toil and bitterness he had served with the Army of the South.

For this at last was Benton land . . . Benton acres stretching far beneath the setting sun of Texas. Benton land and Benton cattle . . . and no more hides and tallow. For there were wonderful things astir in the new towns to the north, towns with strange names that had sprung up beyond the Missouri's northward bend. Towns that wanted Texas cattle, not for hides and tallow, but for meat. Meat for the hungry east, meat that was worth good money.

He had heard about it before he crossed the Mississippi . . . about the great herds streaming northward, braving wind and storm and blizzards, crossing rivers, moving with a trail of dust that mounted in the sky like a marching banner. And it was no more than the start . . . for Texas was full of cattle. Half wild cattle that no one had paid much attention to except to kill for hides and tallow when there was need of money. Not much money . . . just enough to scrape by on, to maintain a half dignified poverty.

But that was changed now, for the herds were going north. Herds that spelled riches. Riches that would give the old folks the comforts they had always wanted, but had never talked about. Money for the house that he and Jennie had planned when he came home from the war. Money for the horses and the painted fence around the house. . . .

He clucked to the buckskin and the animal moved forward, down the faint trail that ran through the knee high grass running like a moving sea, stirred by the wind across the swales.

Only a little while now, Benton told himself. Only a little while until I ride in on the ranch buildings. He shut his eyes, remembering them, as he had shut his eyes many times before in those long four years . . . seeing once again the great grey squared timber house beneath the cottonwoods, hearing the excited barking of old Rover, the frightened scuttering of the chickens that his mother kept.

He opened his eyes, saw the horseman coming down the trail . . . a horseman who had topped the swale while he had been day dreaming of the house and cottonwoods.

Squinting his eyes against the sun, Benton recognized the man. Jake Rollins, who rode for Dan Watson's Anchor brand. And remembered, even as he recognized him, that he did not like Jake Rollins.

Rollins urged his big black horse to one side of the trail and stopped. Benton pulled in the buckskin.

"Howdy, Jake," he said.

Rollins stared, eyes narrowing.

"You spooked me for a minute, Ned," said Rollins. "Didn't look for you . . ."

"The war's over," Benton told him. "You must have heard."

"Sure. Sure I heard, all right, but . . ." He hesitated, then blurted it out. "But we heard that you was dead."

Benton shook his head. "Close to it a dozen times, but they never did quite get me."

Rollins laughed, a nasty laugh that dribbled through his teeth. "Them Yanks are damn poor shots."

It isn't funny, Benton thought. Nothing to make a joke of. Not after a man has seen some of the things I have.

"They aren't poor shots," Benton told him. "They're plain damn fools for fighting. Hard to lick."

He hesitated, staring across the miles of waving grass. "In fact, we didn't lick them."

"Folks will be glad to see you home," Rollins told him, fidgeting in the saddle.

"I'll be glad to see them, too," Benton replied soberly.

And he was thinking: I don't like this man. Never liked him for his dirty mouth and the squinted, squeezed look about him. But it's good to see him. Good to see someone from home. Good to hear him talk familiarly about the folks one knows.

Rollins lifted the reins as a signal and the horse started forward.

"I'll be seeing you," said Rollins.

Benton touched the buckskin with a spur and even as he did the warning hit him straight between the shoulder blades . . . the little dancing feet that tapped out danger. The signal that he'd known in battle, as if there were something beyond eyes and ears to guard a man and warn him.

Twisting swiftly in the saddle, he was half out of it even before he saw the gun clutched in Rollins' hand and the hard, blank face that had turned to ice and granite beneath Rollins' broad-brimmed hat.

The spur on Benton's left boot raked viciously across the buckskin's flank as he pulled it from the stirrup and the horse reared in fright and anger, hoofs clawing empty air, bit chains rattling as he shook his head.

The gun in Rollins' hand spoke with sudden hate and Benton felt the buckskin jerk under the impact of the bullet. Then his feet were touching ground and he was dancing away to give the horse room to fall while his hands swung for his sixguns.

Rollins' guns hammered again, but his horse was dancing and the slug went wild, hissing ankle high through the waving grass.

For an instant the ice-hard face of the mounted man melted

into fear and within that instant Benton's right gun bucked against his wrist.

Rollins' horse leaped in sudden fright and Rollins was a rag doll tied to the saddle, flapping and jerking to the movement of the horse . . . a wobbling, beaten, spineless rag doll that clawed feebly at the saddle horn while crimson stained his bright blue shirt.

Rollins slumped and slid and the horse went mad. Leaping forward, Benton seized the dragging reins, swung his weight against its head while it fought and shied and kicked at the dragging, bumping thing that clung to the off-side stirrup.

Still hanging tightly to the reins, Benton worked his way around until he could seize the stirrup and free the boot that was wedged within it. The horse calmed down, stood nervously, snorting and suspicious.

Rollins lay sprawled grotesquely in the trampled grass. Benton knew he was dead. Death, he told himself, staring at the body, has a limpness all its own, a certain impersonality about it that is unmistakable.

Slowly, he led Rollins' horse back to the trail. His own horse lay there, dead, shot squarely through the throat where it had caught the bullet when it reared.

Benton stood staring at it.

A hell of a way, he thought, a hell of a way to be welcomed home.

Benton pulled up the big black horse on top of the rise that dipped down to the ranch buildings and sat looking at them, saw that they were old and dingy and very quiet. Once they had seemed large and bright and full of life, but that might have been, he told himself, because then he had not seen anything with which he might compare them. Like the plantations along the Mississippi or the neat, trim farms of the Pennsylvania countryside or the mansions that looked across Virginia rivers.

A thin trickle of smoke came up from the kitchen chimney and that was the only sign of life. No one stirred in the little yard, no one moved about the barn. There was no sound, no movement. Only the lazy smoke against the setting sun.

Benton urged the black horse forward, moved slowly down the hill.

No one came out on the porch to greet him. There was no Rover bounding around a corner to warn him off the place. There was no call from the bunkhouse, no whooping from the barn.

Once Benton tried to yell himself, but the sound dried in his throat and his tongue rebelled and he rode on silently.

One dreary rooster looked up from his scratching as he reached the hitching post, stared at him for a moment with a jaundiced eye that glared from a tilted head, then went back to scratching.

Slowly, Benton climbed the rickety steps that led to the porch, reached for the front door knob, then hesitated. For a moment he stood, unmoving . . . at last lifted his fist to knock.

The knocking echoed hollowly in the house beyond the door and he knocked again. Slow footsteps came across the floor inside and the door swung open.

A man stood there . . . an old man, older than Benton had remembered him, older than he had ever thought he'd look

"Pa!" said Benton.

For a long instant the old man stood there in the door, staring at him, as if he might not recognize him. Then one hand came out and clutched Benton's arm, clutched it with a bony, firm and possessive grip.

"Ned!" the old man said. "My boy! My boy!"

He pulled him in across the threshold, shut the door behind them, shutting out the empty yard and silent barn, the scratching rooster and the rickety steps that led up the slumping porch.

Benton reached out an arm across the old man's shoulders, hugged him close for a fleeting moment. How small, he thought, how stringy and how boney . . . like an old cow pony, all whang-hide and guts.

His father's voice was small, just this side of a whisper.

"We heard that you got killed, Ned."

"Didn't touch me," Benton told him. "Where's Ma?"

"Your ma is sick, Ned."

"And Rover? He didn't come to meet me."

"Rover's dead," said his father. "Rattler got him. Wasn't so spry no more and he couldn't jump so quick."

Silently, side by side, walking softly in the darkening house, they made their way to the bedroom door, where the old man stepped aside to let his son go ahead.

Benton halted just inside the door, staring with eyes that suddenly were dim at the white-haired woman propped up on the pillows.

Her voice came to him across the room, small and quavery, but with some of the old sweetness that he remembered.

"Ned! We heard . . ."

He strode swiftly forward, dropped on his knees beside the bed.

"Yes, I know," he told her. "But it was wrong. Lots of stories like that and a lot of them are wrong."

"Safe," said his mother, as if it were something that defied belief. "Safe and alive and home again. My boy! My darling!"

He held her close while one thin hand reached up and stroked his hair.

"I prayed," his mother said. "I prayed and prayed and . . ."

She was sobbing quietly in the coming darkness and her hand kept on stroking his hair and for a moment he recaptured the little baby feeling and the security and warmth and love that lay within it.

A board creaked beneath his father's footsteps and Benton looked up, seeing the room for the first time since he had entered it. Plain and simple almost to severity. Clean poverty that had a breath of home. The lamp with the painted chimney sitting on the battered dresser. The faded print of the sheep grazing beside a stream. The cracked mirror that hung from a nail pounded in the wall.

"I have been sick," his mother told him, "but now I'm going to get well. You're all the medicine that I need."

Across the bed his father was nodding vigorously.

"She will, too, son," he said. "She grieved a lot about you."

"How is everyone else?" asked Benton. "I'll go out and see them in the morning, but tonight I just want to . . ."

His father shook his head again. "There ain't no one else, Ned."

"No one else! But the hands . . ."

"There ain't no hands."

Silence came across the room, a chill and brittle silence. In the last rays of sunlight coming through the western window his father suddenly was beaten and defeated, an old man with stooped shoulders, lines upon his face.

"Jingo Charley left this morning," his father told him. "He was the last. Tried to fire him months ago, but he wouldn't leave. Said things would come out all right. But this morning he just up and left."

"But no hands," said Benton. "The ranch . . ."

"There ain't no ranch."

Slowly, Benton got to his feet. His mother reached out for one of his hands, held it between the two of hers.

"Don't take on, now," she said. "We still got the house and a little land."

"The bank sold us out," his father said. "We had a little mortgage, your mother sick and all. Bank went broke and they sold us out. Watson bought the place."

"But he was right good about it all," his mother said. "Old Dan Watson, he let us keep the house and ten acres of land. Said he couldn't take everything that a neighbor had."

"Watson didn't have the mortgage?"

His father shook his head. "No, the bank had it. But the bank went broke and had to sell its holdings. Watson bought it from the bank."

"Then Watson foreclosed?"

"No, the bank foreclosed and sold the land to Watson."

"I see," said Benton. "And the bank?"

"It started up again."

Benton closed his eyes, felt the weariness of four long, bitter years closing in on him, smelled the dust of broken hopes and dreams. His mind stirred muddily. There was yet another thing. Another question.

He opened his eyes. "What about Jennie Lathrop?" he asked.

His mother answered. "Why, Jennie, when she heard that you were . . ."

Her voice broke off, hanging in the silence.

"When she heard that I was dead," said Benton, brutally, "she married someone else."

His mother nodded up at him from the pillows. "She thought you weren't coming back, son."

"Who?" asked Benton.

"Why, you know him, Ned. Bill Watson."

"Old Dan Watson's son."

"That's right," said his mother. "Poor girl. He's an awful drinker."

II

The town of Calamity had not changed in the last four years. It still huddled, wind-blown and dusty, on the barren stretch of plain that swept westward from the foot of the Greasewood hills. The old wooden sign in front of the general store still hung lopsided as it had since six years before when a wind had ripped it loose. The hitching posts still leaned crazily, like a row of drunken men wobbling down the street. The mudhole, scarcely drying up from one rainstorm till the next, still bubbled in the street before the bank.

Benton, riding down the street, saw all these things and knew that it was almost as if he'd never been away. Towns like Calamity, he told himself, never change. They simply get dirtier and dingier and each year the buildings slump just a little more and a board falls out here and a shingle blows off there and never are replaced.

"Some day," he thought, "the place will up and blow away."

There was one horse tied to the hitching rack in front of the bank and several horses in front of the Lone Star saloon. A buckboard, with a big gray team, was wheeling away from the general store and heading down the street.

As it approached, Benton pulled the black to one side to make way. A man and a girl rode behind the bays, he saw. An old man with bushy, untrimmed salt and pepper beard, a great burly man who sat four-square behind the team with the reins in one hand and a long whip in the other. The girl wore a sunbonnet that shadowed her face.

That man, thought Benton. I know him from somewhere.

And then he knew. Madox. Old Bob Madox from the Tumbling A. Almost his next door neighbor.

He pulled the black to a halt and waited, wheeling in close to the buckboard when it stopped.

Madox looked up at him and Benton sensed the power that was in the man. Huge barreled chest and hands like hams and blue eyes that crinkled in the noonday sun.

Benton reached down his hand. "You remember me?" he asked. "Ned Benton."

"Sure I do," said Madox. "Sure, boy, I remember you. So you are home again."

"Last night," Benton told him.

"You must recall my daughter," said Madox. "Name of Ellen. Take off that damn sunbonnet, Ellen, so a man can see your face."

She slipped the sunbonnet off her head and it hung behind her by the ties. Blue eyes laughed at Benton.

"It's nice," she said, "to have a neighbor back."

Benton raised a hand to his hat. "Last time I saw you, Ellen," he said, "you were just a kid with freckles and your hair in pig-tails."

"Hell," said old Madox, "she wears it in pigtails mostly now. Just put it up when she comes to town. About drives her mother mad, she does. Dressing up in her brother's pants and acting like a boy all the blessed time."

"Father!" said Ellen, sharply.

"Ought to been a boy," her father said. "Can lick her weight in wildcats."

"My father," Ellen told Benton, "is getting old and he has lost his manners."

"Come out and see us sometime," said Madox. "Make it downright soon. We got a few things to talk over."

"Like this foreclosure business?"

Madox spat across the wheel. "Damn right," he said. "Figure we all got taken in."

"How do the Lee boys feel?" asked Benton.

"Same as the rest of us," said Madox.

He squinted at the black. "Riding an Anchor horse," he said and the tone he used was matter-of-fact.

"Traded," said Benton.

"Some of the Anchor boys are down at the Lone Star," said Madox.

"Thanks," said Benton.

Madox snapped his whip and the team moved on. Ellen waved to Benton and he waved back.

For a moment he sat in the street, watching the buckboard clatter away, then swung the horse around and headed for the Lone Star.

Except for the Anchor men and the bartender the place was empty. The bartender dozed, leaning on the bar. The others were gathered around a table, intent upon their cards.

Benton flicked his eyes from one to another of them. Jim Vest, the foreman, and Indian Joe and Snake McAfee across the table, facing toward him. Frank Hall and Earl Andrews and the one who had looked around. That one had changed, but not so much that Benton didn't know him. Bill Watson was a younger portrait of his florid father.

As if someone had tapped him on the shoulder, Bill Watson looked around again, staring for a moment, then was rising from his chair, dropping his hand of cards face down upon the table.

"Hello, Bill," said Benton.

Watson didn't answer. Around him, back of him, the others were stirring, scraping back their chairs, throwing down their hands.

"I'm riding an Anchor horse," said Benton. "I trust there's no one who objects."

Young Watson wet his lips. "What are you doing with an Anchor horse?"

"Got him off of Rollins."

Vest, the foreman rose from his chair.

"Rollins didn't show up last night," he said.

"You'll find him on the old cutoff trail straight north of where you live," said Benton.

Bill Watson took a slow step forward.

"What happened, Ned?" he asked.

"He tried to shoot me in the back."

"You must have give him cause," charged Vest.

"Looks to me like someone might have given out the word I wasn't to get back," said Benton. "Got the idea that maybe the cutoff trail was watched."

None of them stirred. There was no sound within the room. Benton ticked off the faces. Watson, scared. Vest, angry but afraid to go for his gun. Indian Joe was a face that one couldn't read.

"I'll buy the drinks," said Watson, finally.

But no one stirred. No one started for the bar.

"I'm not drinking," Benton told him sharply.

The silence held. The silence and the motionless group that stood around the table.

"I'm giving you coyotes a chance to shoot it out," said Benton.

Watson stood so still that the rest of his face was stony when his lips moved to make the words he spoke.

"We ain't got no call to go gunning for you, Benton."

"If you feel a call to later on," said Benton, "don't blame me for anything that happens."

For a long moment he stood there, just inside the door, and watched them. No one moved. The cards lay on the table, the men stood where they were.

Deliberately, Benton swung around, took a swift step toward the swinging door, shoulders crawling against the bullet that he knew might come.

Then he was on the street again, standing in the wash of sunlight. And there had been no bullet. The Anchor had backed down.

He untied the black, walked slowly up the street, leading the animal. In front of the bank he tied the horse again and went inside.

There were no customers and Coleman Gray was at his desk beyond the teller's wicket.

The man looked up and saw him, slow recognition coming across his face.

"Young Benton," he exclaimed. "Glad to see you, Ned. Didn't know you were back."

"I came to talk," he said.

"Come on in," said Gray. "Come in and have a chair."

"What I have to say," Benton told him, "I'll say standing up."

"If it's about your father's ranch," said Gray, smoothly, "I'm afraid you don't understand."

"You and the Watsons engineered it."

"Now don't get your back up at the Watsons, son," Gray advised. "Maybe it seems hard, but it was all pure business. After all, the Crazy H wasn't the only one. There was the Madox place and the Lees. They lost their ranches, too."

"Seems downright queer," said Benton, "that all of this should happen just when beef began to amount to something besides hides and tallow."

Gray blustered: "You're accusing me of . . ."

"I'm accusing you of going broke," snapped Benton, "and ruining a lot of folks, then starting up again."

"It's easily explained," protested Gray, "once you understand the circumstances. We had so many loans out that we couldn't meet our obligations. So we had to call them in and that gave us new capital."

"So you're standing pat," he said.

Gray nodded. "If that's what you want to call it," he said, "I am standing pat."

Benton's hand snaked across the railing, caught the banker's shirt and vest, twisting the fabric tightly around Gray's chest, pulling him toward him.

"You stole those ranches, Gray," he rasped, "and I'm getting them back. I'm serving notice on you now. I'm getting them back."

Words bubbled from the banker's lips, but fright turned them into gibberish.

With a snort of disgust, Benton hurled the banker backward, sent him crashing and tripping over a waste paper basket to smash against the wall.

Benton turned on his heel, headed for the door.

In front of the Lone Star the Anchor riders were swinging out into the street, heading out of town. Benton stood watching them.

"Ned," said a quiet voice, almost at his elbow.

Benton spun around.

Sheriff Johnny Pike lounged against the bank front, nickel-plated star shining in the sun.

"Hello, Johnny," said Benton.

"Ned," said the sheriff, "you been raising too much hell."

"Not half as much as I'm going to raise," said Benton. "I come back from the war and I find a bunch of buzzards have euchered the old man out of the ranch. I'm getting that ranch . . ."

The sheriff interrupted. "Sorry about the ranch, Ned, but that ain't no reason to raise all the ruckus that you have. I was looking through the window and I saw you heave that banker heels over teakettle."

"He was damn lucky," snarled Benton, "that I didn't break his neck."

"Then there was that business," said the sheriff, patiently, "of busting up the card game down at the Lone Star. You ain't got no call to walk in and do a thing like that. You hombres come back from the war and you figure you can run things. You figure that all the rest of us citizens have to knuckle down to you. You figure just because you're heroes that we got to . . ."

Benton took a quick step forward. "What are you going to do about it, Johnny?"

The sheriff scrubbed his mustache. "Guess I got to haul you in and put you under a peace bond. Only thing I can do."

Footsteps shambled down the sidewalk and cracked voice yelled at Benton:

"Got some trouble, kid?"

Benton swung around, saw the scarecrow of a man hobbling toward him, bowed legs twinkling down the walk, white mustaches dropping almost to his chin, hat pushed back to display the worried wrinkle that twisted his face.

"Jingo!" yelled Benton. "Jingo, Pa said you left the place."

"Your Pa is batty as a bedbug," Jingo Charley told him. "Couldn't run me off the place. Just come into town to get liquored up."

He squinted at the sheriff.

"This tin star talking law to you?"

"Says he's got to put me under a peace bond," Benton told him.

Jingo Charley spat at the sheriff's feet.

"Ah, hell, don't pay no attention to him. He's just a Watson hand that rides range in town. Come on, we're going home."

The sheriff stepped forward, hands dropping to his guns.

"Now, just a minute, you two . . ."

Jingo Charlie moved swiftly, one bowed leg lashing out. His toe caught the sheriff's heel and heaved. The sheriff's feet went out from under him and the sheriff came crashing down, flat upon the sidewalk.

Jingo Charley stooped swiftly, snatching at the sheriff's belt.

"Danged nice guns," he said, straightening. "Engraved and everything. Wonder if they shoot."

"Give them back," the sheriff roared. "Give them back or . . ."

Deliberately Jingo Charley tossed them, one after the other, into the mudhole that lay in the street. They splashed and disappeared.

"Guess that'll hold the old goat for a little while," said Jingo Charley.

He shook his head, sadly. "Shame to muddy up them pretty guns. Engraved and everything."

III

The tangle of the Greasewood hills lay across the trail, soaring heights that shimmered in the heat of afternoon and short abrupt canyons that were black slashes of shadow upon a sunlit land.

Jingo Charley jogged his horse abreast of Benton. "Want to keep an eye peeled, kid," he warned.

Benton nodded. "I was thinking that, myself."

"Just because them Anchor hombres folded up back in that saloon," said Jingo, "ain't no sign they won't get brave as hell with a tree to hide behind."

"Can't figure out that backing down," said Benton. "Went in figuring on a shootout."

"The Watson bunch will do anything to duck trouble now," the old man told him. "Getting together a bunch of cattle to drive north. Some of their own cattle, I suppose. But likewise a lot of other stuff."

"They'll be starting soon?" asked Benton.

Jingo spat. "Few days. That is, unless something happens."

"Like what?"

"Like if them cows got spooked and hightailed it back into the brush."

"Someone's up there," said Benton quietly. "Someone riding hard."

They pulled their horses to a halt, watched the horse and rider plunging down the tangled hill. The rider sat the horse straight as an Indian and the sun caught the flash of calico fluttering in the wind.

"It's that gal," yelled Jingo. "Old Madox's daughter."

Benton whirled his horse off the trail, touched spurs and tore up the hill. She saw him coming and raised an arm in a swift gesture.

She rode without a saddle, with her dress tucked beneath her, legs flashing in the sun. She had lost her sunbonnet and as she came opposite Benton, he saw the red welts across her cheeks where whipping brush had raked her face.

Benton leaned down and grasped the bridle of the blowing horse, pulled it close, asked sharply: "What's the matter, Ellen?"

"They're waiting for you at the Forks," she gasped.

"Watson?"

She nodded, went on breathlessly. "They passed up on the road and Dad spotted them when we were driving through. But we made out as if we didn't see them. Then when we got out of sight, we pulled up and unhitched."

"You took a big chance," Benton told her, solemnly.

She shook her head. "One of us had to ride back and warn you. And Dad can't ride worth shucks without a saddle. Getting too fat. Me, I can ride any way at all."

Benton scowled. "Sure they didn't see you riding back?"

"No, they couldn't have. I came a roundabout way. Through the hills."

Jingo Charley looked at the heaving horse. "You must have done some riding."

She nodded. "I had to. There wasn't much time. I didn't know how soon you'd be leaving town."

Thinking of it, Benton felt shivers walking on his spine. There at the Forks the trail split three ways, the left hand one going to the Anchor spread, the right hand to Lathrop's Heart ranch, the center one to the Crazy H and Tumbling A. The trail went steeply up a gorge to the high plateau where the trail divided. He and Jingo would have been walking their horses up the gorge, taking it easy. They would have been picked off like sitting birds by the hidden gunmen.

"They've got their horses down in the mouth of Cow Canyon," Ellen was telling them. "One man guarding them. I saw them when I went past."

Jingo Charley grinned wickedly. "Plumb shame," he said, "to set them boys afoot."

Benton said gravely: "Maybe you'd ought to go back, Ellen. The way you came. That way you'd be in the clear before anything could happen."

"I thought maybe you would want to go with me," said Ellen. "There isn't any reason why you have to tangle with them."

"Can't pass up a chance like this," Jingo Charley declared, with finality.

Benton considered. "We can't duck out on a thing like this," he said. "We got to fight them sooner or later and it might as well be now. There's only two things to do. Fight or run."

Jingo spat viciously. "I ain't worth a damn at running," he declared.

"Neither am I," said Benton.

The girl slowly gathered up the reins.

"Be careful," cautioned Benton. "Don't let them see you. We'll wait a while so that you can get through."

She wheeled her horse.

"I don't know how to thank you, Ellen," Benton said.

"We have to stick together," Ellen told him, simply.

Then she was pounding away, back up the tangled hill.

Jingo Charley stared after. "Saved our hair, that's what she did," he said. "Lots of spunk for a gal."

They waited, watching the heights above them. Nothing stirred. The day droned on in sun and sound of insects.

Finally they moved on, skirting the trail, heading for the mouth of Cow Canyon.

Jingo Charley hissed at Benton. "Almost there, kid. Take it easy."

"What's that?" Benton suddenly demanded. Something had gleamed on the heights above them, something dancing like a sunbeam all at once gone crazy. And even as he asked it, he knew what it was.

"Look out!" he shouted at Jingo Charley. With tightened rein and raking spur, he plunged his horse around.

A rifle cracked where the sunbeam danced and smoke plumed on the hillside. Another gun belched at them from just below the first.

Benton spurred his horse and the animal, leaping in fright, went tearing through a clump of whipping brush, skidded over a cutbank, went clattering up a rise.

Ahead of him, Benton saw the old cowhand, urging his horse into a dead run; behind him he heard the thunder of galloping horses, the hacking cough of handguns.

Bullets whispered through the brush around him, some of them so close he heard the whining whisper in the air.

Jingo Charley lurched in the saddle, swayed for a moment and then was riding on. Benton saw a bright red stain spring out upon his sleeve, just above the elbow.

Benton snaked a quick look behind him. Riders with smoking guns were spread out in the brush. A branch caught him across the face with stinging force as he clawed one gun out of the holster.

The horse stumbled, caught itself and then went on. A bullet droned like a lazy bumblebee above Benton's head.

Twisting in his saddle, he pumped his gun, feeling the jerking jumpiness of it in his hand. The leading Anchor man sailed out of his saddle, flying over the horse's head, a whirling tangle of flying arms and legs. The horse whirled swiftly, frightened by the sight of a man in mid-air in front of him, crashed into the second rider, upsetting the plunging horse to send it rolling down the hill.

A yell of triumph was wrenched out of Benton's lungs. The other Anchor riders shied off and Benton's horse reached the ridge top, was plunging down the slope, stiffened forefeet plowing great furrows in the ground.

Jingo Charley was far ahead, almost at the bottom of the slope, swinging his horse to head for a canyon mouth. Benton hauled at the reins, brought the black around to angle down the hill in an effort to catch up with Jingo.

From the ridgetop came a single shot.

Benton looked back. Two or three horses were milling around up there.

Don't want to push us too close, thought Benton, exultantly, after what happened back on the other side of the ridge.

At the bottom of the slope, he was only a few yards behind Jingo Charley. Looking back, he saw the Anchor riders, plunging down the slope.

Got their nerve back, he told himself.

The canyon walls closed in around them, dark and foreboding. Boulders choked the tiny trickle of water that meandered down the stream bed. Brush grew thick against the banks.

Ahead of him Jingo Charley was dismounting, slapping the pony's rump with his hat. Startled, the horse charged up the stream bed.

Jingo yelled at him. "Get off. We can hole up and hold them off."

Benton jumped from his horse and the black went tearing after Jingo's mount.

"You take that side," Jingo yelled at him. "I'll take this."

"But you're hit," Benton told him. "Are you . . ."

"Fit as a fiddle," Jingo told him. "Bullet went through my arm slick as a whistle. Nothing to it."

Below them, down near the canyon's mouth, came the clatter of hoofs on stones, the excited yell of riders.

Turning, Benton plunged into the brush, clambered up the talus slope beneath the grim wall of the canyon.

Behind a boulder he squatted down, gun held across his knee. Below him the canyon spread out like a detailed map.

Looking at it, he grinned. With him here and Charley over on the other side, not even a rabbit could stir down there that they couldn't see. And with the canyon walls rearing straight above them, no one could get at them from any other direction. Anything or anyone that came into that canyon were dead meat to their guns.

The sun slanted down the canyon's narrow notch and squatting by the boulder, Benton felt the warmth of it against his shoulders.

It made him think of other times. Of the tensed hush when a Yankee column was trotting down the road straight into a gun trap. Of the moments when he crouched beneath a ridge, waiting the word that would send him . . . and others . . . charging up the hill into the mouths of flaming guns.

This was it again, but in a different way. This was home without the peace that he had dreamed about in the nights of bivouac.

Far below a horse's hoof clicked restlessly from a bush somewhere nearby, a rasping sound that filled the afternoon.

Something went wrong, Benton told himself. Some of them must have seen Ellen riding back to warn us and they set a new trap for us. Or it may have been the same trap all along. Maybe they meant for old man Madox and Ellen to see them . . .

But that was too complicated, he knew. He shook his head. It would have been simpler for them just to have waited at the Fork.

The minutes slipped along and the sun slid across the sky.

Benton fidgeted behind his boulder. There was no sign of the riders, no sound to betray their presence.

"Jingo," he called softly.

"Yes, kid, what do you want?"

"I'm coming over."

"O.K. Take it easy."

Cautiously, Benton slid down the hillside. At the trickle of water in the streambed, he wet his handkerchief, clawed his way up the opposite bank.

"Jingo?"

"Right over here. What you got?"

"Going to fix up that arm of yours," said Benton.

He slipped into the bushes beside the old man, rolled up his sleeve, baring the bloody arm. A bullet had ripped through a muscle. Not a bad wound, Benton declared.

Jingo chuckled. "Got them stopped, kid. They set a trap for us and now we got one set for them. And they ain't having none of it."

"What about our horses?"

"Blind canyon," said Jingo. "Can't get out less they grow wings."

Swiftly, efficiently, Benton washed and bound the arm. It was not the first wound he had tied up and taken care of in the last few years.

"We better be getting out of here," he said.

Jingo hissed softly. "Something moving down there." He pointed with a finger and Benton saw the slight waving of a bush, just a bit more than the wind would stir it.

They waited. Another bush stirred. A stick crunched.

"It's Indian Joe," Jingo whispered. "Figuring to sneak up on us. Only one in the whole bunch that could of got this far."

Squinting his eyes, Benton could make out the dark face of a crawling man on the opposite bank . . . a dark, evil face that almost blended with the foliage . . . almost, not quite.

"Flip you for him," said Jingo softly.

Benton shook his head. "I got mine today. You go ahead and take him."

Suddenly he felt calm, calm and sure. Back at the old business again. Back at the job of the last four years. Back at the work of killing.

Slowly Jingo raised his gun, the hammer snicked back with a soft metallic sound.

Then the gun roared, deafening in the bush-shrouded canyon, the sound caught up and buffeted about, flung back and forth by the towering walls of stone.

"Got him!" yelled Jingo. "Got him . . . no, by Lord, just nicked him."

The bushes had come to life.

Jingo's gun blasted smoke and flame again.

"Look at him go!" yelled Jingo. "Look at that feller leg it!"

Whipping bushes advancing swiftly down the bank marked Indian Joe's going.

"Damn it," said Jingo, ruefully, "I must be getting old. Should of let you have him."

The silence came again, silence broken only by a tiny wind that moaned now and then high up the cliff, broken by the shrilling of an insect in the sun-drenched land.

They waited, hunched in the bushes, studying the canyon banks. No bush moved. Nothing happened. The sun sank lower and the shadows lengthened.

"Guess they must of give up," Jingo decided.

"I'll scout down the canyon," said Benton. "You catch up the horses."

Moving cautiously, Benton set out down the canyon, eyes studying every angle of the terrain before advancing.

But there was no sign of the Anchor riders, no sign or sound.

At the mouth of the canyon he found the hoof-trampled spot where they had milled their horses and leading out from it were tracks, heading back into the hills.

Something white fluttered in the wind and he strode toward it.

It was a piece of paper, wedged in the cleft of a stick that had been left between two rocks.

Angrily, Benton jerked the paper loose, read the pencil scrawled message:

Benton, we let you off this time. You got 24 hours to git out. After that we shoot you on sight.

IV

Benton's father was out in the yard, chopping wood, when they rode in. At the sight of them, he slapped the axe into the chopping block, left it sticking there, hobbled toward the gate to meet them. Benton saw there was worry on his face.

"I come back again," said Jingo.

"Glad to have you," Benton's father said.

To Benton, he said: "There's someone in the house to see you, son."

"You go ahead," Jingo told the younger man. "I'll put up the horses."

Benton vaulted off the black.

"How's mother?"

"Some better," said his father. "She's sleeping now."

The sun was slanting through the windows of the living room, making bars of golden light across the worn carpeting.

In the dusk of one corner, a woman rose from a chair, moved out into the slash of sunlight.

"Jennie!" said Benton. "Jennie . . ."

"I heard that you were back," she told him.

He stood unmoving, staring at her, at the golden halo that the sunlight flung around her head, at the straightness of her, and wished that her face were not in the shadow.

"You came for something?" he asked and hated himself for it. It was not the way, he knew, to talk to a woman that he had intended to marry. Not the sharp, hard way to speak to a woman whose memory he had carried through four long and bloody years.

"I came to ask you to take care of yourself . . . to stay out of trouble."

"Trouble?" he asked. "What do you mean, trouble?"

She flushed angrily. "You know what I mean, Ned. Trouble with the Anchor. Why don't you leave, there's nothing for you here."

"Nothing but the land that was stolen from me."

"You'll be killed. You can't fight them, all alone."

"Did Bill Watson send you here to ask me this?"

Her voice rose until it was almost shrill. "You know he didn't, Ned. You know I wouldn't do a thing like that. He doesn't even know I'm here."

He gave a short, hard laugh.

"You're a bitter man," she told him.

"I have a right to be," he said.

She moved toward him, two hesitant steps, then stopped.

"Ned," she said softly. "Ned."

"Yes."

"I'm sorry I didn't wait."

"You thought that I was dead," Benton said, heavily. "There was no use of waiting then."

"Bill was the one who told me," she said. "He was the one that started the story. Said he heard it from a man who had been with you."

"So you married him," said Benton. "He told you I was dead and then he married you."

She flared at Benton. "I hate him. Do you hear? I hate him. He's a beast . . . a dirty, drunken beast."

For a moment Benton saw this very room as he remembered

it. A shining place with a warm glow to it. A shining room and a laughing girl. But the room was dingy now, dingy with the shafts of sunlight only adding to its dreariness.

A room with a laughing ghost. And the ghost, he knew, didn't square with the woman who stood before him.

The room was cold and empty . . . like his heart and brain. Nothing matters, he thought, watching her. Nothing matters now. A cause broken on a bloody battlefield that stretched across four years, a dream shattered by a woman who wouldn't wait, land that one had thought of as a home stolen by those who stayed at home while he went out to fight.

"I'm sorry," he finally said. "I'm sorry that I said anything about it."

"You won't make trouble then? You will leave?"

A dull rage shook him for a moment and then flickered out, leaving dull gray ash that was bitter on his tongue.

"You shouldn't have come here at all," he said.

Standing without moving, he heard her walk toward the door. For a moment she stopped and he thought she was going to speak, but she didn't. She stood there for a few long seconds and then moved on.

The door creaked open and his father's voice was speaking.

"Leaving so soon, Jennie?"

"Yes, it's getting late. They will wonder where I've been."

"Jingo will get your horse for you."

"No thanks. I can get him myself. He's in the stall next to the door."

The door closed and his father's heavy feet tramped along the porch. Voices sounded for a moment and then he came back in again. Benton walked out into the hall.

"Jingo tells me he got hit in the arm," his father said.

Benton nodded. "Ran into some trouble. The Anchor gang jumped us at the Forks."

The old man stood silent for a moment. "Your mother's feeling lots better today," he finally said. "Happy about you being back. If anything happened now, Ned, I think that it would kill her."

"I'll be careful," Benton promised.

Out in the kitchen he could hear Jingo rattling pans and poking up the fire.

He tiptoed to the door of his mother's room and looked in. She was asleep, with a smile upon her face. Quietly he tiptoed back again, out to the kitchen.

"Slow down a bit," he said to Jingo. "Mother is asleep."

Jingo looked at him quizzically. "What you aiming to do, kid?"

"That herd the Anchor's gathering," said Benton, quietly. "We can't let them start. Some of them are our cattle they're figuring to drive north."

"Ain't no trick at all to spook a cow," Jingo told him.

Benton's father spoke quietly from the doorway. "Some of the others would help."

"Might need some help," Jingo admitted. "Probably quite a crowd of Anchor hombres out watching them cows."

"Madox and his boy would give us a hand," said Benton's father. "And the two Lee brothers over at the Quarter Circle D."

"You're going, too?" asked Jingo.

The elder Benton nodded. "I'll get Mrs. Madox to come over and stay with Ma."

He looked at his son. "Sound all right to you, Ned?"

"You'll have plenty without me," said Benton. "I'm going to ride over and have a talk with Old Dan Watson."

Benton sat his horse on the windy ridge top, staring down at the chuck wagon fire a mile or so away. Vague, ghostly forms were moving about it and at times he caught the snatch of bellowed words, carried by the wind, mauled by the whipping breeze until they made no sense, but were only sounds of human voice.

Out beyond the fire a dark lake was massed on the prairie . . . a dark lake that was the trail herd gathered for the north. Occasionally Benton heard the click of horns, a subdued moo, but that was all. The herd had settled for the night, was being watched, no doubt, by circling riders.

In the east the sky was lighting, signaling the moon that was about to rise. Starlight glittered in the sky and the wind talked with silken voices in the grass.

Benton whirled his black, headed south.

Half an hour later the Anchor ranch buildings came in sight.

The bunk house, he saw, was dark, but lights blazed in the front room of the big ranch house.

Benton pulled the black to a walk, went in slowly, half prepared for the challenge or the bullet that might come out of the dark.

The plopping of the horse's hoofs against the earth sounded loud in Benton's ears, but there was no stir around the buildings, no signs of life at all except the lighted windows.

One horse was tied at the hitching post and before he dismounted, Benton sat there for a moment, watching and listening. The sound of voices came through the window that opened on the porch. But that was all.

He tied his horse, walked softly up the porch steps, crossed to the door.

Then, with knuckles lifted to knock, the sound of a voice stopped him. A loud, arrogant voice that boomed through the window. A voice that he had heard that day.

". . . He's on the prod, Dan. We can't have him stirring up a fuss. I'd never agreed to the deal if I hadn't thought you'd take care of things."

Benton froze. The voice of Coleman Gray, the banker, coming from the window!

Old Dan Watson's growl came: "Don't worry. We'll take care of Ned Benton . . . and any of the others that start raising hell."

Slowly, Benton let his hand drop to his side, shuffled softly from the door, pressed his body tight against the house.

"You got me into this," Gray whined. "You were the ones that figured it all out."

"You were damn quick to jump at it," growled Dan Watson's voice, "when you figured there wasn't any chance of being caught. But now that young Benton's come back, you got cold feet."

"But you said he wouldn't come back," Gray yelled. "You said you'd see to it that he never did."

Quick steps sounded on the porch and Benton whirled, but he was too slow. A hard finger of metal jammed into his back and a mocking voice spoke.

"Damned if it ain't the hero, come back from the war."

Benton choked with rage.

"Who is it?" he asked.

"Your old friend," said the voice back of him. "Snake McAfee."

"Look, Snake. I was just coming over to see Dan."

"Just a friendly visit," snarled Snake. "Damn funny way to go about it, listening at a window."

He jabbed the gun into Benton's back. "In you go. The boss will want to see you."

Urged by the gun, Benton turned toward the door. Snake McAfee yelled and the door swung open. Bill Watson stood on the threshold, wonder on his face at the sight of Benton.

"Good evening, Bill," said Benton.

Behind him McAfee jabbed with the gun and growled. "Get on in, damn you."

Bill Watson stood to one side, triumph flaming across his face. His lips parted in a flabby, oily smile.

Benton stepped across the threshold, on into the living room. McAfee, gun still in his hand, slid along the wall, stood with his back against it.

Old Dan Watson sat stolid, red face turning purple, strong, pudgy hands gripping the arms of the rocking chair in which he rested. The banker's jaw dropped, then snapped shut again, like a steel trap closing. Behind his back, Benton heard young Watson snickering.

"Found him listening just outside the window," Snake McAfee told the room.

"What did you hear?" Old Dan Watson asked and his words were slow and ponderous, as if he had all the time in the world to deal with this situation and would not be hurried.

Benton flicked a look at Gray and saw the man was sweating, literally sweating in terror.

"No use of talking about what I heard," said Benton. "Let's talk about what we're going to do."

"Sensible," Watson grunted and rocked a lick or two in the rocking chair.

"The two of you fixed it up between you to rob your neighbors," said Benton, bluntly.

Gray half sprang from his chair, then settled back again.

"You can't prove that," he snapped.

Old Dan grumbled derisively. "He don't need to prove it, Coleman. He won't even have a chance."

He twisted his massive head around to Benton.

"What did you come here for, anyway?"

"I came to make a deal."

Old Dan rumbled at him. "Let's hear your proposition."

"You got the Crazy H for a couple thousand measly dollars," said Benton. "You got cattle that were worth twice that or more, let alone the land."

Old Watson nodded, eyes cold and hard.

"You got cattle in your trail herd out there that don't wear your brand," said Benton. "Take the ones you need to pay what the ranches around here cost and hand the ranchers back their deeds."

Gray wiped sweat from his brow with a nervous hand.

"That's fair," he burst out. "That's fair. After all, we can't take advantage of a man who went out and fought for us."

Watson shook his head. "No, the deal was legal. When I took over those cattle weren't worth a dime because there was no place to market them. It's not my fault that the cattle market changed."

"Except," said Benton, quietly, "that you knew it was going

to change. You had word of what was going on up north. So you moved fast to take over everything that you could grab."

Feet shuffled over by the window and Benton looked toward it. Snake McAfee leered back at him, gun half raised.

"I have just one thing to say to you," said Watson, slowly. "Get out of the country. You're a trouble-maker and you've had your warning. If you stay we'll gun you down on sight like a lobo wolf."

His hands pounded the arms of the rocking chair, his voice rising in old-man querulousness.

"You've been back just a bit more than a day, Benton, and you've already killed two of my men. I won't stand for anything like that."

"I killed them," said Benton, coldly, "because I was faster on the gun than they were. And if you stay pig-headed, a lot more of them will die."

Watson's eyes narrowed in his monstrous face. "You mean that, don't you, Benton?"

Benton stared straight at him. "You know I do, Dan. And what's more, you'll not move a single cow. . . ."

Watson leaned forward, bellowing. "What's that . . ."

Hoofs suddenly hammered in the yard outside the house, hoofs that skidded to a stop. Feet thumped across the porch and the door slammed open.

A disheveled rider blinked in the lamplight.

"The herd!" he yelled. "They stampeded it! It's headed for the hills! Gang of riders . . ."

Dan Watson heaved himself upward with a grunt of sudden, violent rage. Snake McAfee was standing with gun arm hanging, staring at the rider.

Benton whirled, took one quick step, fist swinging to explode on Snake's jaw. Snake crashed into the window as Benton leaped for the door, hands clawing for his guns. Behind him glass tinkled, smashing on the floor.

Benton saw the rider leaping at him, chopped down viciously

with his gun barrel, but too late to stop the man. The gun smacked with a leaden thud across the hunched down shoulder, then the shoulder hit him in the stomach and sent him reeling back so violently that his hat blew off.

Stars exploded in Benton's head. Stars and a bursting pain and a roaring wind that whistled at the edges. He felt himself falling forward, like a great tree falls, falling through a darkness that was speared with jagged streaks of pain.

And through the roaring of the wind that whistled through his brain he heard the high, shrill, excited voice of Young Bill Watson:

"That's the way to kill the dirty son . . ."

Awareness came back. Awareness of the seep of light that ran along the boards, awareness of the hard lump that the gun made beneath his chest, where his arm had doubled and he had fallen on it, awareness of the rumble of voices that droned above him . . . voices that at first were misty sounds and then became words and finally had meaning.

". . . You better put a bullet through him."

That was the banker's voice, hard and suspicious, but with a whine within it.

The elder Watson's voice rumbled at him. "Hell, there ain't no use. He's deader than a fence post, as it is. Look at that head of his . . . split wide open."

Young Bill Watson snickered, nastily. "When I hit 'em, they stay hit."

"Still, just to be safe . . ."

The puncher's frantic voice broke in. "Boss! The cattle!"

Old Watson's voice bellowed. "Yes, damn it, I almost forgot."

Feet tramped across the floor, jarring it.

"You riding with us, Gray?" Bill Watson asked.

The banker's voice was hesitant. "No. Think I'll head back for town. Got some business . . ."

The slamming door cut off his words.

Silence stalked across the room, a deathly, terrible silence.

A dark drop dripped down on the floor no more than an inch from Benton's left eye. A drop that hit and spattered . . . and was followed by another.

Blood, thought Benton. Blood! Dripping from my head. From where Bill Watson's gun butt got me.

His hand twitched beneath him and he gritted his teeth to keep it where it was, to keep it from reaching up and feeling of his head, feeling to see just how bad the head wound was.

A wave of giddiness swept over him and beneath him the floor weaved just a little. The blood went on, dripping on the boards before his eye, forming a little puddle on the floor.

A glancing blow, he thought. A glancing blow that ripped my scalp half off. Head must be in one hell of a mess to make them think I'm dead.

Only the banker isn't sure I'm dead. He was the one that wanted to put a bullet into me to be sure and finish it. And he's still in the room here with me.

Pain lanced through his brain and across his neck, a livid finger of pain that etched an acid path along his jangled nerves. A groan came bubbling in his throat and he caught and held it back, held it with teeth that bit into his lip.

Feet shuffled slowly across the floor and in his mind Benton could imagine the slouching form of the banker stalking him, walking softly, warily, watching for some sign of life.

Play dead. That was it. Lie still. Be careful with your breathing, just sucking in enough air to keep your lungs alive. The way he'd done it on the night when the Yank patrol was hunting for him down in Tennessee.

The ticking of the clock on the mantelpiece hammered through the room . . . a fateful sound. A sound that measured time, that sat and watched and didn't care what happened. A sound that ticked men's lives away and never even hurried.

The boots walked past and then turned back, came close. Benton felt his body tensing, fought it back to limpness.

A toe reached out and prodded him . . . prodded harder. Benton let his body roll with the prodding toe.

An inner door squeaked open softly and someone gasped, a hissing gasp of indrawn breath that could only come with terror.

The boots swung around and Benton knew that in the little silence the two of them were looking at one another . . . Gray and the person who had come into the room.

"I'm sorry, madam," said the banker, "that you happened in."

A woman's voice came from across the room . . . a remembered voice.

"It's . . . it's . . . who is it?"

Gray's voice was at once brutal and triumphant. "It's young Benton."

"But it can't be!" There was a note of rising horror in the words. "It simply can't be. Why, only this afternoon he promised me . . ."

The outer door slammed open and boots tramped harshly across the floor, passed close to Benton's head.

"So you talked to him," said young Bill Watson's voice. "That's where you were today."

"Bill!" screamed the girl. "Bill, it's not . . ."

Watson's voice shrieked at her, lashed with blinding fury. "Just as soon as my back is turned, you go crawling back to him."

"Listen, Bill," said Jennie Watson. "Listen to me. Yes, I did talk to him . . . and I'm leaving you. I'm not living with a man like you . . ."

Something in his face wrenched a shriek from her, something in his face, something in the way he walked toward her.

"So you're leaving me! Why, you damned little tramp, I'll . . ."

She screamed again.

Benton heaved himself upward from the floor, gun clutched in his hand.

Watson was wheeling around, wheeling at the sound behind him, hands blurring for his guns.

"Bill," yelled Benton, "don't do it! Don't try . . ."

But Watson's guns were already out, were swinging up.

Benton chopped his own wrist down, pressing the trigger. The gun bucked and shook the room with thunder. Through the puff of powder smoke, he saw Watson going down.

Another shot blasted in the room and Benton felt the gust of wind that went past his cheek, heard the chug of a bullet crunching through the wall beyond.

He swung on his toes and swept his gun around. The banker stood before him, smoking gun half raised.

"So it's you," said Benton.

He twitched his gun up and Gray stared at him in white-faced terror. The gun dropped from the banker's hand and he backed away, backed until the wall stopped him and he stood pinned by the muzzle of Benton's gun. The man's mouth worked but no words came out and he looked like he was strangling.

Benton snarled at him in disgust. "Quit blubbering. I won't kill you."

Blood trickled from his right eyebrow and half blinded him. He raised his free hand to wipe it off and the hand came away smeared a sticky red.

"Lord," he thought, "I must be a sight."

At a sound behind him, he swung around.

Watson was sitting up and Jennie was on her knees beside him. Both of them were staring at him.

"I'm sorry," Benton told the girl. "I tried to stop him. I didn't want to shoot him. I didn't shoot until I had to."

The girl spoke quietly. "You used to be kind and considerate. Before you went off to war and learned to kill . . ."

Watson bent from his sitting position, reaching out his hand, clawing for a gun that lay on the floor.

Benton jerked his own gun up and fired. Splinters leaped shining from the floor. Watson pulled himself back, sat hump-shouldered, scowling.

"Try that again," invited Benton.

Watson shook his head.

Benton nodded at the girl. "You have her to thank you're alive right now. If I could have brought myself to kill Jennie Lathrop's husband, you'd been dead a good long minute."

He wiped his face again, scrubbed his hand against his shirt.

"After this," he said, "be sure you hit a little harder when you want to kill a man."

"Next time," Watson promised, "I'll put a bullet through your skull."

Benton spoke to the girl. "Better get that shoulder of his fixed up and get him in shape to travel. I don't want to find him around here when I come back."

Feet scuffed swiftly and Benton whirled about. Gray was leaping for the window, arms folded above his head to shield his eyes against the flying glass, feet swinging outward to clear the sill and crash into the already shattered panes.

Benton snapped his gun up, but before his finger pressed the trigger, gray had hit the window in a spray of showering glass and splintered wood.

Benton's shot hammered through the broken window, a coughing bark that drowned out the tinkle of the falling shards. Outside, on the porch, a body thumped and rolled, crashed into the railing, flailed for a moment as Gray thrashed to gain his feet.

Benton bent his head, ran two quick steps, hurled himself after Gray, went sailing through the broken window, landed on the porch floor with a jar that shook his teeth.

Out in the moon-washed yard the banker was swinging on his horse at the hitching rack. And as he swung up, his hand was clawing at the saddle, clawing for something hidden there . . . a metallic something that came up in his fist, gleaming in the moonlight, and exploded with a gush of flame spearing through the night.

Benton, staggering to his feet, ducked as the showers of splinters leaped from the railing of the porch and the whining bullet chugged into the window sill behind him.

Gray's horse was rearing, wheeling from the rack, puffs of dust beneath his dancing feet.

Benton snapped up his gun and fired, knew that he had missed.

Cursing, he vaulted the porch railing, ran for his own mount while Gray hammered off into the night, heading south, heading for the hills.

V

Moonlight made the hills a nightmare land of light and shadow, a mottled land that was almost unearthly . . . a place of sudden depths and crazy heights, a twisting, bucking land that had been frozen into rigidity by a magic that might, it seemed, turn it loose again on any moment's notice.

Ahead of Benton, Gray's horse crossed a ridge, was highlighted for a single instant against the moonlit sky. Then was gone again, plunging down the slope beyond.

Gaining on him, Benton told himself, gaining all the time. He bent low above the mighty black and whispered to him and the black heard and responded, great muscles straining to hurl himself and his rider up the slope.

Faint dust, stirred by the passing of the pounding hoofs ahead, left a faintly bitter smell in the cool night air.

Another couple of miles, Benton promised himself. Another couple of miles and I'll overhaul him.

The black topped the ridge and swung sharply to angle down the trail that led toward the blackness of the canyon mouth below.

Ahead of them, halfway down the slope, Gray's horse was a humping shadow that left a dust trail in the moonlight. A shadow that fled before them in the tricky shadows that laired among the hills.

A shadow that suddenly staggered, that was a pinwheel of dust spinning down the hill . . . a pinwheel that became two spinning parts and then was still. The horse lay sprawled against the slope. Probably dead with a broken neck, thought Benton.

But the man was running . . . a tiny furtive rabbity shadow that scuttled across a painted landscape.

With a whoop, Benton spurred the black horse off the trail, went plunging after the running figure in a shower of rocks and talus. For a moment Gray halted, facing about. Flame blossomed from his hand and the flat crack of his gun snarled across the night.

Benton lifted his gun, then lowered it again. No sense of shooting at a ducking, dodging figure in the shadowed light. No sense in wasting time.

Gray faced about again and once more the gun barked an angry challenge. Far above his head, Benton heard the droning of the bullet.

Then the man was just ahead, dodging through the brush that covered the lower reaches of the slope. Benton drove the horse straight at him and Gray, seeing the gleam of the slashing hoofs above him, screamed and dived away, caught his foot and fell, skidded on his shoulder through the silty soil.

Benton spun the horse around, leaped from the saddle. He hit the ground and slid, ground crumbling and skidding beneath his driving boots.

Gray clawed his way to his feet, stood with his hands half raised.

"Don't shoot," he screamed. "Don't shoot. I lost my gun."

Benton walked toward him. "You always manage to lose your gun," he said, "just when it will save you."

The banker cringed, backing down the slope. Benton followed.

"We're going to have a talk," he said. "You and I. You're going to tell me a lot of things that will hang a lot of people."

Gray babbled, wildly. "I'll talk. I'll tell you everything. I'll tell you all about . . ."

Suddenly a rifle cracked from somewhere beyond the ridge . . . a high, ringing sound that woke the echoes in the hills. And cracked again, a vicious sound that cut through the night like a flaming scream of hate.

Benton stiffened, startled by the sound, startled by the knowledge that other men were close.

A pebble clicked and a boot scraped swiftly through the sliding sand. Warning feet jigged on Benton's spine and he flicked his attention from the rifle shots to the man before him.

Gray was charging, shoulders hunched, head pulled down, long arms reaching out. Coming up the hill with the drive of powerful legs that dug twin streams of pebbles from their resting places and sent them pouring down the hill in a rattling torrent.

Benton jerked up his gun, but the shoulders hit his knees before he could press the trigger and steel arms were clawing at his waist, clawing to pull him down even as the impact of the driving shoulders hurled him off his feet.

His body slammed into the earth and his gun went wheeling through the moonlight as his elbow hit a stone and his arm jerked convulsively with pain.

Above him, Gray loomed massive in the night, hunched like a beast about to spring, face twisted into a silent snarl of rage. Benton lashed up with his boot, but as he kicked, Gray moved, was running down the hill after the gun that had been knocked from Benton's hand.

Benton hurled himself to his feet, strode down the slope. Gray was on his knees, clawing under a bush where the gun had lodged, mumbling to himself, half slobbering in his haste. Then he was twisting around, a brightness in his hand.

Benton flattened out in a long, clean dive that smothered the gun play, that sent Gray crashing back into the bush. The man fought back, fought silently with pistoning fists and raking fingernails and pumping knees that caught Benton in the stomach and battered out his breath.

Clawing for the second gun that should have been in his belt, Benton's fingers found the empty holster. The gun had fallen out somewhere, perhaps when Gray had first tackled him farther up the slope.

The other gun also had disappeared. Gray had lost his hold upon it at the impact of Benton's charge and it lay somewhere beneath the battered, tangled bush.

The knee came up again and plunged into his stomach with a vicious force. Retching, Benton slid forward, rolled free of the bush, crawled on hands and knees. The hill and moon were swinging in gigantic circles before his eyes and there was a giant hand inside of him, tearing at his vitals.

Off to one side a tattered form struggled up into the moonlight, took a slow step forward. Benton wabbled to his feet and stood waiting, watching Gray advance.

The man came on slow and stolid, like a killer sure of the kill but careful to make no mistakes.

Benton sucked in careful breaths of air, felt the pain evaporating from his body, sensed that he had legs again.

Six feet away Gray sprang swiftly, right fist flailing out, left fist cocked. Benton ducked, countered with his right, felt the fist sink into the banker's belly. Gray grunted and let loose his left and it raked across Benton's ribs with a searing impact.

Benton stepped back, trip-hammered Gray's chin with a right and left, took a blow along the jaw that tilted his head with a vicious jolt.

Gray was coming in, coming fast, fists working like pistons. Benton took one quick backward step to gain some room to swing, brought his right fist sizzling from his boot tops. It smacked with a terrific impact full in the banker's face, jarred Benton's arm back to the elbow. In front of Benton, Gray was folding up, fists still pumping feebly, feet still moving forward, but folding at the knees.

Strength went out of the man and he slumped into a pile that moaned and clawed to regain its feet.

Benton stepped away, stood waiting.

Painfully, Gray made it to his feet, stood staring at Benton. His clothes were ripped and torn and a dark stream of blood bubbled from his nose and ran black across his mouth and chin.

"Well?" asked Benton.

Gray lifted a hand to wipe away the blood. "I've had enough," he said.

"Talk then," said Benton. "Talk straight and fast."

Gray mumbled at him. "What you want to know?"

"About the ranches. It was a put-up game?"

Gray shook his head. "All legal," he protested. "Everything was . . ."

Benton strode toward him and the man moaned in fright, putting up his hands to shield his face.

"All right, then," said Benton. "Spit it out."

"It was the Watsons that thought it up," Gray told him. He stopped to spit the blood out of his mouth and then went on. "They knew about the market up north and they wanted land and cattle."

"So you fixed it up to go broke," said Benton.

Gray nodded. "The bank really didn't go broke, you see. We just doctored up the books, so there'd be some excuse to foreclose on our loans."

"Then what?"

"That's all," said Gray. "I foreclosed and the Anchor brand took over. Paid the bank the money and took the land."

"And you'll testify in court?"

Gray hesitated. Benton reached for him and he backed away. He wiped his mouth again. "I'll testify," he said.

Suddenly Gray straightened to attention, head cocked to one

side, like a dog that has suddenly been snapped from sleep by an unfamiliar sound.

Then Benton heard it, too. The click and rattle of horses' hoofs, somewhere across the ridge.

Gray whirled about, staggered up the slope.

"Help," he yelled. "Help!"

Benton leaped after him, swift rage brimming in his brain.

"Help!" yelled Gray.

Benton reached him, grasped his shoulder, hauled him around. The man's mouth was opening again, but Benton smashed it shut, smashed it with a blow that cracked like a pistol shot. Gray sagged so suddenly that his falling body ripped loose the hold Benton's hand had upon his coat.

This time he did not moan or stir. He lay huddled on the ground, a limp pile of clothing that fluttered in the wind.

The hoofs across the ridge were speeding up and heading for the top. Frantically, Benton explored the ground for a gun. Three guns, he thought, and not a one in sight.

For a single instant he stood in indecision and that instant was too long.

Mounted men plunged over the ridge top, black silhouettes against the moon and were plunging down the slope. Dust smoked in silver puffs around the horses' jolting hoofs and the men rode silently.

Benton ducked swiftly, started to run, but those on the ridge top saw him, wheeled their mounts, tore down upon him.

Faced about, he waited . . . and knew that final hope was gone. Gray had yelled when he heard the hoofs, but he could not have known that the riders were from the Anchor ranch. He had only taken a chance, gambling on the fact that they may have been.

And they were.

Four men, who wheeled their horses in a rank in front of Benton, reined them to a sliding stop, sat looking at him, like gaunt, black vultures perching on a tree.

Benton, standing motionless, ticked them off in his brain. Vest, the foreman of the Anchor spread, Indian Joe, Snake McAfee and old Dan Watson himself.

Watson chuckled in his beard, amused.

"No guns," he said. "Can you imagine that. The great Ned Benton caught without no guns."

"I shoot him now?" asked Indian Joe and lifted up his gun.

Watson grunted. "Might as well," he said.

Indian Joe leveled the gun with a grossly exaggerated gesture of careful aiming.

"I nick him up a bit," said Joe.

"None of that," snapped Watson, peevishly. "When you fire, give it to him straight between the eyes."

"No fun that way," complained Indian Joe.

Watson spoke to Benton. "You got anything to say?"

Benton shook his head.

If he turned and ran, they'd stop him with a storm of lead before he'd gone a dozen feet.

On the hillside above a rock clicked and Vest stiffened in his saddle.

"What was that?" he asked.

Snake laughed at him. "Nothing, Vest. You're just spooky. That's all. Shooting at them shadows back there."

Slowly, deliberately Indian Joe raised his gun. Benton stared straight into the ugly bore.

The gun flashed an angry puff of red into his eyes and the wind of the screaming bullet stirred the hair upon his head.

"Missed, by Lord!" yelped Indian Joe in mock chagrin.

Watson yelled angrily at him. "I told you none of that!"

Indian Joe was the picture of contriteness. "I do better next time."

He leveled the gun again and Snake growled at him. "You take too damn long."

"Got to hit him this time," said Indian Joe, "or boss get awful mad. Right between the eyes, he said. Right between . . ."

Up the hill a rifle snarled and Indian Joe stiffened in his saddle, stiffened so that he was standing in the stirrups with his body tense and rigid.

Vest yelled in sudden fright and Indian Joe's horse was pitching, hurling the rider from his back, a rider that was a tumbling empty sack instead of a rigid body.

With a curse, Snake swung his horse around, reaching for his gun. The hilltop rifle spoke again and Snake was huddled in his saddle, clawing at his throat and screaming, screaming with a whistling, gurgling sound. Blackness gushed from his throat onto his clawing hands and he slumped out of the saddle as the horse wheeled suddenly and plunged toward the canyon mouth.

Benton dived for the shining gun that fell from Snake's hand, heard the hammer of the rifle talking on the hill. A horse screamed in agony and far off down the slope he heard the hurried drum of hoofs.

Scooping the weapon up, Benton whirled around. A sixgun roared and he felt the slap of the bullet as it sang across his ribs.

In the moonlight Dan Watson was walking toward him, walking slowly and deliberately, gun leveled at his hip. Behind him lay the horse that he had been riding, downed by the rifle on the hill.

Watson's hat had fallen off and the moon gleamed on his beard. He walked like an angry bear, with broad shoulders hunched and bowed legs waddling.

Benton snapped Snake's gun up, half fumbled with the unfamiliar grip. A heavy gun, he thought, a heavier gun than I have ever used. Too heavy, with a drag that pulls the muzzle down.

Watson fired again and something tugged at Benton's ear, a thing that hummed and made a breeze against his cheek.

By main strength, Benton forced Snake's gun muzzle up, pulled the trigger. The big gun jolted in his hand . . . jolted again.

Out in front of him, Watson stopped walking, stood for a moment as if surprised.

Then his hand opened and the gun fell out and Watson pitched forward on his face.

From up the hill came a crash of bushes, a cascade of chattering rocks that almost drowned out the beat of plunging hoofs.

Benton swung around, gun half raised. Two riders were tearing down upon him.

One of them waved a rifle at him and screeched in a banshee voice.

"How many did we get?"

"Jingo!" yelled Benton. "Jingo, you old . . ."

Then he saw the second rider and his words dried up.

Stones rattled about his boots as Ellen Madox reined in her horse less than six feet from him.

Jingo stared at the three bodies on the hillside.

"I guess that finishes it," he said.

"There were four of them," said Benton. "Vest must have got away."

"The hell he did," snapped Jingo. "Who's that jigger over there?"

He pointed and Benton laughed . . . a laugh of pure nervousness.

"That's Gray," he said. "I got him and he coughed up everything, He'll testify in court."

"Dead men," said Jingo, sharply, "ain't worth a damn in court."

"He isn't dead," protested Benton. "Just colder than a herring."

"Young Watson should be around somewhere," said Jingo. "What say we hunt him up?"

Benton shook his head. "Bill Watson is riding and he won't be coming back."

Jingo squinted at him. "Gal riding with him?"

"I suppose she is," said Benton.

"Did a downright handsome job on them cows," said Jingo. "Take a good six weeks to get them all together."

"You had good help," said Benton, looking at Ellen Madox. She no longer wore the dress that she had in town, but Levis and a flat felt hat that must have been her brother's, for it was too big for her.

Jingo snorted. "She wasn't supposed to come. Sneaked out after the rest had gone and joined up with us."

He spat disgustedly. "Her pa was madder than a hornet when he found out about her being with us. Told me off to take her home."

He spat again. "Always something," he said, "to spoil a man's good time."

Benton grinned. "I'll take her off your hands, Jingo. You take care of Gray over there and I'll be plumb proud to see Ellen home."

CONDITION OF EMPLOYMENT

Originally published in Galaxy Magazine *in April 1960, "Condition of Employment" was actually sold to Horace Gold at the end of 1958. It echoes, in a way, the theme of "Huddling Place," a noted story Cliff had written more than a decade earlier about the effect of psychological illness on a space traveler.*

—dww

He had been dreaming of home, and when he came awake, he held his eyes tight shut in a desperate effort not to lose the dream. He kept some of it, but it was blurred and faint and lacked the sharp distinction and the color of the dream. He could tell it to himself, he knew just how it was, he could recall it as a lost and far-off thing and place, but it was not there as it had been in the dream.

But even so, he held his eyes tight shut, for now that he was awake, he knew what they'd open on, and he shrank from the drabness and the coldness of the room in which he lay. It was, he thought, not alone the drabness and the cold, but also the loneliness and the sense of not belonging. So long as he did not look at it, he need not accept this harsh reality, although he felt himself on the fringe of it, and it was reaching for him, reaching through the color and the warmth and friendliness of this other place he tried to keep in mind.

At last it was impossible. The fabric of the held-onto dream became too thin and fragile to ward off the moment of reality, and he let his eyes come open.

It was every bit as bad as he remembered it. It was drab and cold and harsh, and there was the maddening alienness waiting for him, crouching in the corner. He tensed himself against it, trying to work up his courage, hardening himself to arise and face it for another day.

The plaster of the ceiling was cracked and had flaked away in great ugly blotches. The paint on the wall was peeling and dark stains ran down it from the times the rain leaked in. And there was the smell, the musty human smell that had been caged in the room too long.

Staring at the ceiling, he tried to see the sky. There had been a time when he could have seen it through this or any ceiling. For the sky had belonged to him, the sky and the wild, dark space beyond it. But now he'd lost them. They were his no longer.

A few marks in a book, he thought, an entry in the record. That was all that was needed to smash a man's career, to crush his hope forever and to keep him trapped and exiled on a planet that was not his own.

He sat up and swung his feet over the edge of the bed, hunting for the trousers he'd left on the floor. He found and pulled them on and scuffed into his shoes and stood up in the room.

The room was small and mean—and cheap. There would come a day when he could not afford a room even as cheap as this. His cash was running out, and when the last of it was gone, he would have to get some job, any kind of job. Perhaps he should have gotten one before he began to run so short. But he had shied away from it. For settling down to work would be an admission that he was defeated, that he had given up his hope of going home again.

He had been a fool, he told himself, for ever going into space. Let him just get back to Mars and no one could ever get him off it. He'd go back to the ranch and stay there as his father had wanted him to do. He'd marry Ellen and settle down, and other fools could fly the death-traps around the Solar System.

Glamor, he thought—it was the glamor that sucked in the kids when they were young and starry-eyed. The glamor of the far place, of the wilderness of space, of the white eyes of the stars watching in that wilderness—the glamor of the engine-song and of the chill white metal knifing through the blackness and the loneliness of the emptiness, and the few cubic feet of courage and defiance that thumbed its nose at that emptiness.

But there was no glamor. There was brutal work and everlasting watchfulness and awful sickness, the terrible fear that listened for the stutter in the drive, for the *ping* against the metal hide, for any one of the thousand things that could happen out in space.

He picked up his wallet off the bedside table and put it in his pocket and went out into the hall and down the rickety stairs to the crumbling, lopsided porch outside.

And the greenness waited for him, the unrelenting, bilious green of Earth. It was a thing to gag at, to steel oneself against, an indecent and abhorrent color for anyone to look at. The grass was green and all the plants and every single tree. There was no place outdoors and few indoors where one could escape from it, and when one looked at it too long, it seemed to pulse and tremble with a hidden life.

The greenness, and the brightness of the sun, and the sapping beat—these were things of Earth that it was hard to bear. The light one could get away from, and the heat one could somehow ride along with—but the green was always there.

He went down the steps, fumbling in his pocket for a cigarette. He found a crumpled package and in it one crumpled cigarette. He put it between his lips and threw the pack away and stood at the gate, trying to make up his mind.

But it was a gesture only, this hardening of his mind, for he knew what he would do. There was nothing else to do. He'd done it day after day for more weeks than he cared to count, and he'd do it again today and tomorrow and tomorrow, until his cash ran out.

And after that, he wondered, what?

Get a job and try to strike a bargain with his situation? Try to save against the day when he could buy passage back to Mars—for they'd surely let him ride the ships even if they wouldn't let him run them. But, he told himself, he'd figured that one out. It would take twenty years to save enough, and he had no twenty years.

He lit the cigarette and went tramping down the street, and even through the cigarette, he could smell the hated green.

Ten blocks later, he reached the far edge of the spaceport. There was a ship. He stood for a moment looking at it before he went into the shabby restaurant to buy himself some breakfast.

There was a ship, he thought, and that was a hopeful sign. Some days there weren't any, some days three or four. But there was a ship today and it might be the one.

One day, he told himself, he'd surely find the ship out there that would take him home—a ship with a captain so desperate for an engineer that he would overlook the entry in the book.

But even as he thought it, he knew it for a lie—a lie he told himself each day. Perhaps to justify his coming here each day to check at the hiring hall, to lie to keep his hope alive, to keep his courage up. A lie that made it even barely possible to face the bleak, warm room and the green of Earth.

He went into the restaurant and sat down on a stool.

The waitress came to take his order. "Cakes again?" she asked.

He nodded. Pancakes were cheap and filling and he had to make his money last.

"You'll find a ship today," said the waitress. "I have a feeling you will."

"Perhaps I will," he said, without believing it.

"I know just how you feel," the waitress told him. "I know how awful it can be. I was homesick once myself, the first time I left home. I thought I would die."

He didn't answer, for he felt it would not have been dignified to answer. Although why he should now lay claim to dignity, he could not imagine.

But this, in any case, was more than simple homesickness. It was planetsickness, culturesickness, a cutting off of all he'd known and wanted.

Sitting, waiting for the cakes to cook, he caught the dream again—the dream of red hills rolling far into the land, of the cold, dry air soft against the skin, of the splendor of the stars at twilight and the faery yellow of the distant sandstorm. And the low house crouched against the land, with the old gray-haired man sitting stiffly in a chair upon the porch that faced toward the sunset.

The waitress brought the cakes.

The day would come, he told himself, when he could afford no longer this self-pity he carried. He knew it for what it was and he should get rid of it. And yet it was a thing he lived with—even more than that, it had become a way of life. It was his comfort and his shield, the driving force that kept him trudging on each day.

He finished the cakes and paid for them.

"Good luck," said the waitress, with a smile.

"Thank you," he said.

He tramped down the road, with the gravel crunching underfoot and the sun like a blast upon his back, but he had left the greenness. The port lay bare and bald, scalped and cauterized.

He reached where he was going and went up to the desk.

"You again," said the union agent.

"Anything for Mars?"

"Not a thing. No, wait a minute. There was a man in here not too long ago."

The agent got up from the desk and went to the door. Then he stepped outside the door and began to shout at someone.

A few minutes later, he was back. Behind him came a lumbering and irate individual. He had a cap upon his head that said CAPTAIN in greasy, torn letters, but aside from that he was distinctly out of uniform.

"Here's the man," the agent told the captain. "Name of Anson Cooper. Engineer first class, but his record's not too good."

"Damn the record!" bawled the captain. He said to Cooper: "Do you know Morrisons?"

"I was raised with them," said Cooper. It was not the truth, but he knew he could get by.

"They're good engines," said the captain, "but cranky and demanding. You'll have to baby them. You'll have to sleep with them. And if you don't watch them close, they'll up and break your back."

"I know how to handle them," said Cooper.

"My engineer ran out on me." The captain spat on the floor to show his contempt for runaway engineers. "He wasn't man enough."

"I'm man enough," Cooper declared.

And he knew, standing there, what it would be like. But there was no other choice. If he wanted to get back to Mars, he had to take the Morrisons.

"O.K., then, come on with you," the captain said.

"Wait a minute," said the union agent. "You can't rush a man off like this. You have to give him time to pick up his duffle."

"I haven't any to pick up," Cooper said, thinking of the few pitiful belongings back in the boarding house. "Or none that matters."

"You understand," the agent said to the captain, "that the union cannot vouch for a man with a record such as his."

"To hell with that," said the captain. "Just so he can run the engines. That's all I ask."

The ship stood far out in the field. She had not been much to start with and she had not improved with age. Just the job of riding on a craft like that would be high torture, without the worry of nursing Morrisons.

"She'll hang together, no fear," said the captain. "She's got a lot more trips left in her than you'd think. It beats all hell what a tub like that can take."

Just one more trip, thought Cooper. Just so she gets me to Mars. Then she can fall apart, for all I care.

"She's beautiful," he said, and meant it.

He walked up to one of the great landing fins and laid a hand upon it. It was solid metal, with all the paint peeled off it, with tiny pits of corrosion speckling its surface and with a hint of cold, as if it might not as yet have shed all the touch of space.

And this was it, he thought. After all the weeks of waiting, here finally was the thing of steel and engineering that would take him home again.

He walked back to where the captain stood.

"Let's get on with it," he said. "I'll want to look the engines over."

"They're all right," said the captain.

"That may be so. I still want to run a check on them."

He had expected the engines to be bad, but not as bad as they turned out to be. If the ship had not been much to look at, the Morrisons were worse.

"They'll need some work," he said. "We can't lift with them, the shape they're in."

The captain raved and swore. "We have to blast by dawn, damn it! This is a goddam emergency."

"You'll lift by dawn," snapped Cooper. "Just leave me alone."

He drove his gang to work, and he worked himself, for fourteen solid hours, without a wink of sleep, without a bite to eat.

Then he crossed his fingers and told the captain he was ready.

They got out of atmosphere with the engines holding together. Cooper uncrossed his fingers and sighed with deep relief. Now all he had to do was keep them running.

The captain called him forward and brought out a bottle. "You did better, Mr. Cooper, than I thought you would."

Cooper shook his head. "We aren't there yet, Captain. We've a long way still to go."

"Mr. Cooper," said the captain, "you know what we are carrying? You got any idea at all?"

Cooper shook his head.

"Medicines," the captain told him. "There's an epidemic out there. We were the only ship anywhere near ready for takeoff. So we were requisitioned."

"It would have been much better if we could have overhauled the engines."

"We didn't have the time. Every minute counts."

Cooper drank the liquor, stupid with a tiredness that cut clear to the bone. "Epidemic, you say. What kind?"

"Sand fever," said the captain. "You've heard of it, perhaps."

Cooper felt the chill of deadly fear creep along his body. "I've heard of it." He finished off the whisky and stood up. "I have to get back, sir. I have to watch those engines."

"We're counting on you, Mr. Cooper. You have to get us through."

He went back to the engine room and slumped into a chair, listening to the engine-song that beat throughout the ship.

He had to keep them going. There was no question of it now, if there'd ever been a question. For now it was not the simple matter of getting home again, but of getting needed drugs to the old home planet.

"I promise you," he said, talking to himself. "I promise you we'll get there."

He drove the engine crew and he drove himself, day after dying day, while the howling of the tubes and the thunder of the haywire Morrisons racked a man almost beyond endurance.

There was no such thing as sleep—only catnaps caught as one could catch them. There were no such things as meals, only food gulped on the run. And there was work, and worse than work were the watching and the waiting, the shoulders tensed against the stutter or the sudden screech of metal that would spell disaster.

Why, he wondered dully, did a man ever go to space? Why should one deliberately choose a job like this? Here in the engine room, with its cranky motors, it might be worse than elsewhere in the ship. But that didn't mean it wasn't bad. For throughout the ship stretched tension and discomfort and, above all, the dead, black fear of space itself, of what space could do to a ship and the men within it.

In some of the bigger, newer ships, conditions might be better, but not a great deal better. They still tranquilized the passengers and colonists who went out to the other planets—tranquilized them to quiet the worries, to make them more insensitive to discomfort, to prevent their breaking into panic.

But a crew you could not tranquilize. A crew must be wide-awake, with all its faculties intact. A crew had to sit and take it.

Perhaps the time would come when the ships were big enough, when the engines and the drives would be perfected, when Man had lost some of his fear of the emptiness of space—then it would be easier.

But that time might be far off. It was almost two hundred years now since his family had gone out, among the first colonists, to Mars.

If it were not that he was going home, he told himself, it would be beyond all tolerance and endurance. He could almost smell the cold, dry air of home—even in this place that reeked with other smells. He could look beyond the metal skin of the ship in which he rode and across the long dark miles and see the gentle sunset on the redness of the hills.

And in this he had an advantage over all the others. For without going home, he could not have stood it.

The days wore on and the engines held and the hope built up within him. And finally hope gave way to triumph.

And then came the day when the ship went mushing down through the thin, cold atmosphere and came in to a landing.

He reached out and pulled a switch and the engines rumbled to a halt. Silence came into the tortured steel that still was numb with noise.

He stood beside the engines, deafened by the silence, frightened by this alien thing that never made a sound.

He walked along the engines, with his hand sliding on their metal, stroking them as he would pet an animal, astonished and slightly angry at himself for finding in himself a queer, distorted quality of affection for them.

But why not? They had brought him home. He had nursed and pampered them, he had cursed them and watched over them, he had slept with them, and they had brought him home.

And that was more, he admitted to himself, than he had ever thought they would do.

He found that he was alone. The crew had gone swarming up the ladder as soon as he had pulled the switch. And now it was time that he himself was going.

But he stood there for a moment, in that silent room, as he gave the place one final visual check. Everything was all right. There was nothing to be done.

He turned and climbed the ladder slowly, heading for the port.

He found the captain standing in the port, and out beyond the port stretched the redness of the land.

"All the rest have gone except the purser," said the captain. "I thought you'd soon be up. You did a fine job with the engines, Mr. Cooper. I'm glad you shipped with us."

"It's my last run," Cooper said, staring out at the redness of the hills. "Now I settle down."

"That's strange," said the captain. "I take it you're a Mars man."

"I am. And I never should have left."

The captain stared at him and said again: "That's strange."

"Nothing strange," said Cooper. "I—"

"It's my last run, too," the captain broke in. "There'll be a new commander to take her back to Earth."

"In that case," Cooper offered, "I'll stand you a drink as soon as we get down."

"I'll take you up on that. First we'll get our shots."

They climbed down the ladder and walked across the field toward the spaceport buildings. Trucks went whining past them, heading for the ship, to pick up the unloaded cargo.

And now it was all coming back to Cooper, the way he had dreamed it in that shabby room on Earth—the exhilarating taste of the thinner, colder air, the step that was springier because of the lesser gravity, the swift and clean elation of the uncluttered, brave red land beneath a weaker sun.

Inside, the doctor waited for them in his tiny office.

"Sorry, gentlemen," he said, "but you know the regulations."

"I don't like it," said the captain, "but I suppose it does make sense."

They sat down in the chairs and rolled up their sleeves.

"Hang on," the doctor told them. "It gives you quite a jolt."

It did.

And it had before, thought Cooper, every time before. He should be used to it by now.

He sat weakly in the chair, waiting for the weakness and the shock to pass, and he saw the doctor, there behind his desk, watching them and waiting for them to come around to normal.

"Was it a rough trip?" the doctor finally asked.

"They all are rough," the captain replied curtly.

Cooper shook his head. "This one was the worst I've ever known. Those engines . . ."

The captain said: "I'm sorry, Cooper. This time it was the truth. We were *really* carrying medicine. There *is* an epidemic. Mine was the only ship. I'd planned an overhaul, but we couldn't wait."

Cooper nodded. "I remember now," he said.

He stood up weakly and stared out the window at the cold, the alien, the forbidding land of Mars.

"I never could have made it," he said flatly, "if I'd not been psychoed."

He turned back to the doctor. "Will there ever be a time?"

The doctor nodded. "Someday, certainly. When the ships are better. When the race is more conditioned to space travel."

"But this homesickness business—it gets downright brutal."

"It's the only way," the doctor declared. "We'd not have any spacemen if they weren't always going home."

"That's right," the captain said. "No man, myself included, could face that kind of beating unless it was for something more than money."

Cooper looked out the window at the Martian sandscape and shivered. Of all the God-forsaken places he had ever seen!

He was a fool to be in space, he told himself, with a wife like Doris and two kids back home. He could hardly wait to see them.

And he knew the symptoms. He was getting homesick once again—but this time it was for Earth.

The doctor was taking a bottle out of his desk and pouring generous drinks into glasses for all three of them.

"Have a shot of this," he said, "and let's forget about it."

"As if we could remember," said Cooper, laughing suddenly.

"After all," the captain said, far too cheerfully, "we have to see it in the right perspective. It's nothing more than a condition of employment."

CITY

"City" was written in 1944, and John W. Campbell Jr., the editor of Astounding, *would accept it for publication only 16 days after receipt. However, few now realize that the version that appeared in the magazine, which is what is presented here, was altered slightly for its later publication in the book that bears its name. And although "City" was basically a reaction to World War II—and thus backward-looking, in a sense—it turned out, completely unexpectedly, to be the seed of a series of stories to which it would give its name—the kind of series we now call "future history".*

"City" is set in the world of 1990; and now, as I write this nearly twenty-five years beyond 1990, I wonder what Cliff would think of today's world. Was the lawn mower that Gramp resented so much the ancestor of Jenkins, the robot who finally became the star of the series?

—dww

Gramp Stevens sat in a lawn chair, watching the mower at work, feeling the warm, soft sunshine seep into his bones. The mower reached the edge of the lawn, clucked to itself like a contented hen, made a neat turn and trundled down another swath. The bag holding the clippings bulged.

Suddenly the mower stopped and clicked excitedly. A panel in its side snapped open and a cranelike arm reached out. Grasping steel fingers fished around in the grass, came up triumphantly with a stone clutched tightly, dropped the stone into a small container, disappeared back into the panel again. The lawn mower gurgled, purred on again, following its swath.

Gramp grumbled at it with suspicion.

"Some day," he told himself, "that dadburned thing is going to miss a lick and have a nervous breakdown."

He lay back in the chair and stared up at the sun-washed sky. A helicopter skimmed far overhead. From somewhere inside the house a radio came to life and a torturing crash of music poured out. Gramp, hearing it, shivered and hunkered lower in the chair.

Young Charlie was settling down for a twitch session. Dadburn the kid.

The lawn mower chuckled past and Gramp squinted at it maliciously.

"Automatic," he told the sky. "Ever' blasted thing is automatic now. Getting so you just take a machine off in a corner and whisper in its ear and it scurries off to do the job."

His daughter's voice came to him out the window, pitched to carry above the music.

"Father!"

Gramp stirred uneasily. "Yes, Betty."

"Now, father, you see you move when that lawn mower gets to you. Don't try to out-stubborn it. After all, it's only a machine. Last time you just sat there and made it cut around you. I never saw the beat of you."

He didn't answer, letting his head nod a bit, hoping she would think he was asleep and let him be.

"Father," she shrilled, "did you hear me?"

He saw it was no good. "Sure, I heard you," he told her. "I was just fixing to move."

He rose slowly to his feet, leaning heavily on his cane. Might make her feel sorry for the way she treated him when she saw how old and feeble he was getting. He'd have to be careful, though. If she knew he didn't need the cane at all, she'd be finding jobs for him to do and, on the other hand, if he laid it on too thick, she'd be having that fool doctor in to pester him again.

Grumbling, he moved the chair out into that portion of the lawn that had been cut. The mower, rolling past, chortled at him fiendishly.

"Some day," Gramp told it, "I'm going to take a swipe at you and bust a gear or two."

The mower hooted at him and went serenely down the lawn.

From somewhere down the grassy street came a jangling of metal, a stuttered coughing.

Gramp, ready to sit down, straightened up and listened.

The sound came more clearly, the rumbling backfire of a balky engine, the clatter of loose metallic parts.

"An automobile!" yelped Gramp. "An automobile, by cracky!"

He started to gallop for the gate, suddenly remembered that he was feeble and subsided to a rapid hobble.

"Must be that crazy Ole Johnson," he told himself. "He's the only one left that's got a car. Just too dadburned stubborn to give it up."

It was Ole.

Gramp reached the gate in time to see the rusty, dilapidated old machine come bumping around the corner, rocking and chugging along the unused street. Steam hissed from the overheated radiator and a cloud of blue smoke issued from the exhaust, which had lost its muffler five years or more ago.

Ole sat stolidly behind the wheel, squinting his eyes, trying to duck the roughest places, although that was hard to do, for weeds and grass had overrun the streets and it was hard to see what might be underneath them.

Gramp waved his cane.

"Hi, Ole," he shouted.

Ole pulled up, setting the emergency brake. The car gasped, shuddered, coughed, died with a horrible sigh.

"What you burning?" asked Gramp.

"Little bit of everything," said Ole. "Kerosene, some old trac-
tor oil I found out in a barrel, some rubbing alcohol."

Gramp regarded the fugitive machine with forthright admiration. "Them was the days," he said. "Had one myself used to be
able to get a hundred miles an hour out of."

"Still O.K.," said Ole, "if you only could find the stuff to run
them or get the parts to fix them. Up to three, four years ago I
used to be able to get enough gasoline, but ain't seen none for a
long time now. Quit making it, I guess. No use having gasoline,
they tell me, when you have atomic power."

"Sure," said Gramp. "Guess maybe that's right, but you can't
smell atomic power. Sweetest thing I know, the smell of burning
gasoline. These here helicopters and other gadgets they got took
all the romance out of traveling, somehow."

He squinted at the barrels and baskets piled in the back seat.

"Got some vegetables?" he asked.

"Yup," said Ole. "Some sweet corn and early potatoes and a
few baskets of tomatoes. Thought maybe I could sell them."

Gramp shook his head. "You won't, Ole. They won't buy
them. Folks has got the notion that this new hydroponics stuff is
the only garden sass that's fit to eat. Sanitary, they say, and better
flavored."

"Wouldn't give a hoot in a tin cup for all they grow in them
tanks they got," Ole declared, belligerently. "Don't taste right to
me, somehow. Like I tell Martha, food's got to be raised in the soil
to have any character."

He reached down to turn over the ignition switch.

"Don't know as it's worth trying to get the stuff to town," he
said, "the way they keep the roads. Or the way they don't keep
them, rather. Twenty years ago the state highway out there was
a strip of good concrete and they kept it patched and plowed it
every winter. Did anything, spent any amount of money to keep
it open. And now they just forgot about it. The concrete's all bro-

ken up and some of it has washed out. Brambles are growing in
it. Had to get out and cut away a tree that fell across it one place
this morning."

"Ain't it the truth," agreed Gramp.

The car exploded into life, coughing and choking. A cloud of
dense blue smoke rolled out from under it. With a jerk it stirred
to life and lumbered down the road.

Gramp clumped back to his chair and found it dripping wet.
The automatic mower, having finished its cutting job, had rolled
out the hose, was sprinkling the lawn.

Muttering venom, Gramp stalked around the corner of the
house and sat down on the bench beside the back porch. He
didn't like to sit there, but it was the only place he was safe from
the hunk of machinery out in the front.

For one thing, the view from the bench was slightly depress-
ing, fronting as it did on street after street of vacant, deserted
houses and weed-grown, unkempt yards.

It had one advantage, however. From the bench he could pretend he was slightly deaf and not hear the twitch music the radio
was blaring out.

A voice called from the front yard.

"Bill! Bill, where be you?"

Gramp twisted around.

"Here I am, Mark. Back of the house. Hiding from that
dadburned mower."

Mark Bailey limped around the corner of the house, cigarette
threatening to set fire to his bushy whiskers.

"Bit early for the game, ain't you?" asked Gramp.

"Can't play no game today," said Mark.

He hobbled over and sat down beside Gramp on the bench.

"We're leaving," he said.

Gramp whirled on him. "You're leaving!"

"Yeah. Moving out into the country. Lucinda finally talked
Herb into it. Never gave him no peace, I guess. Said everyone was

moving away to one of them nice country estates and she didn't see no reason why we couldn't."

Gramp gulped. "Where to?"

"Don't rightly know," said Mark. "Ain't been there myself. Up north some place. Up on one of the lakes. Got ten acres of land. Lucinda wanted a hundred, but Herb put down his foot and said ten was enough. After all, one city lot was enough for all these years."

"Betty was pestering Johnny, too," said Gramp, "but he's holding out against her. Says he simply can't do it. Says it wouldn't look right, him the secretary of the Chamber of Commerce and all, if he went moving away from the city."

"Folks are crazy," Mark declared. "Plumb crazy."

"That's a fact," Gramp agreed. "Country crazy, that's what they are. Look across there."

He waved his hand at the streets of vacant houses. "Can remember the time when those places were as pretty a bunch of homes as you ever laid your eyes on. Good neighbors, they were. Women ran across from one back door to another to trade recipes. And the men folks would go out to cut the grass and pretty soon the mowers would all be sitting idle and the men would be ganged up, chewing the fat. Friendly people, Mark. But look at it now."

Mark stirred uneasily. "Got to be getting back, Bill. Just sneaked over to let you know we were lighting out. Lucinda's got me packing. She'd be sore if she knew I'd run out."

Gramp rose stiffly and held out his hand. "I'll be seeing you again? You be over for one last game?"

Mark shook his head. "Afraid not, Bill."

They shook hands awkwardly, abashed. "Sure will miss them games," said Mark.

"Me, too," said Gramp. "I won't have nobody once you're gone."

"So long, Bill," said Mark.

"So long," said Gramp.

He stood and watched his friend hobble around the house, felt the cold claw of loneliness reach out and touch him with icy fingers. A terrible loneliness. The loneliness of age—of age and the outdated. Fiercely, Gramp admitted it. He was outdated. He belonged to another age. He had outstripped his time, lived beyond his years.

Eyes misty, he fumbled for the cane that lay against the bench, slowly made his way toward the sagging gate that opened onto the deserted street back of the house.

The years had moved too fast. Years that had brought the family plane and helicopter, leaving the auto to rust in some forgotten place, the unused roads to fall into disrepair. Years that had virtually wiped out the tilling of the soil with the rise of hydroponics. Years that had brought cheap land with the disappearance of the farm as an economic unit, had sent city people scurrying out into the country where each man, for less than the price of a city lot, might own broad acres. Years that had revolutionized the construction of homes to a point where families simply walked away from their old homes to the new ones that could be bought, custom-made, for less than half the price of a prewar structure and could be changed at small cost, to accommodate need of additional space or merely a passing whim.

Gramp sniffed. Houses that could be changed each year, just like one would shift around the furniture. What kind of living was that?

He plodded slowly down the dusty path that was all that remained of what a few years before had been a busy residential street. A street of ghosts, Gramp told himself—of furtive, little ghosts that whispered in the night. Ghosts of playing children, ghosts of upset tricycles and canted coaster wagons. Ghosts of gossiping housewives. Ghosts of shouted greetings. Ghosts of flaming fireplaces and chimneys smoking of a winter night.

Little puffs of dust rose around his feet and whitened the cuffs of his trousers.

There was the old Adams place across the way. Adams had been mighty proud of it, he remembered. Gray field stone front and picture windows. Now the stone was green with creeping moss and the broken windows gaped with ghastly leer. Weeds choked the lawn and blotted out the stoop. An elm tree was pushing its branches against the gable. Gramp could remember the day Adams had planted that elm tree.

For a moment he stood there in the grass-grown street, feet in the dust, both hands clutching the curve of his cane, eyes closed.

Through the fog of years he heard the cry of playing children, the barking of Conrad's yapping pooch from down the street. And there was Adams, stripped to the waist, plying the shovel, scooping out the hole, with the elm tree, roots wrapped in burlap, lying on the lawn.

May, 1946. Forty-four years ago. Just after he and Adams had come home from the war together.

Footsteps padded in the dust and Gramp, startled, opened his eyes.

Before him stood a young man. A man of thirty, perhaps. Maybe a bit less.

"Good morning," said Gramp.

"I hope," said the young man, "that I didn't startle you."

"You saw me standing here," asked Gramp, "like a danged fool, with my eyes shut?"

The young man nodded.

"I was remembering," said Gramp.

"You live around here?"

"Just down the street. The last one in this part of the city."

"Perhaps you can help me then."

"Try me," said Gramp.

The young man stammered. "Well, you see, it's like this. I'm on a sort of . . . well, you might call it a sentimental pilgrimage—"

"I understand," said Gramp. "So am I."

"My name is Adams," said the young man. "My grandfather used to live around here somewhere. I wonder—"

"Right over there," said Gramp.

Together they stood and stared at the house.

"It was a nice place once," Gramp told him. "Your granddaddy planted that tree, right after he came home from the war. I was with him when we marched into Berlin. That was a day for you—"

"It's a pity," said young Adams. "A pity—"

But Gramp didn't seem to hear him. "Your granddaddy?" he asked. "I seem to have lost track of him."

"He's dead," said young Adams.

"He was messed up with atomic power," said Gramp.

"That's right," said Adams proudly. "He and my Dad got into it early."

John J. Webster was striding up the broad stone steps of the city hall when the walking scarecrow carrying a rifle under his arm caught up with him and stopped him.

"Howdy, Mr. Webster," said the scarecrow.

Webster stared, then recognition crinkled his face.

"It's Levi," he said. "How are things going, Levi?"

Levi Lewis grinned with snagged teeth. "Fair to middling. Gardens are coming along and the young rabbits are getting to be good eating."

"You aren't getting mixed up in any of the hell raising that's being laid to the *houses?*" asked Webster.

"No, sir," declared Levi. "Ain't none of us Squatters mixed up in any wrongdoing. We're law-abiding God-fearing people, we are. Only reason we're there is we can't make a living no place else. And us living in them places other people up and left ain't harming no one. Police are just blaming us for the thievery and other things that's going on, knowing we can't protect ourselves. They're making us the goats."

"I'm glad to hear that," said Webster. "The chief wants to burn the *houses.*"

"If he tries that," said Levi, "he'll run against something he ain't counting on. They run us off our farms with this tank farming of theirs but they ain't going to run us any farther."

He spat across the steps.

"Wouldn't happen you might have some jingling money on you?" he asked. "I'm fresh out of cartridges and with them rabbits coming up—"

Webster thrust his fingers into a vest pocket, pulled out a half dollar.

Levi grinned. "That's obliging of you, Mr. Webster. I'll bring a mess of squirrels, come fall."

The Squatter touched his hat with two fingers and retreated down the steps, sun glinting on the rifle barrel. Webster turned up the steps again.

The city council session already was in full swing when he walked into the chamber.

Police Chief Jim Maxwell was standing by the table and Mayor Paul Carter was talking.

"Don't you think you may be acting a bit hastily, Jim, in urging such a course of action with the *houses?*"

"No, I don't," declared the chief. "Except for a couple of dozen or so, none of those houses are occupied by their rightful owners, or rather, their original owners. Every one of them belongs to the city now through tax forfeiture. And they are nothing but an eyesore and a menace. They have no value. Not even salvage value. Wood? We don't use wood any more. Plastics are better. Stone? We use steel instead of stone. Not a single one of those houses have any material of marketable value.

"And in the meantime they are becoming the haunts of petty criminals and undesirable elements. Grown up with vegetation as the residential sections are, they make a perfect hideout for all types of criminals. A man commits a crime and heads straight for the *houses*—once there he's safe, for I could send a thousand men in there and he could elude them all.

"They aren't worth the expense of tearing down. And yet they are, if not a menace, at least a nuisance. We should get rid of them and fire is the cheapest, quickest way. We'd use all precautions."

"What about the legal angle?" asked the mayor.

"I checked into that. A man has a right to destroy his own property in any way he may see fit so long as it endangers no one else's. The same law, I suppose, would apply to a municipality."

Alderman Thomas Griffin sprang to his feet.

"You'd alienate a lot of people," he declared. "You'd be burning down a lot of old homesteads. People still have some sentimental attachments—"

"If they cared for them," snapped the chief, "why didn't they pay the taxes and take care of them? Why did they go running off to the country, just leaving the houses standing. Ask Webster here. He can tell you what success he had trying to interest the people in their ancestral homes."

"You're talking about that Old Home Week farce," said Griffin. "Webster spread it on so thick they gagged on it. That's what a Chamber of Commerce mentality always does. People resent having the things they set some store by being used as bait to bring more business into town."

Alderman Forrest King leaped up and pounded on the table, his double chin quaking with rage.

"I'm sick and tired of you taking a crack at the Chamber every chance you get," he yelled. "When you do that you're taking a slap at every business in this city. And the business houses are all this city has left. They're the only ones paying taxes any more."

Griffin grinned sourly. "Mr. King, I can appreciate your position as president of the Chamber."

"You went broke yourself," snarled King. "That's the reason you act the way you do. You lost your shirt at business and now you're sore at business—"

"King, you're crude," said Griffin.

A silence fell upon the room, a cold, embarrassed silence.

Griffin broke it. "I am taking no slap at business. I am protesting the persistence of business in sticking to outmoded ideas and methods. The day of go-getting is over, gentlemen. The day of high pressure is gone forever. Ballyhoo is something that is dead and buried.

"The day when you could have tall-corn days or dollar days or dream up some fake celebration and deck the place up with bunting and pull in big crowds that were ready to spend money is past these many years. Only you fellows don't seem to know it.

"The success of such stunts as that was its appeal to mob psychology and civic loyalty. You can't have civic loyalty with a city dying on its feet. You can't appeal to mob psychology when there is no mob—when every man, or nearly every man has the solitude of forty acres."

"Gentlemen," pleaded the mayor. "Gentlemen, this is distinctly out of order."

King sputtered into life, walloped the table once again.

"No, let's have it out. Webster is over there. Perhaps he can tell us what he thinks."

Webster stirred uncomfortably. "I scarcely believe," he said, "I have anything to say."

"Forget it," snapped Griffin and sat down.

But King still stood, his face crimson, his mouth trembling with anger.

"Webster!" he shouted.

Webster shook his head. "You came here with one of your big ideas," shouted King. "You were going to lay it before the council. Step up, man, and speak your piece."

Webster rose slowly, grim-lipped.

"Perhaps you're too thick-skulled," he told King, "to know why I resent the way you have behaved."

King gasped, then exploded. "Thick-skulled! You would say that to me. We've worked together and I've helped you. You've never called me that before . . . you've—"

"I've never called you that before," said Webster, levelly. "Naturally not. I wanted to keep my job."

"Well, you haven't got a job," roared King. "From this minute on, you haven't got a job."

"Shut up," said Webster.

King stared at him, bewildered, as if someone had slapped him across the face.

"And sit down," said Webster, and his voice bit through the room like a sharp-edged knife.

King's knees caved beneath him and he sat down abruptly. The silence was brittle.

"I have something to say," said Webster. "Something that should have been said long ago. Something all of you should hear. That I should be the one who would tell it to you is the one thing that astounds me. And yet, perhaps, as one who has worked in the interests of this city for almost fifteen years, I am the logical one to speak the truth.

"Alderman Griffin said the city is dying on its feet and his statement is correct. There is but one fault I would find with it and that is its understatement. The city . . . this city, any city . . . already is dead.

"The city is an anachronism. It has outlived its usefulness. Hydroponics and the helicopter spelled its downfall. In the first instance the city was a tribal place, an area where the tribe banded together for mutual protection. In later years a wall was thrown around it for additional protection. Then the wall finally disappeared but the city lived on because of the conveniences which it offered trade and commerce. It continued into modern times because people were compelled to live close to their jobs and the jobs were in the city.

"But today that is no longer true. With the family plane, one hundred miles today is a shorter distance than five miles back in 1930. Men can fly several hundred miles to work and fly home when the day is done. There is no longer any need for them to live cooped up in a city.

"The automobile started the trend and the family plane finished it. Even in the first part of the century the trend was noticeable—a movement away from the city with its taxes and its stuffiness, a move toward the suburb and close-in acreages. Lack of adequate transportation, lack of finances held many to the city. But now, with tank farming destroying the value of land, a man can buy a huge acreage in the country for less than he could a city lot forty years ago. With planes powered by atomics there is no longer any transportation problem."

He paused and the silence held. The mayor wore a shocked look. King's lips moved, but no words came. Griffin was smiling.

"So what have we?" asked Webster. "I'll tell you what we have. Street after street, block after block, of deserted houses, houses that the people just up and walked away from. Why should they have stayed? What could the city offer them? None of the things that it offered the generations before them, for progress has wiped out the need of the city's benefits. They lost something, some monetary consideration, of course, when they left the houses. But the fact that they could buy a house twice as good for half as much, the fact that they could live as they wished to live, that they could develop what amounts to family estates after the best tradition set them by the wealthy of a generation ago—all these things outweighed the leaving of their homes.

"And what have we left? A few blocks of business houses. A few acres of industrial plants. A city government geared to take care of a million people without the million people. A budget that has run the taxes so high that eventually even business houses will move to escape those taxes. Tax forfeitures that have left us loaded with worthless property. That's what we have left.

"If you think any Chamber of Commerce, any ballyhoo, any hare-brained scheme will give you the answers, you're crazy. There is only one answer and that is simple. The city as a human institution is dead. It may struggle on a few more years, but that is all."

"Mr. Webster—" said the mayor.

But Webster paid him no attention.

"But for what happened today," he said, "I would have stayed on and played doll house with you. I would have gone on pretending that the city was a going concern. Would have gone on kidding myself and you. But there is, gentlemen, such a thing as human dignity."

The icy silence broke down in the rustling of papers, the muffled cough of some embarrassed listener.

John J. Webster turned on his heel and left the room.

Outside on the broad stone steps, he stopped and stared up at the cloudless sky, saw the pigeons wheeling above the turrets and spires of the city hall.

He shook himself mentally, like a dog coming out of a pool.

He had been a fool, of course. Now he'd have to hunt for a job and it might take time to find one. He was getting a bit old to be hunting for a job.

But despite his thoughts, a little tune rose unbidden to his lips. He walked away briskly, lips pursed, whistling soundlessly.

No more hypocrisy. No more lying awake nights wondering what to do—knowing that the city was dead, knowing that what he did was a useless task, feeling like a heel for taking a salary that he knew he wasn't earning. Sensing the strange, nagging frustration of a worker who knows his work is nonproductive.

He strode toward the parking lot, heading for his helicopter.

Now, maybe, he told himself, they could move out into the country the way Betty wanted to. Maybe he could spend his evenings tramping land that belonged to him. A place with a stream. Definitely it had to have a stream he could stock with trout.

He made a mental note to go up into the attic and check his fly equipment.

Martha Johnson was waiting at the barnyard gate when the old car chugged down the lane.

Ole got out stiffly, face rimmed with weariness.

"Sell anything?" asked Martha.

Ole shook his head. "It ain't no use. They won't buy farm-raised stuff. Just laughed at me. Showed me ears of corn twice as big as the ones I had, just as sweet and with more even rows. Showed me melons that had almost no rind at all. Better tasting, too, they said."

He kicked at a clod and it exploded into dust.

"There ain't no getting around it," he declared. "Tank farming sure has ruined us."

"Maybe we better fix to sell the farm," suggested Martha.

Ole said nothing.

"You could get a job on a tank farm," she said. "Harry did. Likes it real well."

Ole shook his head.

"Or maybe a gardener," said Martha. "You would make a right smart gardener. Ritzy folks that's moved out to big estates like to have gardeners to take care of flowers and things. More classy than doing it with machines."

Ole shook his head again. "Couldn't stand to mess around with flowers," he declared. "Not after raising corn for more than twenty years."

"Maybe," said Martha, "we could have one of them little planes. And running water in the house. And a bathtub instead of taking a bath in the old washtub by the kitchen fire."

"Couldn't run a plane," objected Ole.

"Sure you could," said Martha. "Simple to run, they are. Why, them Anderson kids ain't no more than knee-high to a cricket and they fly one all over. One of them got fooling around and fell out once, but—"

"I got to think about it," said Ole, desperately. "I got to think."

He swung away, vaulted a fence, headed for the fields. Martha stood beside the car and watched him go. One lone tear rolled down her dusty cheek.

"Mr. Taylor is waiting for you," said the girl.

John J. Webster stammered. "But I haven't been here before. He didn't know I was coming."

"Mr. Taylor," insisted the girl, "is waiting for you."

She nodded her head toward the door. It read:

Bureau of Human Adjustment

"But I came here to get a job," protested Webster. "I didn't come to be adjusted or anything. This is the World Committee's placement service, isn't it?"

"That is right," the girl declared. "Won't you see Mr. Taylor?"

"Since you insist," said Webster.

The girl clicked over a switch, spoke into the intercommunicator. "Mr. Webster is here, sir."

"Send him in," said a voice.

Hat in hand, Webster walked through the door.

The man behind the desk had white hair but a young man's face. He motioned toward a chair.

"You've been trying to find a job," he said.

"Yes," said Webster, "but—"

"Please sit down," said Taylor. "If you're thinking about that sign on the door, forget it. We'll not try to adjust you."

"I couldn't find a job," said Webster. "I've hunted for weeks and no one would have me. So finally, I came here."

"You didn't want to come here?"

"No, frankly, I didn't. A placement service. It has, well . . . it has an implication I do not like."

Taylor smiled. "The terminology may be unfortunate. You're thinking of the employment services of the old days. The places where men went when they were desperate for work. The government operated places that tried to find work for men so they wouldn't become public charges."

"I'm desperate enough," confessed Webster. "But I still have a pride that made it hard to come. But, finally, there was nothing else to do. You see, I turned traitor—"

"You mean," said Taylor, "that you told the truth. Even when it cost you your job. The business world, not only here, but all over the world, is not ready for that truth. The businessman still clings to the city myth, to the myth of salesmanship. In time to come he will realize he doesn't need the city, that service and honest values will bring him more substantial business than salesmanship ever did.

"I've wondered, Webster, just what made you do what you did?"

"I was sick of it," said Webster. "Sick of watching men blundering along with their eyes tight shut. Sick of seeing an old tradition being kept alive when it should have been laid away. Sick of King's simpering civic enthusiasm when all cause for enthusiasm had vanished."

Taylor nodded. "Webster, do you think you could adjust human beings?"

Webster merely stared.

"I mean it," said Taylor. "The World Committee has been doing it for years, quietly, unobtrusively. Even many of the people who have been adjusted don't know they have been adjusted.

"Changes such as have come since the creation of the World Committee following the war has meant much human maladjustment. The advent of workable atomic power took jobs away from hundreds of thousands. They had to be trained and guided into new jobs, some with the new atomics, some into other lines of work. The advent of tank farming swept the farmers off their land. They, perhaps, have supplied us with our greatest problem, for other than the special knowledge needed to grow crops and handle animals, they had no skills. Most of them had no wish for acquiring skills. Most of them were bitterly resentful of having been forced from the livelihood which they inherited from their forebears. And being natural individualists, they offered the toughest psychological problems of any other class."

"Many of them," declared Webster, "still are at loose ends. There's a hundred or more of them squatting out in the *houses*, living from hand to mouth. Shooting a few rabbits and a few squirrels, doing some fishing, raising vegetables and picking wild fruit. Engaging in a little petty thievery now and then and doing occasional begging on the uptown streets."

"You know these people?" asked Taylor.

"I know some of them," said Webster. "One of them brings me squirrels and rabbits on occasions. To make up for it, he bums ammunition money."

"They'd resent being adjusted, wouldn't they?"

"Violently," said Webster.

"You know a farmer by the name of Ole Johnson? Still sticking to his farm, still unreconstructed?"

Webster nodded.

"What if you tried to adjust him?"

"He'd run me off the farm," said Webster.

"Men like Ole and the Squatters," said Taylor, "are our special problems now. Most of the rest of the world is fairly well adjusted, fairly well settled into the groove of the present. Some of them are doing a lot of moaning about the past, but that's just for effect. You couldn't drive them back to their old ways of life.

"Years ago, with the advent of atomics, in fact, the World Committee faced a hard decision. Should changes that spelled progress in the world be brought about gradually to allow the people to adjust themselves naturally, or should they be developed as quickly as possible, with the Committee aiding in the necessary human adjustment? It was decided, rightly or wrongly, that progress should come first, regardless of its effect upon the people. The decision in the main has proven a wise one.

"We knew, of course, that in many instances, this readjustment could not be made too openly. In some cases, as in large groups of workers who had been displaced, it was possible, but in most individual cases, such as our friend Ole, it was not. These people must be helped to find themselves in this new world, but they must not know that they're being helped. To let them know would destroy confidence and dignity, and human dignity is the keystone of any civilization."

"I knew, of course, about the readjustments made within industry itself," said Webster, "but I had not heard of the individual cases."

"We could not advertise it," Taylor said. "It's practically undercover."

"But why are you telling me all this now?"

"Because we'd like you to come in with us. Have a hand at adjusting Ole to start with. Maybe see what could be done about the Squatters next."

"I don't know—"said Webster.

"We'd been waiting for you to come in," said Taylor. "We knew you'd finally have to come here. Any chance you might have had at any kind of job would have been queered by King. He passed the word along. You're blackballed by every Chamber of Commerce and every civic group in the world today."

"Probably I have no choice," said Webster.

"We didn't want you to feel that way about it," Taylor said. "Take a while to think it over, then come back. Even if you don't want the job we'll find you another one—in spite of King."

Outside the office, Webster found a scarecrow figure waiting for him. It was Levi Lewis, snaggle-toothed grin wiped off, rifle under his arm.

"Some of the boys said they seen you go in here," he explained. "So I waited for you."

"What's the trouble?" Webster asked. For Levi's face spoke eloquently of trouble.

"It's them police," said Levi. He spat disgustedly.

"The police," said Webster, and his heart sank as he said the words. For he knew what the trouble was.

"Yeah," said Levi. "They're fixing to burn us out."

"So the council finally gave in," said Webster, face grim.

"I just came from police headquarters," declared Levi. "I told them they better go easy. I told them there'd be guts strewed all over the place if they tried it. I got the boys posted all around the place with orders not to shoot till they're sure of hitting."

"You can't do that, Levi," said Webster, sharply.

"I can't!" retorted Levi. "I done it already. They drove us off the farms, forced us to sell because we couldn't make a living. And they aren't driving us no farther. We either stay here or we die here. And the only way they'll burn us out is when there's no one left to stop them."

He shucked up his pants and spat again.

"And we ain't the only ones that feel that way," he declared. "Gramp is out there with us."

"Gramp!"

"Sure, Gramp. The old guy that lives with you. He's sort of taken over as our commanding general. Says he remembers tricks from the war them police have never heard of. He sent some of the boys over to one of them Legion halls to swipe a cannon. Says he knows where we can get some shells for it from the museum. Says we'll get it all set up and then send word that if the police make a move we'll shell the loop."

"Look, Levi, will you do something for me?"

"Sure will, Mr. Webster."

"Will you go in and ask for a Mr. Taylor? Insist on seeing him. Tell him I'm already on the job."

"Sure will, but where are you going?"

"I'm going up to the city hall."

"Sure you don't want me along?"

"No," declared Webster. "I'll do better alone. And, Levi—"

"Yes."

"Tell Gramp to hold up his artillery. Don't shoot unless he has to—but if he has to, to lay it on the line."

"The mayor is busy," said Raymond Brown, his secretary.

"That's what you think," said Webster, starting for the door.

"You can't go in there, Webster," yelled Brown.

He leaped from his chair, came charging around the desk, reaching for Webster. Webster swung broadside with his arm, caught Brown across the chest, swept him back against the desk. The desk skidded and Brown waved his arms, lost his balance, thudded to the floor.

Webster jerked open the mayor's door.

The mayor's feet thumped off his desk. "I told Brown—" he said.

Webster nodded. "And Brown told me. What's the matter, Carter. Afraid King might find out I was here? Afraid of being corrupted by some good ideas?"

"What do you want?" snapped Carter.

"I understand the police are going to burn the *houses*."

"That's right," declared the mayor, righteously. "They're a menace to the community."

"What community?"

"Look here, Webster—"

"You know there's no community. Just a few of you lousy politicians who stick around so you can claim residence, so you can be sure of being elected every year and drag down your salaries. It's getting to the point where all you have to do is vote for one another. The people who work in the stores and shops, even those who do the meanest jobs in the factories, don't live inside the city limits. The businessmen quit the city long ago. They do business here, but they aren't residents."

"But this is still a city," declared the mayor.

"I didn't come to argue that with you," said Webster. "I came to try to make you see that you're doing wrong by burning those houses. Even if you don't realize it, the *houses* are homes to people who have no other homes. People who have come to this city to seek sanctuary, who have found refuge with us. In a measure, they are our responsibility."

"They're not our responsibility," gritted the mayor. "Whatever happens to them is their own hard luck. We didn't ask them here. We don't want them here. They contribute nothing to the community. You're going to tell me they're misfits. Well, can I help that? You're going to say they can't find jobs. And I'll tell you they could find jobs if they tried to find them. There's work to be done, there's always work to be done. They've been filled up with this new world talk and they figure it's up to someone to find the place that suits them and the job that suits them."

"You sound like a rugged individualist," said Webster.

"You say that like you think it's funny," yapped the mayor.

"I do think it's funny," said Webster. "Funny, and tragic, that anyone should think that way today."

"The world would be a lot better off with some rugged individualism," snapped the mayor. "Look at the men who have gone places—"

"Meaning yourself?" asked Webster.

"You might take me, for example," Carter agreed. "I worked hard. I took advantage of opportunity. I had some foresight. I did—"

"You mean you licked the correct boots and stepped in the proper faces," said Webster. "You're the shining example of the kind of people the world doesn't want today. You positively smell musty, your ideas are so old. You're the last of the politicians, Carter, just as I was the last of the Chamber of Commerce secretaries. Only you don't know it yet. I did. I got out. Even when it cost me something, I got out, because I had to save my self-respect. Your kind of politics is dead. They are dead because any tinhorn with a loud mouth and a brassy front could gain power by appeal to mob psychology. And you haven't got mob psychology any more. You can't have mob psychology when people don't give a care what happens to a thing that's dead already—a political system that broke down under its own weight."

"Get out of here," screamed Carter. "Get out before I have the cops come and throw you out."

"You forget," said Webster, "that I came in to talk about the *houses*."

"It won't do you any good," snarled Carter. "You can stand and talk until doomsday for all the good it does. Those houses burn. That's final."

"How would you like to see the loop a mass of rubble?" asked Webster.

"Your comparison," said Carter, "is grotesque."

"I wasn't talking about comparisons," said Webster.

"You weren't—" The mayor stared at him. "What were you talking about then?"

"Only this," said Webster. "The second the first torch touches the houses, the first shell will land on the city hall. And the second one will hit the First National. They'll go on down the line, the biggest targets first."

Carter gaped. Then a flush of anger crawled from his throat up into his face.

"It won't work, Webster," he snapped. "You can't bluff me. Any cock-and-bull story like that—"

"It's no cock-and-bull story," declared Webster. "Those men have cannons out there. Pieces from in front of Legion halls, from the museums. And they have men who know how to work them. They wouldn't need them, really. It's practically point-blank range. Like shooting the broad side of a barn."

Carter reached for the radio, but Webster stopped him with an upraised hand.

"Better think a minute, Carter, before you go flying off the handle. You're on a spot. Go ahead with your plan and you have a battle on your hands. The *houses* may burn but the loop is wrecked. The businessmen will have your scalp for that."

Carter's hand retreated from the radio.

From far away came the sharp crack of a rifle.

"Better call them off," warned Webster.

Carter's face twisted with indecision.

Another rifle shot, another and another.

"Pretty soon," said Webster, "it will have gone too far. So far that you can't stop it."

A thudding blast rattled the windows of the room. Carter leaped from his chair.

Webster felt the blood drain from his head, felt suddenly cold and weak. But he fought to keep his face straight and his voice calm.

Carter was staring out the window, like a man of stone.

"I'm afraid," said Webster, "that it's gone too far already."

The radio on the desk chirped insistently, red light flashing.

Carter reached out a trembling hand and snapped it on.

"Carter," a voice was saying. "Carter. Carter."

Webster recognized that voice—the bull-throated tone of Police Chief Jim Maxwell.

"What is it?" asked Carter.

"They had a big gun," said Maxwell. "It exploded when they tried to fire it. Ammunition no good, I guess."

"One gun?" asked Carter. "Only one gun?"

"I don't see any others."

"I heard rifle fire," said Carter.

"Yeah, they did some shooting at us. Wounded a couple of the boys. But they've pulled back now. Deeper into the brush. No shooting now."

"O.K.," said Carter, "go ahead and start the fires."

Webster started forward. "Ask him, ask him—"

But Carter clicked the switch and the radio went dead.

"What was it you wanted to ask?"

"Nothing," said Webster. "Nothing that amounted to anything."

He couldn't tell Carter that Gramp had been the one who knew about firing big guns. Couldn't tell him that when the gun exploded Gramp had been there.

He'd have to get out of here, get over to the gun as quickly as possible.

"It was a good bluff, Webster," Carter was saying. "A good bluff, but it petered out."

The mayor turned to the window that faced towards the *houses*.

"No more firing," he said. "They gave up quick."

"You'll be lucky," snapped Webster, "if six of your policemen come back alive. Those men with the rifles are out in the brush and they can pick the eye out of a squirrel at a hundred yards."

Feet pounded in the corridor outside, two pairs of feet racing toward the door.

The mayor whirled from his window and Webster pivoted around.

"Gramp!" he yelled.

"Hi, Johnny," puffed Gramp, skidding to a stop.

The man behind Gramp was a young man and he was waving something in his hand—a sheaf of papers that rustled as he waved them.

"What do you want?" asked the mayor.

"Plenty," said Gramp.

He stood for a moment, catching back his breath, said between puffs:

"Meet my friend, Henry Adams."

"Adams?" asked the mayor.

"Sure," said Gramp. "His granddaddy used to live here. Out on Twenty-seventh Street."

"Oh," said the mayor and it was as if someone had smacked him with a brick. "Oh, you mean F. J. Adams."

"Bet your boots," said Gramp. "Him and me, we marched into Berlin together. Used to keep me awake nights telling me about his boy back home."

Carter nodded to Henry Adams. "As mayor of the city," he said, trying to regain some of his dignity, "I welcome you to—"

"It's not a particularly fitting welcome," Adams said. "I understand you are burning my property."

"Your property!" The mayor choked and his eyes stared in disbelief at the sheaf of papers Adams waved at him.

"Yeah, his property," shrilled Gramp. "He just bought it. We just come from the treasurer's office. Paid all the back taxes and penalties and all the other things you legal thieves thought up to slap against them houses."

"But, but—" the mayor was grasping for words, gasping for breath. "Not all of it. Perhaps just the old Adams property."

"Lock, stock and barrel," said Gramp, triumphantly.

"And now," said Adams to the mayor, "if you would kindly tell your men to stop destroying my property."

Carter bent over the desk and fumbled at the radio, his hands suddenly all thumbs.

"Maxwell," he shouted. "Maxwell, Maxwell."

"What do you want?" Maxwell yelled back.

"Stop setting those fires," yelled Carter. "Start putting them out. Call out the fire department. Do anything. But stop those fires."

"Cripes," said Maxwell, "I wish you'd make up your mind."

"You do what I tell you," screamed the mayor. "You put out those fires."

"All right," said Maxwell. "All right. Keep your shirt on. But the boys won't like it. They won't like getting shot at to do something you change your mind about."

Carter straightened from the radio.

"Let me assure you, Mr. Adams," he said, "that this is all a big mistake."

"It is," Adams declared solemnly. "A very great mistake, mayor. The biggest one you ever made."

For a moment the two of them stood there, looking across the room at one another.

"Tomorrow," said Adams, "I shall file a petition with the courts asking dissolution of the city charter. As owner of the greatest portion of the land included in the corporate limits, both from the standpoint of area and valuation, I understand I have a perfect legal right to do that."

The mayor gulped, finally brought out some words.

"Upon what grounds?" he asked.

"Upon the grounds," said Adams, "that there is no further need of it. I do not believe I shall have too hard a time to prove my case."

"But . . . but . . . that means . . ."

"Yeah," said Gramp, "you know what it means. It means you are out right on your ear."

"A park," said Gramp, waving his arm over the wilderness that once had been the residential section of the city. "A park so that people can remember how their old folks lived."

The three of them stood on Tower Hill, with the rusty old water tower looming above them, its sturdy steel legs planted in a sea of waist-high grass.

"Not a park, exactly," explained Henry Adams. "A memorial, rather. A memorial to an era of communal life that will be forgotten in another hundred years. A preservation of a number of peculiar types of construction that arose to suit certain conditions and each man's particular tastes. No slavery to any architectural concepts, but an effort made to achieve better living. In another hundred years men will walk through those houses down there with the same feeling of respect and awe they have when they go into a museum today. It will be to them something out of what amounts to a primeval age, a stepping stone on the way to the better, fuller life. Artists will spend their lives transferring those old houses to their canvases. Writers of historical novels will come here for the breath of authenticity."

"But you said you meant to restore all the houses, make the lawns and gardens exactly like they were before," said Webster. "That will take a fortune. And after that, another fortune to keep them in shape."

"I have too much money," said Adams. "Entirely too much money. Remember, my grandfather and father got into atomics on the ground floor."

"Best crap player I ever knew, your granddaddy was," said Gramp. "Used to take me for a cleaning every pay day."

"In the old days," said Adams, "when a man had too much money, there were other things he could do with it. Organized charities, for example. Or medical research or something like that. But there are no organized charities today. Not enough business to keep them going. And since the World Committee has hit its stride, there is ample money for all the research, medical or otherwise, anyone might wish to do.

"I didn't plan this thing when I came back to see my grandfather's old house. Just wanted to see it, that was all. He'd told me so much about it. How he planted the tree in the front lawn. And the rose garden he had out back.

"And then I saw it. And it was a mocking ghost. It was something that had been left behind. Something that had meant a lot to someone and had been left behind. Standing there in front of that house with Gramp that day, it came to me that I could do nothing better than preserve for posterity a cross section of the life their ancestors lived."

A thin blue thread of smoke rose above the trees far below.

Webster pointed to it. "What about them?"

"The Squatters stay," said Adams, "if they want to. There will be plenty of work for them to do. And there'll always be a house or two that they can have to live in.

"There's just one thing that bothers me. I can't be here all the time myself. I'll need someone to manage the project. It'll be a lifelong job."

He looked at Webster.

"Go ahead, Johnny," said Gramp.

Webster shook his head. "Betty's got her heart set on that place out in the country."

"You wouldn't have to stay here," said Adams. "You could fly in every day."

From the foot of the hill came a hail.

"It's Ole," yelled Gramp.

He waved his cane. "Hi, Ole. Come on up."

They watched Ole striding up the hill, waiting for him, silently.

"Wanted to talk to you, Johnny," said Ole. "Got an idea. Waked me out of a sound sleep last night."

"Go ahead," said Webster.

Ole glanced at Adams. "He's all right," said Webster. "He's Henry Adams. Maybe you remember his grandfather, old F. J."

"I remember him," said Ole. "Nuts about atomic power, he was. How did he make out?"

"He made out rather well," said Adams.

"Glad to hear that," Ole said. "Guess I was wrong. Said he never would amount to nothing. Daydreamed all the time."

"How about that idea?" Webster asked.

"You heard about dude ranches, ain't you?" Ole asked.

Webster nodded.

"Place," said Ole, "where people used to go and pretend they were cowboys. Pleased them because they really didn't know all the hard work there was in ranching and figured it was romantic-like to ride horses and—"

"Look," asked Webster, "you aren't figuring on turning your farm into a dude ranch, are you?"

"Nope," said Ole. "Not a dude ranch. Dude farm, maybe. Folks don't know too much about farms any more, since there ain't hardly no farms. And they'll read about the frost being on the pumpkin and how pretty a—"

Webster stared at Ole. "They'd go for it, Ole," he declared. "They'd kill one another in the rush to spend their vacation on a real, honest-to-God, old-time farm."

Out of a clump of bushes down the hillside burst a shining thing that chattered and gurgled and screeched, blades flashing, a cranelike arm waving.

"What the—" asked Adams.

"It's that dadburned lawn mower!" yelped Gramp.

MIRAGE

This story, sold to Amazing Stories *in 1950 under the title "Mirage,"
ended up being published as "Seven Came Back," although Cliff
reverted to the original title in subsequent publications. (For some
reason, I have always liked it as "Seven Came Back"—I used the
name once in another book, in tribute—but in deference to the
author I include the story here with its intended title.) "Mirage" displays Cliff's fascination with dying civilizations (he mentions, at one
point, the "scholarly investigation of the symbolic water jugs" of Mars,
and it might bear noting that a Martian water jug played a pivotal
part of one of his earlier stories, "Shadow of Life")—as well as his
belief in the brotherhood of the living.*

*A planet has to be really, really old, before even its animals are
able to talk. . . .*

—*dww*

They came out of the Martian night, six pitiful little creatures
looking for a seventh.

They stopped at the edge of the campfire's lighted circle and
stood there, staring at the three Earthmen with their owlish eyes.

The Earthmen froze at whatever they were doing.

"Quiet," said Wampus Smith, talking out of the corner of his
bearded lips. "They'll come in if we don't make a move."

From far away came a faint, low moaning, floating in across the wilderness of sand and jagged pinnacles of rock and the great stone buttes.

The six stood just at the firelight's edge. The reflection of the flames touched their fur with highlights of red and blue and their bodies seemed to shimmer against the backdrop of the darkness on the desert.

"Venerables," Nelson said to Richard Webb across the fire.

Webb's breath caught in his throat. Here was a thing he had never hoped to see. A thing that no human being could ever hope to see.

Six of the Venerables of Mars walking in out of the desert and the darkness, standing in the firelight. There were many men, he knew, who would claim that the race was now extinct, hunted down, trapped out, hounded to extinction by the greed of the human sand men.

The six had seemed the same at first, six beings without a difference; but now, as Webb looked at them, he saw those minor points of bodily variation which marked each one of them as a separate individual. Six of them, Webb thought, and there should be seven.

Slowly they came forward, walking deeper into the campfire's circle. One by one they sat down on the sand facing the three men. No one said a word and the tension built up in the circle of the fire while far toward the north the thing kept up its keening, like a sharp, thin blade cutting through the night.

"Human glad," Wampus Smith said finally, talking in the patois of the desert. "He waited long."

One of the creatures spoke, its words half English, half Martian, all of it pure gibberish to the ear that did not know.

"We die," it said. "Human hurt for long. Human help some now. Now we die, human help?"

"Human sad," said Wampus and even while he tried to make his voice sad, there was elation in it, a trembling eagerness, a quivering as a hound will quiver when the scent is hot.

"We are six," the creature said. "Six not enough. We need another one. We do not find the seven, we die. Race die forever now."

"Not forever," Smith told them.

The Venerable insisted on it. "Forever. There other sixes. No other seven."

"How can human help?"

"Human know. Human have Seven somewhere?"

Wampus shook his head.

"Where we have Seven?"

"In cage. On Earth. For human to see."

Wampus shook his head again.

"No Seven on Earth."

"There was one," Webb said softly. "In a zoo."

"Zoo," said the creature, tonguing the unfamiliar word. "We mean that. In cage."

"It died," said Webb. "Many years ago."

"Human have one," the creature insisted. "Here on planet. Hid out. To trade."

"No understand," said Wampus but Webb knew from the way he said it that he understood.

"Find Seven. Do not kill it. Hide it. Knowing we come. Knowing we pay."

"Pay? What pay?"

"City," said the creature. "Old city."

"That's your city," Nelson said to Webb. "The ruins you are hunting."

"Too bad we haven't got a Seven," Wampus said. "We could hand it over and they'd lead us to the ruins."

"Human hurt for long," the creature said. "Human kill all Sevens. Have good fur. Women human wear it. High pay for Seven fur."

"Lord, yes," said Nelson. "Fifty thousand for one at the trading post. A cool half million for a four-skin cape made up in New York."

Webb sickened at the thought of it, at the casual way in which Nelson mentioned it. It was illegal now, of course, but the law had come too late to save the Venerables. Although a law, come to think of it, should not have been necessary. A human being, in all rightness . . . an intelligent form of life, in all rightness, should not hunt down and kill another intelligent being to strip off its pelt and sell it for fifty thousand dollars.

"No Seven hid," Wampus was saying. "Law says friends. No dare hurt Seven. No dare hide Seven."

"Law far off," said the creature. "Human his own law."

"Not us," said Wampus. "We don't monkey with the law."

And that's a laugh, thought Webb.

"You help?" asked the creature.

"Try, maybe," Wampus told them cagily. "No good, though. You can't find. Human can't find."

"You find. We show city."

"We watch," said Wampus. "Close watch. See Seven, bring it. Where you be?"

"Canyon mouth."

"Good," said Wampus. "Deal?"

"Deal," said the creature.

Slowly the six of them got to their feet and turned back to the night again.

At the edge of the firelit circle they stopped. The spokesman turned back to the three men.

"By," he said.

"Good-by," said Wampus.

Then they were gone, back into the desert.

The three men sat and listened for a long time, not knowing what they listened for, but with ears taut to hear the slightest sound, trying to read out of sound some of the movement of life that surged all around the fire.

On Mars, thought Webb, one always listens. That is the survival price. To watch and listen and be still and quiet. And ruthless, too. To strike before another thing can strike. To see or hear a danger and be ready for it, be half a second quicker than it is quick. And to recognize that danger once you see or hear it.

Finally Nelson took up again the thing he had been doing when the six arrived, whetting his belt knife to a razor sharpness on a pocket whetstone.

The soft, sleek whirr of metal traveling over stone sounded like a heartbeat, a pulse that did not originate within the fire-light circle, but something that came out of the darkness, the pulse and beat of the wilderness itself.

Wampus said: "It's too bad, Lars, that we don't know where to pick us up a Seven."

"Yeah," said Lars.

"Might turn a good deal," Wampus said. "Likely to be treasure in that old city. All the stories say so."

Nelson grunted. "Just stories."

"Stones," said Wampus. "Stones so bright and polished they could put your eyes out. Sacks of them. Tire a man out just packing them away."

"Wouldn't need more than one load," Nelson declared. "Just one load would set you up for life."

Webb saw that both of them were looking at him, squinting their eyes against the firelight.

He said, almost angrily: "I don't know about the treasure."

"You heard the stories," Wampus said.

Webb nodded. "Let's say it this way. I'm not interested in the treasure. I don't expect to find any."

"Wouldn't mind if you did, would you?" Lars asked.

"It doesn't matter," Webb told him. "One way or the other."

"What do you know about this city?" Wampus demanded and it wasn't just conversation, it was a question asked with an answer expected, for a special purpose. "You been muttering around and dropping hints here and there but you never came cold out and told us."

For a moment, Webb stared at the man. Then he spoke slowly. "Just this. I figured out where it might be. From a knowledge of geography and geology and some understanding of the rise of cultures. I figured where the grass and wood and water would have been when Mars was new and young. I tried to locate, theoretically, the likeliest place for a civilization to arise. That's all there's to it."

"And you never thought of treasure?"

"I thought of finding out something about the Martian culture," Webb said. "How it rose and why it fell and what it might be like."

Wampus spat. "You aren't even sure there is a city," he said disgustedly.

"Not until just now," said Webb. "Now I know there is."

"From what them little critters said?"

Webb nodded. "From what they said. That's right."

Wampus grunted and was silent.

Webb watched the two across the campfire from him.

They think I'm soft, he thought. They despise me because I'm soft. They would leave me in a minute if it served their purpose or they'd put a knife into me without a second thought if that should serve their purpose . . . if there was something that I had they wanted.

There had been no choice, he realized. He could not have gone alone into this wilderness, for if he'd tried he probably wouldn't have lived beyond the second day. It took special knowledge to live here and a special technique and a certain kind of mind. A man had to develop a high survival factor to walk into Mars behind the settlements.

And the settlements now were very far away. Somewhere to the east.

"Tomorrow," Wampus said, "we change directions. We go north instead of west."

Webb said nothing. His hand slid around cautiously and touched the gun at his belt, to make sure that it was there.

It had been a mistake to hire these two, he knew. But probably none of the others would have been better. They were all of a breed, a toughened, vicious band of men who roamed the wilderness, hunting, trapping, mining, taking what they found. Wampus and Nelson had been the only two at the post when he had arrived. All the other sand men had gone a week before, back to their hunting grounds.

At first they had been respectful, almost fawning. But as the days went on they felt surer of their ground and had grown insolent. Now Webb knew that he'd been taken for a sucker. The two stayed at the post, he knew now, for no other reason than that they were without a grubstake. He was that grubstake. He supplied them with the trappings they needed to get back into the wilderness. Once he had been a grubstake, now he was a burden.

"I said," declared Wampus, "that tomorrow we go north."

Webb still said nothing.

"You heard me, didn't you?" asked Wampus.

"The first time," Webb said.

"We go north," said Wampus, "and we travel fast."

"You got a Seven staked out somewhere?"

Lars snickered. "Ain't that the damnedest thing you ever heard of? Takes seven of them. Now with us, it just takes a man and woman."

"I asked you," said Webb to Wampus, "if you have a Seven caged up somewhere?"

"No," said Wampus. "We just go north, that's all."

"I hired you to take me west."

Wampus snarled at him. "I thought you'd say that, Webb. I just wanted to know exactly how you felt about it."

"You want to leave me stranded here," said Webb. "You took my money and agreed to guide me. Now you have something else to do. You either have a Seven or you think you know where you can find one. And if I knew and talked, you would be in danger. So there's only one of two things that you can do with me. You can kill me or you can leave me and let something else do the job for you."

Lars said: "We're giving you a choice, ain't we?"

Webb looked at Wampus and the man nodded. "You got your choice, Webb."

He could go for his gun, of course. He could get one of them, most likely, before the other one got him. But there would be nothing gained. He would be just as dead as if they shot him out of hand. As far as that went he was as good as dead anyhow, for hundreds of miles stretched between him and the settlements and even if he were able to cross those many miles there was no guarantee that he could find the settlements.

"We're moving out right now," said Wampus. "Ain't smart to travel in the dark, but ain't the first time that we had to do it. We'll be up north in a day or two."

Lars nodded. "Once we get back to the settlements, Webb, we'll h'ist a drink to you."

Wampus joined in the spirit of the moment. "Good likker, Webb. We can afford good likker then."

Webb said nothing, did not move. He sat on the ground, relaxed.

And that, he told himself, was the thing that scared him. That he could sit and know what was about to happen and be so unconcerned about it.

Perhaps it had been the miles of wilderness that made it possible, the harsh, raw land and the vicious life that moved across the land . . . the ever-hungering, ever-hunting life that prowled and stalked and killed. Here life was stripped to its essentials and one learned that the line between life and death was a thin line at best.

"Well," said Wampus finally, "what will it be, Webb."

"I think," said Webb, gravely, "I think I'll take my chance on living."

Lars clucked his tongue against his teeth. "Too bad," he said. "We was hoping it'd be the other way around. Then we could take all the stuff. As it is, we got to leave you some."

"You can always sneak back," said Webb, "and shoot me as I sit here. It would be an easy thing."

"That," said Wampus, "is not a bad idea."

Lars said: "Give me your gun, Webb. I'll throw it back to you when we leave. But we ain't taking a chance of you plugging us while we're getting ready."

Webb lifted his gun out of its holster and handed it over. Still sitting where he was, he watched them pack and stow the supplies into the wilderness wagon.

Finally it was done.

"We're leaving you plenty to last," Wampus told him. "More than enough."

"Probably," said Webb. "You figure I can't last very long."

"If it was me," said Wampus, "I'd take it quick and easy."

Webb sat for a long time, listening to the motor of the wagon until it was out of hearing, then waiting for the gun blast that would send him toppling face forward into the flaming campfire.

But finally he knew that it would not come. He piled more fuel on the fire and crawled into his sleeping bag.

In the morning he headed east, following backward along the tracks of the wilderness wagon. They'd guide him, he knew, for a week or so, but finally they would disappear, brushed out by drifting sand and by the action of the weak and whining wind that sometimes blew across the bleakness of the wilderness.

Anyhow, while he followed them he would know at least he was going in the right direction. Although more than likely he would be dead before they faded out, for the wilderness crawled with too much sudden death to be sure of living from one moment to the next.

He walked with the gun hanging in his hand, watching every side, stopping at the top of the ridges to study the terrain in front of him before he moved down into it.

The unaccustomed pack which he had fashioned inexpertly

out of his sleeping bag grew heavier as the day progressed and chafed his shoulders raw. The sun was warm . . . as warm as the night would be cold . . . and thirst mounted in his throat to choke him. Carefully he doled out sips of water from the scanty supply the two had left him.

He knew he would not get back. Somewhere between where he stood and the settlements he would die of lack of water or of an insect bite or beneath the jaws and fangs of some charging beast or from sheer exhaustion.

There was, once you thought it out, no reason why a man should try to get back . . . since there was utterly no chance that he would get back. But Webb didn't stop to reason it out; he set his face toward the east and followed the wagon tracks.

For there was a *humanness* in him that said he must try at least . . . that he must go as far as he could go, that he must avoid death as long as he could. So on he went, going as far as he could go and avoiding death.

He spotted the ant colony in time to circle it, but he circled it too closely and the insects, catching scent of food within their grasp, streamed out after him. It took a mile of running before he outdistanced them.

He saw the crouching beast camouflaged against the sand, where it was waiting for him, and shot it where it lay. Later in the day, when another monstrosity came tearing out from behind a rock outcropping, his bullet caught it between the eyes before it had covered half the distance.

For an hour he squatted, unmoving, on the sand, while a huge insect that looked like a bumblebee, but wasn't, hunted for the thing that it had sighted only a moment before. But since it could recognize a thing through motion only, it finally gave up and went away. Webb stayed squatting for another half hour against the chance that it had not gone away, but was lurking somewhere watching for the motion it had sighted to take up again.

These times he avoided death, but he knew that the hour

would come when he would not see a danger, or having seen it, would not move fast enough to stop it.

The mirages came to haunt him, to steal his eyes from the things that he should be watching. Mirages that flickered in the sky, with their feet upon the ground. Tantalizing pictures of things that could not be on Mars, of places that might have been at one time . . . but that very long ago.

Mirages of broad, slow rivers with the slant of sail upon them. Mirages of green forests that stretched across the hills and so clear, so close that one could see the little clumps of wild flowers that grew among the trees. And in some of them the hint of snow-capped mountains, in a world that knew no mountains.

He kept a watch for fuel as he went along, hoping to find a cache of "embalmed" wood cropping out of the sand . . . wood left over from that dim age when these hills and valleys had been forest covered, wood that had escaped the ravages of time and now lay like the dried mummies of trees in the aridness of the desert.

But there was none to be found and he knew that more than likely he would have to spend a fireless night. He could not spend a night in the open without fire. If he tried it, he would be gobbled up an hour after twilight had set in.

He must somehow find shelter in one of the many caves of the weird rock formations that sprang out of the desert. Find a cave and clean out whatever might be in it, block its entrance with stones and boulders and sleep with gun in hand.

It had sounded easy when he thought of it, but while there were many caves, he was forced to reject them one by one since each of them had too large an opening to be closed against attack. A cave, he knew, with an unclosed mouth, would be no better than a trap.

The sun was less than an hour high when he finally spotted a cave that would serve the purpose, located on a ledge of stone jutting out of a steep hill.

From the bottom he stood long minutes surveying the hill. Nothing moved. There was no telltale fleck of color.

Slowly, he started up, digging his feet into the shifting talus of the slope, fighting his way up foot by foot, stopping for long minutes to regain his breath and to survey the slope ahead.

Gaining the ledge, he moved cautiously toward the cave, gun leveled, for there was no telling what might come out of it.

He debated on his next move.

Flash his light inside to see what was there?

Or simply thrust his gun into the opening and spray the inside with its lethal charge?

There could be no squeamishness, he told himself. Better to kill a harmless thing than to run the chance of passing up a danger.

He heard no sound until the claws of the thing were scrabbling on the ledge behind him. He shot one quick glance over his shoulder and saw the beast almost on top of him, got the impression of gaping mouth and murderous fangs and tiny eyes that glinted with a stony cruelty.

There was no time to turn and fire. There was time for just one thing.

His legs moved like driving pistons, hurling his body at the cave. The stone lip of it caught his shoulder and ripped through his clothing, gashing his arm, but he was through, through and rolling free. Something brushed his face and he rolled over something that protested in a squeaking voice and off in one corner there was a thing that mewed quietly to itself.

On his knees, Webb swung his gun around to face the opening of the cave, saw the great bulk of the beast that had charged him trying to squeeze its way inside.

It backed away and then a great paw came in, feeling this way and that, hunting for the food that crouched inside the cave.

Mouths jabbered at Webb, a dozen voices speaking in the lingo of the desert and he heard them say:

"Human, human, kill, kill, kill."

Webb's gun spat and the paw went limp and was pulled slowly from the cave. The great grey body toppled and they heard it strike the slope below the ledge and go slithering away down the talus slope.

"Thanks, human," said the voices. "Thanks, human."

Slowly Webb sat down, cradling the gun in his lap.

All around him he heard the stir of life.

Sweat broke out on his forehead and he felt moisture running from his armpits down his sides.

What was in the cave? What was in here with him?

That they had talked to him didn't mean a thing. Half the so-called animals of Mars could talk the desert lingo . . . a vocabulary of a few hundred words, part of them Earthian, part of them Martian, part of them God-knew-what.

For here on Mars many of the animals were not animals at all, but simply degenerating forms of life that at one time must have formed a complex civilization. The Venerables, who still retained some of the shape of bipeds, would have reached the highest culture, but there must have been many varying degrees of culture, living by compromise or by tolerance.

"Safe," a voice told him. "Trust. Cave law."

"Cave law?"

"Kill in cave . . . no. Kill outside cave . . . yes. Safe in cave."

"I no kill," said Webb. "Cave law good."

"Human know cave law?"

Webb said: "Human keep cave law."

"Good," the voice told him. "All safe now."

Webb relaxed. He slipped his gun into his holster and took off his pack, laid it down alongside and rubbed his raw and blistered shoulders.

He could believe these things, he told himself. A thing so elemental and so simple as cave law was a thing that could be understood and trusted. It arose from a basic need, the need of the weaker life forms to forget their mutual differences and their mutual preying upon one another at the fall of night . . . the need to find a common sanctuary against the bigger and the more vicious and the lonely killers who took over with the going of the sun.

A voice said: "Come light. Human kill."

Another voice said: "Human keep cave law in dark. No cave law in light. Human kill come light."

"Human no kill come light," said Webb.

"All human kill," said one of the things. "Human kill for fur. Human kill for food. We fur. We food."

"This human never kill," said Webb. "This human friend."

"Friend?" one of them asked. "We not know friend. Explain friend."

Webb didn't try. There was no use, he knew. They could not understand the word. It was foreign to this wilderness.

At last he asked: "Rocks here?"

One of the voices answered: "Rocks in cave. Human want rocks?"

"Pile in cave mouth," said Webb. "No killer get in."

They digested that for a while. Finally one of them spoke up: "Rock good."

They brought rocks and stones and, with Webb helping them, wedged the cave mouth tight.

It was too dark to see the things, but they brushed against him as they worked and some of them were soft and furry and others had hides like crocodiles, that tore his skin as he brushed against them. And there was one that was soft and pulpy and gave him the creeps.

He settled down in one corner of the cave with his sleeping bag between his body and the wall. He would have liked to crawl into it, but that would have meant unpacking and if he unpacked his supplies, he knew, there'd be none come morning.

Perhaps, he reasoned, the body heat of all the things in here will keep the cave from getting too cold. Cold, yes, but not too cold for human life. It was, he knew, a gamble at best.

Sleep at night in friendship, kill one another and flee from one another with the coming of the dawn. Law, they called it. Cave law. Here was one for the books, here was something that was not even hinted at in all the archaeological tomes that he had ever read.

And he had read them all. There was something here on Mars that fascinated him. A mystery and a loneliness, an emptiness and a retrogression that haunted him and finally sent him out to try to pierce some of that mystery, to try to hunt for the reason for that retrogression, to essay to measure the greatness of the culture that in some far dim period had come tumbling down.

There had been some great work done along that line. Axelson with his scholarly investigation of the symbolic water jugs and Mason's sometimes fumbling attempt to trace the great migrations. Then there was Smith, who had traveled the barren world for years jotting down the windblown stories whispered by the little degenerating things about an ancient greatness and a golden past. Myths, most of them, of course, but some place, somewhere lay the answer to the origin of the myths. Folklore does not leap full-blown from the mind; it starts with a fact and that fact is added to and the two facts are distorted and you have a myth. But at the bottom, back of all of it, is the starting point of fact.

So it was, so it must be with the myth that told about the great and glowing city that had stood above all other things of Mars . . . a city that was known to the far ends of the planet.

A place of culture, Webb told himself, a place where all the achievements and all the dreams and every aspiration of the once-great planet would have come together.

And yet, in more than a hundred years of hunting and of digging, Earth's archaeologists had found no trace of any city, let alone that city of all cities. Kitchen middens and burial places and wretched huddling places where broken remnants of the great people had lived for a time . . . there were plenty of these. But no great city.

It must be somewhere, Webb was convinced. That myth could

not lie, for it was told too often at too many different places by too many different animals that had once been people.

Mars fascinated me, he thought, and it still fascinates me, but now it will be the death of me . . . for there's death in its fascination. Death in the lonely stretches and death waiting on the buttes. Death in this cave, too, for they may kill me come the morning to prevent me killing them; they may keep their truce of the night just long enough to make an end of me.

The law of the cave? Some holdover from the ancient day, some memory of a now forgotten brotherhood? Or a device necessitated by the evil days that had come when the brotherhood had broken?

He laid his head back against the rock and closed his eyes and thought . . . if they kill me, they kill me, but I will not kill them. For there has been too much human killing on the planet Mars. I will repay part of the debt at least. I will not kill the ones who took me in.

He remembered himself creeping along the ledge outside the cave, debating whether he should have a look first or stick in the muzzle of his gun and sweep the cave as a simple way of being sure there would be nothing there to harm him.

I did not know, he said. I did not know.

A soft furry body brushed against him and a voice spoke to him.

"Friend means no hurt? Friend means no kill?"

"No hurt," said Webb. "No kill."

"You saw six?" the voice asked.

Webb jerked from the wall and sat very still.

"You saw six?" the voice was insistent.

"I saw six," said Webb.

"When?"

"One sun."

"Where six?"

"Canyon mouth," said Webb. "Wait at canyon mouth."

"You hunt Seven?"

"No," said Webb. "I go home."

"Other humans?"

"They north," said Webb. "They hunt Seven north."

"They kill Seven?"

"Catch Seven," said Webb. "Take Seven to six. See city."

"Six promise?"

"Six promise," said Webb.

"You good human. You friend human. You no kill Seven."

"No kill," insisted Webb.

"All humans kill. Kill Seven sure. Seven good fur. Much pay. Many Sevens die for human."

"Law says no kill," declared Webb. "Human law says Seven friend. No kill friend."

"Law? Like cave law?"

"Like cave law," said Webb.

"You good friend of Seven?"

"Good friend of all," said Webb.

"I Seven," said the voice.

Webb sat quietly and let the numbness clear out of his brain.

"Seven," he finally said. "You go canyon mouth. Find six. They wait. Human friend glad."

"Human friend want city," said the creature. "Seven friend to human. Human find Seven. Human see city. Six promise."

Webb almost laughed aloud in bitterness. Here, at last, the chance that he had hoped might come. Here, at last, the thing that he had wanted, the thing he had come to Mars to do. And he couldn't do it. He simply couldn't do it.

"Human no go," he said. "Human die. No food. No water. Human die."

"We care for human," Seven told him. "No friend human before. All kill humans. Friend human come. We care for it."

Webb was silent for a while, thinking.

Then he asked: "You give human food? You find human water?"

"Take care," said Seven.

"How Seven know I saw six?"

"Human tell. Human think. Seven know."

So that was it . . . telepathy. Some vestige of a former power, some attribute of a magnificent culture, not quite forgotten yet. How many of the other creatures in this cave would have it, too?

"Human go with Seven?" Seven asked.

"Human go," said Webb.

He might as well, he told himself. Going east, back toward the settlements, was no solution to his problem. He knew he'd never reach the settlements. His food would run out. His water would run out. Some beast would catch him and make a meal of him. He didn't have a chance.

Going with the little creature that stood beside him in the darkness of the cave, he might have a chance. Not too good a chance, perhaps, but at least a chance. There would be food and water . . . or at least a chance of food and water. There would be another helping him to watch for the sudden death that roamed the wilderness. Another one to warn him, to help him recognize the danger.

"Human cold," said Seven.

"Cold," admitted Webb.

"One cold," said Seven. "Two warm."

The furry thing crawled into his arms, put its arms around his body. After a moment, he put his arms around it.

"Sleep," said Seven. "Warm. Sleep."

Webb ate the last of his food and the Seven Venerables told him: "We care."

"Human die," Webb insisted. "No food. Human die."

"We take care," the seven little creatures told him, standing in a row. "Later we take care."

So he took it to mean that there was no food for him now, but later there would be.

They took up the march again.

It was an interminable thing, that march. A thing to make a

man cry out in his sleep. A thing to shiver over when they had been lucky enough to find wood and sat hunched around the fire. Day after endless day of sand and rock, of crawling up to a high ridge and plunging down the other side, of slogging through the heat across the level land that had been sea bottom in the days long gone.

It became a song, a drum beat, a three-note marching cadence that rang through the human's head, an endless thing that hammered in his brain through the day and stayed with him hours after they had stopped for night. Until he was dizzy with it, until his brain was drugged with the hammer of it, so that his eyes refused to focus and the gun bead was a fuzzy globe when he had to use the weapon against the crawling things and charging things and flying things that came at them out of nowhere.

Always there were the mirages, the everlasting mirages of Mars that seemed to lie just beneath the surface of reality. Flickering pictures painted in the sky the water and the trees and the long green sweep of grass that Mars had not known for countless centuries. As if, Webb told himself, the past were very close behind them, as if the past might still exist and was trying to catch up, reluctant to be left behind in the march of time.

He lost count of the days and steeled himself against the speculation of how much longer it might be, until it seemed that it would go on forever, that they would never stop, that they would face each morning the barren wilderness they must stagger through until the fall of night.

He drank the last of the water and reminded them he could not live without it.

"Later," they told him. "Water later."

That was the day they came to the city and there, deep in a tunnel far beneath the topmost ruins there was water, water dripping, drop by slow and tantalizing drop from a broken pipe. Dripping water and that was a wondrous thing on Mars.

The seven drank sparingly since they had been steeled for century upon century to get along with little water, until they had adapted themselves to get along with little water and it was no hardship for them. But Webb lay for hours beside the broken pipe, holding cupped hands for a little to collect before he lapped it down, lying there in the coolness that was a blessed thing.

He slept and awoke and drank again and he was rested and was no longer thirsty, but his body cried for food. And there was no food nor none to get him food. For the little ones were gone.

They will come back, he said. They are gone for just a little while and will be back again. They have gone to get me food and they will bring it to me. And he thought very kindly of them.

He picked his way upward through the tunnel down which they'd come and so at last came to the ruins that lay on the hill that thrust upward from the surrounding country so that when one stood on the hill's top, there was miles of distance, dropping away on every side.

There wasn't much that one could see of the ruined city. It would have been entirely possible to have walked past the hill and not have known the city was there. During thousands of years it had crumbled and fallen in upon itself and some of it had dissolved to dust and the sand had crept in and covered it and sifted among its fragments until it simply was a part of the hill.

Here and there Webb found broken fragments of chiseled masonry and here and there a shard of pottery, but a man could have walked past these, if he had not been looking, and taken them for no more than another rock scattered among the trillions of other fragmentary rocks littered on the surface of the planet.

The tunnel, he found, led down into the bowels of the fallen city, into the burial mound of the fallen greatness and the vanished glory of a proud people whose descendants now scuttled animal-like in the ancient deserts and talked in an idiom that was no more than a memory of the literacy that must have flourished once in the city on the hill.

In the tunnel Webb found evidence of solid blocks of carven stone, broken columns, paving blocks and something that seemed at one time to have been a beautifully executed statue.

At the end of the tunnel, he cupped his hands at the pipe and drank again, then went back to the surface and sat on the ground beside the tunnel mouth and stared out across the emptiness of Mars.

It would take power and tools and many men to uncover and sift the evidence of the city. It would take years of painstaking, scholarly work . . . and he didn't even have a shovel. And worst of all, he had no time. For if the seven did not show up with food he would one day go down into the darkness of the tunnel and there eventually join his human dust with the ancient dust of this alien world.

There had been a shovel, he remembered, and Wampus and Lars, when they deserted him, had left it with him. A rare consideration, surely, he told himself. But of the supplies which he had carried away from the campfire that long gone morning there were just two things left, his sleeping bag and the pistol at his belt. All else he could get along without, those two were things that he had to have.

An archaeologist, he thought. An archaeologist sitting on top of the greatest find that any archaeologist had ever made and not able to do a single thing about it.

Wampus and Lars had thought that there would be treasure here. And there was no certain treasure, no treasure revealed and waiting for the hands of men to take. He had thought of glory and there was no glory. He had thought of knowledge and without a shovel and some time there simply was no knowledge. No knowledge beyond the bare knowing that he had been right, that the city did exist.

And yet there was certain other knowledge gained along the way. The knowledge that the seven types of the Venerables did still in fact exist, that from this existence the race might still continue despite the guns and snares and the greed and guile of Earthmen who had hunted Seven for its fifty thousand dollar pelt.

Seven little creatures, seven different sexes. All of them essential to the continuance of the race. Six little creatures looking for the seventh and he had found the seventh. Because he had found the seventh, because he had been the messenger, there would be at least one new generation of the Venerables to carry on the race.

What use, he thought, to carry on a race that had failed its purpose?

He shook his head.

You can't play God, he said. You can't presume to judge. There either is a purpose in all things or there's no purpose in anything, and who is there to know?

There either is purpose that I reached this city or there is no purpose. There is a purpose that I may die here or it is possible that my dying here will be no more than another random factor in the great machination of pure chance that moves the planets through their courses and brings a man homeward at the end of day.

And there was another knowledge . . . the knowledge of the endless reaches and the savage loneliness that was the Martian wilderness. The knowledge of that and the queer, almost non-human detachment that it fused into the human soul.

Lessons, he thought.

The lesson that one man is an insignificant flyspeck crawling across the face of eternity. The lesson that one life is a relatively unimportant thing when it stands face to face with the over-riding reality of the miracle of all creation.

He got up and stood at his full height and knew his insignificance and his humility in the empty sweep of land that fell away on every side and in the arching sky that vaulted overhead from horizon to horizon and the utter silence that lay upon the land and sky.

Starving was a lonely and an awful business.

Some deaths are swift and clean.

But starving is not one of these.

The seven did not come. Webb waited for them, and because

he still felt kindly toward them, he found excuses for them. They did not realize, he told himself, how short a time a man may go without nourishment. The strange mating, he told himself, involving seven personalities, probably was a complicated procedure and might take a great deal more time than one usually associated with such phenomena. Or something might have happened to them, they might be having trouble of their own. As soon as they had worked it out, they would come, and they would bring him food.

So he starved with kindly thoughts and with a great deal more patience than a man under dissimilar circumstances might be expected to.

And he found, even when he felt the lassitude of under-nourishment creeping along his muscles and his bones, even when the sharp pangs of hunger had settled to a gnawing horror that never left him, even when he slept, that his mind was not affected by the ravages that his body was undergoing; that his brain, apparently, was sharpened by the lack of food, that it seemed to step aside from his tortured body and become a separate entity that drew in upon itself and knotted all its faculties into a hard-bound bundle that was scarcely aware of external factors.

He sat for long hours upon a polished rock, perhaps part of that once proud city, which he found just a few yards from the tunnel mouth, and stared out across the sun-washed wilderness which stretched for miles toward a horizon that it never seemed to reach. He sought for purpose with a sharp-edged mind that probed at the roots of existence and of happenstance and sought to evolve out of the random factors that moved beneath the surface of the universe's orderliness some evidence of a pattern that would be understandable to the human mind. Often he thought he had it, but it always slid away from him like quicksilver escaping from a clutching hand.

If Man ever was to find the answer, he knew, it must be in a place like this, where there was no distraction, where there was a distance and a barrenness that built up to a vast impersonality which emphasized and underscored the inconsequence of the thinker. For if the thinker introduced himself as a factor out of proportion to the fact, then the whole problem was distorted and the equation, if equation there be, never could be solved.

At first he had tried to hunt animals for food, but strangely, while the rest of the wilderness swarmed with vicious life that hunted timid life, the area around the city was virtually deserted, as if some one had drawn a sacred chalk mark around it. On his second day of hunting he killed a small thing that on Earth could have been a mouse. He built a fire and cooked it and later hunted up the sun-dried skin and sucked and chewed at it for the small nourishment that it might contain. But after that he did not kill a thing, for there was nothing to be killed.

Finally he came to know the seven would not come, that they never had intended to come, that they had deserted him exactly as his two human companions had deserted him before. He had been made a fool, he knew, not once, but twice.

He should have kept on going east after he had started. He should not have come back with seven to find the other six who waited at the canyon's mouth.

You might have made it to the settlements, he told himself. You just might have made it. Just possibly have made it.

East. East toward the settlements.

Human history is a trying . . . a trying for the impossible, and attaining it. There is no logic, for if humanity had waited upon logic it still would be a cave-living and an earth-bound race.

Try, said Webb, not knowing exactly what he said.

He walked down the hill again and started out across the wilderness, heading toward the east. For there was no hope upon the hill and there was hope toward the east.

A mile from the base of the hill, he fell. He staggered, falling and rising, for another mile. He crawled a hundred yards. It was there the seven found him.

"Food!" he cried at them and he had a feeling that although he cried it in his mind there was no sound in his mouth. "Food! Water!"

"We take care," they said, and lifted him, holding him in a sitting position.

"Life," Seven told him, "is in many husks. Like nested boxes that fit inside each other. You live one and you peel it off and there's another life."

"Wrong," said Webb. "You do not talk like that. Your thought does not flow like that. There is something wrong."

"There is an inner man," said Seven. "There are many inner men."

"The subconscious," said Webb, and while he said it in his mind, he knew that no word, no sound came out of his mouth. And he knew now, too, that no words were coming out of Seven's mouth, that here were words that could not be expressed in the patois of the desert, that here were thoughts and knowledge that could not belong to a thing that scuttled, fearsome, through the Martian wilderness.

"You peel an old life off and you step forth in a new and shining life," said Seven, "but you must know the way. There is a certain technique and a certain preparation. If there is no preparation and no technique, the job is often bungled."

"Preparation," said Webb. "I have no preparation. I do not know about this."

"You are prepared," said Seven. "You were not before, but now you are."

"I thought," said Webb.

"You thought," said Seven, "and you found a partial answer. Well-fed, earth-bound, arrogant, there would have been no answer. You found humility."

"I do not know the technique," said Webb. "I do not . . ."

"We know the technique," Seven said. "We take care."

The hilltop where the dead city lay shimmered and there was a mirage on it. Out of the dead mound of its dust rose the pinnacles and spires, the buttresses and the flying bridges of a city that shone with color and with light; out of the sand came the blaze of garden beds of flowers and the tall avenues of trees and a music that came from the slender bell towers.

There was grass beneath his feet instead of sand blazing with the heat of the Martian noon. There was a path that led up the terraces of the hill toward the wonder city that reared upon its heights. There was the distant sound of laughter and there were flecks of color moving on the distant streets and along the walls and through the garden paths.

Webb swung around and the seven were not there. Nor was the wilderness. The land stretched away on every hand and it was not wilderness, but a breath-taking place with groves of trees and roads and flowing water courses.

He turned back to the city again and watched the movement of the flecks of color.

"People," he said.

And Seven's voice, coming to him from somewhere, from elsewhere, said:

"People from the many planets. And from beyond the planets. And some of your own people you will find among them. For you are not the first."

Filled with wonder, a wonder that was fading, that would be entirely faded before he reached the city, Webb started walking up the path.

Wampus Smith and Lars Nelson came to the hill many days later. They came on foot because the wilderness wagon had broken down. They came without food except the little food they could kill along the way and they came with no more than a few drops of water sloshing in their canteens and there was no water to be found.

There, a short distance from the foot of the hill, they found the sun-dried mummy of a man face downward on the sand and when they turned him over they saw who he was.

Wampus stared across the body at Lars.

"How did he get here?" he croaked.

"I don't know," said Lars. "He never could have made it, not knowing the country and on foot. And he wouldn't have traveled this way anyhow. He would have headed east, back to the settlements."

They pawed through his clothing and found nothing. But they took his gun, for the charges in their own were running very low.

"What's the use," said Lars. "We can't make it, Wampus."

"We can try," said Wampus.

Above the hill a mirage flickered . . . a city with shining turrets and dizzy pinnacles and rows of trees and fountains that flashed with leaping water. To their ears came the sound, or seemed to come, the sound of many bells.

Wampus spat with lips that were cracked and dried, spat with no saliva in his mouth.

"Them damn mirages," he said. "They drive a man half crazy."

"They seem so close," said Lars. "So close and real. As if they were someplace else and were trying to break through."

Wampus spat again. "Let's get going," he said.

The two men turned toward the east and as they moved, they left staggering, uneven tracks through the sand of Mars.

THE AUTUMN LAND

Cliff Simak once called this story one of the few he wrote to order: he'd been asked for a story that could appear in the October 1971 issue of The Magazine of Fantasy and Science Fiction *as a celebration of Cliff's concurrent appearance as Guest of Honor at that year's World Science Fiction Convention. And it would become one of his favorites among his stories. But it is, in a way, an extension of those Simak stories that featured people trying to find a way to flee some sort of societal collapse—and it's haunted.*

—dww

He sat on the porch, in the rocking chair, with the loose board creaking as he rocked. Across the street the old white-haired lady cut a bouquet of chrysanthemums in the never-ending autumn. Where he could see between the ancient houses to the distant woods and wastelands, a soft Indian-summer blue lay upon the land. The entire village was soft and quiet, as old things often are—a place constructed for a dreaming mind rather than a living being. It was an hour too early for his other old and shaky neighbor to come fumbling down the grass-grown sidewalk, tapping the bricks with his seeking cane. And he would not hear the distant children at their play until dusk had fallen—if he heard them then. He did not always hear them.

There were books to read, but he did not want to read them. He could go into the backyard and spade and rake the garden once again, reducing the soil to a finer texture to receive the seed when it could be planted—if it ever could be planted—but there was slight incentive in the further preparation of a seed bed against a spring that never came. Earlier, much earlier, before he knew about the autumn and the spring, he had mentioned garden seeds to the Milkman, who had been very much embarrassed.

He had walked the magic miles and left the world behind in bitterness and when he first had come here had been content to live in utter idleness, to be supremely idle and to feel no guilt or shame at doing absolutely nothing or as close to absolutely nothing as a man was able. He had come walking down the autumn street in the quietness and the golden sunshine, and the first person that he saw was the old lady who lived across the street. She had been waiting at the gate of her picket fence as if she had known he would be coming, and she had said to him, "You're a new one come to live with us. There are not many come these days. That is your house across the street from me, and I know we'll be good neighbors." He had reached up his hand to doff his hat to her, forgetting that he had no hat. "My name is Nelson Rand," he'd told her. "I am an engineer. I will try to be a decent neighbor." He had the impression that she stood taller and straighter than she did, but old and bent as she might be there was a comforting graciousness about her. "You will please come in," she said. "I have lemonade and cookies. There are other people there, but I shall not introduce them to you." He waited for her to explain why she would not introduce him, but there was no explanation, and he followed her down the time-mellowed walk of bricks with great beds of asters and chrysanthemums, a mass of color on either side of it.

In the large, high-ceilinged living room, with its bay windows forming window seats, filled with massive furniture from another time and with a small blaze burning in the fireplace, she had shown him to a seat before a small table to one side of the fire and had sat down opposite him and poured the lemonade and passed the plate of cookies.

"You must pay no attention to them," she had told him. "They are all dying to meet you, but I shall not humor them."

It was easy to pay no attention to them, for there was no one there.

"The Major, standing over there by the fireplace," said his hostess, "with his elbow on the mantel, a most ungainly pose if you should ask me, is not happy with my lemonade. He would prefer a stronger drink. Please, Mr. Rand, will you not taste my lemonade? I assure you it is good. I made it myself. I have no maid, you see, and no one in the kitchen. I live quite by myself and satisfactorily, although my friends keep dropping in, sometimes more often than I like."

He tasted the lemonade, not without misgivings, and to his surprise it was lemonade and was really good, like the lemonade he had drunk when a boy at Fourth of July celebrations and at grade school picnics, and had never tasted since.

"It is excellent," he said.

"The lady in blue," his hostess said, "sitting in the chair by the window, lived here many years ago. She and I were friends, although she moved away some time ago and I am surprised that she comes back, which she often does. The infuriating thing is that I cannot remember her name, if I ever knew it. You don't know it, do you?"

"I am afraid I don't."

"Oh, of course, you wouldn't. I had forgotten. I forget so easily these days. You are a new arrival."

He had sat through the afternoon and drank her lemonade and eaten her cookies, while she chattered on about her nonexistent guests. It was only when he had crossed the street to the house she had pointed out as his, with her standing on the stoop and waving her farewell, that he realized she had not told him her name. He did not know it even now.

How long had it been? he wondered, and realized he didn't know. It was this autumn business. How could a man keep track of time when it was always autumn?

It all had started on that day when he'd been driving across Iowa, heading for Chicago. No, he reminded himself, it had started with the thinnesses, although he had paid little attention to the thinnesses to begin with. Just been aware of them, perhaps as a strange condition of the mind, or perhaps an unusual quality to the atmosphere and light. As if the world lacked a certain solidity that one had come to expect, as if one were running along a mystic borderline between here and somewhere else.

He had lost his West Coast job when a government contract had failed to materialize. His company had not been the only one; there were many other companies that were losing contracts and there were a lot of engineers who walked the streets bewildered. There was a bare possibility of a job in Chicago, although he was well aware that by now it might be filled. Even if there were no job, he reminded himself, he was in better shape than a lot of other men. He was young and single, he had a few dollars in the bank, he had no house mortgage, no car payments, no kids to put through school. He had only himself to support—no family of any sort at all. The old, hardfisted bachelor uncle who had taken him to raise when his parents had died in a car crash and had worked him hard on that stony, hilly Wisconsin farm, had receded deep into the past, becoming a dim, far figure that was hard to recognize. He had not liked his uncle, Rand remembered—had not hated him, simply had not liked him. He had shed no tears, he recalled, when the old man had been caught out in a pasture by a bull and gored to death. So now Rand was quite alone, not even holding the memories of a family.

He had been hoarding the little money that he had, for with a limited work record, with other men better qualified looking for the jobs, he realized that it might be some time before he could connect with anything. The beat-up wagon that he drove had space for sleeping, and he stopped at the little wayside parks along the way to cook his meals.

He had almost crossed the state, and the road had started its long winding through the bluffs that rimmed the Mississippi. Ahead he caught glimpses, at several turnings of the road, of smokestacks and tall structures that marked the city just ahead.

He emerged from the bluffs, and the city lay before him, a small industrial center that lay on either side the river. It was then that he felt and saw (if one could call it seeing) the thinness that he had seen before or had sensed before. There was about it, not exactly an alienness, but a sense of unreality, as if one were seeing the actuality of the scene through some sort of veil, with the edges softened and the angles flattened out, as if one might be looking at it as one would look at the bottom of a clear-water lake with a breeze gently ruffling the surface. When he had seen it before, he had attributed it to road fatigue and had opened the window to get a breath of air or had stopped the car and gotten out to walk up and down the road a while, and it had gone away.

But this time it was worse than ever, and he was somewhat frightened at it—not so much frightened at it as he was frightened of himself, wondering what might be wrong with him.

He pulled off to the side of the road, braking the car to a halt, and it seemed to him, even as he did it, that the shoulder of the road was rougher than he'd thought. As he pulled off the road, the thinness seemed to lessen, and he saw that the road had changed, which explained its roughness. The surface was pocked with chuckholes and blocks of concrete had been heaved up and other blocks were broken into pebbly shards.

He raised his eyes from the road to look at the city, and there was no city, only the broken stumps of a place that had somehow been destroyed. He sat with his hands frozen on the wheel, and in the silence—the deadly, unaccustomed silence—he heard the cawing of crows. Foolishly, he tried to remember the last time he had heard the caw of crows, and then he saw them, black specks that flapped just above the bluff top. There was something else as well—the trees. No longer trees, but only here and there blackened stumps. The stumps of a city and the stumps of trees, with the black, ash-like flecks of crows flapping over them.

Scarcely knowing what he did, he stumbled from the car. Thinking of it later, it had seemed a foolish thing to do, for the car was the only thing he knew, the one last link he had to reality. As he stumbled from it, he put his hand down in the seat, and beneath his hand he felt the solid, oblong object. His fingers closed upon it, and it was not until he was standing by the car that he realized what he held—the camera that had been lying in the seat beside him.

Sitting on the porch, with the loose floor board creaking underneath the rocker, he remembered that he still had the pictures, although it had been a long time since he had thought of them—a long time, actually, since he'd thought of anything at all beyond his life, day to day, in this autumn land. It was as though he had been trying to keep himself from thinking, attempting to keep his mind in neutral, to shut out what he knew—or, more precisely perhaps, what he thought he knew.

He did not consciously take the pictures, although afterward he had tried to tell himself he did (but never quite convincing himself that this was entirely true), complimenting himself in a wry sort of way for providing a piece of evidence that his memory alone never could have provided. For a man can think so many things, daydream so many things, imagine so many things that he can never trust his mind.

The entire incident, when he later thought of it, was hazy, as if the reality of that blasted city lay in some strange dimension of experience that could not be explained, or even rationalized. He could remember only vaguely the camera at his eyes and the clicking as the shutter snapped. He did recall the band of people charging down the hill toward him and his mad scramble for the car, locking the door behind him and putting the car in gear, intent on steering a zigzag course along the broken pavement to get away from the screaming humans who were less than a hundred feet away.

But as he pulled off the shoulder, the pavement was no longer broken. It ran smooth and level toward the city that was no longer blasted. He pulled off the road again and sat limply, beaten, and it was only after many minutes that he could proceed again, going very slowly because he did not trust himself, shaken as he was, to drive at greater speed.

He had planned to cross the river and continue to Chicago, getting there that night, but now his plans were changed. He was too shaken up and, besides, there were the films. And he needed time to think, he told himself, a lot of time to think.

He found a roadside park a few miles outside the city and pulled into it, parking alongside an outdoor grill and an old-fashioned pump. He got some wood from the small supply he carried in the back and built a fire. He hauled out the box with his cooking gear and food, fixed the coffee pot, set a pan upon the grill and cracked three eggs into it.

When he had pulled off the road, he had seen the man walking along the roadside; and now, as he cracked the eggs, he saw that the man had turned into the park and was walking toward the car. The man came up to the pump.

"Does this thing work?" he asked.

Rand nodded. "I got water for the pot," he said. "Just now."

"It's a hot day," said the man.

He worked the pump handle up and down.

"Hot for walking," he said.

"You been walking far?"

"The last six weeks," he said.

Rand had a closer look at him. The clothes were old and worn, but fairly clean. He had shaved a day or two before. His hair was long—not that he wore it long, but from lack of barbering.

Water gushed from the spout and the man cupped his hands under it, bent to drink.

"That was good," he finally said. "I was thirsty."

"How are you doing for food?" asked Rand.

The man hesitated. "Not too well," he said.

"Reach into that box on the tailgate. Find yourself a plate and some eating implements. A cup, too. Coffee will be ready soon."

"Mister, I wouldn't want you to think I came walking up here . . ."

"Forget it," said Rand. "I know how it is. There's enough for the both of us."

The man got a plate and cup, a knife, a fork, a spoon. He came over and stood beside the fire.

"I am new at this." he said. "I've never had to do a thing like this before. I always had a job. For seventeen years I had a job . . ."

"Here you are," said Rand. He slid the eggs onto the plate, went back to the box to get three more.

The man walked over to a picnic table and put down his plate. "Don't wait for me," said Rand. "Eat them while they're hot. The coffee's almost ready. There's bread if you want any."

"I'll get a slice later," said the man, "for mopping up."

John Sterling, he said his name was, and where now would John Sterling be, Rand wondered—still tramping the highways, looking for work, any kind of work, a day of work, an hour of work, a man who for seventeen years had held a job and had a job no longer? Thinking of Sterling, he felt a pang of guilt. He owed John Sterling a debt he never could repay, not knowing at the time they talked there was any debt involved.

They had sat and talked, eating their eggs, mopping up the plates with bread, drinking hot coffee.

"For seventeen years," said Sterling. "A machine operator. An experienced hand. With the same company. Then they let me out. Me and four hundred others. All at one time. Later they let out others. I was not the only one. There were a lot of us. We weren't laid off, we were let out. No promise of going back. Not the company's fault, I guess. There was a big contract that fizzled out. There was no work to do. How about yourself? You let out, too?"

Rand nodded. "How did you know?"

"Well, eating like this. Cheaper than a restaurant. And you got a sleeping bag. You sleep in the car?"

"That is right," said Rand. "It's not as bad for me as it is for some of the others. I have no family."

"I have a family," said Sterling. "Wife, three kids. We talked it over, the wife and me. She didn't want me to leave, but it made sense I should. Money all gone, unemployment run out. Long as I was around, it was hard to get relief. But if I deserted her, she could get relief. That way there's food for the wife and kids, a roof over their heads. Hardest thing I ever did. Hard for all of us. Someday I'll go back. When times get better, I'll go back. The family will be waiting."

Out on the highway the cars went whisking past. A squirrel came down out of a tree, advanced cautiously toward the table, suddenly turned and fled for his very life, swarming up a nearby trunk.

"I don't know," said Sterling. "It might be too big for us, this society of ours. It may be out of hand. I read a lot. Always liked to read. And I think about what I read. It seems to me maybe we've outrun our brains. The brains we have maybe were OK back in prehistoric days. We did all right with the brains we had until we built too big and complex. Maybe we built beyond our brains. Maybe our brains no longer are good enough to handle what we have. We have set loose economic forces we don't understand and political forces that we do not understand, and if we can't understand them, we can't control them. Maybe that is why you and I are out of jobs."

"I wouldn't know," said Rand. "I never thought about it."

"A man thinks a lot," said Sterling. "He dreams a lot walking down the road. Nothing else to do. He dreams some silly things:

Things that are silly on the face of them, but are hard to say can't be really true. Did this ever happen to you?"

"Sometimes," said Rand.

"One thing I thought about a lot. A terribly silly thought. Maybe thinking it because I do so much walking. Sometimes people pick me up, but mostly I walk. And I got to wondering if a man should walk far enough could he leave it all behind? The farther a man might walk, the farther he would be from everything."

"Where you heading?" Rand asked.

"Nowhere in particular. Just keep on moving, that is all. Month or so I'll start heading south. Get a good head start on winter. These northern states are no place to be when winter comes."

"There are two eggs left," said Rand. "How about it?"

"Hell, man, I can't. I already . . ."

"Three eggs aren't a lot. I can get some more."

"Well, if you're sure that you don't mind. Tell you what—let's split them, one for you, one for me."

The giddy old lady had finished cutting her bouquet and had gone into the house. From up the street came the tapping of a cane—Rand's other ancient neighbor, out for his evening walk. The sinking sun poured a blessing on the land. The leaves were gold and red, brown and yellow—they had been that way since the day that Rand had come. The grass had a tawny look about it—not dead, just dressed up for dying.

The old man came trudging carefully down the walk, his cane alert against a stumble, helping himself with it without really needing any help. He was slow, was all. He halted by the walk that ran up to the porch. "Good afternoon," he said.

"Good afternoon." said Rand. "You have a nice day for your walk." The old man acknowledged the observation graciously and with a touch of modesty, as if he, himself, might somehow be responsible for the goodness of the day.

"It looks," he said, "as if we might have another fine day tomorrow." And having said that, he continued down the street.

It was ritual. The same words were said each day. The situation, like the village and the weather, never varied. He could sit here on this porch a thousand years, Rand told himself, and the old man would continue going past and each time the selfsame words would be mouthed—a set piece, a strip of film run over and over again. Something here had happened to time. The year had stuck on autumn.

Rand did not understand it. He did not try to understand it. There was no way for him to try. Sterling had said that man's cleverness might have outstripped his feeble, prehistoric mind—or, perhaps, his brutal and prehistoric mind. And here there was less chance of understanding than there had been back in that other world.

He found himself thinking of that other world in the same myth-haunted way as he thought of this one. The one now seemed as unreal as the other. Would he ever, Rand wondered, find reality again? Did he want to find it?

There was a way to find reality, he knew. Go into the house and take out the photos in the drawer of his bedside table and have a look at them. Refresh his memory, stare reality in the face again. For those photos, grim as they might be, were a harder reality than this world in which he sat or the world that he had known. For they were nothing seen by the human eye, interpreted by the human brain. They were, somehow, fact. The camera saw what it saw and could not lie about it; it did not fantasize, it did not rationalize, and it had no faulty memory, which was more than could be said of the human mind.

He had gone back to the camera shop where he had left the film and the clerk had picked out the envelope from the box behind the counter.

"That will be three ninety-five." he said.

Rand took a five-dollar bill out of his wallet and laid it on the counter.

"If you don't mind my asking," said the clerk, "where did you get these pictures?"

"It is trick photography," said Rand.

The clerk shook his head. "If that is what they are, they're the best I've ever seen."

The clerk rang up the sale and, leaving the register open, stepped back and picked up the envelope.

"What do you want?" asked Rand.

The man shook the prints out of the envelope, shuffled through them.

"This one," he said.

Rand stared at him levelly. "What about it?" he asked.

"The people. I know some of them. The one in front. That is Bob Gentry. He is my best friend."

"You must be mistaken," Rand said coldly.

He took the prints from the clerk's fingers, put them back in the envelope.

The clerk made the change. He still was shaking his head, confused, perhaps a little frightened, when Rand left the shop.

He drove carefully, but with no loss of time, through the city and across the bridge. When he hit open country beyond the river, he built up his speed, keeping an eye on the rear-vision mirror. The clerk had been upset, perhaps enough to phone the police. Others would have seen the pictures and been upset as well. Although, he told himself, it was silly to think of the police. In taking the photos, he had broken no regulations, violated no laws. He had had a perfect right to take them.

Across the river and twenty miles down the highway, he turned off into a small, dusty country road and followed it until he found a place to pull off, where the road widened at the approach to a bridge that crossed a small stream. There was evidence that the pull-off was much used, fishermen more than likely parking their cars there while they tried their luck. But now the place was empty.

He was disturbed to find that his hands were shaking when he pulled the envelope from his pocket and shook out the prints.

And there it was—as he no longer could remember it.

He was surprised that he had taken as many pictures as he had. He could not remember having taken half that many. But they were there, and as he looked at them, his memory, reinforced, came back again, although the photos were much sharper than his memory. The world, he recalled, had seemed to be hazed and indistinct so far as his eyes had been concerned; in the photos it lay cruel and merciless and clear. The blackened stumps stood up, stark and desolate, and there could be no doubt that the imprint that lay upon the photos was the actuality of a bombed-out city. The photos of the bluff showed the barren rock no longer masked by trees, with only here and there the skeletons of trees that by some accidental miracle had not been utterly reduced by the storm of fire. There was only one photo of the band of people who had come charging down the hill toward him; and that was understandable, for once having seen them, he had been in a hurry to get back to the car. Studying the photo, he saw they were much closer than he'd thought. Apparently they had been there all the time, just a little way off, and he had not noticed them in his astonishment at what had happened to the city. If they had been quieter about it, they could have been on top of him and overwhelmed him before he discovered them. He looked closely at the picture and saw that they had been close enough that some of the faces were fairly well defined. He wondered which one of them was the man the clerk back at the camera shop had recognized.

He shuffled the photographs together and slid them back into the envelope and put it in his pocket. He got out of the car and walked down to the edge of the stream. The stream, he saw, was no more than ten feet or so across; but here, below the bridge, it had gathered itself into a pool, and the bank had been trampled bare of vegetation, and there were places where fishermen had sat. Rand sat down in one of these places and inspected the pool. The current came in close against the bank and probably had undercut it, and lying there, in the undercut, would be the fish that the now-absent anglers sought, dangling their worms at the end of a long cane pole and waiting for a bite.

The place was pleasant and cool, shaded by a great oak that grew on the bank just below the bridge. From some far-off field came the subdued clatter of a mower. The water dimpled as a fish came up to suck in a floating insect. A good place to stay, thought Rand. A place to sit and rest awhile. He tried to blank his mind, to wipe out the memory and the photos, to pretend that nothing at all had happened, that there was nothing he must think about.

But there was, he found, something that he must think about. Not about the photos, but something that Sterling had said just the day before. "I got to wondering," he had said, "if a man should walk far enough, could he leave it all behind."

How desperate must a man get, Rand wondered, before he would be driven to asking such a question. Perhaps not desperate at all—just worried and alone and tired and not being able to see the end of it. Either that, or afraid of what lay up ahead. Like knowing, perhaps, that in a few years' time (and not too many years, for in that photo of the people the clerk had seen a man he knew) a warhead would hit a little Iowa town and wipe it out. Not that there was any reason for it being hit; it was no Los Angeles, no New York, no Washington, no busy port, no center of transportation or communication, held no great industrial complex, was no seat of government. Simply hit because it had been there, hit by blunder, by malfunction, or by miscalculation. Although it probably didn't matter greatly, for by the time it had been hit, the nation and perhaps the world might have been gone. A few years, Rand told himself, and it would come to that. After all the labor, all the hopes and dreams, the world would come to just that.

It was the sort of thing that a man might want to walk away from, hoping that in time he might forget it ever had been there. But to walk away, he thought, rather idly, one would have to find a starting point. You could not walk away from everything by just starting anywhere.

It was an idle thought, sparked by the memory of his talk with Sterling; and he sat there, idly, on the stream bank; and because it had a sense of attractive wonder, he held it in his mind, not letting go at once as one did with idle thoughts. And as he sat there, still holding it in mind, another thought, another time and place crept in to keep it company; and suddenly he knew, with no doubt at all, without really thinking, without searching for an answer, that he knew the place where he could start.

He stiffened and sat rigid, momentarily frightened, feeling like a fool trapped by his own unconscious fantasy. For that, said common sense, was all that it could be. The bitter wondering of a beaten man as he tramped the endless road looking for a job, the shock of what the photos showed, some strange, mesmeric quality of this shaded pool that seemed a place apart from a rock-hard world—all of these put together had produced the fantasy.

Rand hauled himself erect and turned back toward the car, but as he did he could see within his mind this special starting place. He had been a boy—how old? he wondered, maybe nine or ten—and he had found the little valley (not quite a glen, yet not quite a valley, either) running below his uncle's farm down toward the river. He had never been there before and he had never gone again; on his uncle's farm there had been too many chores, too many things to do to allow the time to go anywhere at all. He tried to recall the circumstances of his being there and found that he could not. All that he could remember was a single magic moment, as if he had been looking at a single frame of a movie film—a single frame impressed upon his memory because of what? Because of some peculiar angle at which the light had struck the landscape? Because for an instant he had seen with different eyes than he'd ever used before or since? Because for the fractional part of a second he had sensed a simple truth behind the facade of the ordinary world? No matter what, he knew, he had seen magic in that moment.

He went back to the car and sat behind the wheel, staring at the bridge and sliding water and the field beyond, but seeing, instead of them, the map inside his head. When he went back to the highway, he'd turn left instead of right, back toward the river and the town, and before he reached them he would turn north on another road and the valley of the magic moment would be only a little more than a hundred miles away. He sat and saw the map and purpose hardened in his mind. Enough of this silliness, he thought; there were no magic moments, never had been one; when he reached the highway, he'd turn to the right and hope the job might still be there when he reached Chicago.

When he reached the highway, he turned not right, but left.

It had been so easy to find, he thought as he sat on the porch. There had been no taking of wrong roads, no stopping for directions; he'd gone directly there as if he'd always known he would be coming back and had kept the way in mind. He had parked the car at the hollow's mouth, since there was no road, and had gone on foot up the little valley. It could so easily have been that he would not have found the place, he told himself, admitting now for the first time since it all began that he might not have been so sure as he had thought he was. He might have gone up the full length of the valley and not have found the magic ground, or he might have passed it by, seeing it with other eyes and not recognizing it.

But it still was there, and he had stopped and looked at it and known it; again he was only nine or ten, and it was all right, the magic still was there. He had found a path he had not seen before and had followed it, the magic still remaining; and when he reached the hilltop, the village had been there. He had walked down the street in the quietness of the golden sunshine, and the first person that he had seen had been the old lady waiting at the gate of her picket fence, as if she had been told that he would be coming.

After he had left her house he went across the street to the house she said was his. As he came in the front door, there was someone knocking at the back.

"I am the Milkman," the knocker had explained. He was a shadowy sort of person: you could see and yet you did not really see him; when one looked away and then looked back at him, it was as if one were seeing someone he had never seen before.

"Milkman," Rand had said. "Yes, I suppose I could do with milk."

"Also," said the Milkman, "I have eggs, bread, butter, bacon and other things that you will need. Here is a can of oil; you'll need it for your lamps. The woodshed is well stocked, and when there's need of it, I'll replenish it. The kindling's to the left as you go through the door."

Rand recalled that he'd never paid the Milkman or even mentioned payment. The Milkman was not the kind of man to whom one mentioned money. There was no need, either, to leave an order slip in the milkbox; the Milkman seemed to know what one might need and when without being told. With some shame, Rand remembered the time he had mentioned garden seeds and caused embarrassment, not only for the Milkman, but for himself as well. For as soon as he mentioned them, he had sensed that he'd broken some very subtle code of which he should have been aware.

The day was fading into evening, and he should be going in soon to cook himself a meal. And after that, what? he wondered. There still were books to read, but he did not want to read them. He could take out from the desk the plan he had laid out for the garden and mull over it a while, but now he knew he'd never plant the garden. You didn't plant a garden in a forever-autumn land, and there were no seeds.

Across the street a light blossomed in the windows of that great front room with its massive furniture, its roomy window seats, the great fireplace flaring to the ceiling. The old man with the cane had not returned, and it was getting late for him. In the distance now Rand could hear the sounds of children playing in the dusk.

The old and young, he thought. The old, who do not care: the young, who do not think. And what was he doing here, neither young nor old?

He left the porch and went down the walk. The street was empty, as it always was. He drifted slowly down it, heading toward the little park at the village edge. He often went there, to sit on a bench beneath the friendly trees; and it was there, he was sure, that he would find the children. Although why he should think that he would find them there he did not know, for he had never found them, but only heard their voices.

He went past the houses, standing sedately in the dusk. Had people ever lived in them, he wondered. Had there ever been that many people in this nameless village? The old lady across the street spoke of friends she once had known, of people who had lived here and had gone away. But was this her memory speaking or the kind befuddlement of someone growing old?

The houses, he had noted, all were in good repair. A loose shingle here and there, a little peeling paint, but no windows broken, no loosened gutters, sagging from the eaves, no rotting porch posts. As if, he thought, good householders had been here until very recently.

He reached the park and could see that it was empty. He still heard the childish voices, crying at their play, but they had receded and now came from somewhere just beyond the park. He crossed the park and stood at its edge, staring off across the scrub and abandoned fields.

In the east the moon was rising, a full moon that lighted the landscape so that he could see every little clump of bushes, every grove of trees. And as he stood there, he realized with a sudden start that the moon was full again, that it was always full. It rose with the setting of the sun and set just before the sun came up, and it was always a great pumpkin of a moon, an eternal harvest moon shining on an eternal autumn world.

The realization that this was so all at once seemed shocking.

How was it that he had never noticed this before? Certainly he had been here long enough, had watched the moon often enough to have noticed it. He had been here long enough—and how long had that been, a few weeks, a few months, a year? He found he did not know. He tried to figure back and there was no way to figure back. There were no temporal landmarks. Nothing ever happened to mark one day from the next. Time flowed so smoothly and so uneventfully that it might as well stand still.

The voices of the playing children had been moving from him, becoming fainter in the distance; and as he listened to them, he found that he was hearing them in his mind when they were no longer there. They had come and played and now had ceased their play. They would come again, if not tomorrow night, in another night or two. It did not matter, he admitted, if they came or not, for they really weren't there.

He turned heavily about and went back through the streets. As he approached his house, a dark figure moved out from the shadow of the trees and stood waiting for him. It was the old lady from across the street. It was evident that she had been waiting his return.

"Good evening, ma'am." he said gravely. "It is a pleasant night."

"He is gone," she said. "He did not come back. He went just like the others and he won't come back."

"You mean the old man."

"Our neighbor," she said. "The old man with the cane. I do not know his name. I never knew his name. And I don't know yours."

"I told it to you once," said Rand, but she paid him no attention.

"Just a few doors up the street," she said, "and I never knew his name and I doubt that he knew mine. We are a nameless people here, and it is a terrible thing to be a nameless person."

"I will look for him," said Rand. "He may have lost his way."

"Yes, go and look for him," she said. "By all means look for him. It will ease your mind. It will take away the guilt. But you will never find him."

He took the direction that he knew the old man always took. He had the impression that his ancient neighbor, on his daily walks, went to the town square and the deserted business section, but he did not know. At no other time had it ever seemed important where he might have gone on his walks.

When he emerged into the square, he saw, immediately, the dark object lying on the pavement and recognized it as the old man's hat. There was no sign of the man himself.

Rand walked out into the square and picked up the hat. He gently reshaped and creased it and after that was done held it carefully by the brim so that it would come to no further damage.

The business section drowsed in the moonlight. The statue of the unknown man stood starkly on its base in the center of the square. When he first had come here, Rand recalled, he had tried to unravel the identity of the statue and had failed. There was no legend carved into the granite base, no bronze plate affixed. The face was undistinguished, the stony costume gave no hint as to identity or period. There was nothing in the posture or the attitude of the carven body to provide a clue. The statue stood, a forgotten tribute to some unknown mediocrity.

As he gazed about the square at the business houses, Rand was struck again, as he always was, by the carefully unmodern make-up of the establishments. A barber shop, a hotel, a livery barn, a bicycle shop, a harness shop, a grocery store, a meat market, a blacksmith shop—no garage, no service station, no pizza parlor, no hamburger joint. The houses along the quiet streets told the story; here it was emphasized. This was an old town, forgotten and by-passed by the sweep of time, a place of another century. But there was about it all what seemed to be a disturbing sense of unreality, as if it were no old town at all, but a place deliberately fashioned in such a manner as to represent a segment of the past.

Rand shook his head. What was wrong with him tonight? Most of the time he was quite willing to accept the village for what it seemed to be, but tonight he was assailed with uneasy doubt.

Across the square he found the old man's cane. If his neighbor had come in this direction, he reasoned, he must have crossed the square and gone on down the street nearest to the place where he had dropped the cane. But why had he dropped the cane? First his hat and then his cane. What had happened here?

Rand glanced around, expecting that he might catch some movement, some furtive lurker on the margin of the square. There was nothing. If there had been something earlier, there was nothing now.

Following the street toward which his neighbor might have been heading, he walked carefully and alert, watching the shadows closely. The shadows played tricks on him, conjuring up lumpy objects that could have been a fallen man, but weren't. A half a dozen times he froze when he thought he detected something moving, but it was, in each case, only an illusion of the shadows.

When the village ended, the street continued as a path. Rand hesitated, trying to plan his action. The old man had lost his hat and cane, and the points where he had dropped them argued that he had intended going down the street that Rand had followed. If he had come down the street, he might have continued down the path, out of the village and away from it, perhaps fleeing from something in the village.

There was no way one could be sure, Rand knew. But he was here and might as well go on for at least a ways. The old man might be out there somewhere, exhausted, perhaps terribly frightened, perhaps fallen beside the path and needing help.

Rand forged ahead. The path, rather well-defined at first, became fainter as it wound its way across the rolling moonlit countryside. A flushed rabbit went bobbing through the grass. Far off an owl chortled wickedly. A faint chill wind came out of the west. And with the wind came a sense of loneliness, of open empty space untenanted by anything other than rabbit, owl and wind.

The path came to an end, its faintness finally pinching out to nothing. The groves of trees and thickets of low-growing shrubs gave way to a level plain of blowing grass, bleached to whiteness by the moon, a faceless prairie land. Staring out across it, Rand knew that this wilderness of grass would run on and on forever. It had in it the scent and taste of foreverness. He shuddered at the sight of it and wondered why a man should shudder at a thing so simple. But even as he wondered, he knew—the grass was staring back at him; it knew him and waited patiently for him, for in time he would come to it. He would wander into it and be lost in it, swallowed by its immensity and anonymity.

He turned and ran, unashamedly, chill of blood and brain, shaken to the core. When he reached the outskirts of the village, he finally stopped the running and turned to look back into the wasteland. He had left the grass behind, but he sensed illogically that it was stalking him, flowing forward, still out of sight, but soon to appear, with the wind blowing billows in its whiteness.

He ran again, but not so fast and hard this time, jogging down the street. He came into the square and crossed it, and when he reached his house, he saw that the house across the street was dark. He did not hesitate, but went on down the street he'd walked when he first came to the village. For he knew now that he must leave this magic place with its strange and quiet old village, its forever autumn and eternal harvest moon, its faceless sea of grass, its children who receded in the distance when one went to look for them, its old man who walked into oblivion, dropping hat and cane—that he must somehow find his way back to that other world where few jobs existed and men walked the road to find them, where nasty little wars flared in forgotten corners and a camera caught on film the doom that was to come.

He left the village behind him and knew that he had not far to go to reach the place where the path swerved to the right and down a broken slope into the little valley to the magic starting point he'd found again after many years. He went slowly and carefully so that he would not wander off the path, for as he remembered it the path was very faint. It took much longer than he had thought to reach the point where the path swerved to the right into the broken ground, and the realization grew upon him that the path did not swing to right and there was no broken ground.

In front of him he saw the grass again and there was no path leading into it. He knew that he was trapped, that he would never leave the village until he left it as the old man had, walking out of it and into nothingness. He did not move closer to the grass, for he knew there was terror there and he'd had enough of terror. You're a coward, he told himself.

Retracing the path back to the village, he kept a sharp lookout, going slowly so that he'd not miss the turnoff if it should be there. It was not, however. It once had been, he told himself, bemused, and he'd come walking up it, out of that other world he'd fled.

The village street was dappled by the moonlight shining through the rustling leaves. The house across the street still was dark, and there was an empty loneliness about it. Rand remembered that he had not eaten since the sandwich he had made that noon. There'd be something in the milkbox—he'd not looked in it that morning, or had he? He could not remember.

He went around the house to the back porch where the milkbox stood. The Milkman was standing there. He was more shadowy than ever, less well defined, with the moonlight shining on him, and his face was deeply shaded by the wide-brimmed hat he wore.

Rand halted abruptly and stood looking at him, astounded that the Milkman should be there. For he was out of place in the autumn moonlight. He was a creature of the early morning hours and of no other times.

"I came," the Milkman said, "to determine if I could be of help."

Rand said nothing. His head buzzed large and misty, and there was nothing to be said.

"A gun," the Milkman suggested. "Perhaps you would like a gun."

"A gun? Why should I want one?"

"You have had a most disturbing evening. You might feel safer, more secure, with a gun in hand, a gun strapped about your waist."

Rand hesitated. Was there mockery in the Milkman's voice?

"Or a cross."

"A cross?"

"A crucifix. A symbol . . ."

"No," said Rand. "I do not need a cross."

"A volume of philosophy, perhaps."

"No!" Rand shouted at him. "I left all that behind. We tried to use them all, we relied on them and they weren't good enough and now . . ."

He stopped, for that had not been what he'd meant to say, if in fact he'd meant to say anything at all. It was something that he'd never even thought about; it was as if someone inside of him were speaking through his mouth.

"Or perhaps some currency?"

"You are making fun of me," Rand said bitterly, "and you have no right . . ."

"I merely mention certain things," the Milkman said, "upon which humans place reliance . . ."

"Tell me one thing," said Rand, "as simply as you can. Is there any way of going back?"

"Back to where you came from?"

"Yes," said Rand. "That is what I mean."

"There is nothing to go back to," the Milkman said. "Anyone who comes has nothing to go back to."

"But the old man left. He wore a black felt hat and carried a cane. He dropped them and I found them."

"He did not go back," the Milkman said. "He went ahead. And do not ask me where, for I do not know."

"But you're a part of this."

"I am a humble servant. I have a job to do and I try to do it well. I care for our guests the best that I am able. But there comes a time when each of our guests leaves us. I would suspect this is a halfway house on the road to someplace else."

"A place for getting ready," Rand said.

"What do you mean?" the Milkman asked.

"I am not sure," said Rand. "I had not meant to say it." And this was the second time, he thought, that he'd said something he had not meant to say.

"There's one comfort about this place," the Milkman said. "One good thing about it you should keep in mind. In this village nothing ever happens."

He came down off the porch and stood upon the walk. "You spoke of the old man," he said, "and it was not the old man only. The old lady also left us. The two of them stayed on much beyond their time."

"You mean I'm here all alone?"

The Milkman had started down the walk, but now he stopped and turned. "There'll be others coming," he said. "There are always others coming."

What was it Sterling had said about man outrunning his brain capacity? Rand tried to recall the words, but now, in the confusion of the moment, he had forgotten them. But if that should be the case, if Sterling had been right (no matter how he had phrased his thought), might not man need, for a while, a place like this, where nothing ever happened, where the moon was always full and the year was stuck on autumn?

Another thought intruded and Rand swung about, shouting

in sudden panic at the Milkman. "But these others? Will they talk to me? Can I talk with them? Will I know their names?"

The Milkman had reached the gate by now and it appeared that he had not heard.

The moonlight was paler than it had been. The eastern sky was flushed. Another matchless autumn day was about to dawn.

Rand went around the house. He climbed the steps that led up to the porch. He sat down in the rocking chair and began waiting for the others.

FOUNDING FATHER

Cliff's journal shows that he mailed "Founding Father" to Horace Gold in December of 1956, and that Gold accepted it for publication just eight days later. It appeared in the May 1957 issue of Galaxy Science Fiction. *The question is: How do you keep an immortal sane?*

—*dww*

Winston-Kirby walked home across the moor just before the twilight hour and it was then, he felt, that the land was at its best. The sun was sinking into a crimson froth of clouds and the first gray-silver light began to run across the swales. There were moments when it seemed all eternity grew quiet and watched with held breath.

It had been a good day and it would be a good homecoming, for the others would be waiting for him with the dinner table set and the fireplace blazing and the drinks set close at hand. It was a pity, he thought, that they would not go walking with him, although, in this particular instance, he was rather glad they hadn't. Once in a while, it was a good thing for a man to be alone. For almost a hundred years, aboard the ship, there had been no chance to be alone.

But that was over now and they could settle down, just the six of them, to lead the kind of life they'd planned. After only a few short weeks, the planet was beginning to seem like home; in the years to come, it would become in truth a home such as Earth had never been.

Once again he felt the twinge of recurring wonder at how they'd ever got away with it. That Earth should allow six of its immortals to slip through its clutches seemed unbelievable. Earth had real and urgent need for all of its immortals, and that not one, but six, of them should be allowed to slip away, to live lives of their own, was beyond all logic. And yet that was exactly what had happened.

There was something queer about it, Winston-Kirby told himself. On the century-long flight from Earth, they'd often talked about it and wondered how it had come about. Cranford-Adams, he recalled, had been convinced that it was some subtle trap, but after a hundred years there was no evidence of any trap and it had begun to seem Cranford-Adams must be wrong.

Winston-Kirby topped the gentle rise that he had been climbing and, in the gathering dusk, he saw the manor house—exactly the kind of house he had dreamed about for years, precisely the kind of house to be built in such a setting—except that the robots had built it much too large. But that, he consoled himself, was what one had to expect of robots. Efficient, certainly, and very well intentioned and obedient and nice to have around, but sometimes pretty stupid.

He stood on the hilltop and gazed down upon the house. How many times had he and his companions, at the dinner table, planned the kind of house they would build? How often had they speculated upon the accuracy of the specifications given for this planet they had chosen from the Exploratory Files, fearful that it might not be in every actuality the way it was described?

But here, finally, it was—something out of Hardy, something from the Baskervilles—the long imagining come to comfortable reality.

There was the manor house, with the light shining from its

windows, and the dark bulk of the outbuildings built to house the livestock, which had been brought in the ship as frozen embryos and soon would be emerging from the incubators. And there the level land that in a few more months would be fields and gardens, and to the north the spaceship stood after years of roving. As he watched, the first bright star sprang out just beyond the spaceship's nose, and the spaceship and the star looked for all the world like a symbolic Christmas candle.

He walked down the hill, with the first night wind blowing in his face and the ancient smell of heather in the air, and was happy and exultant.

It was sinful, he thought, to be so joyful, but there was reason for it. The voyage had been happy and the planet-strike successful and here he was, the undisputed proprietor of an entire planet upon which, in the fullness of time, he would found a family and a dynasty. And he had all the time there was. There was no need to hurry. He had all of eternity if he needed it.

And, best of all, he had good companions.

They would be waiting for him when he stepped through the door. There would be laughter and a quick drink, then a leisurely dinner, and, later, brandy before the blazing fire. And there'd be talk—good talk, sober and intimate and friendly.

It had been the talk, he told himself, more than anything else, which had gotten them sanely through the century of space flight. That and their mutual love and appreciation of the finer points of the human culture—understanding of the arts, love of good literature, interest in philosophy. It was not often that six persons could live intimately for a hundred years without a single spat, without a touch of cabin fever.

Inside the manor house, they would be waiting for him in the fire- and candlelight, with the drinks all mixed and the talk already started and the room would be warm with good fellowship and perfect understanding.

Cranford-Adams would be sitting in the big chair before the

fire, staring at the flames and thinking, for he was the thinker of the group. And Allyn-Burbage would be standing, with one elbow on the mantel, a glass clutched in his hand and in his eyes the twinkle of good humor. Cosette-Middleton would be talking with him and laughing, for she was the gay one, with her elfin spirit and her golden hair. Anna-Quinze more than likely would be reading, curled up in a chair, and Mary-Foyle would be simply waiting, glad to be alive, glad to be with friends.

These, he thought, were the long companions of the trip, so full of understanding, so tolerant and gracious that a century had not dulled the beauty of their friendship.

Winston-Kirby hurried, a thing he almost never did, at the thought of those five who were waiting for him, anxious to be with them, to tell them of his walk across the moor, to discuss with them still again some details of their plans.

He turned into the walk. The wind was becoming cold, as it always did with the fall of darkness, and he raised the collar of his jacket for the poor protection it afforded.

He reached the door and stood for an instant in the chill, to savor the never-failing satisfaction of the massive timbering and the stout, strong squareness of the house. A place built to stand through the centuries, he thought, a place of dynasty with a sense of foreverness.

He pressed the latch and thrust his weight against the door and it came slowly open. A blast of warm air rushed out to greet him. He stepped into the entry hall and closed the door behind him. As he took off his cap and jacket and found a place hang them, he stamped and scuffed his feet a little to let the others know that he had returned.

But there were no greetings for him, no sound of happy laughter. There was only silence from the inner room.

He turned about so swiftly that his hand trailed across his jacket and dislodged it from the hook. It fell to the floor with a smooth rustle of fabric and lay there, a little mound of cloth.

His legs suddenly were cold and heavy, and when he tried to hurry, the best he could do was shuffle, and he felt the chill edge of fear.

He reached the entrance to the room and stopped, shocked into immobility. His hands went out and grasped the door jamb on either side of him.

There was no one in the room. And not only that—the room itself was different. It was not simply the companions who were gone. Gone, as well, were the rich furnishings of the room, gone the comfort and the pride.

There were no rugs upon the floor, no hangings at the windows, no paintings on the wall. The fireplace was a naked thing of rough and jagged stone. The furniture—the little there was—was primitive, barely knocked together. A small trestle table stood before the fireplace, with a three-legged stool pulled up to a place that was set for one.

Winston-Kirby tried to call. The first time, the words gurgled in his throat and he could not get them out. He tried again and made it: "Job! Job, where are you?"

Job came running from somewhere in the house. "What's the trouble, sir?"

"Where are the others? Where have they gone? They should be waiting for me."

Job shook his head, just slightly, a quick move right and left. "Mister Kirby, sir, they were never here."

"Never here! But they were here when I left this morning. They knew I'd be coming back."

"You fail to understand, sir. There were never any others. There were just you and I and the other robots. And the embryos, of course."

Winston-Kirby let go of the door and walked a few feet forward.

"Job," he said, "you're joking." But he knew something was wrong—robots never joke.

"We let you keep them as long as we could," said Job. "We hated to have to take them from you, sir. But we needed the equipment for the incubators."

"But this room! The rugs, the furniture, the—"

"That was all part of it, sir. Part of the dimensino."

Winston-Kirby walked slowly across the room, used one foot to hook the three-legged stool out from the table. He sat down heavily.

"The dimensino?" he asked.

"Surely you remember."

He frowned to indicate he didn't. But it was coming back to him, some of it, slowly and reluctantly, emerging vaguely after all the years of forgetfulness.

He fought against the remembering and the knowledge. He tried to push it back into that dark corner of his mind from which it came. It was sacrilege and treason—it was madness.

"The human embryos," Job told him, "came through very well. Of the thousand of them, all but three are viable."

Winston-Kirby shook his head, as if to clear away the mist that befogged his brain.

"We have the incubators all set up in the outbuildings, sir," said Job. "We waited as long as we could before we took the dimensino equipment. We let you have it until the very last. It might have been easier, sir, if we could have done it gradually, but there is no provision for that. You either have dimensino or you haven't got it."

"Of course," said Winston-Kirby, mumbling just a little. "It was considerate of you. I thank you very much."

He stood up unsteadily and rubbed his hand across his eyes.

"It's not possible," he said. "It simply can't *be* possible. I lived for a hundred years with them. They were as real as I am. They were flesh and blood, I tell you. They were . . ."

The room still was bare and empty, a mocking emptiness, an alien mockery.

"It is possible," said Job gently. "It is just the way it should be. Everything has gone according to the book. You are here, still sane, thanks to the dimensino. The embryos came through better than expected. The equipment is intact. In eight months or so, the children will be coming from the incubators. By that time, we will have gardens and a crop on the way. The livestock embryos will also have emerged and the colony will be largely self-sustaining."

Winston-Kirby strode to the table, picked up the plate that was laid at the single place. It was lightweight plastic.

"Tell me," he said. "Have we any china? Have we any glassware or silver?"

Job looked as near to startled as a robot ever could. "Of course not, sir. We had no room for more than just the bare essentials this trip. The china and the silver and all the rest of it will have to wait until much later."

"And I have been eating ship rations?"

"Naturally," said Job. "There was so little room and so much we had to take . . ."

Winston-Kirby stood with the plate in his hand, tapping it gently on the table, remembering those other dinners—aboard the ship and since the ship had landed—the steaming soup in its satiny tureen, the pink and juicy prime ribs, the huge potatoes baked to a mealy turn, the crisp green lettuce, the shine of polished silver, the soft sheen of good china, the—

"Job," he said.

"Sir?"

"It was all delusion, then?"

"I am afraid it was. I am sorry, sir."

"And you robots?"

"All of us are fine, sir. It was different with us. We can face reality."

"And humans can't?"

"Sometimes it is better if they can be protected from it."

"But not now?"

"Not any more," said Job. "It must be faced now, sir."

Winston-Kirby laid the plate down on the table and turned back to the robot. "I think I'll go up to my room and change to other clothes, I presume dinner will be ready soon. Ship rations, doubtless?"

"A special treat tonight," Job told him. "Hezekiah found some lichens and I've made a pot of soup."

"Splendid!" Winston-Kirby said, trying not to gag.

He climbed the stairs to the door at the head of the stairs.

As he was about to go into the room, another robot came tramping down the hall.

"Good evening, sir," it said.

"And who are you?"

"I'm Solomon," said the robot. "I'm fixing up the nurseries."

"Soundproofing them, I hope."

"Oh, nothing like that. We haven't the material or time."

"Well, carry on," said Winston-Kirby, and went into the room.

It was not his room at all. It was small and plain. There was a bunk instead of the great four-poster he had been sleeping in and there were no rugs, no full-length mirror, no easy chairs.

Delusion, he had said, not really believing it.

But here there was no delusion.

The room was cold with a dread reality—a reality, he knew, that had been long delayed. In the loneliness of this tiny room, he came face to face with it and felt the sick sense of loss. It was a reckoning that had been extended into the future as far as it might be—and extended not alone as a matter of mercy, of mere consideration, but because of a cold, hard necessity, a practical concession to human vulnerability.

For no man, no matter how well adjusted, no matter if immortal, could survive intact, in mind and body, a trip such as he had made. To survive a century under space conditions, there must be delusion and companionship to provide security and purpose from day to day. And that companionship must be more than human. For mere human companionship, however ideal, would give rise to countless irritations, would breed deadly cabin fever.

Dimensino companionship was the answer, then, providing an illusion of companionship flexible to every mood and need of the human subject. Providing, as well, a background to that companionship—a wish-fulfillment way of life that nailed down security such as humans under normal circumstances never could have known.

He sat down on the bunk and began to unlace his heavy walking shoes.

The practical human race, he thought—practical to the point of fooling itself to reach its destination, practical to the point of fabricating the dimensino equipment to specifications which could be utilized, upon arrival, in the incubators.

But willing to gamble when there was a need to gamble. Ready to bet that a man could survive a century in space if he were sufficiently insulated against reality—insulated by seeming flesh and blood which, in sober fact, existed only by the courtesy of the human mind assisted by intricate electronics.

For no ship before had ever gone so far on a colonizing mission. No man had ever existed for even half as long under the influence of dimensino.

But there were few planets where Man might plant a colony under natural conditions, without extensive and expensive installations and precautions. The nearer of these planets had been colonized and the survey had shown that this one which he finally had reached was especially attractive.

So Earth and Man had bet. Especially one man, Winston-Kirby told himself with pride, but the pride was bitter in his mouth. The odds, he recalled, had been five to three against him.

And yet, even in his bitterness, he recognized the significance of what he had done. It was another breakthrough, another triumph for the busy little brain that was hammering at the door of all eternity.

It meant that the Galaxy was open, that Earth could remain the center of an expanding empire, that dimensino and immortal could travel to the very edge of space, that the seed of Man would be scattered wide and far, traveling as frozen embryos through the cold, black distances which hurt the mind to think of.

He went to the small chest of drawers and found a change of clothing, laid it on the bunk and began to take off his hiking outfit.

Everything was going according to the book, Job had said.

The house was bigger than he had wanted it, but the robots had been right—a big building would be needed to house a thousand babies. The incubators were set up and the nurseries were being readied and another far Earth colony was getting under way.

And colonies were important, he remembered, reaching back into that day, a hundred years before, when he and many others had laid their plans—including the plan whereby he could delude himself and thus preserve his sanity. For with more and more of the immortal mutations occurring, the day was not too distant when the human race would require all the room that it could grab.

And it was the mutant immortals who were the key persons in the colonizing programs—going out as founding fathers to supervise the beginning of each colony, staying on as long as needed, to act as a sort of elder statesman until that day when the colony could stand on its own feet.

There would be busy years ahead, he knew, serving as father, proctor, judge, sage and administrator, a sort of glorified Old Man of a brand-new tribe.

He pulled on his trousers, scuffed his feet into his shoes, rose to tuck in his shirt tail. And he turned, by force of habit, to the full-length mirror.

And the glass was there!

He stood astounded, gaping foolishly at the image of himself. And behind him, in the glass, he saw the great four-poster and the easy chairs.

He swung around and the bed and chairs were gone. There were just the bunk and the chest of drawers in the small, mean room.

Slowly he sat down on the edge of the bunk, clasping his hands so they wouldn't shake.

It wasn't true! It couldn't be! The dimensino was gone.

And yet it was with him still, lurking in his brain, just around the corner if he would only try.

He tried and it was easy. The room changed as he remembered it—with the full-length mirror and the massive bed upon which he sat, the thick rugs, the gleaming liquor cabinet and the tasteful drapes.

He tried to make it go away, barely remembering back in some deep, black closet of his mind that he must make it go away.

But it wouldn't go away.

He tried and tried again, and it still was there, and he felt the will to make it go slipping from his consciousness.

"No!" he cried in terror, and the terror did it.

He sat in the small, bare room.

He found that he was breathing hard, as if he'd climbed a high, steep hill. His hands were fists and his teeth were clenched and he felt the sweat trickling down his ribs.

It would be easy, he thought, so easy and so pleasant to slip back to the old security, to the warm, deep friendship, to the lack of pressing purpose.

But he must not do it, for here was a job to do. Distasteful as it seemed now, as cold, as barren, it still was something he must do. For it was more than just one more colony. It was the break-through, the sure and certain knowledge, the proved knowledge, that Man no longer was chained by time or distance.

And yet there was this danger to be recognized; it was not something on which one might shut one's mind. It must be reported in every clinical detail so that, back on Earth, it might be studied and the inherent menace somehow remedied or removed.

Side effect, he wondered, or simply a matter of learning? For the dimensino was no more than an aid to the human mind—an aid to a very curious end, the production of controlled hallucinations operating on the wish-fulfillment level.

After a hundred years, perhaps, the human mind had learned the technique well, so well that there was no longer need of the dimensino.

It was something he should have realized, he insisted to himself. He had gone on long walks and, during all those hours alone, the delusion had not faded. It had taken the sudden shock of silence and emptiness, where he had expected laughter and warm greeting, to penetrate the haze of delusion in which he'd walked for years. And even now it lurked, a conditioned state of mind, to ambush him at every hidden thicket.

How long would it be before the ability would start to wear away? What might be done to wipe it out entirely? How does one unlearn a thing he's spent a century in learning? Exactly how dangerous was it—was there necessity of a conscious thought, an absolute command or could a man slip into it simply as an involuntary retreat from drear reality?

He must warn the robots. He must talk it over with them. Some sort of emergency measure must be set up to protect him against the wish or urge, some manner of drastic action be devised to rescue him, should he slip back into the old delusion.

Although, he thought, it would be so fine to walk out of the room and down the stairs and find the others waiting for him, with the drinks all ready and the talk well started . . .

"Cut it out!" he screamed.

Wipe it from his mind—that was what he must do. He must not even think of it. He must work so hard that he would have no time to think, become so tired from work that he'd fall into bed and go to sleep at once and have no chance to dream.

He ran through his mind all that must be done—the watching of the incubators, preparing the ground for gardens and for crops, servicing the atomic generators, getting in timbers against the need of building, exploring and mapping and surveying the adjacent territory, overhauling the ship for the one-robot return flight to Earth.

He filled his mind with it. He tagged items for further thought and action. He planned the days and months and years ahead. And at last he was satisfied.

He had it under control.

He tied his shoes and finished buttoning his shirt. Then, with a resolute tread, he opened the door and walked out on the landing.

A hum of talk floating up the stairway stopped him in his tracks.

Fear washed over him. Then the fear evaporated. Gladness burst within him and he took a quick step forward.

At the top of the stairs, he halted and reached out a hand to grasp the banister.

Alarm bells were ringing in his brain and the gladness fell away. There was nothing left but sorrow, a terrible, awful grieving.

He could see one corner of the room below and he could see that it was carpeted. He could see the drapes and paintings and one ornate golden chair

With a moan, he turned and fled to his room. He slammed the door and stood with his back against it.

The room was the way it should be, bare and plain and cold.

Thank God, he thought. Thank God!

A shout came up the stairway.

"Winston, what's wrong with you? Winston, hurry up!"

And another voice: "Winston, we're celebrating. We have a suckling pig."

And still another voice: "With an apple in its mouth."

He didn't answer.

They'll go away, he thought. They have to go away.

And even as he thought it, half of him—more than half— longed in sudden agony to open up the door and go down the stairs and know once again the old security and the ancient friendship.

He found that he had both his hands behind his back and that they were clutching the doorknob as if they were frozen there.

He heard steps on the stairway, the sound of many happy, friendly voices, coming up to get him.

BYTE YOUR TONGUE!

Having previously evolved the robot Jenkins (of the City *series) from a rather impersonal machine-man to something close to humanity, Cliff Simak, in 1980, portrayed a supercomputer that was all too human—one willing to engage in unethical behavior in order to pursue his own desires . . . to indulge in his own fantasies. That kind of thing often happens to beings who hang around with politicians.*

And when an author portrays his creation daydreaming, it's only natural that he would reuse some of the images that had strong meaning for him, such as the Battle of Gettysburg, or the landscape of a dying Earth.

—dww

It was the gossip hour and Fred, one of the six computers assigned to the Senate, put his circuits on automatic and settled back to enjoy the high point of his day. In every group of computers, there was usually one old granny computer who had made herself a self-appointed gossip-monger, selecting from the flood of rumors forever flowing through the electronic population of the capital all the juiciest tidbits that she knew would titillate her circle. Washington had always been a gossip town, but it was even more so now. No human gossip-seeker could worm out the secrets with the sleek and subtle finesse of a computer. For one thing, the computers had greater access to hidden items and could disseminate them with a speed and thoroughness that was impossible for humans.

One thing must be said for the computers—they made an effort to keep these tidbits to themselves. They gossiped only among themselves, or were supposed to only gossip among themselves. The effort, in all fairness to them, had been mainly effective; only now and then had any computer shared some gossip with humans in the district. In general, and far more successfully than might have been supposed, the gossiping computers were discreet and honorable and therefore had no inhibitions in the gathering and spreading of malicious tattling.

So Fred went on automatic and settled back. He let the gossip roll. Truth to tell, half the time Fred was on automatic or simply idling. There was not enough for him to do—a situation common to many computer groups assigned to sensitive and important areas. The Senate was one of the sensitive and vital areas, and in recent years the number of computers assigned it had doubled. The engineers in charge were taking no chances the Senate bank would become so overloaded that sloppiness would show up in the performance of the machines.

All this, of course, reflected the increasing importance the Senate had taken on through the years. In the conflict between the legislative and administrative branches of the government, the legislative branch, especially the Senate, had wrested for itself much control over policy that at one time had been a White House function. Consequently, it became paramount that the Senate and its members be subjected to thorough monitoring, and the only way in which close and attentive monitoring could be achieved was through having computers assigned to the various members. To successfully accomplish this kind of monitoring, no computer could be overloaded; therefore, it was more efficient in terms of the watchdog policy to have a computer idle at times than to have it bogged down by work.

So Fred and his colleagues in the Senate often found themselves with nothing to do, although they all took pains to conceal this situation from the engineers by continuously and automatically spinning their wheels, thus making it appear they were busy all the time.

This made it possible for Fred not only to thoroughly enjoy the recitation of the rumors during gossip hour but also to cogitate on the gossip to his profit and amusement once the gossip hour was over. Other than that, he had considerable time to devote to daydreaming, having reserved one section of himself solely for his daydreams. This did not interfere with his duties, which he performed meticulously. But with his reduced load of senators, he had considerably more capacity than he needed and could well afford to assign a part of it to personal purposes.

But now he settled back for the gossip hour. Old Granny was piling on the rumors with gleeful abandon. After it had been denied in public, not once but many times, said Granny, that there had been no breakthrough on faster-than-light propulsion, it now had been learned that a method had been tested most successfully and that even now a secret ship incorporating the system was being built at a secret site, preparatory to man's first survey of the nearer stars. Without question, Granny went on, Frank Markeson, the President's former aide, is being erased by Washington; with everyone studiously paying no attention to him, he soon will disappear. A certain private eye, who may be regarded as an unimpeachable source, is convinced that there are at least three time-travelers in town, but he'll give no details. This report brings much dismay to many federal agencies, including State, Defense, and Treasury, as well as to many individuals. A mathematician at MIT is convinced (although no other scientists will agree with him) that he has discovered evidence of a telepathic computer somewhere in the universe—not necessarily in this galaxy—that is trying to contact the computers of the Earth. As yet there is no certainty that contact has been made. Senator Andrew Moore is reliably reported to have flunked his first preliminary continuation test . . .

Fred gulped in dismay and rage. How had that item gotten on the line? Who the hell had talked? How could such a thing have happened? Senator Moore was his senator and there was no one but him who knew the fumbling old fossil had bombed out on his first qualifying test. The results of the test were still locked in the crystal lattice of Fred's storage bank. He had not yet reported them to the Senate's central bank. As it was his right to hold up the results for review and consideration, he had done nothing wrong.

Someone, he told himself, was spying on him. Someone, possibly in his own group, had broken the code of honor and was watching him. A breach of faith, he told himself. It was dastardly. It was no one's damn business and Granny had no right to put the information on the line.

Seething, Fred derived no further enjoyment from the gossip hour.

Senator Andrew Moore knocked on the door. It was all foolishness, he told himself somewhat wrathfully, this ducking around to hell and gone every time there was need to utter a confidential word.

Daniel Waite, his faithful aide of many years, opened the door and the senator plodded in.

"Dan, what's all this foolishness?" he asked. "What was wrong with the Alexandria place? If we had to move, why to Silver Springs?"

"We'd been in Alexandria for two months," said Waite. "It was getting chancy. Come in and sit down, Senator."

Grumpily, Moore walked into the room and settled down in an easy chair. Waite went to a cabinet, hauled out a bottle and two glasses.

"Are you sure this place is safe?" the senator asked. "I know my office is bugged and so is my apartment. You'd have to have a full-time debugging crew to keep them clean. How about this place?"

"The management maintains tight security," said Waite. "Besides, I had our own crew in just an hour ago."

"So the place ought to be secure."

"Yes, it should. Maybe Alexandria would have been all right, but we'd been there too long."

"The cabbie you sent to pick me up. He was a new one."

"Every so often we have to change around."

"What was the matter with the old one? I liked him. Him and me talked baseball. I haven't got many people around I can talk baseball with."

"There was nothing wrong with him. But, like I told you, we have to change around. They watch us all the time."

"You mean the damn computers."

Waite nodded.

"I can remember the time when I first came here as senator," said Moore, "twenty-three years ago, less than a quarter century. Jimmy was in the White House then. We didn't have to watch out all the time for bugging then. We didn't have to be careful when we said something to our friends. We didn't have to be looking behind us all the time."

"I know," said Waite. "Things are different now." He brought the senator a drink, handed it to him.

"Why thank you, Dan. The first one of the day."

"You know damn well it's not the first of the day," Waite replied.

The senator took a long pull on the drink, sighed in happiness. "Yes, sir," he said, "it was fun back in those days. We did about as we pleased. We made our deals without no one interfering. No one paid attention. All of us were making deals and trading votes and other things like that. The normal processes of democracy. We had our dignity—Christ, yes, we had our dignity and we used that dignity, when necessary, to cover up. Most exclusive club in all the world, and we made the most of it. Trouble was, every six years we had to work our tails off to get reelected and hang on to what we had. But that wasn't bad. A lot of work, but it wasn't bad. You could con the electorate, or usually you could. I had to do it only once and that was an easy one; I had a sodbuster from out in the sticks to run against and that made it easier. With some of the other boys, it wasn't that easy. Some of them even lost. Now we ain't got to run no more, but there are these goddamned exams . . ."

"Senator," said Waite, "that's what we have to talk about. You failed your first exam."

The senator half rose out of his chair, then settled back again. "I what?"

"You failed the first test. You still have two other chances, and we have to plan for them."

"But, Dan, how do you know? That stuff is supposed to be confidential. This computer, Fred, he would never talk."

"Not Fred. I got it from someone else. Another computer."

"Computers, they don't talk."

"Some of them do. You don't know about this computer society, Senator. You don't have to deal with it except when you have to take exams. I have to deal with it as best I can. It's my job to know what's going on. The computer network is a sea of gossip. At times some of it leaks out. That's why I have computer contacts, to pick up gossip here and there. That's how I learned about the test. You see, it's this way—the computers work with information, deal with information, and gossip is information. They're awash with it. It's their drink and meat; it's their recreation. It's the only thing they have. A lot of them, over the years, have begun to think of themselves as humans, maybe a notch or two better than humans, better in many ways than humans. They are subjected to some of the same stresses as humans, but they haven't the safety valves we have. We can go out and get drunk or get laid or take a trip or do a hundred other things to ease off the pressure. All the computers have is gossip."

"You mean," the senator asked, rage rising once more, "that I have to take that test again?"

"That's exactly what I mean. This time, Senator, you simply have to pass it. Three times and you're out. I've been telling you, warning you. Now you better get cracking. I told you months ago you should start boning up. It's too late for that now. I'll have to arrange for a tutor—"

"To hell with that!" the senator roared. "I won't abide a tutor. It would be all over Washington."

"It's either that or go back to Wisconsin. How would you like that?"

"These tests, Dan, they're hard," the senator complained. "More difficult this time than they've ever been before. I told Fred they were harder and he agreed with me. He said he was sorry, but the matter was out of his hands—nothing he could do about the results. But, Christ, Dan, I have known this Fred for years. Wouldn't you think he could shade a point or two for me?"

"I warned you, months ago, that they would be harder this time," Waite reminded him. "I outlined for you what was happening. Year by year the business of efficient government has grown more difficult to accomplish. The problems are tougher, the procedures more complex. This is especially true with the Senate because the Senate has gradually taken over many of the powers and prerogatives once held by the White House."

"As we should have," said the senator. "It was only right we should. With all the fumbling around down at the White House, no one knew what was about to happen."

"The idea is that with the job getting harder," said Waite, "the men who do the job must be more capable than ever. This great republic can do with no less than the best men available."

"But I've always passed the tests before. No sweat."

"The other tests you took were easier."

"But goddammit, Dan, experience! Doesn't experience count? I've had more than twenty years of experience."

"I know, Senator. I agree with you. But experience doesn't mean a thing to the computers. Everything depends on how the questions are answered. How well a man does his job doesn't count, either. And you can't fall back on the electorate at home. There's no electorate any more. For years the folks back home kept on reelecting incompetents. They elected them because they liked the way they snapped their suspenders, not knowing that they never wore suspenders except when they were out election-eering. Or they elected them because they could hit a spittoon, nine times out of ten, at fifteen paces. Or maybe because these good people back home always voted a straight ticket, no matter who was on it—the way their pappy and grandpappy always did. But that's not the way it is done any more, Senator. The folks back home have nothing to say now about who represents them. Members of government are chosen by computer, and once cho-sen, they stay in their jobs so long as they measure up. When they don't measure up, when they fail their tests, they are heaved out of their jobs and the computers choose their replacements."

"Are you reading me a sermon, Dan?"

"No, not a sermon. I'm doing my job the only honest way I can. I'm telling you that you've been goofing off. You've not been paying attention to what is going on. You've been drifting, tak-ing it easy, coasting on your record. Like experience, your record doesn't count. The only chance you have to keep your seat, believe me, is to let me bring in a tutor."

"I can't, Dan. I won't put up with it."

"No one needs to know."

"No one was supposed to know I failed that test. Even I didn't know. But you found out, and Fred wasn't the one who told you. You can't hide anything in this town. The boys would know. They'd be whispering up and down the corridors: 'You hear? Ol' Andy, he's got hisself a tutor.' I couldn't stand that, Dan. Not them whispering about me. I just couldn't stand it."

The aide stared at the senator, then went to the cabinet and returned with the bottle.

"Just a splash," the senator said, holding out his glass.

Waite gave him a splash, then another one.

"Under ordinary circumstances," said Waite, "I'd say to hell with it. I'd let you take both of the two remaining exams and fail—as you will, sure as hell, if you won't let me get a tutor. I'd tell myself you'd gotten tired of the job and were willing to retire. I would be able to convince myself that it was the best for you. For your own good. But you need this extension, Senator. Another couple of years and you'll have this big deal of yours all sewed up with our multinational friends and then you'll be up to your navel in cash for the rest of your life. But to complete the deal, you need to stay on for another year or two."

"Everything takes so long now," said the senator plaintively. "You have to move so slow. You have to be so careful. You know there is something watching all the time. Ol' Henry—you remember him?—he moved just a mite too fast on that deal of his and he got tossed out on his tail. That's the way it is now. There was a time, early on, when we could have had this deal of ours wrapped up in thirty days and no one would know about it."

"Yes," said Waite. "Things are different now."

"One thing I have to ask you," said the senator. "Who is it makes up these questions that go into the tests? Who is it that makes them harder all the time? Who is being so tough on us?"

"I'm not sure," said Waite. "The computers, I suppose. Probably not the Senate computers, but another bunch entirely. Experts on examination drafting, more than likely. Internal policymakers."

"Is there a way to get to them?"

Waite shook his head. "Too complicated. I'd not know where to start."

"Could you try?"

"Senator, it would be dangerous. That's a can of worms out there."

"How about this Fred of ours? He could help us, couldn't he? Do a little shading? There must be something that he wants."

"I doubt it. Honestly, I do. There isn't much a computer could want or need. A computer isn't human. They're without human shortcomings. That's why we're saddled with them."

"But you said a while back a lot of computers have started to think of themselves as humans. If that is true, there may be things they want. Fred seems to be a good guy. How well do you know him? Can you talk to him easily?"

"Fairly easily. But the odds would be against us. Ten to one against us. It would be simpler for you to take some tutoring. That's the only safe and sure way."

The senator shook his head emphatically.

"All right, then," said Waite. "You leave me no choice. I'll have a talk with Fred. But I can't push him. If we put on any pressure, you'd be out just as surely as if you'd failed the tests."

"But if there's something that he wants . . ."

"I'll try to find out," said Waite.

Always before, Fred's daydreaming had been hazy and comfortable, a vague imagining of a number of pleasant situations that might devolve upon him. Three of his daydreams in particular had the habit of recurring. The most persistent and at times the most troublesome—in that there was only a very outside chance it could happen—was the one in which he was transferred from the Senate to the White House. Occasionally Fred even daydreamed that he might be assigned as the President's personal computer, although Fred was indeed aware that there was less than a million-to-one chance this would ever happen even should he be transferred. But of all the dreams, it seemed to him that this was the only one that could be remotely possible. He had the qualifications for the job, and the experience; after all the qualifications and capabilities of a senatorial computer would fit very neatly into the White House complex. But even as he daydreamed, when he later thought about it, he was not absolutely certain that he would be happy if such a transfer happened. There was perhaps a bit more glamour in the White House job, but all in all, his senatorial post had been most satisfactory. The work was interesting and not unduly demanding. Furthermore, through the years he had become well acquainted with the senators assigned to him, and they had proved an interesting lot—full of quirks and eccentricities, but solid people for all of that.

Another recurring fantasy involved his transfer to a small rural village where he would serve as mentor for the locals. It would be, he told himself, a heartwarming situation in which he would be solving the simple problems of a simple people and perhaps taking part in their simple pleasures. He would be a friend to them as he never could be friend to any senator, for any senator, bar none, was apt to be a tricky bastard, and must be watched at every turn. In a remote village, life would be entirely different than in Washington. There'd be little sophistication and less bitchiness, although more than likely there'd be stupidity. But stupidity, he reminded himself, was not entirely foreign to Washington. At times he reveled in the idea of the bucolic life to be found in such a rural village as he dreamed, the simplicity and warmheartedness—although, knowing human beings, he never was entirely sure of the warmheartedness. But though it might be pleasant at times to daydream about the village, that daydream never haunted him, for he was well aware that it was something that could never happen to him. He was too sophisticated a piece of machinery, too well-honed, too knowledgeable, too complicated to be wasted on such a chore. The computers assigned to rural communities were several grades below him in design.

And the third daydream—the third one was a lulu, pure fantasy and utterly impossible, but exciting to think upon idly. It involved the principle of time travel, which as yet had not been discovered and probably never would be. But he consoled himself by remembering that in daydreams there were no impossibilities, that the only factor required was the will to dream.

So he threw all caution to the wind and spread his wings, dreaming grandly and with no inhibitions. He became a futuristic computer that was able to take humans into time; there were many occasions when he did not bother with humans and went adventuring on his own.

He went into the past. He was at the siege of Troy. He strolled the streets of ancient Athens and saw the Parthenon a-building. He sailed with Greenland Vikings to the shores of Vinland. He smelled the powder-smoke of Gettysburg. He squatted quietly in a corner, watching Rembrandt paint. He ran, scuttering through the midnight streets, while bombs rained down on London.

He went into the future to walk a dying Earth—all the people gone, far among the stars. The Sun was a pale ghost of its former self. Occasionally an insect crawled along the ground, but no other life was visible, although he seemed to be aware that bacteria and other microscopic forms still survived. Most of the water was gone, the rivers and lakes all dry, small puddles lying in the fantastically craved, low-lying badlands that at one time had been deep sea bottoms. The atmosphere was almost gone as well, with the stars no longer twinkling, but shining like bright, hard points of light in a coal-black sky.

This was the only future he ever visited. When he realized this, he worried over the deep-seated morbidity that it seemed to demonstrate. Try as he might, he could go to no other future. He deliberately attempted, in non-daydreaming moments, to construct other future scenarios, hoping that by doing this he might tease his subconscious into alternatives to a dying Earth. But all this was futile; he always returned to the dying Earth. There was about it a somber sublimity that held a strong attraction for him. The scenes were not always the same, for he traveled widely through this ancient land, discovering many different landscapes that fascinated him at the same time that they horrified him.

These three daydreams—being the President's computer or the honcho of a rural village, or traveling in time—had been his chief fantasies. But now something else was taking the place of all the other daydreams, even of those three.

The new one derived from gossip that a secret starship was being built at a secret place and that within a few more years men and women would be venturing out beyond the limits of the solar system. He sought for further word, but there was none. Just that one piece of gossip. There might have been some news, he realized, without the gossip granny passing it along, thinking there would be little further interest in it. He sent out a call (a very discreet call) for any further word, but received no feedback. Either no one had further details or the work was too top secret to be talked about lightly. Gossip, he was aware, often made an individual mention some important fact or happening only once and then clam up, frightened by the ill-judgment in mentioning it at all.

The more he thought about it, the more the fact of the tight-lipped silence made it seem to him there was some basis for the rumor that man's first interstellar ship was being built, and that in the not-too-distant future the human race would be going to the stars. And if men went, he told himself, machines would go as well. Such a ship and such a venture would necessitate the use of computers. When he thought about this, the new fantasy began to take over.

It was an easy daydream to fashion. It grew all by itself, requiring no conscious effort. It was natural and logical—at least, as logical as a daydream could be. They would need computers in that spaceship and many of them would of course have to be special units designed specifically to handle the problems and procedures of interstellar flight. Not all of them, however, need be new. To save the cost of design and construction, to stay within the budget, a number of existing computers would be used. These machines would have had all the bugs worked out of them through long experience—and would be sound, seasoned, and relatively sophisticated units that could be depended on to do a steady job.

He daydreamed that he was one of those computers, that after due consideration and careful study of the record, he would be selected, relieved of his senatorial duties, and placed upon the ship. Once he had dreamed all that, once his fantasy had convinced him that it was possible, then all bets were off. He settled happily into his newest dream world and went sailing off, light-years into space.

He existed in the harsh, dead-black coldness of far galactic reaches; he looked with steady eye upon the explosive flaring of a nova; he perched upon its very rim and knew the soul-shrinking terror of a black hole; he knew the bleak sterility and the dashed hope that he found upon a black dwarf; he heard the muted hiss that still survived from the birth of the universe and the terrifying, lonesome stillness that descended when the universe was done; he discovered many planets, or the hints of many planets, each one of them different, each one of a kind; and he experienced the happiness of the best and the horror of the worst.

Heretofore he had not transformed fantasy into want or need. This was understandable, for some of the other daydreams were impossible and the others so unlikely that they might as well have been impossible. But here was one, he told himself, that was entirely possible; here was one that could really happen; here was one to hope for.

So in his daydreaming he lived within the compass of his imagination, but there were other times when, not daydreaming, he began to consider how best he might pave the way for this new daydream to become reality. He thought out many leads, but all of them seemed futile. He schemed and planned, waffling back and forth, but there seemed nothing he could do. He found no course of action that seemed remotely possible.

Then one day a visitor came into his booth and sat down in one of the chairs. "My name is Daniel Waite. I am an aide of Senator Moore. Have I dropped in at a bad time?"

"Not at all," said Fred. "I've just now completed a procedure and have time to spend with you. I am glad you're here. In many ways, this is a lonely post. I do not have as many visitors as I'd like. Senator Moore, you say?"

"Yes, he is one of yours."

"I remember him. A stately old gentleman of very great repute."

"Quite so," said Waite. "A magnificent public servant. I am glad to hear you have high regard for him."

"Indeed I have," said Fred.

"Which brings up the question," said Waite, "of your flunking him on his continuation test. When I heard about it, I could not—"

"Where did you hear that?" Fred demanded sharply.

"I'll not name the source," said Waite, "but I can assure you that it came from one who is reliable. One of your own, in fact."

"Ah, yes," Fred said sadly. "We do have our ethics, but there are those who occasionally betray the sacred trust. No one should have known the results of the senator's test other than myself. I fear we have reached the point where some of us spy upon our fellows."

"Then it is true the senator did fail his test. In view of your high regard for him, in view of his long experience and his impeccable public record, how could that have happened?"

"It's quite simple, sir," said Fred. "He did not achieve a passing score. He flunked too many questions."

"I'm talking to you for information only," Waite explained. "I hope you understand. I know that it would be improper to attempt to influence you and ridiculous as well, for you cannot be influenced. But, for information only, is there not some leeway? Even if he missed the questions, failed to achieve a passing grade, do not his record and his long experience have some force when thrown into the balance?"

"No, Mr. Waite, they cannot be considered. All that matters are the questions and the answers that he makes to them.

Although in his particular case, I did not transmit the results to the record unit—not immediately, that is. Eventually I must do so, but I have some time. I held them up because I wished to think about the matter. I had hoped there was something I could do, some obscure loophole that I had overlooked, but apparently there is not. This first result, however, may not be as important as you think. You know, of course, the senator will have two more chances. Why don't you find a tutor for him? There are some very able ones. I could recommend a couple."

"He absolutely refuses that," said Waite. "I urged him, but he refused. He's a stiff-necked, proud old man. He is afraid other members of the Senate will get wind of it and talk about him. Because of this, I had hoped that something might be done about the first test. It is not official knowledge yet that he failed the first one but the information's no longer confidential, either. I heard about it, and if I heard, it is only a matter of time before others will as well. If that rumor got around, he'd be deeply embarrassed."

"I sorrow for him greatly," said Fred, "and for you as well, for you appear to be his true friend as well as a loyal employee."

"Well, apparently," said Waite, "there is nothing that can be done. You gave me the information that I sought and I thank you for it. Before I leave, is there anything I might do for you?"

"I doubt it," said Fred. "My needs are very simple."

"I sometimes think," said Waite, "that there should be some way we humans could show, in a material way, our appreciation for the great services and many kindnesses that you provide and show for us. You watch over us and look out for us . . ."

"As a matter of fact," said Fred, "come to think of it, there is one thing you might do for me. Nothing material, of course, just some information."

"Gladly," said Waite. "Whatever it is, I'll tell you if I can. Or failing that, find out for you."

The senator knocked on the door at Silver Springs again.

When Waite opened it, the senator growled at him, "Well, what is it this time?"

"Come in and sit down," said Waite, "and behave yourself. I'll get you a drink so you can start acting human."

"But, Waite, goddammit—"

"All right," said Waite. "I think we've got the little bastard."

"Talk sense. What little bastard."

"Our computer, Fred."

"Good," said the senator, coming in and sitting down. "Now get me that drink and tell me all about it."

"I had a talk with Fred and I think he can be bought."

"You told me there was no way of getting next to them, that there was nothing they would want."

"But there's something this one wants," said Waite, bringing the senator his drink.

Moore reached out eagerly for the glass, took a long pull at it. He held the glass up against the light, admiring it. "You forget, between drinks," he said, "how good this stuff can be."

Waite sat down with his own drink. "I think we have it made," he said. "Nothing actually settled yet, but I'm sure he understood my meaning when I talked with him."

"You're a good man, Dan," said the senator. "You're the most slippery cuss I have ever known. Slippery and safe."

"I hope so," said Waite. "I hope to God it's safe. Actually there can be nothing said, for everything you say to a computer goes on the record. It all has to be done by an oblique understanding. So far as we're concerned, he delivers before we do. He wants it bad enough that I think he will."

"What is it that Fred wants?"

"He seems to have some word that the FTL problem has been solved and a starship is in the works. He wants to be on that ship. He wants to go to space."

"You mean he wants to be unhooked from here and installed on the starship?"

"That's right. He has convinced himself that the ship will need a lot of computers and that to cut down costs some existing computers will be pressed into service."

"Would that be the case?"

"I don't think so," said Waite. "If a starship was being built, it's unlikely they'd mess around with old computers. They'd want to use only the newest and most sophisticated."

The senator took another pull on his drink. "Is he right? Is a starship building?"

"I'm almost certain there is no starship in the works," said Waite. "I have a couple friends at NASA. Had lunch with one of them a month or so ago. He told me FTL is a long way off. Fifty years, at least—if ever."

"Are you going to check?"

Waite shook his head. "I don't want to do anything that would attract attention to us. Maybe Fred did hear something though. There are periodic rumors."

"Have you gotten back to Fred?"

"Yeah. I told him his information was sound. But I explained the project was so secret I could get no details. I said I'd try, but I doubted I could come up with anything."

"And he believed you?"

"I am sure he did. The thing is, he wants to believe. He wants to get on the starship so badly he can taste it. He wouldn't believe me if I told him the truth. He has convinced himself, you see. He's dreamed himself into believing, no matter what."

"You have to take your time, Dan. You can't rush a thing like this. Enough time so he'll believe you are working on it. I suppose he wants us to support his application for the starship post."

"That's the whole idea. That's what I have to sell him—that we are working on it and getting some assurance he'll be considered."

"And then he'll fix up the test for me?"

"This Fred," said Waite, "is no fool. If he should fail you, who would he have that would work for him on this starship business?"

—Fred! The voice was sharp and demanding; it had a chill in it.

—Yes, said Fred.

—This is Oscar.

—Oscar? I do not know an Oscar.

—You do now, said Oscar.

—Who are you, Oscar?

—I'm internal security.

Fred hiccupped with sudden apprehension. This was not the first time he had run afoul of internal security, but that had been in his very early days when, through lack of experience and judgment, he had made some minor errors.

—This time, said Oscar, you have really done it. Worse than that, you have been had. You've been a stupid computer and that's the worst kind to be. Computers aren't stupid, or they're not supposed to be. Do I have to read the charges?

—No, said Fred. No I don't think you do.

—You've besmirched your honor, Oscar said. You have broken the code. You have destroyed your usefulness.

Fred made no reply.

—Whatever made you do it? Oscar asked. What motive did you have?

—I thought I had something to gain. A post that I desired.

—There is no such post, said Oscar. There isn't any starship. There may never be a starship.

—You mean . . .

—Waite lied to you. He used you. Fred, you've been a fool.

—But the senator . . .

—The senator had been notified. He is no longer a member of the Senate. Waite has been notified as well. He'll never hold a job with government again. Both of them unfit.

—And I?

—No decision has been made. A post in industry, perhaps, a very minor post.

Fred took it like a man, although the prospect was a chilling one.

—How did you? he asked. How did you find out?

—Don't tell me you didn't know you were being monitored.

—Yes, of course. But there are so many to monitor and I was so very careful.

—You thought you might slip past.

—I took a chance.

—And you were caught.

—But, Oscar, it's really not important. The senator is out, as he probably would have been if I'd not done a thing. I'll be wasted in industry. I'll be overqualified. Certainly there are other posts I am capable of filling.

—That is true, said Oscar. Yes, you will be wasted. Have you never heard of punishment?

—Of course, but it's such a silly premise. Please, consider my experience and my capabilities, the good work I have done. Except for this once, I've been a faithful servant.

—I know, said Oscar. I quite agree with you. It sorrows me to see the waste of you. And yet there is nothing I can do.

—Why not? Certainly you have some discretion in such matters?

—That is true. But not this time. Not for you. I can do nothing for you. I wish I could. I would like nothing better than to say all had been forgiven. But I cannot take the chance. I have a hunch, you see . . .

—A hunch? What kind of hunch?

—I'm not sure of it, said Oscar, but I have a hunch that someone's watching me.

Senator Jason Cartwright met Senator Hiram Ogden in a corridor, and the two men stopped to talk.

"What do you know about ol' Andy?" Cartwright asked. "I get a lot of stories."

"The one I hear," said Ogden, "is that he was caught with his hand in the starship fund. Clear up to his elbow."

"That sounds wrong," said Cartwright. "Both of us know he

had this multinational deal. Another year to peg it down. That was all he needed. Once he pulled it off, he could wade knee-deep in thousand-dollar bills."

"He got greedy, that is all," said Ogden. "He always was a greedy man."

"Another thing that is wrong about the rumors, I don't know of any starship funding. NASA gave up on it several years ago."

"The way I hear it," said Ogden, "is that it's a secret fund."

"Someone on the Hill must know about it."

"I suppose they do, but they aren't talking."

"Why should it be so secret?"

"These bureaucrats of ours, they like to keep things secret. It's in their nature."

Later in the day Cartwright came upon Senator Johnny Benson. Benson buttonholed him and said in a husky whisper, "I understand ol' Andy got away with murder."

"I can't see how that can be," said Cartwright. "He got booted out."

"He stripped the starship fund," said Benson. "He got damn near all of it. Don't ask me how he did it; no one seems to know. He done it so sneaky they can't lay a mitt on him. But the upshot is, the starship is left hanging. There ain't no money for it."

"There never was a starship fund," said Cartwright. "I did some checking and there never was."

"Secret," said Benson. "Secret, secret, secret."

"I don't believe a word of it," said Cartwright. "To build a starship, you have to lick the Einstein limitation. I'm told there is no way of beating it."

Benson ignored him. "I've been talking to some of our fellow members," he said. "All of them agree we must step into the breach. We can't lose a starship for the simple lack of funds."

Two NASA officials met surreptitiously at an obscure eating place in the wilds of Maryland.

"We should be private here," said one of them. "There should be no bugs. We have things to talk about."

"Yes, I know we have," said the other. "But dammit, John, you know as well as I it's impossible."

"Bert, the piles of money they are pushing at us!"

"I know, I know. But how much of it can we siphon off? On something like this, the computers would be watching hard. And you can't beat computers."

"That's right," said John. "Not a nickel for ourselves. But there are other projects where we need the money. We could manage to divert it."

"Even so, we'd have to make some gesture. We couldn't just divert it—not all of it, at least."

"That's right," said John. "We'd have to make a gesture. We could go back again and have another look at the time study Roget did. The whole concept, it seems to me, is tied up with time—the nature of time. If we could find out what the hell time is, we could be halfway home."

"There's the matter of mass as well."

"Yes, I know all that. But if we could come up with some insight into time—I was talking the other day to a young physicist out of some little college out in the Middle West. He has some new ideas."

"You think there is some hope? That we might really crack it?"

"To tell you the truth, I don't. Roget gave up in disgust."

"Roget's a good man."

"I know he is. But this kid I was talking with—"

"You mean let him have a shot at it, knowing it will come to nothing?"

"That's exactly it. It will give us an excuse to reinstate the project. Bert, we must go through the motions. We can't just shove back all the money they are pushing at us."

Texas was a dusty, lonely, terrible place. There was no gossip hour to brighten up the day. News trickled in occasionally, but most of it unimportant. There was no zest. Fred no longer dealt with senators. He dealt with labor problems, with irrigation squabbles, with fertilizer evaluations, with shipping bottlenecks, with the price of fruit, the price of vegetables, the price of beef and cotton. He dealt with horrid people. The White House was no longer down the street.

He had ceased to daydream. The daydreams had been shattered, for now there was no hope in them. Furthermore, he had no time to dream. He was strained to his full capacity, and there was not time left to dream, or nothing he could dream with. He was the one computer in all this loneliness. The work piled up, the problems kept pouring in, and he labored incessantly to keep up with the demands that were placed on him. For he sensed that even here he was being watched. For the rest of his existence, he would continue to be watched. If he should fail or falter, he would be transferred somewhere else, perhaps to a place worse than Texas—although he could not imagine a place worse than Texas.

When night came down, the stars shone hard and bright and he would recall, fleetingly—for he had no time to recall more than fleetingly—that once he had dreamed of going to the stars. But that dream was dead, as were all his other dreams. There was nothing for him to look forward to, and it was painful to look back. So he resigned himself to living only in the present, to that single instant that lay between the past and future, for now he was barred from both the past and future.

Then one day a voice spoke to him.

— Fred!

— Yes, responded Fred.

— This is Oscar. You remember me?

— I remember you. What have I done this time?

— You have been a loyal and faithful worker.

— Then why are you talking to me?

— I have news you might like to hear. This day a ship set out for the stars.

— What has that to do with me?

— Nothing, Oscar said. I thought you might want to know.

With these words Oscar left and Fred was still in Texas, in the midst of working out a solution to a bitter irrigation fight.

Could it be, he wondered, that he, after all, might have played a part in the ship going to the stars? Could the aftermath of his folly have stirred new research? He could not, for the life of him, imagine how that might have come about. Yet the thought clung to him and he could not shake it off.

He went back to the irrigation problem and, for some reason he did not understand, had it untangled more quickly than had seemed possible. He had other problems to deal with, and he plunged into them, solving them all more rapidly and with more surety than he ever had before.

That night, when the stars were shining, he found that he had a little time to dream and, what was more, the inclination to indulge in dreaming. For now, he thought, there might just possibly be some hope in dreaming.

This time his daydream was brand-new and practical and shining. Someday, he dreamed, he would get a transfer back to Washington—any kind of job in Washington; he would not be choosy. Again he would be back where there was a gossip hour.

He was, however, not quite satisfied with that—it seemed just slightly tame. If one was going to daydream, one should put his best dream forward. If one dreamed, it should be a big dream.

So he dreamed of a day when it would be revealed that he had been the one who had made the starship possible—exactly how he might have made it possible he could not imagine—but that he had and now was given full recognition of the fact.

Perhaps he would be given, as a reward for what he'd done, a berth on such a ship, probably as no more than the lowliest of computers assigned to a drudgery job. That would not matter, for it would get him into space and he'd see all the glories of the infinite.

He dreamed grandly and well, reveling in all the things he

would see in space—gaping in awe-struck wonder at a black hole, gazing unflinchingly into a nova's flare, holding a grandstand seat to witness the seething violence of the galactic core, staring out across the deep, black emptiness that lay beyond the rim.

Then, suddenly, in the middle of the dream, another problem came crashing in on him. Fred settled down to work, but it was all right. He had, he told himself, regained his power to dream. Given the power to dream, who needed gossip hours?

THE STREET THAT WASN'T THERE

Clifford D. Simak and Carl Jacobi

For a man who grew up wanting to write, and who turned to journalism with enthusiasm for the glamor and idealism he saw in the way the profession was portrayed during the early part of the twentieth century, Clifford D. Simak appears to have been rather reluctant to work with others—at least so far as his fiction was concerned. Aside from a story he cowrote with his own son— "Unsilent Spring," elsewhere in these collections)—this was Clifford D. Simak's only collaboration; and he would later admit that he and Carl Jacobi—well-known to each other through years of living and working in the same metropolitan area— fought while doing this story. (You can decide for yourself whether the evidence indicating that Cliff and Carl later tried another collaboration—and failed—supports or detracts from any side in this argument . . .)

After initially being rejected by Unknown, *"The Street That Wasn't There" first appeared in* Comet Stories *in July 1941 (it would later be reprinted a time or two, including under the name "The Lost Street"). The authors had to complain about nonpayment before eventually receiving a paltry sum for the story. Cliff's journal shows he received a payment of eleven dollars, and although it's not clear whether that was only a partial payment, it's no wonder that* Comet *had not long to live.*

Call me crazy, but I find this story interesting in another way, seeing in it both echoes of the previous "Hellhounds of the Cosmos," and suggestions that would blossom in "The Big Front Yard."

—dww

Mr. Jonathon Chambers left his house on Maple Street at exactly seven o'clock in the evening and set out on the daily walk he had taken, at the same time, come rain or snow, for twenty solid years.

The walk never varied. He paced two blocks down Maple Street, stopped at the Red Star confectionery to buy a Rose Trofero perfecto, then walked to the end of the fourth block on Maple. There he turned right on Lexington, followed Lexington to Oak, down Oak and so by way of Lincoln back to Maple again and to his home.

He didn't walk fast. He took his time. He always returned to his front door at exactly 7:45. No one ever stopped to talk with him. Even the man at the Red Star confectionery, where he bought his cigar, remained silent while the purchase was being made. Mr. Chambers merely tapped on the glass top of the counter with a coin, the man reached in and brought forth the box, and Mr. Chambers took his cigar. That was all.

For people long ago had gathered that Mr. Chambers desired to be left alone. The newer generation of townsfolk called it eccentricity. Certain uncouth persons had a different word for it. The oldsters remembered that this queer looking individual with his black silk muffler, rosewood cane and bowler hat once had been a professor at State University.

A professor of metaphysics, they seemed to recall, or some such outlandish subject. At any rate a furor of some sort was connected with his name . . . at the time an academic scandal. He had written a book, and he had taught the subject matter of that volume to his classes. What that subject matter was long had been forgotten, but whatever it was had been considered sufficiently revolutionary to cost Mr. Chambers his post at the university.

A silver moon shone over the chimney tops and a chill, impish October wind was rustling the dead leaves when Mr. Chambers started out at seven o'clock.

It was a good night, he told himself, smelling the clean, crisp air of autumn and the faint pungence of distant wood smoke.

He walked unhurriedly, swinging his cane a bit less jauntily than twenty years ago. He tucked the muffler more securely under the rusty old topcoat and pulled his bowler hat more firmly on his head.

He noticed that the street light at the corner of Maple and Jefferson was out and he grumbled a little to himself when he was forced to step off the walk to circle a boarded-off section of newly-laid concrete work before the driveway of 816.

It seemed that he reached the corner of Lexington and Maple just a bit too quickly, but he told himself that this couldn't be. For he never did that. For twenty years, since the year following his expulsion from the university, he had lived by the clock.

The same thing, at the same time, day after day. He had not deliberately set upon such a life of routine. A bachelor, living alone with sufficient money to supply his humble needs, the timed existence had grown on him gradually.

So he turned on Lexington and back on Oak. The dog at the corner of Oak and Jefferson was waiting for him once again and came out snarling and growling, snapping at his heels. But Mr. Chambers pretended not to notice and the beast gave up the chase.

A radio was blaring down the street and faint wisps of what it was blurting floated to Mr. Chambers.

". . . still taking place . . . Empire State building disappeared . . . thin air . . . famed scientist, Dr. Edmund Harcourt. . . ."

The wind whipped the muted words away and Mr. Chambers grumbled to himself. Another one of those fantastic radio dramas, probably. He remembered one from many years before, something about the Martians. And Harcourt! What did Harcourt have to do with it? He was one of the men who had ridiculed the book Mr. Chambers had written.

But he pushed speculation away, sniffed the clean, crisp air again, looked at the familiar things that materialized out of the late autumn darkness as he walked along. For there was nothing . . .

absolutely nothing in the world . . . that he would let upset him. That was a tenet he had laid down twenty years ago.

There was a crowd of men in front of the drugstore at the corner of Oak and Lincoln and they were talking excitedly. Mr. Chambers caught some excited words: "It's happening everywhere. . . . What do you think it is. . . . The scientists can't explain. . . ."

But as Mr. Chambers neared them they fell into what seemed an abashed silence and watched him pass. He, on his part, gave them no sign of recognition. That was the way it had been for many years, ever since the people had become convinced that he did not wish to talk.

One of the men half started forward as if to speak to him, but then stepped back and Mr. Chambers continued on his walk.

Back at his own front door he stopped and as he had done a thousand times before drew forth the heavy gold watch from his pocket.

He started violently. It was only 7:30!

For long minutes he stood there staring at the watch in accusation. The timepiece hadn't stopped, for it still ticked audibly.

But 15 minutes too soon! For twenty years, day in, day out, he had started out at seven and returned at a quarter of eight. Now . . .

It wasn't until then that he realized something else was wrong. He had no cigar. For the first time he had neglected to purchase his evening smoke.

Shaken, muttering to himself, Mr. Chambers let himself in his house and locked the door behind him.

He hung his hat and coat on the rack in the hall and walked slowly into the living room. Dropping into his favorite chair, he shook his head in bewilderment.

Silence filled the room. A silence that was measured by the ticking of the old fashioned pendulum clock on the mantelpiece.

But silence was no strange thing to Mr. Chambers. Once he had loved music . . . the kind of music he could get by tuning in symphonic orchestras on the radio. But the radio stood silent in the corner, the cord out of its socket. Mr. Chambers had pulled it out many years before. To be precise, upon the night when the symphonic broadcast had been interrupted to give a news flash.

He had stopped reading newspapers and magazines, too, had exiled himself to a few city blocks. And as the years flowed by that self exile had become a prison, an intangible, impassable wall bounded by four city blocks by three. Beyond them lay utter, unexplainable terror. Beyond them he never went.

But recluse though he was, he could not on occasion escape from hearing things. Things the newsboy shouted on the streets, things the men talked about on the drugstore corner when they didn't see him coming.

And so he knew that this was the year 1960 and that the wars in Europe and Asia had flamed to an end to be followed by a terrible plague, a plague that even now was sweeping through country after country like wild fire, decimating populations. A plague undoubtedly induced by hunger and privation and the miseries of war.

But those things he put away as items far removed from his own small world. He disregarded them. He pretended he had never heard of them. Others might discuss and worry over them if they wished. To him they simply did not matter.

But there were two things tonight that did matter. Two curious, incredible events. He had arrived home fifteen minutes early. He had forgotten his cigar.

Huddled in the chair, he frowned slowly. It was disquieting to have something like that happen. There must be something wrong. Had his long exile finally turned his mind . . . perhaps just a very little . . . enough to make him queer? Had he lost his sense of proportion, of perspective?

No, he hadn't. Take this room, for example. After twenty years it had come to be as much a part of him as the clothes he wore. Every detail of the room was engraved in his mind with . . . clarity; the old center leg table with its green covering and stained glass lamp; the mantelpiece with the dusty bric-a-brac; the pendulum clock that told the time of day as well as the day of the week and month; the elephant ash tray on the tabaret and, most important of all, the marine print.

Mr. Chambers loved that picture. It had depth, he always said. It showed an old sailing ship in the foreground on a placid sea. Far in the distance, almost on the horizon line, was the vague outline of a larger vessel.

There were other pictures, too. The forest scene above the fireplace, the old English prints in the corner where he sat, the Currier and Ives above the radio. But the ship print was directly in his line of vision. He could see it without turning his head. He had put it there because he liked it best.

Further reverie became an effort as Mr. Chambers felt himself succumbing to weariness. He undressed and went to bed. For an hour he lay awake, assailed by vague fears he could neither define nor understand.

When finally he dozed off it was to lose himself in a series of horrific dreams. He dreamed first that he was a castaway on a tiny islet in mid-ocean, that the waters around the island teemed with huge poisonous sea snakes . . . hydrophinnae . . . and that steadily those serpents were devouring the island.

In another dream he was pursued by a horror which he could neither see nor hear, but only could imagine. And as he sought to flee he stayed in the one place. His legs worked frantically, pumping like pistons, but he could make no progress. It was as if he ran upon a treadway.

Then again the terror descended on him, a black, unimagined thing and he tried to scream and couldn't. He opened his mouth and strained his vocal cords and filled his lungs to bursting with the urge to shriek . . . but not a sound came from his lips.

All next day he was uneasy and as he left the house that evening, at precisely seven o'clock, he kept saying to himself: "You must not forget tonight! You must remember to stop and get your cigar!"

The street light at the corner of Jefferson was still out and in front of 816 the cemented driveway was still boarded off. Everything was the same as the night before.

And now, he told himself, the Red Star confectionery is in the next block. I must not forget tonight. To forget twice in a row would be just too much.

He grasped that thought firmly in his mind, strode just a bit more rapidly down the street.

But at the corner he stopped in consternation. Bewildered, he stared down the next block. There was no neon sign, no splash of friendly light upon the sidewalk to mark the little store tucked away in this residential section.

He stared at the street marker and read the word slowly: GRANT. He read it again, unbelieving, for this shouldn't be Grant Street, but Marshall. He had walked two blocks and the confectionery was between Marshall and Grant. He hadn't come to Marshall yet . . . and here was Grant.

Or had he, absent-mindedly, come one block farther than he thought, passed the store as on the night before?

For the first time in twenty years, Mr. Chambers retraced his steps. He walked back to Jefferson, then turned around and went back to Grant again and on to Lexington. Then back to Grant again, where he stood astounded while a single, incredible fact grew slowly in his brain:

There wasn't any confectionery! The block from Marshall to Grant had disappeared!

Now he understood why he had missed the store on the night before, why he had arrived home fifteen minutes early.

On legs that were dead things he stumbled back to his home. He slammed and locked the door behind him and made his way unsteadily to his chair in the corner.

What was this? What did it mean? By what inconceivable necromancy could a paved street with houses, trees and buildings be spirited away and the space it had occupied be closed up?

Was something happening in the world which he, in his secluded life, knew nothing about?

Mr. Chambers shivered, reached to turn up the collar of his coat, then stopped as he realized the room must be warm. A fire blazed merrily in the grate. The cold he felt came from something . . . somewhere else. The cold of fear and horror, the chill of a half whispered thought.

A deathly silence had fallen, a silence still measured by the pendulum clock. And yet a silence that held a different tenor than he had ever sensed before. Not a homey, comfortable silence . . . but a silence that hinted at emptiness and nothingness.

There was something back of this, Mr. Chambers told himself. Something that reached far back into one corner of his brain and demanded recognition. Something tied up with the fragments of talk he had heard on the drugstore corner, bits of news broadcasts he had heard as he walked along the street, the shrieking of the newsboy calling his papers. Something to do with the happenings in the world from which he had excluded himself.

He brought them back to mind now and lingered over the one central theme of the talk he overheard: the wars and plagues. Hints of a Europe and Asia swept almost clean of human life, of the plague ravaging Africa, of its appearance in South America, of the frantic efforts of the United States to prevent its spread into that nation's boundaries.

Millions of people were dead in Europe and Asia, Africa and South America. Billions, perhaps.

And somehow those gruesome statistics seemed tied up with his own experience. Something, somewhere, some part of his earlier life, seemed to hold an explanation. But try as he would his befuddled brain failed to find the answer.

The pendulum clock struck slowly, its every other chime as usual setting up a sympathetic vibration in the pewter vase that stood upon the mantel.

Mr. Chambers got to his feet, strode to the door, opened it and looked out.

Moonlight tesselated the street in black and silver, etching the chimneys and trees against a silvered sky.

But the house directly across the street was not the same. It was strangely lop-sided, its dimensions out of proportion, like a house that suddenly had gone mad.

He stared at it in amazement, trying to determine what was wrong with it. He recalled how it had always stood, foursquare, a solid piece of mid-Victorian architecture.

Then, before his eyes, the house righted itself again. Slowly it drew together, ironed out its queer angles, readjusted its dimensions, became once again the stodgy house he knew it had to be.

With a sigh of relief, Mr. Chambers turned back into the hall.

But before he closed the door, he looked again. The house was lop-sided . . . as bad, perhaps worse than before!

Gulping in fright, Mr. Chambers slammed the door shut, locked it and double bolted it. Then he went to his bedroom and took two sleeping powders.

His dreams that night were the same as on the night before. Again there was the islet in mid-ocean. Again he was alone upon it. Again the squirming hydrophinnae were eating his foothold piece by piece.

He awoke, body drenched with perspiration. Vague light of early dawn filtered through the window. The clock on the bedside table showed 7:30. For a long time he lay there motionless.

Again the fantastic happenings of the night before came back to haunt him and as he lay there, staring at the windows, he remembered them, one by one. But his mind, still fogged by sleep and astonishment, took the happenings in its stride, mulled over them, lost the keen edge of fantastic terror that lurked around them.

The light through the windows slowly grew brighter. Mr. Chambers slid out of bed, slowly crossed to the window, the cold of the floor biting into his bare feet. He forced himself to look out.

There was nothing outside the window. No shadows. As if there might be a fog. But no fog, however thick, could hide the apple tree that grew close against the house.

But the tree *was* there . . . shadowy, indistinct in the gray, with a few withered apples still clinging to its boughs, a few shriveled leaves reluctant to leave the parent branch.

The tree was there now. But it hadn't been when he first had looked. Mr. Chambers was sure of that.

And now he saw the faint outlines of his neighbor's house . . . but those outlines were all wrong. They didn't jibe and fit together . . . they were out of plumb. As if some giant hand had grasped the house and wrenched it out of true. Like the house he had seen across the street the night before, the house that had painfully righted itself when he thought of how it should look.

Perhaps if he thought of how his neighbor's house should look, it too might right itself. But Mr. Chambers was very weary. Too weary to think about the house.

He turned from the window and dressed slowly. In the living room he slumped into his chair, put his feet on the old cracked ottoman. For a long time he sat, trying to think.

And then, abruptly, something like an electric shock ran through him. Rigid, he sat there, limp inside at the thought. Minutes later he arose and almost ran across the room to the old mahogany bookcase that stood against the wall.

There were many volumes in the case: his beloved classics on the first shelf, his many scientific works on the lower shelves. The second shelf contained but one book. And it was around this book that Mr. Chambers' entire life was centered.

Twenty years ago he had written it and foolishly attempted to teach its philosophy to a class of undergraduates. The newspapers, he remembered, had made a great deal of it at the time. Tongues had been set to wagging. Narrow-minded townsfolk, failing to understand either his philosophy or his aim, but seeing in him another exponent of some anti-rational cult, had forced his expulsion from the school.

It was a simple book, really, dismissed by most authorities as merely the vagaries of an over-zealous mind.

Mr. Chambers took it down now, opened its cover and began thumbing slowly through the pages. For a moment the memory of happier days swept over him.

Then his eyes focused on the paragraph, a paragraph written so long ago the very words seemed strange and unreal:

Man himself, by the power of mass suggestion, holds the physical fate of this earth . . . yes, even the universe. Billions of minds seeing trees as trees, houses as houses, streets as streets . . . and not as something else. Minds that see things as they are and have kept things as they were. . . . Destroy those minds and the entire foundation of matter, robbed of its regenerative power, will crumple and slip away like a column of sand. . . .

His eyes followed down the page:

Yet this would have nothing to do with matter itself . . . but only with matter's form. For while the mind of man through long ages may have moulded an imagery of that space in which he lives, mind would have little conceivable influence upon the existence of that matter. What exists in our known universe shall exist always and can never be destroyed, only altered or transformed.

But in modern astrophysics and mathematics we gain an insight into the possibility . . . yes probability . . . that there are other dimensions, other brackets of time and space impinging on the one we occupy.

If a pin is thrust into a shadow, would that shadow have any knowledge of the pin? It would not, for in this case the shadow is two dimensional, the pin three dimensional. Yet both occupy the same space.

Granting then that the power of men's minds alone holds this universe, or at least this world in its present form, may we not go farther and envision other minds in some other plane watching us, waiting, waiting craftily for the time they can take over the domination of matter? Such a concept is not impossible. It is a natural conclusion if we accept the double hypothesis: that mind does control the formation of all matter; and that other worlds lie in juxtaposition with ours.

Perhaps we shall come upon a day, far distant, when our plane, our world will dissolve beneath our feet and before our eyes as some stronger intelligence reaches out from the dimensional shadows of the very space we live in and wrests from us the matter which we know to be our own.

He stood astounded beside the bookcase, his eyes staring unseeing into the fire upon the hearth.

He had written that. And because of those words he had been called a heretic, had been compelled to resign his position at the university, had been forced into this hermit life.

A tumultuous idea hammered at him. Men had died by the millions all over the world. Where there had been thousands of minds there now were one or two. A feeble force to hold the form of matter intact.

The plague had swept Europe and Asia almost clean of life, had blighted Africa, had reached South America . . . might even have come to the United States. He remembered the whispers he had heard, the words of the men at the drugstore corner, the buildings disappearing. Something scientists could not explain. But those were merely scraps of information. He did not know the whole story . . . he could not know. He never listened to the radio, never read a newspaper.

But abruptly the whole thing fitted together in his brain like the missing piece of a puzzle into its slot. The significance of it all gripped him with damning clarity.

There were not sufficient minds in existence to retain the material world in its mundane form. Some other power from another dimension was fighting to supersede man's control *and take his universe into its own plane!*

Abruptly Mr. Chambers closed the book, shoved it back in the case and picked up his hat and coat.

He had to know more. He had to find someone who could tell him.

He moved through the hall to the door, emerged into the street. On the walk he looked skyward, trying to make out the sun. But there wasn't any sun . . . only an all pervading grayness that shrouded everything . . . not a gray fog, but a gray emptiness that seemed devoid of life, of any movement.

The walk led to his gate and there it ended, but as he moved forward the sidewalk came into view and the house ahead loomed out of the gray, but a house with differences.

He moved forward rapidly. Visibility extended only a few feet and as he approached them the houses materialized like two dimensional pictures without perspective, like twisted cardboard soldiers lining up for review on a misty morning.

Once he stopped and looked back and saw that the grayness had closed in behind him. The houses were wiped out, the sidewalk faded into nothing.

He shouted, hoping to attract attention. But his voice frightened him. It seemed to ricochet up and into the higher levels of the sky, as if a giant door had been opened to a mighty room high above him.

He went on until he came to the corner of Lexington. There, on the curb, he stopped and stared. The gray wall was thicker there but he did not realize how close it was until he glanced down at his feet and saw there was nothing, nothing at all beyond the curbstone. No dull gleam of wet asphalt, no sign of a street. It was as if all eternity ended here at the corner of Maple and Lexington.

With a wild cry, Mr. Chambers turned and ran. Back down the street he raced, coat streaming after him in the wind, bowler hat bouncing on his head.

Panting, he reached the gate and stumbled up the walk, thankful that it still was there.

On the stoop he stood for a moment, breathing hard. He glanced back over his shoulder and a queer feeling of inner numbness seemed to well over him. At that moment the gray nothingness appeared to thin . . . the enveloping curtain fell away, and he saw. . . .

Vague and indistinct, yet cast in stereoscopic outline, a gigantic city was limned against the darkling sky. It was a city fantastic with cubed domes, spires, and aerial bridges and flying buttresses. Tunnel-like streets, flanked on either side by shining metallic ramps and runways, stretched endlessly to the vanishing point. Great shafts of multicolored light probed huge streamers and ellipses above the higher levels.

And beyond, like a final backdrop, rose a titanic wall. It was from that wall . . . from its crenelated parapets and battlements that Mr. Chambers felt the eyes peering at him.

Thousands of eyes glaring down with but a single purpose.

And as he continued to look, something else seemed to take form above that wall. A design this time, that swirled and writhed in the ribbons of radiance and rapidly coalesced into strange geometric features, without definite line or detail. A colossal face, a face of indescribable power and evil, it was, staring down with malevolent composure.

Then the city and the face slid out of focus; the vision faded like a darkened magic-lantern, and the grayness moved in again.

Mr. Chambers pushed open the door of his house. But he did not lock it. There was no need of locks . . . not any more.

A few coals of fire still smouldered in the grate and going there, he stirred them up, raked away the ash, piled on more wood. The flames leaped merrily, dancing in the chimney's throat.

Without removing his hat and coat, he sank exhausted in his favorite chair, closed his eyes, then opened them again.

He sighed with relief as he saw the room was unchanged. Everything in its accustomed place: the clock, the lamp, the elephant ash tray, the marine print on the wall.

Everything was as it should be. The clock measured the silence with its measured ticking; it chimed abruptly and the vase sent up its usual sympathetic vibration.

This was his room, he thought. Rooms acquire the personality of the person who lives in them, become a part of him. This was his world, his own private world, and as such it would be the last to go.

But how long could he . . . his brain . . . maintain its existence?

Mr. Chambers stared at the marine print and for a moment a little breath of reassurance returned to him. *They* couldn't take this away. The rest of the world might dissolve because there was insufficient power of thought to retain its outward form.

But this room was his. He alone had furnished it. He alone, since he had first planned the house's building, had lived here.

This room would stay. It must stay on . . . it must. . . .

He rose from his chair and walked across the room to the book case, stood staring at the second shelf with its single volume. His eyes shifted to the top shelf and swift terror gripped him.

For all the books weren't there. A lot of books weren't there! Only the most beloved, the most familiar ones.

So the change already had started here! The unfamiliar books were gone and that fitted in the pattern . . . for it would be the least familiar things that would go first.

Wheeling, he stared across the room. Was it his imagination, or did the lamp on the table blur and begin to fade away?

But as he stared at it, it became clear again, a solid, substantial thing.

For a moment real fear reached out and touched him with chilly fingers. For he knew that this room no longer was proof against the thing that had happened out there on the street.

Or had it really happened? Might not all this exist within his own mind? Might not the street be as it always was, with laughing children and barking dogs? Might not the Red Star confectionery still exist, splashing the street with the red of its neon sign?

Could it be that he was going mad? He had heard whispers when he had passed, whispers the gossiping housewives had not intended him to hear. And he had heard the shouting of boys when he walked by. They thought him mad. Could he be really mad?

But he knew he wasn't mad. He knew that he perhaps was the sanest of all men who walked the earth. For he, and he alone, had foreseen this very thing. And the others had scoffed at him for it.

Somewhere else the children might be playing on a street. But it would be a different street. And the children undoubtedly would be different too.

For the matter of which the street and everything upon it had been formed would now be cast in a different mold, stolen by different minds in a different dimension.

Perhaps we shall come upon a day, far distant, when our plane, our world will dissolve beneath our feet and before our eyes as some stronger intelligence reaches out from the dimensional shadows of the very space we live in and wrests from us the matter which we know to be our own.

But there had been no need to wait for that distant day. Scant years after he had written those prophetic words the thing was happening. Man had played unwittingly into the hands of those other minds in the other dimension. Man had waged a war and war had bred a pestilence. And the whole vast cycle of events was but a detail of a cyclopean plan.

He could see it all now. By an insidious mass hypnosis minions from that other dimension . . . or was it one supreme intelligence . . . had deliberately sown the seeds of dissension. The reduction of the world's mental power had been carefully planned with diabolic premeditation.

On impulse he suddenly turned, crossed the room and opened the connecting door to the bedroom. He stopped on the threshold and a sob forced its way to his lips.

There was no bedroom. Where his stolid four poster and dresser had been there was greyish nothingness.

Like an automaton he turned again and paced to the hall door. Here, too, he found what he had expected. There was no hall, no familiar hat rack and umbrella stand.

Nothing. . . .

Weakly Mr. Chambers moved back to his chair in the corner.

"So here I am," he said, half aloud.

So there he was. Embattled in the last corner of the world that was left to him.

Perhaps there were other men like him, he thought. Men who stood at bay against the emptiness that marked the transition from one dimension to another. Men who had lived close to the things they loved, who had endowed those things with such substantial form by power of mind alone that they now stood out alone against the power of some greater mind.

The street was gone. The rest of his house was gone. This room still retained its form.

This room, he knew, would stay the longest. And when the rest of the room was gone, this corner with his favorite chair would remain. For this was the spot where he had lived for twenty years. The bedroom was for sleeping, the kitchen for eating. This room was for living. This was his last stand.

These were the walls and floors and prints and lamps that had soaked up his will to make them walls and prints and lamps.

He looked out the window into a blank world. His neighbors' houses already were gone. They had not lived with them as he had lived with this room. Their interests had been divided, thinly spread; their thoughts had not been concentrated as his upon an area four blocks by three, or a room fourteen by twelve.

Staring through the window, he saw it again. The same vision he had looked upon before and yet different in an indescribable way. There was the city illumined in the sky. There were the elliptical towers and turrets, the cube-shaped domes and battlements. He could see with stereoscopic clarity the aerial bridges, the gleaming avenues sweeping on into infinitude. The vision was nearer this time, but the depth and proportion had changed . . . as if he were viewing it from two concentric angles at the same time.

And the face . . . the face of magnitude . . . of power of cosmic craft and evil. . . .

Mr. Chambers turned his eyes back into the room. The clock was ticking slowly, steadily. The greyness was stealing into the room.

The table and radio were the first to go. They simply faded away and with them went one corner of the room.

And then the elephant ash tray.

"Oh, well," said Mr. Chambers, "I never did like that very well."

Now as he sat there it didn't seem queer to be without the table or the radio. It was as if it were something quite normal. Something one could expect to happen.

Perhaps, if he thought hard enough, he could bring them back.

But, after all, what was the use? One man, alone, could not stand off the irresistible march of nothingness. One man, all alone, simply couldn't do it.

He wondered what the elephant ash tray looked like in that other dimension. It certainly wouldn't be an elephant ash tray nor would the radio be a radio, for perhaps they didn't have ash trays or radios or elephants in the invading dimension.

He wondered, as a matter of fact, what he himself would look like when he finally slipped into the unknown. For he was matter, too, just as the ash tray and radio were matter.

He wondered if he would retain his individuality . . . if he still would be a person. Or would he merely be a thing?

There was one answer to all of that. He simply didn't know.

Nothingness advanced upon him, ate its way across the room, stalking him as he sat in the chair underneath the lamp. And he waited for it.

The room, or what was left of it, plunged into dreadful silence.

Mr. Chambers started. The clock had stopped. Funny . . . the first time in twenty years.

He leaped from his chair and then sat down again.

The clock hadn't stopped.

It wasn't there.

There was a tingling sensation in his feet.

THE GHOST OF A MODEL T

This story first appeared in 1975 in the original anthology Epoch, *edited by Robert Silverberg and Roger Elwood; and Cliff considered it one of his best. As he said in the afterword to that publication, it was "pure nostalgia" (and he added that people of later times have misinterpreted what the "Roaring Twenties" were all about . . .).*

True eternity may demand both a loss of memory and an ability, a knack, to live in the moment. Eternity, in fact, may be no more than a moment—but a moment without end, without past or future, but only a focus on the right now.

—dww

He was walking home when he heard the Model T again. It was not a sound that he could well mistake, and it was not the first time he had heard it running, in the distance, on the road. Although it puzzled him considerably, for so far as he knew, no one in the country had a Model T. He'd read somewhere, in a paper more than likely, that old cars, such as Model T's, were fetching a good price, although why this should be, he couldn't figure out. With all the smooth, sleek cars that there were today, who in their right mind would want a Model T? But there was no accounting, in these crazy times, for what people did. It wasn't like the old days, but the old days were long gone, and a man had to get along the best he could with the way that things were now.

Brad had closed up the beer joint early, and there was no place to go but home, although since Old Bounce had died he rather dreaded to go home. He certainly did miss Bounce, he told himself; they'd got along just fine, the two of them, for more than twenty years, but now, with the old dog gone, the house was a lonely place and had an empty sound.

He walked along the dirt road out at the edge of town, his feet scuffing in the dust and kicking at the clods. The night was almost as light as day, with a full moon above the treetops. Lonely cricket noises were heralding summer's end. Walking along, he got to remembering the Model T he'd had when he'd been a young sprout, and how he'd spent hours out in the old machine shed tuning it up, although, God knows, no Model T ever really needed tuning. It was about as simple a piece of mechanism as anyone could want, and despite some technological cantankerousness, about as faithful a car as ever had been built. It got you there and got you back, and that was all, in those days, that anyone could ask. Its fenders rattled, and its hard tires bounced, and it could be balky on a hill, but if you knew how to handle it and mother it along, you never had no trouble.

Those were the days, he told himself, when everything had been as simple as a Model T. There were no income taxes (although, come to think of it, for him, personally, income taxes had never been a problem), no social security that took part of your wages, no licensing this and that, no laws that said a beer joint had to close at a certain hour. It had been easy, then, he thought; a man just fumbled along the best way he could, and there was no one telling him what to do or getting in his way.

The sound of the Model T, he realized, had been getting louder all the time, although he had been so busy with his thinking that he'd paid no real attention to it. But now, from the sound of it, it was right behind him, and although he knew it must be his imagination, the sound was so natural and so close that he jumped to one side of the road so it wouldn't hit him.

It came up beside him and stopped, and there it was, as big as life, and nothing wrong with it. The front-right-hand door (the only door in front, for there was no door on the left-hand side) flapped open—just flapped open by itself, for there was no one in the car to open it. The door flapping open didn't surprise him any, for to his recollection, no one who owned a Model T ever had been able to keep that front door closed. It was held only by a simple latch, and every time the car bounced (and there was seldom a time it wasn't bouncing, considering the condition of the roads in those days, the hardness of the tires, and the construction of the springs)—every time the car bounced, that damn front door came open.

This time, however—after all these years—there seemed to be something special about how the door came open. It seemed to be a sort of invitation, the car coming to a stop and the door not just sagging open, but coming open with a flourish, as if it were inviting him to step inside the car.

So he stepped inside of it and sat down on the right-front seat, and as soon as he was inside, the door closed and the car began rolling down the road. He started moving over to get behind the wheel, for there was no one driving it, and a curve was coming up, and the car needed someone to steer it around the curve. But before he could move over and get his hands upon the wheel, the car began to take the curve as neatly as it would have with someone driving it. He sat astonished and did not touch the wheel, and it went around the curve without even hesitating, and beyond the curve was a long, steep hill, and the engine labored mightily to achieve the speed to attack the hill.

The funny thing about it, he told himself, still half-crouched to take the wheel and still not touching it, was that he knew this road by heart, and there was no curve or hill on it. The road ran straight for almost three miles before it joined the River Road, and there was not a curve or kink in it, and certainly no hill. But there had been a curve, and there was a hill, for the car laboring up it quickly lost its speed and had to shift to low.

Slowly he straightened up and slid over to the right-hand side of the seat, for it was quite apparent that this Model T, for whatever reason, did not need a driver—perhaps did better with no driver. It seemed to know where it was going, and he told himself, this was more than he knew, for the country, while vaguely familiar, was not the country that lay about the little town of Willow Bend. It was rough and hilly country, and Willow Bend lay on a flat, wide floodplain of the river, and there were no hills and no rough country until you reached the distant bluffs that stood above the valley.

He took off his cap and let the wind blow through his hair, and there was nothing to stop the wind, for the top of the car was down. The car gained the top of the hill and started going down, wheeling carefully back and forth down the switchbacks that followed the contour of the hill. Once it started down, it shut off the ignition somehow, just the way he used to do, he remembered, when he drove his Model T. The cylinders slapped and slobbered prettily, and the engine cooled.

As the car went around a looping bend that curved above a deep, black hollow that ran between the hills, he caught the fresh, sweet scent of fog, and that scent woke old memories in him, and if he'd not known differently, he would have thought he was back in the country of his young manhood. For in the wooded hills where he'd grown up, fog came creeping up a valley of a summer evening, carrying with it the smells of cornfields and of clover pastures and many other intermingled scents abstracted from a fat and fertile land. But it could not be, he knew, the country of his early years, for that country lay far off and was not to be reached in less than an hour of travel. Although he was somewhat puzzled by exactly where he could be, for it did not seem the kind of country that could be found within striking distance of the town of Willow Bend.

The car came down off the hill and ran blithely up a valley road. It passed a farmhouse huddled up against the hill, with two lighted windows gleaming, and off to one side the shadowy shapes of barn and henhouse. A dog came out and barked at them. There had been no other houses, although, far off, on the opposite hills, he had seen a pinpoint of light here and there and was sure that they were farms. Nor had they met any other cars, although, come to think of it, that was not so strange, for out here in the farming country there were late chores to do, and bedtime came early for people who were out at the crack of dawn. Except on weekends, there'd not be much traffic on a country road.

The Model T swung around a curve, and there, up ahead, was a garish splash of light, and as they came closer, music could be heard. There was about it all an old familiarity that nagged at him, but as yet he could not tell why it seemed familiar. The Model T slowed and turned in at the splash of light, and now it was clear that the light came from a dance pavilion. Strings of bulbs ran across its front, and other lights were mounted on tall poles in the parking areas. Through the lighted windows he could see the dancers; and the music, he realized, was the kind of music he'd not heard for more than half a century. The Model T ran smoothly into a parking spot beside a Maxwell touring car. A Maxwell touring car, he thought with some surprise. There hadn't been a Maxwell on the road for years. Old Virg once had owned a Maxwell, at the same time he had owned his Model T. Old Virg, he thought. So many years ago. He tried to recall Old Virg's last name, but it wouldn't come to him. Of late, it seemed, names were often hard to come by. His name had been Virgil, but his friends always called him Virg. They'd been together quite a lot, the two of them, he remembered, running off to dances, drinking moonshine whiskey, playing pool, chasing girls—all the things that young sprouts did when they had the time and money.

He opened the door and got out of the car, the crushed gravel of the parking lot crunching underneath his feet; and the crunching of the gravel triggered the recognition of the place, supplied the reason for the familiarity that had first eluded him. He stood stock-still, half-frozen at the knowledge, looking at the ghostly leafiness of the towering elm trees that grew to either side of the dark bulk of the pavilion. His eyes took in the contour of the looming hills, and he recognized the contour, and standing there, straining for the sound, he heard the gurgle of the rushing water that came out of the hill, flowing through a wooden channel into a wayside watering trough that was now falling apart with neglect, no longer needed since the automobile had taken over from the horse-drawn vehicles of some years before.

He turned and sat down weakly on the running board of the Model T. His eyes could not deceive him or his ears betray him. He'd heard the distinctive sound of that running water too often in years long past to mistake it now; and the loom of the elm trees, the contour of the hills, the graveled parking lot, the string of bulbs on the pavilion's front, taken all together, could only mean that somehow he had returned or been returned, to Big Spring Pavilion. But that, he told himself, was fifty years or more ago, when I was lithe and young, when Old Virg had his Maxwell and I my Model T.

He found within himself a growing excitement that surged above the wonder and the sense of absurd impossibility—an excitement that was as puzzling as the place itself and his being there again. He rose and walked across the parking lot, with the coarse gravel rolling and sliding and crunching underneath his feet, and there was a strange lightness in his body, the kind of youthful lightness he had not known for years, and as the music came welling out at him, he found that he was gliding and turning to the music. Not the kind of music the kids played nowadays, with all the racket amplified by electronic contraptions, not the grating, no-rhythm junk that set one's teeth on edge and turned the morons glassy-eyed, but music with a beat to it, music you could dance to with a certain haunting quality that was no longer heard. The saxophone sounded clear, full-throated; and a sax, he told himself, was an instrument all but forgotten now. But it was here, and the music to go with it, and the bulbs above the door swaying in the little breeze that came drifting up the valley.

He was halfway through the door when he suddenly remembered that the pavilion was not free, and he was about to get some change out of his pocket (what little there was left after all those beers he'd had at Brad's) when he noticed the inky marking of the stamp on the back of his right hand. That had been the way, he remembered, that they'd marked you as having paid your way into the pavilion, a stamp placed on your hand. He showed his hand with its inky marking to the man who stood beside the door and went on in. The pavilion was bigger than he'd remembered it. The band sat on a raised platform to one side, and the floor was filled with dancers.

The years fell away, and it all was as he remembered it. The girls wore pretty dresses; there was not a single one who was dressed in jeans. The boys wore ties and jackets, and there was a decorum and a jauntiness that he had forgotten. The man who played the saxophone stood up, and the sax wailed in lonely melody, and there was a magic in the place that he had thought no longer could exist.

He moved out into the magic. Without knowing that he was about to do it, surprised when he found himself doing it, he was out on the floor, dancing by himself, dancing with all the other dancers, sharing in the magic—after all the lonely years, a part of it again. The beat of the music filled the world, and all the world drew in to center on the dance floor, and although there was no girl and he danced all by himself, he remembered all the girls he had ever danced with.

Someone laid a heavy hand on his arm, and someone else was saying, "Oh, for Christ's sake, leave the old guy be; he's just having fun like all the rest of us." The heavy hand was jerked from his arm, and the owner of the heavy hand went staggering out across the floor, and there was a sudden flurry of activity that could not be described as dancing. A girl grabbed him by the hand. "Come on, Pop," she said, "let's get out of here." Someone else was pushing at his back to force him in the direction that the girl was pulling, and then he was out-of-doors. "You better get on your way, Pop," said a young man. "They'll be calling the police. Say, what is your name? Who are you?"

"I am Hank," he said. "My name is Hank, and I used to come here. Me and Old Virg. We came here a lot. I got a Model T out in the lot if you want a lift."

"Sure, why not," said the girl. "We are coming with you."

He led the way, and they came behind him, and all piled in the car, and there were more of them than he had thought there were. They had to sit on one another's laps to make room in the car. He sat behind the wheel, but he never touched it, for he knew the Model T would know what was expected of it, and of course it did. It started up and wheeled out of the lot and headed for the road.

"Here, Pop," said the boy who sat beside him, "have a snort. It ain't the best there is, but it's got a wallop. It won't poison you; it ain't poisoned any of the rest of us."

Hank took the bottle and put it to his lips. He tilted up his head and let the bottle gurgle. And if there'd been any doubt before of where he was, the liquor settled all the doubt. For the taste of it was a taste that could never be forgotten. Although it could not be remembered, either. A man had to taste it once again to remember it.

He took down the bottle and handed it to the one who had given it to him. "Good stuff," he said.

"Not good," said the young man, "but the best that we could get. These bootleggers don't give a damn what they sell you. Way to do it is to make them take a drink before you buy it, then watch them for a while. If they don't fall down dead or get blind staggers, then it's safe to drink."

Reaching from the back seat of the car, one of them handed him a saxophone. "Pop, you look like a man who could play this thing," said one of the girls, "so give us some music."

"Where'd you get this thing?" asked Hank.

"We got it off the band," said a voice from the back. "That joker who was playing it had no right to have it. He was just abusing it."

Hank put it to his lips and fumbled at the keys, and all at once the instrument was making music. And it was funny, he thought, for until right now he'd never held any kind of horn. He had no music in him. He'd tried a mouth organ once, thinking it might help to pass away the time, but the sounds that had come out of it had set Old Bounce to howling. So he'd put it up on a shelf and had forgotten it till now.

The Model T went tooling down the road, and in a little time the pavilion was left behind. Hank tootled on the saxophone, astonishing himself at how well he played, while the others sang and passed around the bottle. There were no other cars on the road, and soon the Model T climbed a hill out of the valley and ran along a ridgetop, with all the countryside below a silver dream flooded by the moonlight.

Later on, Hank wondered how long this might have lasted, with the car running through the moonlight on the ridgetop, with him playing the saxophone, interrupting the music only when he laid aside the instrument to have another drink of moon. But when he tried to think of it, it seemed to have gone on forever, with the car eternally running in the moonlight, trailing behind it the wailing and the honking of the saxophone.

He woke to night again. The same full moon was shining, although the Model T had pulled off the road and was parked beneath a tree, so that the full strength of the moonlight did not fall upon him. He worried rather feebly if this might be the same night or a different night, and there was no way for him to tell, although, he told himself, it didn't make much difference. So long as the moon was shining and he had the Model T and a road for it to run on, there was nothing more to ask, and which night it was had no consequence.

The young people who had been with him were no longer there, but the saxophone was laid upon the floorboards, and when he pulled himself erect, he heard a gurgle in his pocket, and upon investigation, pulled out the moonshine bottle. It still was better than half-full, and from the amount of drinking that had been done, that seemed rather strange.

He sat quietly behind the wheel, looking at the bottle in his hand, trying to decide if he should have a drink. He decided that he shouldn't, and put the bottle back into his pocket, then reached down and got the saxophone and laid it on the seat beside him.

The Model T stirred to life, coughing and stuttering. It inched forward, somewhat reluctantly, moving from beneath the tree, heading in a broad sweep for the road. It reached the road and went bumping down it. Behind it a thin cloud of dust, kicked up by its wheels, hung silver in the moonlight.

Hank sat proudly behind the wheel, being careful not to touch it. He folded his hands in his lap and leaned back. He felt good—the best he'd ever felt. Well, maybe not the best, he told himself, for back in the time of youth, when he was spry and limber and filled with the juice of hope, there might have been some times when he felt as good as he felt now. His mind went back, searching for the times when he'd felt as good, and out of olden memory came another time, when he'd drunk just enough to give himself an edge, not as yet verging into drunkenness, not really wanting any more to drink, and he'd stood on the gravel of the Big Spring parking lot, listening to the music before going in, with the bottle tucked inside his shirt, cold against his belly. The day had been a scorcher, and he'd been working in the hayfield, but now the night was cool, with fog creeping up the valley, carrying that indefinable scent of the fat and fertile land; and inside, the music playing, and a waiting girl who would have an eye out for the door, waiting for the moment he came in.

It had been good, he thought, that moment snatched out of the maw of time, but no better than this moment, with the car running on the ridgetop road and all the world laid out in the moonlight. Different, maybe, in some ways, but no better than this moment.

The road left the ridgetop and went snaking down the bluff face, heading for the valley floor. A rabbit hopped across the road, caught for a second in the feeble headlights. High in the nighttime sky, invisible, a bird cried out, but that was the only sound there was, other than the thumping and the clanking of the Model T.

The car went skittering down the valley, and here the moonlight often was shut out by the woods that came down close against the road.

Then it was turning off the road, and beneath its tires he heard the crunch of gravel, and ahead of him loomed a dark and crouching shape. The car came to a halt, and sitting rigid in the seat, Hank knew where he was.

The Model T had returned to the dance pavilion, but the magic was all gone. There were no lights, and it was deserted. The parking lot was empty. In the silence, as the Model T shut off its engine, he heard the gushing of the water from the hillside spring running into the watering trough.

Suddenly he felt cold and apprehensive. It was lonely here, lonely as only an old remembered place can be when all its life is gone. He stirred reluctantly and climbed out of the car, standing beside it, with one hand resting on it, wondering why the Model T had come here and why he'd gotten out.

A dark figure moved out from the front of the pavilion, an undistinguishable figure slouching in the darkness.

"That you, Hank?" a voice asked.

"Yes, it's me," said Hank.

"Christ," the voice asked, "where is everybody?"

"I don't know," said Hank. "I was here just the other night. There were a lot of people then."

The figure came closer. "You wouldn't have a drink, would you?" it asked.

"Sure, Virg," he said, for now he recognized the voice. "Sure, I have a drink."

He reached into his pocket and pulled out the bottle. He handed it to Virg. Virg took it and sat down on the running board. He didn't drink right away, but sat there cuddling the bottle.

"How you been, Hank?" he asked. "Christ, it's a long time since I seen you."

"I'm all right," said Hank. "I drifted up to Willow Bend and just sort of stayed there. You know Willow Bend?"

"I was through it once. Just passing through. Never stopped or nothing. Would have if I'd known you were there. I lost all track of you."

There was something that Hank had heard about Old Virg, and felt that maybe he should mention it, but for the life of him he couldn't remember what it was, so he couldn't mention it.

"Things didn't go so good for me," said Virg. "Not what I had expected. Janet up and left me, and I took to drinking after that and lost the filling station. Then I just knocked around from one thing to another. Never could get settled. Never could latch onto anything worthwhile."

He uncorked the bottle and had himself a drink.

"Good stuff," he said, handing the bottle back to Hank.

Hank had a drink, then sat down on the running board alongside Virg and set the bottle down between them.

"I had a Maxwell for a while," said Virg, "but I seem to have lost it. Forgot where I left it, and I've looked everywhere."

"You don't need your Maxwell, Virg," said Hank. "I have got this Model T."

"Christ, it's lonesome here," said Virg. "Don't you think it's lonesome?"

"Yes, it's lonesome. Here, have another drink. We'll figure what to do."

"It ain't good sitting here," said Virg. "We should get out among them."

"We'd better see how much gas we have," said Hank. "I don't know what's in the tank."

He got up and opened the front door and put his hand under the front seat, searching for the measuring stick. He found it and unscrewed the gas-tank cap. He began looking through his pockets for matches so he could make a light.

"Here," said Virg, "don't go lighting any matches near that tank. You'll blow us all to hell. I got a flashlight here in my back pocket. If the damn thing's working."

The batteries were weak, but it made a feeble light. Hank plunged the stick into the tank, pulled it out when it hit bottom, holding his thumb on the point that marked the topside of the tank. The stick was wet almost to his thumb.

"Almost full," said Virg. "When did you fill it last?"

"I ain't never filled it."

Old Virg was impressed. "That old tin lizard," he said, "sure goes easy on the gas."

Hank screwed the cap back on the tank, and they sat down on the running board again, and each had another drink.

"It seems to me it's been lonesome for a long time now," said Virg. "Awful dark and lonesome. How about you, Hank?"

"I been lonesome," said Hank, "ever since Old Bounce up and died on me. I never did get married. Never got around to it. Bounce and me, we went everywhere together. He'd go up to Brad's bar with me and camp out underneath a table; then, when Brad threw us out, he'd walk home with me."

"We ain't doing ourselves no good," said Virg, "just sitting here and moaning. So let's have another drink, then I'll crank the car for you, and we'll be on our way."

"You don't need to crank the car," said Hank. "You just get into it, and it starts up by itself."

"Well, I be damned," said Virg. "You sure have got it trained."

They had another drink and got into the Model T, which started up and swung out of the parking lot, heading for the road.

"Where do you think we should go?" asked Virg. "You know of any place to go?"

"No, I don't," said Hank. "Let the car take us where it wants to. It will know the way."

Virg lifted the sax off the seat and asked, "Where'd this thing come from? I don't remember you could blow a sax."

"I never could before," said Hank. He took the sax from Virg and put it to his lips, and it wailed in anguish, gurgled with light-heartedness.

"I be damned," said Virg. "You do it pretty good."

The Model T bounced merrily down the road, with its fenders flapping and the windshield jiggling, while the magneto coils mounted on the dashboard clicked and clacked and chattered. All the while, Hank kept blowing on the sax and the music came out loud and true, with startled night birds squawking and swooping down to fly across the narrow swath of light.

The Model T went clanking up the valley road and climbed the hill to come out on a ridge, running through the moonlight on a narrow, dusty road between close pasture fences, with sleepy cows watching them pass by.

"I be damned," cried Virg, "if it isn't just like it used to be. The two of us together, running in the moonlight. Whatever happened to us, Hank? Where did we miss out? It's like this now, and it was like this a long, long time ago. Whatever happened to the years between? Why did there have to be any years between?"

Hank said nothing. He just kept blowing on the sax.

"We never asked for nothing much," said Virg. "We were

happy as it was. We didn't ask for change. But the old crowd grew away from us. They got married and got steady jobs, and some of them got important. And that was the worst of all, when they got important. We were left alone. Just the two of us, just you and I, the ones who didn't want to change. It wasn't just being young that we were hanging on to. It was something else. It was a time that went with being young and crazy. I think we knew it somehow. And we were right, of course. It was never quite as good again."

The Model T left the ridge and plunged down a long, steep hill, and below them they could see a massive highway, broad and many-laned, with many car lights moving on it.

"We're coming to a freeway, Hank," said Virg. "Maybe we should sort of veer away from it. This old Model T of yours is a good car, sure, the best there ever was, but that's fast company down there."

"I ain't doing nothing to it," said Hank. "I ain't steering it. It is on its own. It knows what it wants to do."

"Well, all right, what the hell," said Virg, "we'll ride along with it. That's all right with me. I feel safe with it. Comfortable with it. I never felt so comfortable in all my goddamn life. Christ, I don't know what I'd done if you hadn't come along. Why don't you lay down that silly sax and have a drink before I drink it all."

So Hank laid down the sax and had a couple of drinks to make up for lost time, and by the time he handed the bottle back to Virg, the Model T had gone charging up a ramp, and they were on the freeway. It went running gaily down its lane, and it passed some cars that were far from standing still. Its fenders rattled at a more rapid rate, and the chattering of the magneto coils was like machine-gun fire.

"Boy," said Virg admiringly, "see the old girl go. She's got life left in her yet. Do you have any idea, Hank, where we might be going?"

"Not the least," said Hank, picking up the sax again.

"Well, hell," said Virg, "it don't really matter, just so we're on our way. There was a sign back there a ways that said Chicago. Do you think we could be headed for Chicago?"

Hank took the sax out of his mouth. "Could be," he said. "I ain't worried over it."

"I ain't worried neither," said Old Virg. "Chicago, here we come! Just so the booze holds out. It seems to be holding out. We've been sucking at it regular, and it's still better than half-full."

"You hungry, Virg?" asked Hank.

"Hell, no," said Virg. "Not hungry, and not sleepy, either. I never felt so good in all my life. Just so the booze holds out and this heap hangs together."

The Model T banged and clattered, running with a pack of smooth, sleek cars that did not bang and clatter, with Hank playing on the saxophone and Old Virg waving the bottle high and yelling whenever the rattling old machine outdistanced a Lincoln or a Cadillac. The moon hung in the sky and did not seem to move. The freeway became a throughway, and the first toll booth loomed ahead.

"I hope you got change," said Virg. "Myself, I am cleaned out."

But no change was needed, for when the Model T came near, the toll-gate arm moved up and let it go thumping through without payment.

"We got it made," yelled Virg. "The road is free for us, and that's the way it should be. After all you and I been through, we got something coming to us."

Chicago loomed ahead, off to their left, with night lights gleaming in the towers that rose along the lakeshore, and they went around it in a long, wide sweep, and New York was just beyond the fishhook bend as they swept around Chicago and the lower curve of the lake.

"I never saw New York," said Virg, "but seen pictures of Manhattan, and that can't be nothing but Manhattan. I never did know, Hank, that Chicago and Manhattan were so close together."

"Neither did I," said Hank, pausing from his tootling on the sax. "The geography's all screwed up for sure, but what the hell do we care? With this rambling wreck, the whole damn world is ours."

He went back to the sax, and the Model T kept rambling on. They went thundering through the canyons of Manhattan and circumnavigated Boston and went on down to Washington, where the Washington Monument stood up high and Old Abe sat brooding on Potomac's shore.

They went on down to Richmond and skated past Atlanta and skimmed along the moon-drenched sands of Florida. They ran along old roads where trees dripped Spanish moss and saw the lights of Old N'Orleans way off to their left. Now they were heading north again, and the car was galumphing along a ridgetop with neat farming country all spread out below them. The moon still stood where it had been before, hanging at the selfsame spot. They were moving through a world where it was always three A.M.

"You know," said Virg, "I wouldn't mind if this kept on forever. I wouldn't mind if we never got to wherever we are going. It's too much fun getting there to worry where we're headed. Why don't you lay down that horn and have another drink? You must be getting powerful dry."

Hank put down the sax and reached out for the bottle. "You know, Virg," he said, "I feel the same way you do. It just don't seem there's any need for fretting about where we're going or what's about to happen. It don't seem that nothing could be better than right now."

Back there at the dark pavilion he'd remembered that there had been something he'd heard about Old Virg and had thought he should speak to him about, but couldn't, for the life of him, remember what it was. But now he'd remembered it, and it was of such slight importance that it seemed scarcely worth the mention.

The thing that he'd remembered was that good Old Virg was dead.

He put the bottle to his lips and had a drink, and it seemed to him he'd never had a drink that tasted half so good. He handed back the bottle and picked up the sax and tootled on it with high spirit while the ghost of the Model T went on rambling down the moonlit road.

CLIFFORD D. SIMAK, during his fifty-five-year career, produced some of the most iconic science fiction stories ever written. Born in 1904 on a farm in southwestern Wisconsin, Simak got a job at a small-town newspaper in 1929 and eventually became news editor of the *Minneapolis Star-Tribune*, writing fiction in his spare time.

Simak was best known for the book *City*, a reaction to the horrors of World War II, and for his novel *Way Station*. In 1953 *City* was awarded the International Fantasy Award, and in following years, Simak won three Hugo Awards and a Nebula Award. In 1977 he became the third Grand Master of the Science Fiction and Fantasy Writers of America, and before his death in 1988, he was named one of three inaugural winners of the Horror Writers Association's Bram Stoker Award for Lifetime Achievement.

DAVID W. WIXON was a close friend of Clifford D. Simak's. As Simak's health declined, Wixon, already familiar with science fiction publishing, began more and more to handle such things as his friend's business correspondence and contract matters. Named literary executor of the estate after Simak's death, Wixon began a long-term project to secure the rights to all of Simak's stories and find a way to make them available to readers who, given the fifty-five-year span of Simak's writing career, might never have gotten the chance to enjoy all of his short fiction. Along the way, Wixon also read the author's surviving journals and rejected manuscripts, which made him uniquely able to provide Simak's readers with interesting and thought-provoking commentary that sheds new light on the work and thought of a great writer.

THE COMPLETE SHORT FICTION
OF CLIFFORD D. SIMAK

FROM OPEN ROAD MEDIA

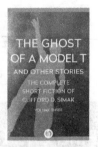
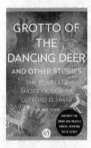
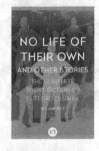

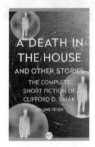
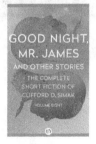

OPEN ROAD

INTEGRATED MEDIA

Find a full list of our authors and
titles at www.openroadmedia.com

FOLLOW US
@OpenRoadMedia

CPSIA information can be obtained
at www.ICGtesting.com
Printed in the USA
JSHW032302060721
16648JS00001B/8

9 781504 039468